THE THREE IMPOSTORS
OR THE TRANSMUTATIONS

broadview editions
series editor: Martin R. Boyne

THE THREE IMPOSTORS
OR THE TRANSMUTATIONS

Arthur Machen

edited by Stefania Forlini

broadview editions

BROADVIEW PRESS – www.broadviewpress.com
Peterborough, Ontario, Canada

Founded in 1985, Broadview Press remains a wholly independent publishing house. Broadview's focus is on academic publishing; our titles are accessible to university and college students as well as scholars and general readers. With over 800 titles in print, Broadview has become a leading international publisher in the humanities, with world-wide distribution. Broadview is committed to environmentally responsible publishing and fair business practices.

2023 Stefania Forlini

Library and Archives Canada Cataloguing in Publication

Title: The three imposters : or, The transmutations / Arthur Machen ; edited by Stefania Forlini.
Other titles: Transmutations
Names: Machen, Arthur, 1863-1947, author. | Forlini, Stefania, editor.
Series: Broadview editions.
Description: Series statement: Broadview editions | Includes bibliographical references.
Identifiers: Canadiana (print) 20220400288 | Canadiana (ebook) 2022040030X |
   ISBN 9781554815043 (softcover) | ISBN 9781770488717 (PDF) |
   ISBN 9781460408070 (EPUB)
Subjects: LCSH: Machen, Arthur, 1863-1947—Criticism and interpretation. |
   LCGFT: Novels. | LCGFT: Horror fiction.
Classification: LCC PR6025.A245 T47 2022 | DDC 823/.912—dc23

Broadview Editions
The Broadview Editions series is an effort to represent the ever-evolving canon of texts in the disciplines of literary studies, history, philosophy, and political theory. A distinguishing feature of the series is the inclusion of primary source documents contemporaneous with the work.

Advisory editor for this volume: Michel Pharand

Broadview Press handles its own distribution in North America:
PO Box 1243, Peterborough, Ontario K9J 7H5, Canada
555 Riverwalk Parkway, Tonawanda, NY 14150, USA
Tel: (705) 743-8990; Fax: (705) 743-8353
email: customerservice@broadviewpress.com

For all territories outside of North America, distribution is handled by Eurospan Group.

Broadview Press acknowledges the financial support of the Government of Canada for our publishing activities.

Canadä

Cover design by Lisa Brawn
Typesetting: George Kirkpatrick

PRINTED IN CANADA

Contents

Acknowledgements

Many thanks to the librarians at the University of Calgary's Taylor Family Digital Library for supporting research remotely while the library itself was closed due to pandemic restrictions. Thanks also to Broadview editor Marjorie Mather for considering the initial proposal for this critical edition and to the many persons at or affiliated with Broadview who helped shape and refine it, including but not limited to Michel Pharand, Martin Boyne, Tara Lowes, and anonymous peer reviewers.

Introduction

Arthur Machen (1863–1947) lived a relatively long life, earning his sometimes-meagre living by his writing and achieving only brief moments of fame during his lifetime. Across five decades (1880s–1930s), he produced a substantial body of work, including translations, novels, short stories, autobiographies, and a vast array of short periodical-based pieces. Although most often associated with the British *fin de siècle* and remembered for his formative influence on the modern genres of weird, horror, and occult fiction, Machen's heterogeneous body of work spans several traditional literary historical periods and does not easily fit any one form, genre category, or style. In the 1890s, when some of his most popular works were first published, critics often compared Machen to Edgar Allan Poe (1809–49), Sheridan Le Fanu (1814–73), Robert Louis Stevenson (1850–94), as well as French and English Decadent authors. Today Machen is most often associated with those he influenced, including writers H.P. Lovecraft (1890–1937) and Stephen King (b. 1947), and film director Guillermo del Toro (b. 1964). Although Machen's work is receiving increasing attention, his unusual novel *The Three Impostors* (1895) remains somewhat obscure, in part because of the circumstances surrounding its original publication, the ways in which it has been re-issued since, and not least because it ill fits many of the categories through which readers might attempt to make sense of it.

The Three Impostors borrows a centuries-old transnational form—the story-cycle, consisting of a frame narrative with multiple shorter narratives embedded within it—and infuses it with generic tendencies as diverse as supernatural, horror, and science fiction, detective fiction, tragedy, and farce, all while self-reflexively calling attention to the artifice of its design. Some critics then and since have wondered whether this is a weakness of the text,[1] but in effect it is part of its power. *The Three Impostors* operationalizes and undermines assumed borders of all kinds, borders between human and animal, between past and present, between the local and the global, between an imagined "us" and "them,"

---

1 According to Machen himself, "the farce and the tragedy in it were not well mixed" (*Things Near and Far* 115).

and even between discursive genres of fiction and non-fiction. It puts on display the very mechanics of storytelling—of how acts of storytelling can compel certain effects: visceral effects such as disgust and horror, truth effects that attempt to compel belief, and even satirical effects that compel critical questioning and awareness. Acts of storytelling and their world-shaping powers are the primary focus of *The Three Impostors* and its many embedded narratives, many of them "tall" tales told by nefarious impostors. If Machen's text has a claim to our renewed attention today, it is both because its exploration of storytelling makes it especially resonant with our supposedly "post-truth" times and because it might help us grapple with an undead past.

Although firmly rooted in its own time, *The Three Impostors* is clearly oriented toward a past that fundamentally shapes the present. As if in response to evolutionary anthropologist E.B. Tylor's suggestion that digging into the ground beneath London unearths artefacts that provide "the history of human civilisation" (*Primitive Culture* 59), Machen's *The Three Impostors* reanimates the buried histories of one of the most modern cities of the world through ancient artefacts, peoples, and occult rituals that mysteriously reappear in the heart of London. In doing so, it effectively troubles the Victorian belief in progress by presenting cultural "survivals" that speak not of a long-gone past but of how the past *persists*, fundamentally shaping modernity.[1] If Machen's work offers a complication of time, it is no less effective in offering complications of place. It is perhaps more accurate to say that Machen is specifically drawn to probing the mysteries (hidden delights and horrors) of what we might call "mixed places" and "mixed times," of places constituted by interlocking cultures and histories.

Machen was born in Caerleon-on-Usk (Gwent), located in what some call "border country," that "region between England and Wales" (Ward 144). In his writings, Machen most often identifies as Welsh and cherishes ties to his birthplace (esteeming it as

---

1 Both *The Three Impostors* and *The Great God Pan* display an interest in survivals, a term that Machen employs in much the same way as it was employed by E.B. Tylor, who used it to refer to "processes, opinions, and so forth, which have been carried on by force of habit into a new state of society different from that in which they had their original home, and they thus remain as proofs and examples of an older condition of culture out of which a newer has been evolved" (*Primitive Culture* 16). See Appendix D, especially pp. 232–33.

the creative source of his best work) but at other times he identifies as English. It may be that for Machen the experience of being from the border country also means inhabiting and becoming attuned to potentially disorienting border identities. He comes to London as an outsider. Although initially he idealizes London as a magical city in an Eastern tale, when he moves there, he experiences it as "rather a goblin's castle than a city of delights" and even as "a place of punishment wherein [he] was condemned to hard labour through many dreary and hopeless years" (*Far Off Things* 109), suffering in poverty and isolation as he tries to make a living from writing. London (much like the fashionable Strand) is a place accessible only to those who can afford to be there—that is, it was not for him (130). Indeed, he recalls that when he happens to meet someone in the "great desert of London" whom he knows from those "old days" in Gwent, they reminisce together and "feel as if [they] were surviving tribesmen of some sept [clan] that has been 'literally annihilated' or 'almost decimated' to use our modern English" (32); he felt strangely out of place and out of time, outmoded in one of the most modern cities in the world.

If London remains locked in ambivalence for Machen—a place both of magic and horror—strangely, it is much like his birthplace, which he describes, in his autobiographical writings, as a fairy land seen through the wonder of a child's eyes even as it becomes, in several of his stories, a place haunted by its history. The ancient Roman ruins and pre-Celtic monuments and burial mounds discovered in his native Gwent speak to Machen of peoples who came before and, Machen speculates, might still be around, even if hidden, unknown to most except as they have been preserved and distorted through fairy lore. As one of his biographers notes, from a very young age, Machen saw that "these relics of ancient civilisations were visible realities" and this had a very important effect on his understanding of history: "to him history was not a series of disjointed events, but a steady flow, merging the past with the present" (Sweetser 18).[1] It is this attentiveness to the ways in which the past merges with the present that primarily captivates Machen. If his birthplace is haunted by ancient ruins and

---

1 More details on Machen's life and writings can be found in his own autobiographical writing—*Far Off Things* (1922), *Things Near and Far* (1923), and *The London Adventure, Or The Art of Wandering* (1924)—as well as in Aidan Reynolds and William Charlton's *Arthur Machen: A Short Account of his Life and Work* (1963), Wesley D. Sweetser's *Arthur Machen* (1964), and Mark Valentine's *Arthur Machen* (1995).

peoples, London is haunted by the debris of past civilizations as the British face their own possible decadence.[1] Machen's London and Caerleon-ọn-Usk are mixed places in which distant times and peoples meet and in which the past is not dead and modernity is not new.

For Machen, the earth, its peoples, their artefacts, and their stories are the media of history, not so much because they tell histories forthright but rather because they hold scraps of histories congealed, just as amber is a medium that holds ancient insects, as rock is a medium that can hold fossil traces of long extinct species, or as the earth itself is (to borrow Walter Benjamin's words) "the medium in which ancient cities lie buried." (*Selected Writings* 576). In Machen's own time, science was unearthing rocks that told of the earth's ancient age, fossils that "spoke" of giant monsters (dinosaurs) that rivalled any dragon or magical beast of age-old legends, and the material remnants of ancient cities and civilizations that "told" of peoples who came before. But as Machen's tales often suggest, these remnants of past times, no less than the specimens of science, or the modern commodities that London has on offer, are about as easily readable as ancient hieroglyphs from a little-known ancient civilization. If Machen is sceptical about their very readability, or at least human beings' abilities to read or interpret them accurately, he is also fascinated by the stories they *might* tell.

In *The Three Impostors*, material artefacts are the primary focus of characters who are collectors, antiquaries, and fetish-worshippers as much as they are the focus of detectives who hunt for material clues of crimes and of scientists who study objects to learn about the histories of the earth, its species, and its many civilizations. As objects take centre stage in this text, they sometimes

---

1 In this introduction, decadence (uncapitalized) refers to a civilization's period of decline, while Decadence (capitalized) refers to the artistic movement associated with the *fin de siècle*. The two terms overlap, however, as the former was part of a widespread belief that civilizations progressed as natural organisms do (they are born, develop, and then decline and die), and the latter was first employed by a French critic to refer disparagingly to a particular kind of French literature that seemed symptomatic of the decline of French civilization. The authors so disparaged reclaimed the term as a badge of honour, and thus Decadence became an often counter-cultural movement whose practitioners do not shy away from—indeed, often take pride in—offending the sensibilities of their contemporaries.

display a strange agency that allows them to compete with and displace human characters. Characters appear caught between different valuations of things, and some even enter circuits of exchange typically reserved for things. Bodies and body parts are stolen, bought and sold, and exhibited in museums, apparently violating a fundamental tendency in Western thought—"that of conceptually separating people from things, and of seeing people as the natural preserve for individuation (that is singularization) and things as the natural preserve for commoditization" (Kopytoff 84). For readers of Victorian literature, who have been trained to pay attention to "subjects and plots" (Freedgood, *Ideas* 1), this text's insistent focus on objects can seem distracting, even superfluous. However, this is a text for which—to paraphrase French Decadent poet Théophile Gautier (1811–72)—the superfluous is necessary. But what are readers to make of a text that resists in-depth reading protocols, returning readers repeatedly to a play of surfaces? Perhaps it is best to begin with the appeal of surfaces and to attempt to understand how Victorians might have learned to read (and misread) them.

The Beautiful Book of Horrors: The Keynotes Series and Beyond

During his first trip to London, a young Arthur Machen purchased a book that he would later describe as "cataclysmic" (*Far Off Things* 92). The book's "tremendous boldness" captivated Machen; its "very cover" was more "provocative" than any he had seen (91) and its "literary manner" was "wholly strange and new and wonderful" (92). It was "a denial of everything [he] had been brought up to believe most sure and sacred" (92). This ground-shifting book moved him to begin writing. Although he would later deny and downplay his part in *fin-de-siècle* Decadence, this was one of several instances in which he was drawn into its orbit. In a bookshop in London in 1880, he was drawn, more specifically, to some of its stylistic experiments in both the production of beautiful books and the boldness of their content.

Written by "earth-shaking, heaven-storming poet" (*Far Off Things* 92) Algernon Charles Swinburne (1837–1909), the copy of *Songs Before Sunrise* (1871) that Machen purchased was likely adorned with an elegant and unconventionally sparse design by Pre-Raphaelite poet and artist Dante Gabriel Rossetti (1828–82) that consisted of three roundels depicting the rising sun, moon, and stars blocked in gold onto the upper and lower covers and spine of the book. Machen may not have known it, but this was one of only about eleven book bindings designed by Rossetti, and it was based on a design Rossetti had made for a frame of one of his paintings (Royal Academy 58–59) now transposed to frame the book itself as aesthetic artefact. Both Rossetti and Swinburne were already controversial figures, famously criticized as part of the morbid and overly sensual "fleshly school of poetry" and key influences on the Aesthetes and Decadents of the British *fin de siècle*, who sought (among other things) to free art from the constraints of middle-class Victorian morality and to free the artist to explore any and all forms of embodied experience, beauty, and strangeness.[1] For Machen, Swinburne's book was precisely that kind of subversive book; it "was positively strewn with the fragments of shattered altars and the torn limbs of kings and priests" (*Far Off Things* 92).

Machen would gain his first real notice as a writer through a beautifully designed book that featured its own kind of fleshly boldness. That book, *The Great God Pan* (1894), and the one that soon followed, *The Three Impostors*, would place him firmly among the supposedly depraved sensibilities of the "Gospel of Intensity" (Quilter). Both books were first published as part of John Lane's Keynotes series, and this had a bigger impact on these works than critics generally acknowledge, even if it affected each work quite differently. In total, the series would consist of thirty-three volumes printed between 1894 and 1897, and Machen would be one of only four authors to have two works published in the series. Although Lane (1854–1925) initially intended the Keynotes as a series of cheaply bound works of fiction, they soon became "a distinguished set of books" with several signature features such as their "slim format, the excellent paper and typography, [and] the blended colours chosen for cloth and blocking" (Sadleir, qtd. in Stetz and Lasner 42). Perhaps most significantly, the

---

1 Even if Decadence has a complex international history and is admittedly difficult to define, it has nonetheless been associated with a number of themes, images, and textual strategies, including "the imagery of imperial Rome and the *femme fatale*, ... sensual indulgence, philosophical pessimism, ... sexual nonconformism" (Potolsky v), "morbidity, a cult of artificiality, [and] exoticism" (Constable et al. 2), "the perennial decay of boundaries—the insistence on *at once* mobilizing and undermining boundaries and differences" (21), contradiction (Freedman), and "unsettling commonly held assumptions" (Dellamora 529).

Keynotes were distinguished by cover and title-page illustrations designed by Aubrey Beardsley (1872–98), one of the most infamous, instantly recognizable, and widely imitated (and parodied) illustrators of the 1890s, who was already notoriously associated with Decadence since illustrating the English translation of Oscar Wilde's *Salomé* (1894) and becoming co-editor of the infamous avant-garde periodical *The Yellow Book*, also published by Lane. In short, the Keynotes were uniquely positioned to garner much public attention. As highlighted in an advertising pamphlet for the series, showcasing the Beardsley cover designs, reviewers of the series saw it as "daringly original" and commended its "cleverness," its "style," and "uncommonness" (*Keynotes Series of Novels and Short Stories*). Beardsley's covers (shown in Appendix A1) were both art and advertisement, and Machen was among the "school of brilliant storytellers" that the Keynotes series first introduced to the public, even if he would ride this wave of popularity for only a short time.

Sporting "a suitably sinister faun" (Reynolds and Charlton 43) described by one contemporary critic as a "nasty little naked figure of dubious sex and humanity" (Quilter 773), Machen's *The Great God Pan* was clearly marked as Decadent, as Beardsley's art was recognized as "the handmaid of a very morbid species of literature" (Quilter 778). The tales contained in *The Great God Pan*—featuring supernatural horrors unleashed through neurological experiments, neo-pagan rituals, and unspeakable acts of depravity—further reinforced the connection.[1] The book was what the time might call a *succès de scandale*—earning Machen compliments from Oscar Wilde (1854–1900) himself. Arthur Conan Doyle (1859–1930) thought Machen a genius and claimed that the book gave him nightmares. In addition to counting these famous writers among its first readers, *The Great God Pan* reached enough of a popular readership to require an immediate second edition. Reviews selected by Lane to help advertise the second edition play up its most sensational features; they describe the work as appalling, weird, powerful, and uncanny, and they highlight the visceral responses it elicits and that are still associated with the genre of horror (blood curdling, bodily shudders, shivers, and creeps). These same reviewers compared Machen with the likes of Poe, Le Fanu, and the Stevenson of *Dr. Jekyll and Mr. Hyde* (1886),

---

1 For more on the connection between Decadence and neo-paganism, see Denisoff.

helping define him as an author of particularly sensational genres, including horror, "borderland fiction" treating unexplained mysteries often of a supernatural or occult kind, and the kind of fiction that "played with the crucibles of science" (*Pall Mall Gazette*, qtd. in *Keynotes Series*) that would eventually become more widely known as science fiction.

When *The Three Impostors* appeared the next year—again in Lane's Keynotes series and with a cover and title design by Beardsley—it seemed reasonable to expect that it would garner a similar response. After all, *The Three Impostors* continued to cultivate the eerie, dread-filled atmosphere of the earlier work while featuring some of the same characters and dealing with similarly dark subject matter in which ancient peoples, pagan rituals, and occult powers collide with modern city-dwellers, artistic crimes, decadent detectives, and modern science. In some ways, reviewers' assessment of *The Three Impostors* was comparable to that of *The Great God Pan*, and several reviews mention both texts to underline the connection (see, for example, Appendices B2, B3, B7, and B8). The book was often described as full of horrors and terrors, as gruesome, weird, uncanny, and grim, and as having the tell-tale visceral effects of horror (fascinating, gripping, and thrilling its readers). And yet, even if *The Three Impostors* was published only a short time after *The Great God Pan* and shared many of the same ingredients that had made *The Great God Pan* notorious, it was something of a flop by comparison. No immediate second edition was required, and, indeed, it would not be reprinted again for about a decade.

The poor performance of *The Three Impostors* was likely tied to the timing of its publication. As one reviewer for *The Saturday Review* points out, Machen "is an unfortunate man" in that he "has determined to be weird, horrible, and as outspoken as his courage permits in an age which is noisily resolved to be ''ealthy'''" (Appendix B2, p. 209). In the brief time between the publication of *The Great God Pan* in 1894 and that of *The Three Impostors* in 1895, much had changed, particularly in late-Victorian readers' openness to "unhealthy" literature—and Decadence had been defined by contemporary poet and critic Arthur Symons (1865–1945) as precisely that: "a new and beautiful and interesting disease" ("Decadent" 859). Only months before *The Three Impostors* first appeared, Oscar Wilde—the "high priest" of Aestheticism and Decadence—had been arrested, reportedly while holding a yellow book that many (incorrectly) assumed was a copy of *The Yellow Book*. During his trial, his own book *The Picture of Dorian*

Gray (1891) was famously employed as "evidence" against him, and he was convicted of homosexual behaviour and jailed. If books helped mark Wilde as Decadent and "degenerate," Beardsley's drawings similarly marked Lane's Keynotes (and *The Yellow Book*). The resulting backlash against any literature deemed "unhealthy" was swift, as was the repercussion for anyone associated with Wilde. Beardsley was let go from his post with *The Yellow Book* because his illustrations for Wilde's *Salomé* (which had launched him into public prominence) meant that he and his unusual aesthetic were associated with Wilde. Machen had met Wilde and maintained an acquaintance with him for a brief time, but his book's association with both Beardsley and, by extension, Wilde and all he represented was enough to negatively affect the sales of *The Three Impostors*.

After its Keynotes series debut in 1895, *The Three Impostors* would not be printed again until 1906. In this second printing, *The Three Impostors* appeared in an altered version (with a few episodes removed), and not on its own but rather as part of a collection of Machen's works under the title *The House of Souls*, published by Grant Richards and with a uniquely strange cover and spine image—this time by Sidney H. Sime (1865–1941), an illustrator heavily influenced by Beardsley who would go on to develop his own unique style and gain fame through his illustrations of weird and fantastical creatures. Indeed, the "Sime Zoology" of fantastic "Beasts that Might Have Been" was a series that ran in the London-based illustrated weekly *The Sketch* in 1905, and the figures on the cover and spine of the 1906 *House of Souls* would easily fit among them (see Appendices A4 and A5). If Beardsley's black and white drawings branded the Keynotes series *Three Impostors* as Decadent, Sime's illustrations, which retain certain resemblances to Beardsley's strange figures, re- invoke this history and further entrench Machen's association with genres of the weird, horror, and the fantastic. The next reprinting of *The Three Impostors*, by Knopf in 1923, would feature a yellow cover, perhaps an echo of the novel's provenance in the so-called "yellow" nineties.

In general, though, *The Three Impostors* was—and is still—much more likely to be reprinted in parts, with one or more of the impostors' tales excerpted from the novel for inclusion in collections of horror and/or supernatural tales or in edited compilations of Machen's work that help accentuate Machen's contributions to the horror genre and/or British Decadence. The impostors' tales can certainly stand on their own—as they did before the first publication of *The Three Impostors* and have done since[1]—but, as discussed below, the meaning and effects of the individual tales appear very different when examined within the larger frame narrative of this story-cycle. What appear to be tales of supernatural horror on their own are much more difficult to categorize as part of a highly self-reflexive whole that seems to undermine the horrors it presents. Strangely, Machen's beautiful book and its horrors are perhaps best understood in tandem, and not just because this appears to have affected its reception, as discussed above, but also because the human attraction to and relationship with beautiful objects are central to the novel's concerns.

The Art(ifice) of Visceral Effects

The original cover design for *The Three Impostors* was perhaps not nearly so provocative as the sexually charged Pan figure that adorned Machen's first Keynotes volume. Nonetheless, its sleek lines and seemingly self-perpetuating design certainly signal a commitment to a carefully wrought style—one that is as apparent in the finely crafted phrases that characters speak[2] as it is built into the structure of the text itself. With its frame narrative containing several embedded narratives that themselves often contain further embedded texts, the structure of *The Three Impostors* appears carefully designed to attract readers' notice. Although this is not fully apparent until the end of the novel, the text resembles nothing so much as an ouroboros, an ancient symbol depicting a snake devouring its own tail. The text's beginning devours its ending: the first section ("Prologue") presents what is in effect the end of the story, an ending that will be repeated in the final section of the novel ("Adventure of the Deserted Residence"). In between these two stagings of the ending, readers witness a series of chance encounters and the telling of fantastic tales between characters incompletely introduced in

---

1 "The Novel of the Iron Maid" appeared in the *St James's Gazette* before the publication of *The Three Impostors*. Some collections that republished one or more of the impostors' tales separately after 1895 include Knopf's *Tales of Horror and the Supernatural by Arthur Machen* (1948) and, more recently, both Joshi and Denisoff.

2 Characters often speak in elevated or ornate styles (sometimes employing French or Latin terms) and discuss the importance of style directly, claiming, for example, that for them "style is absolutely everything" (p. 184).

the Prologue. Each tale is intriguing in and of itself, but it also functions as part of a larger whole in which repeating patterns and resonating forms of dread invite readers to piece together a puzzle (trap) whose picture becomes clearer only at the very end.[1]

In the Prologue, readers overhear a conversation already in progress among three persons (impostors), partners in a mysterious mission involving a certain "young man with spectacles" (p. 55), before leaving an old, deserted house. After they leave, two friends—Dyson and Phillipps—happen upon this same house while out for a stroll on the edges of London. Mesmerized by the "heavy desolation of the place," they begin to "moralise" in "great style" and, looking up from outside the house to one of its upper-floor windows, Dyson claims, "that very room, I tell you, is within all blood and fire" (pp. 57–58). When readers read the Prologue, they do not—indeed cannot—know its significance. It appears tantalizingly intriguing, but ultimately perplexing for readers unfamiliar with the story context and characters necessary to make sense of it.

Readers then move from the Prologue to the next section, "Adventure of the Gold Tiberius," which, in addition to filling in background details on Dyson (a Decadent writer) and Phillipps (an amateur ethnologist), also recounts a peculiar incident framed by the section title as the adventure of a coin and hence invokes the popular genre of the it-narrative.[2] One evening, while out for a stroll, an unsuspecting Dyson sees a man (with spectacles!) running for his life. As the man runs, desperately fleeing his pursuer, he throws something away, and by chance it falls into the path of Dyson, who desperately peels after it and pockets it without knowing what it is. When he tells his friend Phillipps about this strange occurrence, Phillipps informs him that the object he has found is *the* Gold Tiberius, a "storied" object with a history that stretches back to the Roman empire. Phillipps explains, "It glints through history and legend, appearing and disappearing,

---

1 Readers should be aware that this Introduction might contain plot details.

2 An eighteenth-century genre that continued to be popular in the Victorian period, the "it-narrative" is a narrative told from the perspective of an inanimate object or an animal. For more on it-narratives generally, see Blackwell, "The It-Narrative in Eighteenth-Century England" (2004). For a discussion of the genre in the nineteenth-century, see Freedgood, "What Objects Know" (2010).

with intervals of a hundred years in time, and continents in place" (p. 63). Dyson believes they have been called upon to solve a great mystery, while Phillipps refuses to have anything more to do with it. Nevertheless, they are both drawn in by what seems to be the power of the coin, described as having unusual agency and magnetism. In a series of chance encounters by each character in subsequent sections, they are called to listen to the three impostors (in various guises) as these spin one or more extraordinary tales.

Somewhat like Dyson and Phillipps (who act as surrogate readers as they listen to the impostors' tales), readers are also lured into the tales, all of them full of carefully drawn-out details and increasing in suspense, violence, and ultimately horror. Each tale proceeds by subtle suggestions, forebodings, and intense intimations of horror while carefully delaying the revelations of the suggested horrors. Because strange occurrences are described in detail, each tale resembles detective fiction in its accumulation of clues that at first appear not to add up. It is only at the very end of the tale that the supernatural, occult, or otherwise inexplicable phenomena that are the basis of the tale are revealed, albeit more through suggestion (and thus still shrouded in mystery) than through the explicit explication one might expect from a Sherlock Holmesian detective. This technique would make Machen famous. In addition to keeping Conan Doyle up at night, it would lead H.P. Lovecraft to dub Machen a "modern master" of supernatural horror and to characterize his work of the 1890s as "stand[ing] alone in its class, and mark[ing] a distinct epoch in the history of [supernatural horror]" (159). From there, Machen's work would continue to captivate generations of readers.

As Lovecraft claims, the "charm" of Machen's tales is "in the telling" (160), in the carefully cultivated effects on its readers. Although distinct, the different impostors' tales resonate with one another and seem to point to larger patterns and themes that lure readers further and further along into its design, even if this design is ultimately revealed to be something of a trap. Several tales gravitate around the notion of circulation and exchange (as in the "Novel of the Dark Valley," in which unspeakable crimes are committed in exchange for gold, and in "The Incident," in which a dealer in curiosities tells of how a priceless precious stone was obtained for a trifle under false pretenses), and around processes of "transmutation"—the novel's subtitle. The tales most clearly focused on transmutations are also the two most often excerpted from *The Three Impostors* for collections of horror and occult tales. These are also the tales that most strongly support claims that

Machen's stories are specimens of Decadent gothic, featuring Darwinian fears of degeneration and the mutability of matter (see especially Punter; Hurley). They are worth examining more carefully to better understand the novel's subtitle before proceeding to explore how these (and other) tales function somewhat like red herrings in readers' attempts to understand the larger work as a whole.

"The Novel of the Black Seal" is one of several works that Machen wrote featuring what he calls the "little people." Machen did not invent the idea that the fairies of old folklore may have existed (indeed, he speculates that they may still exist), that rather than being entirely imaginary, the fairies preserved in folklore were based on memories of an actual race that inhabited the British Isles before they were driven away by the invading Celts. As Carole G. Silver has shown, this idea has a long and complex history, and by the end of the nineteenth century, what Machen would call the "little people" were the product of an amalgam of discourses, folklore, ethnology, Darwinian evolution, fantastic fiction, and even fantastic illustrations such as Beardsley's that conflated natural and supernatural dwarves with various kinds of pygmy and/or aboriginal races (see Appendix A3). As readers eventually learn, the character of Cradock, the young man that Professor Gregg suspects might be a member of that ancient race of supernatural beings, was born eight months after the disappearance of his mother in the Grey Hills where these beings were thought to have dwelled. Cradock is possessed of features that are otherwise inexplicable: his hissing language unintelligible to anyone else and his ability to move material objects from a distance through what are effectively "ectoplasmic pseudopodia"—or slimy projections from his body (more on this fascinating theory later). Cradock's body (as part human and part little person) retains certain abilities recorded in its very matter that most people can no longer access. Matter has its mysteries, at the heart of which lies horror. In fact, the black seal at the centre of this tale supposedly tells (in a virtually indecipherable ancient form of writing) of such mysteries, of "how man can be reduced to the slime from which he came, and be forced to put on the flesh of the reptile and the snake" (p. 128); the horror here appears in how matter itself is given to transmutations, and it plays more specifically on Victorian fears of regression and reversion as much as on xenophobic fears of racialized others.

The "Novel of the White Powder" reinvokes fears of regression and the instability of matter, but this time with a focus on the powers of ancient pagan rituals to initiate the transmutation. In this tale a young man begins a spectacular regression that reduces him to primordial ooze after he mistakenly ingests a corrupted compound that he assumes is a prescribed medicine but turns out to be a chemical akin to the wine used in the ancient witches' Sabbath rituals. This tale, often compared to *Dr. Jekyll and Mr. Hyde*, most blatantly features the "transmutations" of the novel's subtitle, a term that surfaces repeatedly, accumulating multiple meanings across tales. Most notably, the term is associated with the ancient art of alchemy and its aim to transmute baser metals into gold, with the more recent theory of the transmutations of species (a controversial theory of evolution that predates Darwin's[1]), and with the transmutations, including inter-species transformations, that supposedly occurred during certain pagan rituals.[2] If we could combine the meanings of transmutation here briefly described, we would come closest to the power of that term for Machen, who appears fascinated by the potential for radical transformation.

And yet, as tempting as it might be to use such tales as evidence that *The Three Impostors* is an anxious text that (much like other Victorian Gothic texts) plays with Victorian fears, such an interpretation is only partially convincing, as it does not account for the many ways in which the text self-reflexively works to undermine such tales and their implicit fears. At the end of each impostor's tale, our surrogate reader expresses doubt about the veracity of the recounted tale that readers will likely share. Phillipps, for instance, remains largely unmoved by the tales, often offering a rational explanation for the seemingly marvellous events recounted, as one might very well expect from a "man of science." Even Dyson, who we know is partial to the marvellous, finds himself unable to believe and after listening to a few tales becomes so exasperated with what he strongly suspects are nothing but "tall tales" that he even considers subscribing to Mudie's, a circulating library known for providing the kind of family-friendly middle-class reading that a Decadent would abhor.

---

1 This continental theory was widely disseminated to an English audience through Robert Chambers's best-selling *Vestiges of the Natural History of Creation* (1844). This book, which went through multiple editions, had a wide-ranging impact on the time, including on Arthur Waite (1857–1942), one of Machen's closest lifelong friends, who was a researcher in all things occult. Waite "read Chambers' *Vestiges* which set him on his mystical investigations" (Reynolds and Charlton 167).

2 See, for example, the description of such transmutations in Pater.

Readers have even more reason to doubt the impostors' tales. Unlike Dyson and Phillipps, who are approached individually by different impostors on different occasions, readers attend to *all* the tales, so they would inevitably notice not only the accumulating resonances across tales that suggest a finely crafted design but also the fact that each of the tales told by the different impostors features a young man with spectacles, although no two tales agree on who he is or why he is being sought. It becomes obvious that the tales are made up, finely drawn out, and told for strategic purposes on the part of the impostors, even if their purposes remain largely unclear until the end. In explicitly revealing the gruesome tales to be false, Machen undermines the carefully crafted atmosphere of dread and horror for which he would become famous. If an impostor's story manages to give readers "the creeps," it is not long before such a visceral response is explicitly revealed to be the effect of artifice and manipulation.

While Machen was often congratulated for the cleverness of this work, he was also chastised for being the kind of magician that lets his audience see "how the thing is done" (as qtd. in *Precious Balms* 28). Why overtly reveal the artifice of the whole and risk undermining the very effects of horror that Machen cultivates so carefully throughout the work? Why be the kind of magician who lets viewers see how the magic trick is done? It seems an odd approach to horror, as readers are more likely to be moved by a tale that seems at least plausibly true than by one that is patently false. Perhaps Machen here shows his allegiance to other writers in the Decadent cult of artifice: he is a "true artist in artificial things" who delights to see his artifice as artifice (Symons, "Apology" 5). At the same time, however, Machen's insistence on showing readers how his horror tricks are done also aligns with aesthetic techniques employed in horror genres today.

Consider, for instance, the sudden appearance of blood splattering across a viewer's screen during particularly violent or gory scenes in a variety of films and TV series in recent years. This "special effect" appears to lend immediacy to the scene and elicits a visceral response in viewers (perhaps shock and/or disgust and/or horror), while at the same time, or very soon after, reminding viewers of the presence of the screen itself, as the blood remains on it for a few moments after the violence has subsided. This special effect calls attention to a paradox: in general, the "visceral" effect (one that seems to come from one's gut or viscera) requires that we forget the technological mediation and become immersed in the scene, but here the very technique that elicits a visceral response is also one that reminds viewers they are being manipulated. Albeit briefly, viewers switch from looking *through* their screen (forgetting that they are watching something fake), to looking *at* their screen when the blood appears to hit and linger on its surface (and thus remembering that they are watching something fake). However fleetingly, the visceral effect turns into a meta-fictional moment whose ultimate effect is uncertain: are viewers supposed to be shocked by the effect even as they are called to attend to the pleasure (?!) of the spectacle of gratuitous horror and violence, to appreciate the "special effects"? With his overt references to Decadent writers (themselves known for their obsession with artifice), the orthographic separation of the all-caps titles of stories told within the story, and the explicit revelation that the tales are false, Machen calls attention to the book as mediating the visceral effects of the impostors' stories, although the effect in Machen's case is not so fleeting as the blood-splatter visual technique of our own time.

In Machen's text, the self-reflexive effect is not only repeated with every tale told but is sustained to the point of climax at the end of the text, when the design of the whole is finally revealed. Upon completing the text, readers realize that the last and most gruesome, most horrific scene of all, which shows the results of the artistic torture of the poor man with spectacles, is one that has been carefully staged by Machen, twice!—once as a kind of teaser scene at the very beginning and again at the end—with enough similarity and difference to make sure readers notice the theatricality of the scene, even if they happen to miss the theatrical language that accompanies it.[1] When readers behold the blood and fire in the artistically tortured and burned body of the unfortunate man with spectacles in the final paragraphs of the novel, they will likely recall Dyson's impossibly prophetic claim from the Prologue—"that very room, I tell you, is within all blood and fire"—a claim he makes *from outside the deserted house before* he and Phillipps enter it! In addition to making plain how well Machen has manipulated everyone (characters and readers alike), this final scene also allows readers to become retrospectively aware of newly conspicuous patterns.

---

1 Dyson comments on how the "stage is decked out" and on the elements of the whole "scene" (p. 193). The two scenes echo each other with the repetition of words such as "moralise," "cedarn gloom," and "dissolution," and the resonance between the repeated words "mouldering" and "smouldering."

Having made their way through every tale and sub-tale through to the repeated ending, readers can now see what would not be apparent to anyone reading the impostors' tales excerpted out of context: that their tales function as counterfeit coin exchanged in the hope of "buying" information about the man with spectacles. This suggests that readers would waste their time delving into the details of any one of the tales, as we have done briefly above; the tales are a trap, so to speak, part of an elaborate ruse, a gratuitous distraction from the impostors' true intent, which readers (together with Dyson and Phillipps) eventually learn is to capture and torture the man with spectacles and retrieve the Gold Tiberius he had stolen on behalf of the secret society to which he and the impostors belong. But the tales fail to make the desired purchase: the three impostors eventually find the man with spectacles, but not through any information provided by the hapless Dyson and Phillipps, and they never retrieve the coin. When the impostors cannot find the coin anywhere on their victim, they decide instead to take one of his fingers from the hand that took the coin. The finger is intended for the secret society's museum collection—much like the body of the ill-fated Mr. Headley—the antiquary from whom the man with spectacles first stole the coin and who ends up mummified in Egyptian fashion to be sold to a museum by the secret society. Indeed, upon learning the fate of Mr. Headley, the man with spectacles flees the secret society's headquarters in a panic and, without "thought or design of action," he takes the "accursed coin" (p. 189) with him and then unknowingly throws it away into the path of an unsuspecting, casually strolling Dyson.

The exchange of false tales is part of a larger pattern of exchanges that focus readers' attention on peculiar relations between persons and things in which they appear to exchange properties: persons (or parts of persons) are objectified and objects appear lifelike, sometimes seeming to have more agency than humans. Both persons and things enter circuits of displacements, substitutions, and exchanges often under false pretenses and everywhere laced with violence. This pattern is pervasive, self-amplifying, and seemingly self-perpetuating, much like Beardsley's design for the cover.[1] But given that the "playful"

---

1 There is no evidence that Machen discussed the covers for his Keynotes books with Beardsley. Rather than a direct link between Beardsley's image and Machen's stories, they are parallel representations of the British *fin de siècle*'s obsession with all things stylized and artificial.

exchanges ultimately land human bodies and body parts in museums, the pattern, much like Machen's highly stylized text, is not just clever and ingenious, as critics have so often noted. It changes everything. When read as a whole and in the broader context of Victorian object practices, *The Three Impostors* reveals new horrors only hinted at in its individual tales.

Material, Scientific, and Decadent Cultures

Machen's text (featuring a Decadent writer as well as several antiquaries, ethnologists, and other kinds of collectors and dealers in curiosities) suggests that seemingly unrelated Victorian trends are indeed interrelated: the Decadent cult of artifice, the emergence of commodity culture, the Victorian craze for collecting, collections, and museums, and the increasingly specimen-oriented sciences of the time converge in this text and appear entangled with seemingly gratuitous violence. Although the connection to violence is most apparent in the text's invocation of museums, somewhat surprisingly it also pervades other forms of Victorian object practices represented in the novel.

Museums and their practices of collecting and exhibiting artefacts are quintessentially associated with the Victorian era, an era well known for its intertwined ventures of scientific and colonial expansion that filled Victorian museums and homes with a wide range of "exotic" objects. Museums and exhibits helped bring the world to Britain and to frame it from a British perspective. Many of the most famous British museums have their origins in the period, some of which are referred to directly in Machen's text. The many things (e.g., fossils, archeological artefacts, etc.) that were brought or bequeathed by wealthy collectors to British museums came from distant places and/or times and seemed to harbour tantalizing pieces of stories—seemingly marvellous stories about the vast history of the earth, the origin and evolution of its many species, and its current and long-lost civilizations. The vast array of cultural artefacts and scientific specimens in Victorian museums were actively sought-after, "highly storied" objects often implicated in a history of violence, much like the Gold Tiberius at the centre of Machen's novel.

As Anne McClintock has shown, museums and their collections became central to consolidating and promoting practices of imperial and epistemic violence through what she calls a "global science of the surface" (34). As she explains, the Victorian era remained committed to a particular project of knowledge that began in the Enlightenment—one that "imagined drawing the whole world into a single 'science of order'" (34). Borrowing the template established by Carl Linnaeus's (1707–78) attempt "to organize all plant forms into a single genesis narrative," "hosts of explorers, botanists, natural historians and geographers set out with the vocation of ordering the world's forms into a global science of the surface and an optics of truth" (34). This science of the surface is entangled with the imperial project of expanding territorial control over much of the surface of the globe and becomes intimately tied to racist pseudo-sciences that sought, for example, to "measure" racial differences and ultimately rank races into a hierarchy of supposedly self-evident, visually apparent, and quantifiable evidence of evolutionary progress from "primitive" to "modern." In McClintock's words, the science of the surface was "a *conversion* project, dedicated to transforming the earth into a single economic currency, a single pedigree of history and a universal standard of cultural value—set and managed by Europe" (34). Thus, in addition to having become an established imperial acquisitive practice associated with the appropriation of cultural and historical artefacts, the practice of collecting and displaying objects was also an increasingly important part of the professionalization of emerging sciences (such as anthropology) and also propelled such sciences and their racist assumptions into more general public visibility, converting narratives of imperial and evolutionary progress into easily consumable spectacles (33). Museums and major exhibits became places through which (to borrow Roger Luckhurst's words) the British could "[master] the globe in an afternoon" (388); they were effectively a training ground in what Luckhurst calls "global space-time," which centred a British view of the world and its history and implicitly promoted both formal and informal colonial practices of domination.

The collecting and display of objects and the practices of "reading" people through them were not limited to major museums and exhibits. Indeed, collecting was so pervasive and seemingly coextensive with "modern" Victorian culture that Henry James (1843–1916) referred to it as "that *most modern* of our current passions" (xliii; emphasis added); this modern craze was visible as much in "chinamania" as it was in "going in for aesthetics" or the intense consumption of beautiful objects, both practices repeatedly ridiculed by *Punch* (see Appendix C6). Oddly, collections of objects became "symptoms" of a variety of disorders; they were "signs" that could be read, that seemed to tell of an underlying condition. *Punch* may very well playfully point out chronic and acute forms of "chinamania," but some, like Max Nordau (1849–1923), seriously diagnosed the Decadents (among other artists) as degenerate, based, at least in part, on their collecting of things. His highly popular *Degeneration* (1892)[1] contains a chapter entitled "Symptoms" that effectively lists the kinds of clothing, fashion accessories, elements of interior décor, and "the piling up in dwellings of aimless *bric-à-brac*" as indicators of degeneration (537). Although Nordau's work is certainly peculiar in earnestly diagnosing Decadents based on their things, the connection between Decadence and collecting was also cultivated by Decadents themselves, who prized, among other things, beautiful books and a wide range of beautiful objects, from jewel-encrusted tortoises to hot-house flowers. Arguably, their collected things were part of a larger pattern of the Decadent valuing of artificial things over natural ones, or the cult of artifice, itself intertwined with the rise of urban lifestyles and the refinements of advanced (decadent) civilization.

Some of the most infamous Decadent protagonists were collectors, and their stories often include long, detailed lists of collected things: Wilde's *The Picture of Dorian Gray*, for instance, devotes a whole chapter to listing the many items in Dorian's collection, and J.-K. Huysmans's *À Rebours* (1884)[2]—the so-called "breviary of the decadence" (Symons, *Symbolist* 76)—has more lists than plot. This is the book that likely "poisoned" Dorian Gray, who conspicuously collects it in nine differently bound copies to suit different moods (Wilde 161). Throughout this "novel without a plot" (Wilde 159), Huysmans painstakingly details the many things that help the main character, Des Esseintes, create an artificial paradise for himself.

In some ways, both Dorian and Des Esseintes are model consumers; they appear to model sensual attraction to beautiful things and material acquisitiveness as the basis of identity formation that becomes typical of consumer culture. They thus showcase how Decadence (much like Aestheticism) may be "part of the process whereby objects take on what Marx calls their 'enigmatical character,' whereby they become objects of desire and identification,

---

1 *Degeneration* was first published in German in 1892. It was a widely popular work, translated into several languages (including English in 1895) and running through multiple editions (Mosse xvi).

2 Often translated as *Against Nature* or *Against the Grain*, Huysmans's novel was recognized as a key Decadent text in its own time and has long retained this reputation. See Cevasco.

rather than the center of economic transactions" (Psomiades 16). At the same time, however, they also model a particular Decadent "type" that Dorian describes as one "in whom the romantic temperament and the scientific temperament were so strangely blended" (Wilde 161). Dorian, like Des Esseintes, will cultivate a romantic hypersensibility and a penchant for scientific experimentation as he searches for new sensations artificially induced, in part, by collecting things that would elicit different forms of Decadent pleasure. This hybrid of the Decadent consumer/aesthete/scientist highlights what they have in common: a desire for complete freedom (especially from usefulness) in the pursuit of knowledge (Ferguson 470) and a decidedly materialist perspective.[1] Both characters seek freedom from usefulness in their experiments with things; they list and categorize them in ways that align them not only with Decadent *flâneurs* who went "botanizing on the sidewalk" (Benjamin, *Charles Baudelaire* 39) but also with scientists—who collected, categorized, and built (scientific and pseudo-scientific) narratives based on things like rocks, fossils, bones, and cultural artefacts of ancient civilizations. Notably, as the excerpt in Appendix C5 shows, Dorian's collection is full of "exotic" objects and thus—not coincidentally—inflected with the broader imperialist acquisitiveness and orientalism of his time.

The many varied Victorian practices of collecting briefly discussed here are thus entangled with imperialist, consumerist, and scientific acquisitiveness, as well as with certain aesthetic tendencies, modes of attention, and narrative forms, including the list-heavy works such as those of Huysmans and Wilde that some have read as precursors to modernist fiction,[2] but also with those of writers such as Richard Marsh (1857–1915) and Vernon Lee

---

1 A materialist is a proponent of materialism, which was "not a coherent doctrine" at this time, although it did generally refer to the "fundamental proposition ... that nothing exists independently of matter." The term was often used as an insult or "pejorative label" to "tarnish the reputation of those who challenged the old tradition of natural theology" (Dawson 114) but also to refer to artists (like the Aesthetes and Decadents) who appeared overly concerned with the body and its sensual, embodied experiences.

2 See especially Weir. Although many Modernists would distance themselves from Decadence, critics in recent decades have helped revise our understanding of the many ways in which Decadence and Modernism are entangled. See, for example, among others, Hext and Murray; Murray.

(1856–1935), who, much like Machen, explore the stories (and hauntings) that accrue around the exchange and collection of things.[1]

Given the entanglement of collecting and museums with practices of interpretation of things as signs (of aesthetic sophistication, of disease or degeneration, of one's place in evolutionary time, etc.) and with the telling of stories about others, the violence of Machen's text, which lands bodies and body parts in museums, no longer appears gratuitous—it is not simply violence for violence's sake. Machen's text—which refers to the Linnean system of classification from which the science of the surface takes inspiration and often (especially through the character of Professor Gregg) aligns the colonizing explorer who "discovers" new lands with the scientist who ventures into new, potentially occult territories of knowledge—seems to have absorbed this wider tendency rampant at this time. But if Machen adopts the codes of the science of the surface of his time, he also frequently undercuts them by staging what appears to be the revenge of the surface—the surface that cannot be read. His text is full of objects whose value and meaning are not immediately evident, cannot be easily ascertained. Machen's text questions the readability of material artefacts: What might they mean? What relationships do they have to humans? What evidentiary, economic, or other kind of value might they have and for whom? How do we know? Who gets to decide? This questioning is nowhere more blatant than in Machen's invocation of two quintessentially nineteenth-century types of objects: the *bibelot* and the fetish.

It is telling that Machen employs the term *bibelot*, especially in the context of what appears to be a superfluous conversation between Dyson and one of his friends, Russell, a realist writer. In a somewhat ridiculous discussion about the appropriate binding for Russell's yet-to-be-written series of books on the history of a street, Dyson observes that because of current bindings, books increasingly appear indistinguishable from *bibelots* (p. 153), a French term that encompasses a wide variety of material things, from trifles to priceless objects. As Janell Watson explains, "[b]y the 1880's, the medieval French word *bibelot* (knick-knack), which in the fifteenth century designated miscellaneous household items of little value, is revived by the most elite among Parisian collectors

---

1 See, for example, Marsh's collection of stories *Curios: Some Strange Adventures of Two Bachelors* (1898) and Lee's "A Worldly Woman" (1892) and "The Doll" (1927).

to designate the objects most precious to them, even though the term is also used to refer to the cheapest industrial kitsch. The term is not only revived and reinvented during the nineteenth century, it is also associated with the century" (5). Machen shows himself to be *au courant*, finely attuned to the material culture of his time and its practices of collecting by employing the French term, but he also shows an awareness of books themselves (perhaps much like his own beautifully designed Keynotes books) as aesthetic objects that are themselves highly collectible, fetishized items—collected not for their content so much as for their beautiful material form and what that form appears to say about their owner's taste, sophistication, and class. The *bibelot* in Machen's text appears akin to the fetish.

Although students of literature today are most likely to encounter the fetish and fetishism through the theories of Sigmund Freud (1856–1939) and Karl Marx (1818–83), and indeed both kinds of fetishism are relevant to Machen's text, it is important to note that both Freud and Marx are nineteenth-century writers who would have developed their own notion of fetishism from a much longer history of the term that is most significant in understanding Machen's text. The term fetish derives from the Latin *facticius*—"made by art" or "manufactured." The term evolved through the Portuguese *feitiço*—"which in the Middle Ages meant 'magical practice' or 'witch-craft' performed, often innocently, by the simple, ignorant classes" (Bernheimer 63). It then took on added significance as the Portuguese *feitiço* developed into the pidgin *fetisso* at the site of cross-cultural trading on the West African coast in the sixteenth century, where the term was employed by Europeans to describe Africans' conflation of the value of things, specifically, what they perceived as the Africans' tendency to "overestimate the economic value of trifles" and "attribute religious value to trifling objects" (Pietz, "Problem of the Fetish II" 41). From there, the term was incorporated into eighteenth-century fetish theory, which was disseminated into nineteenth-century popular scientific discourses that helped propagate an opposition between supposedly "primitive" societies (characterized by the practice of fetish-worship and associated with an "unenlightened" view of the world that was based on a belief in chance and/or supernatural intervention) and supposedly more advanced "modern" societies (characterized by science and the "enlightened" view of the world based on rational causality). In short, the fetish and the associated belief in animism (attributing lifelike qualities, powers, and agencies to inanimate objects) came to the fore in nineteenth-century Britain as a means of placing people into a hierarchy—a hierarchy that Machen's text troubles by aligning (rather than opposing) supposedly modern tendencies with supposedly primitive ones.

The fetish is everywhere in Machen's London, this most modern of cities that is itself a place governed by "Chance, the blind Madonna of the Pagan" (Stevenson and Stevenson 8). Dyson, a Decadent author, is writing a book on fetish-worshippers; the man with spectacles was recently initiated into a secret society of pagan fetish-worshippers; and Phillipps has a fetish from the South Seas as the dominant note of décor in his room (p. 85). Even if we do not count all the ways in which different characters across the novel's many tales (collectors, dealers in curiosities, antiquaries, etc.) fetishize specific kinds of objects, the fetish is particularly implied in the strange powers of the ancient coin— the Gold Tiberius—which is repeatedly framed as a seemingly magical object animated with unusual agency and magnetic powers that pull people into its orbit and may be ultimately responsible for orchestrating the whole plot.

Recall that the novel's plot is effectively launched by a chance encounter between Dyson and the coin. Dyson recounts being inexplicably and powerfully drawn to the object thrown in his path before he even knows what it is; he hardly attends to the man with spectacles who is clearly fleeing for his life and "in spite of [himself, he] could not help tearing after [the coin]" (p. 62). As Dyson indicates to Phillipps, he is thoroughly convinced that the coin has "chosen" them to solve its mystery, and he happily acquiesces, welcoming the adventures it will bring him. Phillipps "resolutely decline[s] to have any more to do with the matter," insisting that he "will not be enslaved by a gold Tiberius, even though it swims into [his] ken in a manner which is somewhat melodramatic" (p. 65).

And yet even Phillipps (with his supposedly superior scientific mode of meaning making) is not impervious to the power of the fetish, as he too gets drawn into the coin's orbit and the orbit of the impostors who unceasingly search for it. Machen marks him (no less than Dyson) as a fetish worshipper, not only by the South Seas fetish in his apartment but also through a seemingly minor interaction that he has with his landlady concerning his collection of flint arrowheads. His landlady thinks they are rubbish and throws them out; he prizes them highly and grudgingly retrieves them from a "malodorous" dustbin (p. 87). In this moment, it is as if Phillipps and his landlady were from completely different cultures. Even in this seemingly minor, superfluous interaction, the drastic contrast in their valuing the same things encapsulates the problem of value that is inherent in the fetish. Are these pieces of shaped rock trifling things that might very well belong in the dustbin, or are they museum-worthy objects that might further our knowledge of the history of human societies? Who gets to decide? How do we know? Phillipps himself is uncertain, as he does not yet know if the arrowheads are real or fake. He inspects them as a Victorian ethnologist or anthropologist would, reading them as potential evidence of peoples and cultures that existed long ago.

This practice of reading people's place in evolution based on their things is invoked by the flint arrowheads themselves, which likely had a broader range of resonance than they might have for readers today. A collection of flint arrowheads had recently been examined by Victorian anthropologist E.B. Tylor (1832–1917), who concluded that the Tasmanians—who had been almost annihilated from contact with European colonizers—were representatives of prehistoric people. Tylor's "On the Tasmanians as Representatives of Palæolithic Man" (1894; see Appendix D2) famously produced what I have elsewhere called an "object-driven narrative" that Machen imitates and satirizes in his own object-driven *The Three Impostors* (see Forlini). In Tylor's "scientific" tall tale, objects (flint arrowheads) are used to narrate a people's place in what Machen would call "the grand march of evolution" (p. 122). As historian of anthropology George Stocking explains, Tylor's assessment helped the Victorians justify the horror of the Tasmanians' fate:

> Left behind long since by the ancestors of the Europeans, they [the Tasmanians] had outlived their time by many thousands of years. And when the two ends of the cultural time-scale were finally forced into spatial contact there at the furthest reaches of the antipodes, extinction was simply a matter of straightening out the scale, and placing the Tasmanians back into the dead prehistoric world where they belong. Not only did the paleolithic equation help to distance the horror of the Tasmanians' extinction;[1]

---

1 Stocking notes that while the "extinction" of the Tasmanians may have "seemed a clearly defined 'event' to Victorians inclined to construe 'race' in quasi-polygenetic terms," it would be incorrect to employ the term, since "Europeans and Tasmanian Aboriginals did in fact produce numerous offspring, who survived primarily on the islands in Bass Strait to the north of Tasmania" (283).

it seemed even to set the seal of anthropological science on
their fate. (283)

If Tylor's narrative about the Tasmanians helped assuage European guilt, it was also a repression of the violence inherent in
colonial expansion. By landing the British antiquarian Mr.
Headley and (part of) the man with spectacles in museums,
Machen's text stages the return of repressed violence against
objectified others; its seemingly gratuitous violence is aligned
with the violence of colonialism.[1]

The fetish and the *bibelot* encapsulate at least two kinds of crises
that Machen's text obsessively probes. First, they highlight a crisis
of value that is revealed most blatantly in cross-cultural exchange,
which shows that any value that appears inherent in an object
is culturally constructed. This doesn't mean that value does not
exist but rather that it is culturally and historically specific instead
of universal—itself a significant realization, given the imperial
"conversion project" that McClintock details. Second, it suggests
a crisis in meaning making: How can we best make sense of the
world? Are the events of the world governed primarily by chance,
by divine intervention, by evil design and conspiracy, or by physical laws of the universe that are understandable through rational,
causal explanation? How do we know? Who decides? Both crises
(of value and of meaning) are edged in violence in Machen's text,
as he shows that both value and meaning are highly contested, cut
across by conflict as culturally and historically specific frames of
reference often clash and different peoples have varying levels of
power to secure and influence value and meaning.

Different modes of meaning making are put in tension in
Machen's text as different narrative models in the world of the
novel—the "primitive" model based on contingency, chance, and
supernatural intervention, and the "modern" model based on
rational causality. In Machen's text these two seemingly opposed
extremes meet and become difficult to disentangle. Are the events
of the story driven by chance encounters? By the power of the
coin? Or is the whole thing finely orchestrated by Lipsius's network of spies who function as "a relentless mechanism" (p. 189)?
In his own play of surfaces, Machen opposes and then conflates
narratives of causality (associated with "modern" enlightened

---

1 The "return of the repressed," famously associated with the literature
    of fear, revulsion, and horror by Freud in "The Uncanny" (1919),
    continues to be central in critical discussions of the Gothic.

science) with narratives of chance (the "blind Madonna of the Pagan"). For Machen, the assumed linear temporality of Western scientific and historical narratives implicit in the primitive/modern divide does not hold; appropriately, Machen's narrative implies a more circular (ouroboros-like) temporality that self-reflexively calls attention to its design as something "made by art."

Machen's text goes so far as to suggest that science has its own style and that science's style is as much an affectation as Decadent style. Consider that Phillipps, who prides himself on being a man of science, disbelieves everything unless it comes "neatly draped in the robes of Science" and its "severe and irreproachable" language (p. 85). Our narrator makes this observation rather pointedly, suggesting that science is a style to which Phillipps is partial, no less than Dyson is partial to the style of the marvellous. Phillipps and Dyson repeatedly disagree about who sees things as they really are. Phillipps accuses Dyson of "using a kaleidoscope instead of a telescope in the view of things" (p. 86), suggesting that he distorts reality with a child-like perception,[1] instead of depending, as Phillipps does, on the accuracy of a scientific optical instrument. However, it is not so easy to decide whether the text itself takes a side, as it appears to ridicule both characters. Moreover, it appears to play at both science—a kind of "speculative anthropology" (Joshi xv)—and a Decadent art of overloaded style. What is apparent, however, is that the "styles" of both the Decadent artist and scientist characters appear similarly concerned with surfaces—surfaces that at once attract them even as they repel any easy interpretation. Moreover, it becomes clear that if such disagreements occur between friends from the same culture, city, and time, imagine how such discord might be amplified in cross-cultural or even cross-historical encounters.

The self-reflexivity of *The Three Impostors* is a key aspect of this text even if it has displeased, perplexed, or otherwise struck readers and critics as ill fitting the horror genre of the tales the novel contains. If Machen is the type of magician that likes to show how the thing is done, it is because he seeks to demonstrate how narratives function—not so much what they mean as much as what they *do* and *how* they do it. In some ways, the cult of artifice and its obsessive interest in surfaces (especially jewel-like or reflective

---

1 Phillipps may be alluding to French Decadent poet Charles Baudelaire's (1821–67) definition of the modern artist as a "kaleidoscope gifted with consciousness" (9) in his "The Painter of Modern Life" (1863).

surfaces that appear to resist understanding or depth) constitute a perfectly apt way to probe the mechanics/dynamics of meaning and cultural value, revealing both to be something that emerges as if from a play of mirrors, rather than being based on any stable, underlying essence. If the relationships between persons and things are at the centre of this text, the relationship of both persons and things to practices of storytelling is where this text ultimately lands. Machen's text effectively showcases a complication of time and place that both is itself profoundly emblematic of the British Decadence (which often compared itself with the demise of Rome) and everywhere gestures beyond it to an implied global historical reframing of the same, as discussed in the next section.

Form and Genre: Transnational Peoples, Stories, and Histories

Critics most often refer to *The Three Impostors* as an episodic novel, a form consisting of a frame narrative that contains multiple smaller narratives embedded within it. In Machen's case, these smaller narratives themselves often contain further nested narratives, as a glance at the text's prominent headings and subheadings will make plain. These prominent headings also suggest that *The Three Impostors* is a collection of *nouvelles*—a French term used to refer to short stories or tales. It is in this sense that readers might understand Machen's headings that begin with the word "Novel" (*Nouvelle*). In practice, as mentioned previously, many editors and publishers have treated *The Three Impostors* rather like a collection of short stories, lifting one or more stories from the frame narrative and republishing them separately.

In the context of Machen's other writings from the 1880s and 1890s, *The Three Impostors* is perhaps best understood in terms of the *short-story cycle*—a form that is not specifically British or modern or postmodern. It is rather of centuries-old, transnational provenance, much like the occult and mystical theories that Machen invokes and the artefacts (like the ancient coin) that attract him most. The connection to his own and other episodic narratives places his work in broader, transnational currents that helped produce narrative models in an explicitly global context. Considering some of the literary precedents that Machen engages with and the ways in which he mines and mixes his contemporary and historical sources to produce his chilling tales provides insight into Machen's own approach to storytelling and to the profound investment by *The Three Impostors* in—and its critique of—practices of storytelling and their world-building effects.

Machen draws on richly layered and interlocking traditions of storytelling that circulate across times, places, and cultures, resonating, transmuting, and continuing to be told even today. Machen not only alludes to other story cycles throughout *The Three Impostors*; he also actively worked with the form in multiple ways. By the time he came to write *The Three Impostors*, Machen had already translated other episodic works, including notably Marguerite de Navarre's *L'Heptaméron* (first published in 1559, Machen's trans. published in 1886), and published his own episodic work, *The Chronicles of Clemendy* (1888), described as "the Welsh *Heptameron*" (Starrett, qtd. in Valentine 17). *The Three Impostors* itself was written (as Machen freely admitted) in imitation of Robert Louis Stevenson and Fanny Van de Grift Stevenson's *The Dynamiter*,[1] which consists of a frame narrative with multiple embedded narratives that is part of a larger collection entitled *More New Arabian Nights*, inspired by the world-famous story cycle *The Arabian Nights*. Machen, who had read *The Arabian Nights* in translation and prized it as one of his favourite works, emulates some of its most recognizable features, including its use of narrative as distraction, the seemingly endless narrative possibilities of embedding narratives within narratives, and the presence of the extraordinary in seemingly ordinary circumstances, including magical objects with powers to transmute everyday life.

The Arabian Nights has the kind of richly complex history that would likely attract someone like Machen, who was captivated by overlapping cross-cultural histories that remain ever-present. *Alf Layla wa-Layla* (*One Thousand Nights and a Night*)—also known in English as *The Thousand and One Nights*, *The Arabian Nights' Entertainment*, or simply *The Arabian Nights*—is more of a phenomenon than a single, single-authored work. Some of its most well-known tales (of Ali Baba and Aladdin) have been attributed to eighteenth-century Syrian storyteller Hanna Diyab, who apparently told the tales to the first European translator of *The Arabian Nights*, Antoine Galland (1646–1715), who in turn incorporated them—without acknowledging Diyab as their source—into his multi-volume French translation of *The Arabian Nights*

---

1 Although Fanny Stevenson (1840–1914) claimed that "the whole idea of The Dynamiter was her work," she "never claimed responsibility for the final draft" (Harman 271–72).

published beginning in 1704. However, well before Galland's translation, *The Arabian Nights* had travelled large portions of the globe (including Europe), influencing some of its earliest canonical works. In fact, *The Arabian Nights* "had been one of the great examples of a book that could move across the world (from India to Baghdad, Cairo, and Damascus), picking up new stories and features at every pause along the way" (Johnson et al. 246); it is "a programmatically cosmopolitan form, integrating narratives from a range of cultures" (247). The oldest preserved version is a fourteenth-century Syrian manuscript, but some components of the tales have been dated to as far back as the eighth century. There is evidence that the tales originate in an Indian and/or Iranian context but that they travelled across borders for centuries, changing and growing as they did, circulating throughout the Middle East and into "medieval Spain and then Western Europe, where they influenced omnibus fictions like *The Decameron* and *The Canterbury Tales*" (247). When they were re-introduced to the West in translation, many saw *The Arabian Nights* as an alternative version of *Don Quixote* (1604), itself a story cycle that purports to be based on a discovered manuscript from an Arabic source (246).

Machen's work is tied to *The Arabian Nights* from multiple directions. He translated and then imitated (in *The Chronicles of Clemendy*) Navarre's work, which was influenced by the *Decameron*, itself influenced by the already circulating *Arabian Nights*. Machen wrote in the vein of the Stevensons' work, itself in imitation of (and an apparent addition to) *The Arabian Nights*. Whether or not Machen knew of the complex history of *The Arabian Nights* tales, his work is entangled with it as part of the larger European obsession with this world-famous text, and thus it is perhaps best understood, not only in the context of (often limited and limiting) literary histories that are focused primarily on national or temporal delineations (e.g., the British *fin de siècle*) but also with an eye to the complex interactivity and intertwining of cultural forms and histories that develop across national and temporal lines.

And yet, even if Machen's text is recontextualized in what one critic calls "a horizontally integrative 'geography' of transnational influence and exchange, rather than the more familiar vertical and genealogical 'history' of the national model" (Aravamudan 71), Machen's attraction to *The Arabian Nights* cannot be disentangled from what Edward Said famously theorized as orientalism, any more than Machen's representations of the "little people" could be disentangled from the orientalist motifs of Victorian Gothic that represent often orientalized Others as the locus of horror.

As some Arabist scholars argue, European interest in *The Arabian Nights* ultimately "exemplifies Europe's obsession with itself" since the West's interest in the East is primarily in its status as "Not Europe" (Johnson et al. 244). Across centuries, the West's efforts to delineate and define the East, to make "the strange familiar and the distant proximate," were at bottom a project of domination through which "the West [extended] its reach" (Ahmed 126) and worked to establish its own assumed superiority. It is important to note that for Machen and his contemporaries the "Orient" was a conceptual more than a geographical distinction; it "does not refer to a specific place, even if we can find it on a map ... The Orient is the 'not Europe' through which the boundaries between Europe and what is 'not Europe' are established as a way of 'locating' a distinction between self and other" (Ahmed 114). Indeed, as Sara Ahmed reminds us, the very division of the world into "Orient" and "Occident" speaks of processes through which persons are "oriented" in the world. The very ways in which the West framed the "Orient" imply that it is being viewed from the Occident, which then appears to install itself as a kind of invisible, pervasive universal subject position that centres the Occident precisely by the Othering of the Orient. Machen, who saw London as a magical city in an Eastern tale, turns London itself into a kind of Orient, at once repeating the efforts through which the West sought to extend its reach and through which it "Othered" not only other cultures but also others in Western society, including "delinquents, the insane, women, the poor" (Said 207). At the same time, however, if *The Three Impostors* adopts the orientalist codes of Machen's time, it also disrupts them by laying bare how projects of attempted domination depend on the manipulation of discursive designs, and how specific frames of reference (such as those through which objects and persons come to be imbued with more or less value and meaning) are decidedly not universal.

In other words, Machen's orientalism is also a disorienting one. Much like some of his contemporaries, who felt themselves marginalized in Victorian society, Machen not only identifies with the Other (he is himself a stranger in London both by virtue of his poverty and his being from the "border country") but also "blurs the typical binary opposition between us and them, West and East" (Im 369). He does this in part by complicating notions of time and space and parading different, sometimes conflicting narrative forms of making sense of the world as discussed above, and by showcasing how narratives themselves can be transmuted—their effects fundamentally dependent on their specific context, such that shifting the context effectively shifts the effects and meanings of the stories. The intrusiveness of the frame narrative that Machen borrows from *The Arabian Nights* is perhaps most effective at showcasing precisely this kind of textual transmutation, or the ways in which meanings depend on context and specific frames of reference.

In Machen's text, discourses are always entangled with other discourses as much as texts are always embedded in other texts, and this embedding is explicitly employed for strategic effects. Most obviously, as discussed above, the ouroboros-like frame narrative is embedded in itself. The embeddedness of texts also occurs in each section, which often contains its own sub-sections, many of which are employed to help bolster the credibility of the impostors' dubious tales. Consider that each of the impostors tells one or more tales that clearly strain credulity, but each also contains some further text provided as "evidence" by the impostors in the hopes of producing a "truth" effect. "The Encounter on the Pavement" contains a tale called "Novel of the Dark Valley," which itself contains a newspaper clipping that appears to legitimate the Novel of the Dark Valley. "The Recluse of Bayswater" contains the "Novel of the White Powder," which itself incorporates a report by Dr. Chambers, itself bolstered with a note by Dr. Haberden. Similarly, "Adventure of the Missing Brother" contains the "Novel of the Black Seal," a tale that concludes with the written statement of Professor Gregg, again as "proof" of the veracity of an unbelievable tale.

In all three cases, multiple genres are combined and recontextualized in the hopes of creating a kind of reality or truth effect. However, in all but one of these, they fail to convince. And yet even the exception is quite telling of the complexity of discursive proliferation and transmutation that Machen's text stages. If the first two examples fail to convince, their efforts nonetheless show how horror is transmuted into farce. By contrast, in the last example, the listener (Phillipps) goes on to write *Protoplasmic Reversion*, a supposedly scientific treatise written by a man of science (albeit an amateur) that is based on what is likely a tall tale told by an impostor. The implication here is not only that Phillipps will go on to write a highly questionable "scientific" treatise but also that what may appear unbelievable in a tale told by an impostor may in a different context—and in a different style—compel a truth effect, that is, it will appear believable and compel belief from some readers.

Machen knew all too well that if he "were writing in the Middle Ages [he] should need no scientific basis [for his tales]," but in his own time, "the supernatural per se is entirely incredible" and as such "to believe, we must link our wonders to some scientific or pseudo-scientific fact, or basis, or method" (Dobson et al. 218). He understands that frames of reference change, that contextual cues have power, that changing notions of authority can be manipulated, and that the current material practices of evidence gathering and interpretation would compel belief in his contemporaries in ways the supernatural on its own could not. He uses what he knows to move his readers accordingly.

If *The Three Impostors* appears to be difficult to categorize in terms of both form and genre, it is precisely because it plays with the mechanics of both—of how they can be manipulated to activate certain visceral responses and modes of interpretation in readers who are (no less than authors) trained in the repeated cultural structures that underlie meaning making. Although genres have often been defined in terms of textual characteristics, more recently critics have tended to view them as fluid, historically specific constructions that emerge through the interaction of a variety of claims and practices by fans, critics, writers, publishers, and others (Vint and Bould 48). If, as Carolyn Miller suggests, we consider genre "as typified rhetorical action" (151), then we can better assess not only what genre is but what it *does*. A genre such as horror, for example, may very well be a label that refers to repeated and repeatable strategies for writing and reading, but these strategies are forms of *social practice* that emerge and change through repeated and repeatable use in specific contexts. Machen's text, which repeatedly showcases the interaction between storyteller and reader/listener, also highlights the mobilizing of cues that invite certain forms of interpretive practice, raising awareness about the very practices through which we make sense of this and other forms of discourse. Does reading science and (Decadent) literature require a similar suspension of disbelief? How do different narrative genres (newspaper reports, medical reports, letters, journals, etc.) produce—or fail to produce—a certain desired effect, such as a visceral effect, a truth effect, a sense of authority that compels trust and belief, or alternatively a satirical or humorous effect? These are newly pressing questions in our own time of, for example, climate change denial and vaccine hesitancy. In *The Three Impostors* the telling (practice) and the context (embeddedness) always transmute the tale, shifting its meanings and its effects.

Machen not only exposes this contextual transmutation again and again; he also practises it in the very crafting of his stories, in which he borrows and recontextualizes bits and pieces of existing sources and transmutes them into something newly strange. Consider, for instance, his use of "ectoplasmic pseudopodia" in the "Novel of the Black Seal." The idea that Cradock's body is able to move an object from an inaccessibly high shelf (leaving a slimy trail) is based on a theory by physicist and member of the Society for Psychical Research[1] Sir Oliver Lodge (1851–1940), to whom Machen refers directly in his text. Machen had read a paper in which Lodge sought to explain the movement of objects from remote parts of the room during séances, suggesting they may have been moved by "a kind of extension of the medium's body" (*Things Near and Far* 110) or extensions of "ectoplasm." Machen recalls imagining the medium's body as having extensions akin to the "protrusion and withdrawal of a snail's horns" (110). Although Machen was highly sceptical about Lodge's theory, he used it in his stories, combining it with other elements of uncertain existence to produce something new that might move his readers: "In all probability the whole theory is a pack of nonsense, and the 'phenomena' are the tricks of clever cheats: still, what do we know? At all events, I worked it all into my fairy tale, mixing up the old view that the fairy tales, the stories of Little People, are in fact traditions of the aborigines of these islands, small, dark men who took refuge under the hills from the invading Celt with this view of the capacities of the human body, and my view, still newer, that the fairies may still be found under the hills, and that they are far from being pleasant little people. That was the recipe for the tale" (110–11). Machen borrows and imaginatively transmutes Lodge's theory by combining it with euhemeristic theories[2] about fairies to suggest that Cradock is a living specimen of a (wrongly assumed) long-lost race.

The Sixtystone is another example in which Machen recontextualizes and thus transmutes an existing text—but this time it

---

1 First established in 1882, the Society for Psychical Research conducted scientific research into supernatural phenomena, including communication with the dead, mesmerism, apparitions, etc.

2 Euhemeristic theories, or "the belief that myths and folk beliefs arise from actual historical persons or events," "became a major explanation of fairy origins—raising issues related to Victorian ideas of race and empire" (Silver 7). Such theories climaxed in the 1890s with "David MacRitchie's once famous, now discredited, 'pigmy theory' of fairy origins" (7). See Leslie-McCarthy for more on the relevance of such theories for Machen's work.

is not a recent scientific speculation that is recast, but rather an ancient speculation about little-known, ancient cultures. Machen borrows the Sixtystone from an ancient geographer, Solinus (fl. third century CE), but the passage that Machen quotes and translates from Solinus is a pastiche of several different parts of Solinus's work combined *out of context* to produce the myth told by Machen about the "little people." As Christopher Josiffe points out, the passage itself is an impostor (4). Indeed, Miss Lally (the impostor who recounts the tale) attributes this "odd mixture of fact and fancy" (p. 105) to the ancient geographer himself, whose work combines the seemingly factual (geographical and historical information) with the mythological, but Machen apparently compounded the generic indeterminacy of the original text by transmuting it for his own purposes. Mixing folklore, ancient texts, evolutionary sciences, and the supernatural is typical of Machen's writing, both here and elsewhere.[1] Machen's use of sources, allusions, and references enacts the kind of entanglement between past and present, "primitive" and "modern," scientific and occult that pervades *The Three Impostors*. The novel may suggest that meaning is unstable, even that there is perhaps no inherent meaning, but it also suggests that there are context-specific cultivated meanings and that the cultivation of meaning is part of what defines the human for Machen.

While he can imagine other species communicating with each other (his example is ants who may very well warn other ants of the destruction of one of their anthills), only the human species is given to writing poetry and building places of worship; it is, Machen suggests, instinctual for humans to do so. His proof is that even in his age (not unlike our own), which judged all value as economic value ("does it pay?"), poets still write poetry and artists still produce art (*Far Off Things* 95), even though it only rarely pays—as Machen himself knew all too painfully well. Machen claimed his own desire to write "was more like the instinct of a bird or a beetle than the reasoned scheme of a man" (qtd. in Valentine 14). For Machen, who sees in the earliest discovered prehistoric cave drawings the centrally human impulse to create, it is part of human nature to transmute things and in so doing transmute ourselves.

---

1 Arguably, it is also typical of the writings of the British *fin de siècle*, perhaps indicative of the still-developing distinctions between sciences and pseudo-sciences at the time and of efforts to grapple with the many strange revelations of science, using whatever genres were at hand.

The Three Impostors, which seems to both pull readers in and push them back out again, is perhaps most effective in raising questions about how narratives function, what they *do*. For Machen, stories and storytelling are not only instinctual expressions of fundamental human creativity (how we fashion ourselves and our world); they also record the myriad ways we come to understand—*and misunderstand*—each other and our "shared" world, how we exist in (to borrow a phrase from American playwright Lynn Nottage) in "a fractured togetherness." Significantly, for Machen, this fractured togetherness plays out in *both space and time*. "We" (meaning every human or humanoid being to have ever walked the earth past, present, and to come) may very well share a world in the sense that we all inhabit the planet earth, but our perspectives, understandings, and lived experiences of this world vary greatly; it is in part the stories we hear and tell that help fashion "the world" and the very interpretive strategies through which we try to understand it. *The Three Impostors* exposes the processes through which stories help construct—and fail to construct—a shared world. Its characters may inhabit the same city, but they are worlds apart; they are strangers who happen to cross paths but make only superficial connections.

It is not often noted (but no less relevant for all that) that characters in Machen's novel lack even a basic sense of empathy toward others, but this is certainly part of what is flaunted in Machen's text, with its insistent treatment of persons as things. This is repeated within and across stories: Dyson seems to intuit that the man with spectacles is running for his life, but his attention (and that of readers!) is redirected to the shiny coin; Phillipps is annoyed when he encounters a visibly distraught woman weeping on a park bench and only reluctantly agrees to listen to her tale of great loss and grief. Rather than eliciting his empathy and compassion, listening to the stranger's story motivates him to seek his own potential gain; he takes her tale and makes it the basis of his own work (the pseudo-scientific *Protoplasmic Reversion*). She, for her part, is only pretending to grieve to gain information about a man she will ultimately help torture, kill, and mutilate. This is one of the many ways in which the text shows how stories (and things) redirect our attention, eliciting, redirecting, or interfering with empathy, the basis of our relatedness to others.

Notably, it is exceedingly difficult to identify with any of the characters in this novel, most (if not all) of whom appear more like caricatures or types (e.g., the Decadent writer, the amateur ethnologist, the fetish-worshipper, the landlady, the curiosity dealer, etc.) than full-bodied characters. There is little, if any, sense of characters' psychological depth or interiority. The journal of the man with spectacles (another text embedded in this text) provides perhaps the only extended insight into the interiority of any character, but even that more personal account appears distanced. His first-person account is titled the "History of the Man with Spectacles" rather than, say, Joseph Walters's Journal, which is what it is—the personal journal of the man with spectacles whose name (Joseph Walters) readers do not learn until Dyson reads the journal that Walters drops as he attempts to flee the impostors for the last time. This first real glance at a character's interiority comes very late in the novel and is sardonically followed by the literal exposure of the character's "interiority" in the final scene, where his bodily integrity is literally burned open. To "enjoy" the novel's "artistic" crimes, to witness the finely crafted spectacle of torture, readers must assume a kind of detached superiority or desensitized apathy that they see in two of the three impostors. The fact that only one of the impostors is sickened by the torture of a fellow human being helps accentuate the sociopathic coolness of the other two, who continue their glib chatter while holding the severed bloody finger of their victim.

If, for Machen, storytelling is a practice that unites all members of the human species across the globe from ancient times to the present, this same practice of storytelling is also often intertwined with violence—from the relatively subtle violence of inattention to the suffering of fellow human beings to the more blatant violence that appropriates stories and other cultural artefacts, bodies, and body parts for museums, institutions of knowledge and memory that are also—or at least they have been historically—institutions of horror, preserving unevenly the suffering of so many who enter historical records only obliquely. This is what Walter Benjamin (1892–1940) meant when he claimed that "[t]here is no document of civilization which is not at the same time a document of barbarism" ("Theses" 256)—and that the greatest achievements of human civilizations are always underwritten by the sufferings of millions whose stories remain untold, written over, imperfectly preserved, and/or actively distorted, if they leave any traces at all. The intertwining of storytelling and violence in Machen's tales of horror regards unevenly preserved things and histories with a steady eye that opens the novel to another level of horrors—not the horror of evil fairies and goblins or even the horrors of the dissecting room that seemed to be revealing all life is but matter, stuff that will in time become other stuff—but the horrors of human history, horrors that persist and continue to haunt us today, as we in our own fractured togetherness continue to deal with the undead past—or, to borrow Christine Sharpe's highly evocative phrase, "the past that is not past" (9)—of colonialism, of slavery, and of the genocide of Indigenous peoples.

The horror of *The Three Impostors* is less about returning to primordial ooze than it is about how people, things, and tales circulate, how they are used for different ends, valued differently or not at all, how distanced apathy invades social relations such that we avert our eyes to human suffering and follow instead, like Dyson, a shiny coin. In an age defined by its concerted efforts in all branches of knowledge to "see the object as in itself it really is" (as Matthew Arnold famously claimed), Machen's text highlights the contingent, haphazard, ultimately unstable, and at times violent ways in which people read and build narratives upon material, cultural artefacts—whether a stone implement from the paleolithic period, an artefact from a little-known, distant culture, or even a decadently clad book.

Arthur Machen: A Brief Chronology

1863   (3 March) Arthur Llewelyn Jones-Machen is born
        to Janet Robina Machen and clergyman John
        Edward Jones at Caerleon-on-Usk, in the medieval
        district of Gwent (Monmouthshire, Wales); an only
        child, he spends his early years in Llanddewi (north
        of Caerleon), where his father becomes rector

1874   Begins formal schooling at Hereford Cathedral
        School (classical education including French and
        Latin), completed in 1880

1880   First trip to London, where he fails the examina-
        tion for the Royal College of Surgeons; returns to
        Llanddewi for several months; inspired by Swin-
        burne's *Songs Before Sunrise* (1871), he begins to
        write poetry

1881   Publishes a collection of poems, *Eleusinia*

1881–84 Lives in London, learning shorthand with the
        aim of becoming a journalist while tutoring young
        children to support himself; struggles with extreme
        poverty and loneliness; begins writing *The Anatomy
        of Tobacco* (1884)

1884–88 Works as a translator, editor, proofreader, and
        cataloguer for publishers, completing a catalogue
        of *The Literature of Occultism and Archeology* in
        1885; publisher George Redway commissions him
        to translate Marguerite, Queen of Navarre's *The
        Heptameron*

1885   (10 November) Mother, who was an invalid since
        he was a child, dies

1886   Publishes *The Heptameron* (translation)

1887   Marries independent bohemian Amelia Hogg,
        13 years his senior; father dies (29 September);
        receives inheritance that offers him economic sta-
        bility for the next 14 years

1888   Publishes *The Chronicles of Clemendy*; Amelia
        Machen introduces him to Arthur Waite, who will
        become a well-known scholar of the occult and one
        of Machen's closest lifelong friends

1888–89 Translates *The Memoirs of Jacques Casanova* and de
        Verville's *Le Moyen de Parvenir*

1889–90	Begins writing for *The Globe, St James's Gazette*, and *The Queen*; his first published stories appear in *St James's Gazette*
1890	Meets Oscar Wilde; publishes *Fantastic Tales* (his translation of *Le Moyen de Parvenir*)
1890–91	Composes *The Great God Pan*
1890–94	Composes *The Three Impostors*
1894	Publishes *The Great God Pan* (and *The Inmost Light*) in John Lane's Keynotes series, and his translation of *The Memoirs of Jacques Casanova*
1895	Publishes *The Three Impostors* (John Lane, Keynotes)
1898–99	Works as an assistant editor and reviewer for *Literature* magazine
1899	(31 July) Amelia Machen dies after a long illness
1900	Joins the Hermetic Order of the Golden Dawn (his friend Arthur Waite is already a member)
1900–09	Works as an actor (especially with the Benson Shakespeare Repertory Company); publishes *Hieroglyphics* (1902), *The House of the Hidden Light* (1904), *Dr. Stiggins* (1906), *The House of Souls* (1906, with cover design by S.H. Sime), and *The Hill of Dreams* (1907); writes for *Academy* (1907–08) and for *T.P.'s Weekly*; works that had previously appeared in *T.P.'s Weekly* from 1908 to 1909 are later published as *Notes and Queries* (1926)
1903	Marries fellow actor Dorothie Purefoy Hudleston (25 June); they have two children: Hilary (b. 1912) and Janet (b. 1917)
1910–21	Works as a reporter for *The Evening News*; publishes "The Bow Men" (1914), *The Angel of Mons* (1915), *The Great Return* (1915), *The Terror* (1917), and *War and the Christian Faith* (1918)
1920s	Machen's works enjoy renewed attention, as they are republished by Martin Secker (London) and Knopf (New York); publishes *The Secret Glory* (1922), *Far Off Things* (1922), *Things Near & Far* (1923), *The Shining Pyramid* (1923), *Strange Roads* (1923), *Dog and Duck* (1924), *The London Adventure* (1924), *The Glorious Mystery* (1924), *Precious Balms* (1924), *Ornaments in Jade* (1924), *The Canning Wonder* (1925), *Dreads and Drolls* (1926), and *Notes and Queries* (1926)

1927–30	Lives in poverty at 28 Loudoun Road, London, but receives some financial assistance thanks to the intervention of friends (1928–30); moves to Old Amersham (Buckinghamshire) in 1929, where he remains until his death
1930s	Publishes *Tom O'Bedlam and His Song* (1930); composes *Bridles and Spurs* (1931–34), published in 1951; receives civil list pension (1932) which is increased in 1938; publishes *A Few Letters from Arthur Machen* (1932), *The Green Round* (1933), *The Cosy Room and Other Stories* (1936), *The Children of the Pool* (1936)
1945	Penguin publishes a selection of Machen's stories under the title *Holy Terrors*
1947	(30 March) Purefoy Machen dies; (15 December) Arthur Machen dies, aged 84

A Note on the Text

The text of this Broadview edition is based on the first edition of *The Three Impostors* as published by John Lane in 1895. Dialogue is presented with double quotation marks rather than the single ones of the original text; original spelling has been for the most part preserved, except in cases where an obvious typographical error has been corrected.

THE THREE IMPOSTORS
OR THE TRANSMUTATIONS

PROLOGUE

"And Mr. Joseph Walters is going to stay the night?" said the smooth clean-shaven man to his companion, an individual not of the most charming appearance, who had chosen to make his ginger-coloured moustache merge into a pair of short chin-whiskers.

The two stood at the hall door, grinning evilly at each other; and presently a girl ran quickly down the stairs, and joined them. She was quite young, with a quaint and piquant rather than a beautiful face, and her eyes were of a shining hazel. She held a neat paper parcel in one hand, and laughed with her friends.

"Leave the door open," said the smooth man to the other, as they were going out. "Yes, by—," he went on with an ugly oath, "we'll leave the front door on the jar. He may like to see company, you know."

The other man looked doubtfully about him.

"Is it quite prudent, do you think, Davies?" he said, pausing with his hand on the mouldering knocker. "I don't think Lipsius would like it. What do you say, Helen?"

"I agree with Davies. Davies is an artist, and you are commonplace, Richmond, and a bit of a coward. Let the door stand open, of course. But what a pity Lipsius had to go away! He would have enjoyed himself."

"Yes," replied the smooth Mr. Davies, "that summons to the west was very hard on the doctor."

The three passed out, leaving the hall door, cracked and riven with frost and wet, half-open, and they stood silent for a moment under the ruinous shelter of the porch.

"Well," said the girl, "it is done at last. We shall hurry no more on the track of the young man with spectacles."

"We owe a great deal to you," said Mr. Davies politely; "the doctor said so before he left. But have we not all three some farewells to make? I, for my part, propose to say good-bye, here, before this picturesque but mouldy residence, to my friend Mr. Burton, dealer in the antique and curious," and the man lifted his hat with an exaggerated bow.

"And I," said Richmond, "bid adieu to Mr. Wilkins, the private secretary, whose company has, I confess, become a little tedious."

"Farewell to Miss Lally, and to Miss Leicester also," said the girl, making as she spoke a delicious curtsy. "Farewell to all occult adventure; the farce is played."

Mr. Davies and the lady seemed full of grim enjoyment, but Richmond tugged at his whiskers nervously.

"I feel a bit shaken up," he said. "I've seen rougher things in the States, but that crying noise he made gave me a sickish feeling. And then the smell—; but my stomach was never very strong."

The three friends moved away from the door, and began to walk slowly up and down what had been a gravel path, but now lay green and pulpy with damp mosses. It was a fine autumn evening, and a faint sunlight shone on the yellow walls of the old deserted house, and showed the patches of gangrenous decay, and all the stains, the black drift of rain from the broken pipes, the scabrous blots where the bare bricks were exposed, the green weeping of a gaunt laburnum that stood beside the porch, and ragged marks near the ground where the reeking clay was gaining on the worn foundations. It was a queer, rambling old place, the centre perhaps two hundred years old, with dormer windows sloping from the tiled roof, and on each side there were Georgian wings; bow windows had been carried up to the first floor, and two dome-like cupolas that had once been painted a bright green were now grey and neutral. Broken urns lay upon the path, and a heavy mist seemed to rise from the unctuous clay; the neglected shrubberies, grown all tangled and unshapen, smelt dank and evil, and there was an atmosphere all about the deserted mansion that proposed thoughts of an opened grave. The three friends looked dismally at the rough grasses and the nettles that grew thick over lawn and flower-beds; and at the sad water-pool in the midst of the weeds. There, above green and oily scum instead of lilies, stood a rusting Triton[1] on the rocks, sounding a dirge through a shattered horn; and beyond, beyond the sunk fence and the far meadows, the sun slid down and shone red through the bars of the elm-trees.

Richmond shivered and stamped his foot.

"We had better be going soon," he said; "there is nothing else to be done here."

"No," said Davies, "it is finished at last. I thought for some time we should never get hold of the gentleman with the spectacles. He was a clever fellow, but, Lord! he broke up badly at last. I can tell you he looked white at me when I touched him on the arm in the bar. But where could he have hidden the thing? We can all swear it was not on him."

---

1 In Greek mythology, Triton is a merman capable of calming the seas with his conch trumpet.

The girl laughed, and they turned away, when Richmond gave a violent start.

"Ah!" he cried, turning to the girl, "what have you got there? Look, Davies, look; it's all oozing and dripping."

The young woman glanced down at the little parcel she was carrying, and partially unfolded the paper.

"Yes, look both of you," she said; "it's my own idea. Don't you think it will do nicely for the doctor's museum? It comes from the right hand, the hand that took the Gold Tiberius."

Mr. Davies nodded with a good deal of approbation, and Richmond lifted his ugly high-crowned bowler, and wiped his forehead with a dingy handkerchief.

"I'm going," he said; "you two can stay if you like."

The three went round by the stable-path, past the withered wilderness of the old kitchen garden, and struck off by a hedge at the back, making for a particular point in the road. About five minutes later two gentlemen, whom idleness had led to explore these forgotten outskirts of London, came sauntering up the shadowy carriage drive. They had spied the deserted house from the road, and as they observed all the heavy desolation of the place they began to moralise in the great style, with considerable debts to Jeremy Taylor.[1]

"Look, Dyson," said the one, as they drew nearer; "look at those upper windows; the sun is setting, and, though the panes are dusty, yet—

'The grimy sash an oriel burns.'"[2]

"Phillipps," replied the elder and (it must be said) the more pompous of the two, "I yield to fantasy; I cannot withstand the influence of the grotesque. Here, where all is falling into dimness and dissolution, and we walk in cedarn[3] gloom, and the very air of heaven goes mouldering to the lungs, I cannot remain

---

1 Episcopalian theologian (1613–67) noted for the eloquence and style of his preaching and devotional writing.

2 Line from the poem "All-Saints," by James Russell Lowell (1819–91), in which a "den" of "Sin and Famine" is transmuted into a shrine as a recessed window (oriel) burns with light: "The den they enter grows a shrine, / The grimy sash an oriel burns."

3 One of many instances of Dyson's preference for highly stylized poetic language. Cedarn is a poetic term meaning "Of or pertaining to cedar-trees; made of cedar" (*OED*).

commonplace. I look at that deep glow on the panes, and the house lies all enchanted; that very room, I tell you, is within all blood and fire."

ADVENTURE OF THE GOLD TIBERIUS

The acquaintance between Mr. Dyson and Mr. Charles Phillipps arose from one of those myriad chances which are every day doing their work in the streets of London. Mr. Dyson was a man of letters, and an unhappy instance of talents misapplied. With gifts that might have placed him in the flower of his youth among the most favoured of Bentley's favourite novelists,[1] he had chosen to be perverse; he was, it is true, familiar with scholastic logic, but he knew nothing of the logic of life, and he flattered himself with the title of artist, when he was in fact but an idle and curious spectator of other men's endeavours. Amongst many delusions, he cherished one most fondly, that he was a strenuous worker; and it was with a gesture of supreme weariness that he would enter his favourite resort, a small tobacco-shop[2] in Great Queen Street, and proclaim to any one who cared to listen that he had seen the rising and setting of two successive suns. The proprietor of the shop, a middle-aged man of singular civility, tolerated Dyson partly out of good nature, and partly because he was a regular customer. He was allowed to sit on an empty cask, and to express his sentiments on literary and artistic matters till he was tired, or the time for closing came; and if no fresh customers were attracted, it is believed that none were turned away by his eloquence. Dyson was addicted to wild experiments in tobacco; he never wearied of trying new combinations; and one evening he had just entered the shop, and given utterance to his last preposterous formula, when a young fellow, of about his own age, who had come in a moment later, asked the shop-man to duplicate the order on his account, smiling politely, as he spoke, to Mr. Dyson's address. Dyson felt profoundly flattered,

---

1 The Bentley publishing firm was perhaps best known for its highly successful series Bentley's Standard Novels. Unlike Lane's Keynotes series, which introduced new works by new authors, Bentley's series consisted of cheap reprints of previously published works by well-known authors.

2 The work that Machen admitted to imitating in writing *The Three Impostors* similarly begins with a chance meeting of main characters in a cigar shop. See Appendix E1 for an excerpt of Robert Louis Stevenson and Fanny Van de Grift Stevenson's *The Dynamiter* (1885).

and after a few phrases the two entered into conversation, and in an hour's time the tobacconist saw the new friends sitting side by side on a couple of casks, deep in talk.

"My dear sir," said Dyson, "I will give you the task of the literary man in a phrase. He has got to do simply this: to invent a wonderful story, and to tell it in a wonderful manner."

"I will grant you that," said Mr. Phillipps, "but you will allow me to insist that in the hands of the true artist in words all stories are marvellous, and every circumstance has its peculiar wonder. The matter is of little consequence, the manner is everything. Indeed, the highest skill is shown in taking matter apparently commonplace and transmuting[1] it by the high alchemy of style into the pure gold of art."

"That is indeed a proof of great skill, but it is great skill exerted foolishly, or at least unadvisedly. It is as if a great violinist were to show us what marvellous harmonies he could draw from a child's banjo."

"No, no, you are really wrong. I see you take a radically mistaken view of life. But we must thresh this out. Come to my rooms; I live not far from here."

It was thus that Mr. Dyson became the associate of Mr. Charles Phillipps, who lived in a quiet square not far from Holborn. Thenceforth they haunted each other's rooms at intervals, sometimes regular, and occasionally the reverse, and made appointments to meet at the shop in Queen Street, where their talk robbed the tobacconist's profit of half its charm. There was a constant jarring of literary formulas, Dyson exalting the claims of the pure imagination, while Phillipps, who was a student of physical science and something of an ethnologist, insisted that all literature ought to have a scientific basis.[2] By the mistaken benevolence of deceased relatives both young men were placed out of reach of hunger, and so, meditating high achievements, idled their time pleasantly away, and revelled in the careless joys of a

---

1 The first of numerous occasions where Machen employs the terms "transmuting" or "transmutation" that offer insight into the novel's subtitle "The Transmutations." Here it alludes to the use of the term in alchemy (in the medieval and early Renaissance periods) to refer to the transformation of base metals into gold.

2 The characters of Dyson and Phillipps and the antagonism (and alignment) they seem to represent between art and science appear in other Machen stories published before and after *The Three Impostors*. See Appendices E2–3 for examples.

Bohemianism devoid of the sharp seasoning of adversity.

One night in June Mr. Phillipps was sitting in his room in the calm retirement of Red Lion Square. He had opened the window, and was smoking placidly, while he watched the movement of life below. The sky was clear, and the afterglow of sunset had lingered long about it. The flushing twilight of a summer evening vied with the gas-lamps in the square, had fashioned a chiaroscuro[1] that had in it something unearthly; and the children, racing to and fro upon the pavement, the lounging idlers by the public, and the casual passers-by rather flickered and hovered in the play of lights than stood out substantial things. By degrees in the houses opposite one window after another leapt out a square of light; now and again a figure would shape itself against a blind and vanish, and to all this semi-theatrical magic the runs and flourishes of brave Italian opera played a little distance off on a piano-organ seemed an appropriate accompaniment, while the deep-muttered bass of the traffic of Holborn never ceased. Phillipps enjoyed the scene and its effects; the light in the sky faded and turned to darkness, and the square gradually grew silent, and still he sat dreaming at the window, till the sharp peal of the house-bell roused him, and looking at his watch, he found that it was past ten o'clock. There was a knock at the door, and his friend Mr. Dyson entered, and, according to his custom, sat down in an arm-chair and began to smoke in silence.

"You know, Phillipps," he said at length, "that I have always battled for the marvellous. I remember your maintaining in that chair that one has no business to make use of the wonderful, the improbable, the odd coincidence in literature, and you took the ground that it was wrong to do so, because as a matter of fact the wonderful and the improbable don't happen, and men's lives are not really shaped by odd coincidence. Now, mind you, if that were so, I would not grant your conclusion, because I think the 'criticism-of-life' theory is all nonsense; but I deny your premiss. A most singular thing has happened to me to-night."

"Really, Dyson, I am very glad to hear it. Of course, I oppose your argument, whatever it may be; but if you would be good enough to tell me of your adventure, I should be delighted."

"Well, it came about like this. I have had a very hard day's work; indeed, I have scarcely moved from my old bureau since seven o'clock last night. I wanted to work out that idea we discussed last

---

1 A sketch produced using black and white to represent light and shade; here it is used figuratively to refer to how the gas-lamps transmute the scene into a black-and-white sketch.

Tuesday, you know, the notion of the fetish-worshipper."[1]

"Yes, I remember. Have you been able to do anything with it?"

"Yes; it came out better than I expected; but there were great difficulties, the usual agony between the conception and the execution. Anyhow, I got it done at about seven o'clock to-night, and I thought I should like a little of the fresh air. I went out and wandered rather aimlessly about the streets; my head was full of my tale, and I didn't much notice where I was going. I got into those quiet places to the north of Oxford Street as you go west, the genteel residential neighbourhood of stucco and prosperity. I turned east again without knowing it, and it was quite dark when I passed along a sombre little by-street, ill-lighted and empty. I did not know at the time in the least where I was, but I found out afterwards that it was not very far from Tottenham Court Road. I strolled idly along, enjoying the stillness; on one side there seemed to be the back premises of some great shop; tier after tier of dusty windows lifted up into the night, with gibbet-like contrivances for raising heavy goods, and below large doors, fast closed and bolted, all dark and desolate. Then there came a huge pantechnicon[2] warehouse; and over the way a grim blank wall, as forbidding as the wall of a gaol, and then the headquarters of some volunteer regiment, and afterwards a passage leading to a court where wagons were standing to be hired; it was, one might almost say, a street devoid of inhabitants, and scarce a window showed the glimmer of a light. I was wondering at the strange peace and dimness there, where it must be close to some roaring main artery of London life, when suddenly I heard the noise of dashing feet tearing along the pavement at full speed, and from a narrow passage, a mews or something of that kind, a man was discharged as from a catapult under my very nose, and rushed past me, flinging something from him as he ran. He was gone, and down another street in an instant, almost before I knew what had happened, but I didn't much bother about him, I was watching something else. I told you he had thrown something away; well, I watched what seemed a line of flame flash through the air and fly quivering over

---

1 The first of many references to fetishes and fetish-worship. In the nineteenth century, the term was primarily employed in ethnological or anthropological writings to refer to objects worshipped and/or believed to have special powers by supposedly "primitive" peoples. See Introduction, pp. 31–34, and Appendix D1.

2 A building that contains numerous shops or stalls with a range of merchandise, especially of an "exotic" nature.

the pavement, and in spite of myself I could not help tearing after it. The impetus lessened, and I saw something like a bright half-penny roll slower and slower, and then deflect towards the gutter, hover for a moment on the edge, and dance down into a drain. I believe I cried out in positive despair, though I hadn't the least notion what I was hunting; and then, to my joy, I saw that, instead of dropping into the sewer, it had fallen flat across two bars. I stooped down and picked it up and whipped it into my pocket, and I was just about to walk on when I heard again that sound of dashing footsteps. I don't know why I did it, but as a matter of fact I dived down into the mews, or whatever it was, and stood as much in the shadow as possible. A man went by with a rush a few paces from where I was standing, and I felt uncommonly pleased that I was in hiding. I couldn't make out much feature, but I saw his eyes gleaming and his teeth showing, and he had an ugly-looking knife in one hand, and I thought things would be very unpleasant for gentleman number one if the second robber, or robbed, or what you like, caught him up. I can tell you, Phillipps, a fox-hunt is exciting enough, when the horn blows clear on a winter morning, and the hounds give tongue, and the red-coats charge away, but it's nothing to a man-hunt, and that's what I had a slight glimpse of to-night. There was murder in the fellow's eyes as he went by, and I don't think there was much more than fifty seconds between the two. I only hope it was enough."

Dyson leant back in his arm-chair, relit his pipe, and puffed thoughtfully. Phillipps began to walk up and down the room, musing over the story of violent death fleeting in chase along the pavement, the knife shining in the lamplight, the fury of the pursuer, and the terror of the pursued.

"Well," he said at last, "and what was it, after all, that you rescued from the gutter?"

Dyson jumped up, evidently quite startled. "I really haven't a notion. I didn't think of looking. But we shall see."

He fumbled in his waistcoat pocket, drew out a small and shining object, and laid it on the table. It glowed there beneath the lamp with the radiant glory of rare old gold; and the image and the letters stood out in high relief, clear and sharp, as if it had but left the mint a month before. The two men bent over it, and Phillipps took it up and examined it closely.

"Imp. Tiberius Cæsar Augustus,"[1] he read the legend, and then

---

1 "Imperator" or Emperor Tiberius Caesar Augustus, who ruled the Roman empire for 23 years (14–37 CE).

looking at the reverse of the coin, he stared in amazement, and at last turned to Dyson with a look of exultation.

"Do you know what you have found?" he said.

"Apparently a gold coin of some antiquity," said Dyson coolly.

"Quite so, a gold Tiberius. No, that is wrong. You have found *the* gold Tiberius. Look at the reverse."

Dyson looked and saw the coin was stamped with the figure of a faun[1] standing amidst reeds and flowing water. The features, minute as they were, stood out in delicate outline; it was a face lovely and yet terrible, and Dyson thought of the well-known passage of the lad's playmate, gradually growing with his growth and increasing with his stature, till the air was filled with the rank fume of the goat.

"Yes," he said, "it is a curious coin. Do you know it?"

"I know about it. It is one of the comparatively few historical objects in existence; it is all storied like those jewels we have read of. A whole cycle of legend has gathered round the thing; the tale goes that it formed part of an issue struck by Tiberius to commemorate an infamous excess. You see the legend on the reverse: 'Victoria.' It is said that by an extraordinary accident the whole issue was thrown into the melting-pot, and that only this one coin escaped. It glints through history and legend, appearing and disappearing, with intervals of a hundred years in time, and continents in place. It was 'discovered' by an Italian humanist, and lost and rediscovered. It has not been heard of since 1727, when Sir Joshua Byrde,[2] a Turkey merchant, brought it home from Aleppo, and vanished with it a month after he had shown it to the virtuosi, no man knew or knows where. And here it is!"

"Put it into your pocket, Dyson," he said, after a pause. "I would not let any one have a glimpse of the thing if I were you. I would not talk about it. Did either of the men you saw see you?"

"Well, I think not. I don't think the first man, the man who was vomited out of the dark passage, saw anything at all; and I am sure that the second could not have seen me."

---

1 Classical Greek and Roman mythical beings associated with rural or woodland areas, "at first represented like men with horns and the tail of a goat, afterwards with goats' legs like the Satyrs, to whom they were assimilated in lustful character" (*OED*). Often associated with the Greek god Dionysus or the Roman god Bacchus, they are known for their drunkenness, "lustful character" (*OED*), and rituals involving transmutations.

2 Apparently a fictional, rather than an actual, historical person.

"And you didn't really see them. You couldn't recognise either the one or the other if you met him in the street to-morrow?"

"No, I don't think I could. The street, as I said, was dimly lighted, and they ran like madmen."

The two men sat silent for some time, each weaving his own fancies of the story; but lust of the marvellous was slowly overpowering Dyson's more sober thoughts.

"It is all more strange than I fancied," he said at last. "It was queer enough what I saw; a man is sauntering along a quiet, sober, everyday London street, a street of grey houses and blank walls, and there, for a moment, a veil seems drawn aside, and the very fume of the pit steams up through the flagstones, the ground glows, red-hot, beneath his feet, and he seems to hear the hiss of the infernal caldron. A man flying in mad terror for his life, and furious hate pressing hot on his steps with knife drawn ready; here indeed is horror; but what is all that to what you have told me? I tell you, Phillipps, I see the plot thicken; our steps will henceforth be dogged with mystery, and the most ordinary incidents will teem with significance. You may stand out against it, and shut your eyes, but they will be forced open; mark my words, you will have to yield to the inevitable. A clue, tangled if you like, has been placed by chance in our hands; it will be our business to follow it up. As for the guilty person or persons in this strange case, they will be unable to escape us, our nets will be spread far and wide over this great city, and suddenly, in the streets and places of public resort, we shall in some way or other be made aware that we are in touch with the unknown criminal. Indeed, I almost fancy I see him slowly approaching this quiet square of yours; he is loitering at street corners, wandering, apparently without aim, down far-reaching thoroughfares, but all the while coming nearer and nearer, drawn by an irresistible magnetism, as ships were drawn to the Loadstone Rock in the Eastern tale."[1]

"I certainly think," replied Phillipps, "that if you pull out that coin and flourish it under people's noses as you are doing at the present moment, you will very probably find yourself in touch with the criminal, or a criminal. You will undoubtedly be robbed

---

1 A loadstone, or lodestone, is a naturally occurring magnet. Dyson compares the coin's apparent magnetism to the enormous loadstone rock that draws a ship to it in one of the *Arabian Nights* tales. See Introduction, pp. 37–40, for more on *The Arabian Nights* and its significance for Machen's work.

with violence. Otherwise, I see no reason why either of us should be troubled. No one saw you secure the coin, and no one knows you have it. I, for my part, shall sleep peacefully, and go about my business with a sense of security and a firm dependence on the natural order of things. The events of the evening, the adventure in the street, have been odd, I grant you, but I resolutely decline to have any more to do with the matter, and, if necessary, I shall consult the police. I will not be enslaved by a gold Tiberius, even though it swims into my ken in a manner which is somewhat melodramatic."

"And I for my part," said Dyson, "go forth like a knight-errant[1] in search of adventure. Not that I shall need to seek; rather adventure will seek me; I shall be like a spider in the midst of his web, responsive to every movement, and ever on the alert."

Shortly afterwards Dyson took his leave, and Mr. Phillipps spent the rest of the night in examining some flint arrow-heads which he had purchased. He had every reason to believe that they were the work of a modern and not a palæolithic man;[2] still he was far from gratified when a close scrutiny showed him that his suspicions were well founded. In his anger at the turpitude which would impose on an ethnologist, he completely forgot Dyson and the gold Tiberius; and when he went to bed at first sunlight, the whole tale had faded utterly from his thoughts.

THE ENCOUNTER ON THE PAVEMENT

Mr. Dyson, walking leisurely along Oxford Street, and staring with bland inquiry at whatever caught his attention, enjoyed in all its rare flavours the sensation that he was really very hard at work. His observation of mankind, the traffic, and the shop windows tickled his faculties with an exquisite bouquet; he looked serious, as one looks on whom charges of weight and moment are laid, and he was attentive in his glances to right and left, for fear lest he should miss some circumstance of more acute significance. He had narrowly escaped being run over at a crossing by

---

1 In medieval romance, a knight who wanders in search of adventure and opportunities to perform acts of bravery and chivalry. The term is also used in the Stevensons' *The Dynamiter*.

2 Flint arrow-heads associated with "primitive" cultures at this time (see Introduction, pp. 33–34, and Appendices D1 and D2). Phillipps suspects these particular specimens to be (like so much else in this novel) fakes, counterfeits, impostors.

a charging van, for he hated to hurry his steps,[1] and indeed the afternoon was warm; and he had just halted by a place of popular refreshment, when the astounding gestures of a well-dressed individual on the opposite pavement held him enchanted and gasping like a fish. A treble line of hansoms, carriages, vans, cabs, and omnibuses was tearing east and west, and not the most daring adventurer of the crossings would have cared to try his fortune; but the person who had attracted Dyson's attention seemed to rage on the very edge of the pavement, now and then darting forward at the hazard of instant death, and at each repulse absolutely dancing with excitement, to the rich amusement of the passers-by. At last a gap that would have tried the courage of a street-boy appeared between the serried lines of vehicles, and the man rushed across in a frenzy, and escaping by a hair's breadth, pounced upon Dyson as a tiger pounces on her prey. "I saw you looking about you," he said, sputtering out his words in his intense eagerness; "would you mind telling me this! Was the man who came out of the Aerated Bread Shop[2] and jumped into the hansom three minutes ago a youngish-looking man with dark whiskers and spectacles? Can't you speak, man? For heaven's sake, can't you speak? Answer me; it's a matter of life and death."

The words bubbled and boiled out of the man's mouth in the fury of his emotion, his face went from red to white, and the beads of sweat stood out on his forehead; he stamped his feet as he spoke, and tore with his hand at his coat, as if something swelled and choked him, stopping the passage of his breath.

"My dear sir," said Dyson, "I always like to be accurate. Your observation was perfectly correct. As you say, a youngish man—a man, I should say, of somewhat timid bearing—ran rapidly out of the shop here, and bounced into a hansom that must have been waiting for him, as it went eastwards at once. Your friend also wore spectacles, as you say. Perhaps you would like me to call a hansom for you to follow the gentleman?"

---

1   Dyson is presented as a *flâneur*, a French term referring to one who strolls unhurriedly and that has come to be associated with the (male) artist in modernity who remains detached from the urban life he carefully observes.

2   A chain of bread shops and tea rooms that employed a new "carbolic acid process" rather than yeast for making bread, originated in the early 1860s by Scotsman Dr. John Dauglish (1824–66) as a supposedly healthier method.

"No, thank you; it would be a waste of time." The man gulped down something which appeared to rise in his throat, and Dyson was alarmed to see him shaking with hysterical laughter; he clung hard to a lamp-post, and swayed and staggered like a ship in a heavy gale.

"How shall I face the doctor?" he murmured to himself. "It is too hard to fail at the last moment." Then he seemed to recollect himself; he stood straight again, and looked quietly at Dyson.

"I owe you an apology for my violence," he said at last. "Many men would not be so patient as you have been. Would you mind adding to your kindness by walking with me a little way? I feel a little sick; I think it's the sun."

Dyson nodded assent, and devoted himself to a quiet scrutiny of this strange personage as they moved on together. The man was dressed in quiet taste, and the most scrupulous observer could find nothing amiss with the fashion or make of his clothes; yet, from his hat to his boots, everything seemed inappropriate. His silk hat, Dyson thought, should have been a high bowler of odious pattern, worn with a baggy morning-coat, and an instinct told him that the fellow did not commonly carry a clean pocket-handkerchief. The face was not of the most agreeable pattern, and was in no way improved by a pair of bulbous chin-whiskers of a ginger hue, into which moustaches of like colour merged imperceptibly. Yet, in spite of these signals hung out by nature, Dyson felt that the individual beside him was something more than compact of vulgarity. He was struggling with himself, holding his feelings in check; but now and again passion would mount black to his face, and it was evidently by a supreme effort that he kept himself from raging like a madman. Dyson found something curious, and a little terrible, in the spectacle of an occult emotion thus striving for the mastery, and threatening to break out at every instant with violence; and they had gone some distance before the person whom he had met by so odd a hazard was able to speak quietly.

"You are really very good," he said. "I apologise again; my rudeness was really most unjustifiable. I feel my conduct demands an explanation, and I shall be happy to give it you. Do you happen to know of any place near here where one could sit down? I should really be very glad."

"My dear sir," said Dyson solemnly, "the only café in London is close by. Pray do not consider yourself as bound to offer me any explanation, but at the same time I should be most happy to listen to you. Let us turn down here."

They walked down a sober street and turned into what seemed a narrow passage past an iron-barred gate thrown back. The passage was paved with flagstones, and decorated with handsome shrubs in pots on either side, and the shadow of the high walls made a coolness which was very agreeable after the hot breath of the sunny street. Presently the passage opened out into a tiny square, a charming place, a morsel of France transplanted into the heart of London. High walls rose on either side, covered with glossy creepers, flower-beds beneath were gay with nasturtiums, geraniums, and marigolds, and odorous with mignonette,[1] and in the centre of the square a fountain, hidden by greenery, sent a cool shower continually plashing into the basin beneath. The very noise made this retreat delightful. Chairs and tables were disposed at convenient intervals, and at the other end of the court broad doors had been thrown back; beyond was a long, dark room, and the turmoil of traffic had become a distant murmur. Within the room one or two men were sitting at the tables, writing and sipping, but the courtyard was empty.

"You see, we shall be quiet," said Dyson. "Pray sit down here, Mr.—?"

"Wilkins. My name is Henry Wilkins."

"Sit here, Mr. Wilkins. I think you will find that a comfortable seat. I suppose you have not been here before? This is the quiet time; the place will be like a hive at six o'clock, and the chairs and tables will overflow into that little alley there."

A waiter came in response to the bell; and after Dyson had politely inquired after the health of M. Annibault, the proprietor, he ordered a bottle of the wine of Champigny.[2]

"The wine of Champigny," he observed to Mr. Wilkins, who was evidently a good deal composed by the influence of the place, "is a Tourainian wine of great merit. Ah, here it is; let me fill your glass. How do you find it?"

"Indeed," said Mr. Wilkins, "I should have pronounced it a fine Burgundy. The bouquet is very exquisite. I am fortunate in lighting upon such a good Samaritan as yourself: I wonder you did not think me mad. But if you knew the terrors that assailed me, I

---

1 *Reseda odorata*, a kind of plant with fragrant yellowish-white flowers (*OED*).

2 Wine from Champagne region of France or reminiscent of wines produced in that area; in this case the wine is said to be from Touraine, a historical area of France named after the Turones, a tribe that inhabited the area when Caesar conquered Gaul (Paxton).

am sure you would no longer be surprised at conduct which was certainly most unjustifiable."

He sipped his wine, and leant back in his chair, relishing the drip and trickle of the fountain, and the cool greenness that hedged in this little port of refuge.

"Yes," he said at last, "that is indeed an admirable wine. Thank you; you will allow me to offer you another bottle?"

The waiter was summoned, and descended through a trap-door in the floor of the dark apartment and brought up the wine. Mr. Wilkins lit a cigarette, and Dyson pulled out his pipe.

"Now," said Mr. Wilkins, "I promised to give you an explanation of my strange behaviour. It is rather a long story, but I see, sir, that you are no mere cold observer of the ebb and flow of life. You take, I think, a warm and an intelligent interest in the chances of your fellow-creatures, and I believe you will find what I have to tell not devoid of interest."

Mr. Dyson signified his assent to these propositions; and though he thought Mr. Wilkins's diction a little pompous, prepared to interest himself in his tale. The other, who had so raged with passion half an hour before, was now perfectly cool, and when he had smoked out his cigarette, he began in an even voice to relate the

NOVEL OF THE DARK VALLEY.

I am the son of a poor but learned clergyman in the West of England—but I am forgetting, these details are not of special interest. I will briefly state, then, that my father, who was, as I have said, a learned man, had never learnt the specious arts by which the great are flattered, and would never condescend to the despicable pursuit of self-advertisement. Though his fondness for ancient ceremonies and quaint customs, combined with a kindness of heart that was unequalled and a primitive and fervent piety, endeared him to his moorland parishioners, such were not the steps by which clergy then rose in the Church, and at sixty my father was still incumbent of the little benefice he had accepted in his thirtieth year. The income of the living was barely sufficient to support life in the decencies which are expected of the Anglican parson; and when my father died a few years ago, I, his only child, found myself thrown upon the world with a slender capital of less than a hundred pounds, and all the problem of existence before me. I felt that there was nothing for me to do in the country, and as usually happens in such cases, London drew me like a magnet. One day in August, in the early morning, while the dew still glittered on the turf, and on the high green banks of the lane, a neighbour drove me to the railway station, and I bade good-bye to the land of the broad moors and unearthly battlements of the wild tors. It was six o'clock as we neared London; the faint, sickly fume of the brickfields about Acton came in puffs through the open window, and a mist was rising from the ground. Presently the brief view of successive streets, prim and uniform, struck me with a sense of monotony; the hot air seemed to grow hotter; and when we had rolled beneath the dismal and squalid houses, whose dirty and neglected back-yards border the line near Paddington, I felt as if I should be stifled in this fainting breath of London. I got a hansom and drove off, and every street increased my gloom; grey houses with blinds drawn down, whole thoroughfares almost desolate, and the foot-passengers who seemed to stagger wearily along rather than walk, all made me feel a sinking at heart. I put up for the night at a small hotel in a street leading from the Strand,[1] where my father had stayed on his few brief visits to town; and when I went out after dinner, the real gaiety and bustle of the Strand and Fleet Street[2] could cheer me but little, for in all this great city there was no single human being whom I could claim even as an acquaintance. I will not weary you with the history of the next year, for the adventures of a man who sinks are too trite to be worth recalling. My money did not last me long; I found that I must be neatly dressed, or no one to whom I applied would so much as listen to me; and I must live in a street of decent reputation if I wished to be treated with common civility. I applied for various posts, for which, as I now see, I was completely devoid of qualification; I tried to become a

---

1   By the end of the nineteenth century, the Strand (a street in central London that runs parallel to the Thames River) was well known for the entertainments it offered, including numerous theatres, music halls, and restaurants (Ayto et al.). In his autobiographical writing, Machen writes fondly about this street in London, wishing he could have afforded to partake of what it had to offer (but he could not): "To be in the Strand was like drinking punch and reading Dickens. One felt it was such a warmhearted, hospitable street, if one only had a little money. Unfortunately, I was never on dining terms, as it were, with the Strand" (*Far Off Things* 130).

2   Street in London long associated with the printing trade, booksellers, and newspapers (Ayto et al.).

clerk without having the smallest notion of business habits, and I found, to my cost, that a general knowledge of literature and an execrable style of penmanship are far from being looked upon with favour in commercial circles. I had read one of the most charming of the works of a famous novelist of the present day, and I frequented the Fleet Street taverns in the hope of making literary friends, and so getting the introductions which I understood were indispensable in the career of letters. I was disappointed; I once or twice ventured to address gentlemen who were sitting in adjoining boxes, and I was answered, politely indeed, but in a manner that told me my advances were unusual. Pound by pound, my small resources melted; I could no longer think of appearances; I migrated to a shy quarter, and my meals became mere observances. I went out at one and returned to my room at two, but nothing but a milk-cake had occurred in the interval. In short, I became acquainted with misfortune; and as I sat amidst slush and ice on a seat in Hyde Park,[1] munching a piece of bread, I realised the bitterness of poverty, and the feelings of a gentleman reduced to something far below the condition of a vagrant. In spite of all discouragement I did not desist in my efforts to earn a living. I consulted advertisement columns, I kept my eyes open for a chance, I looked in at the windows of stationers' shops, but all in vain. One evening I was sitting in a Free Library,[2] and I saw an advertisement in one of the papers. It was something like this: "Wanted by a gentleman a person of literary taste and abilities as secretary and amanuensis.[3] Must not object to travel." Of course I knew that such an advertisement would have answers by the hundred, and I thought my own chances of securing the post extremely small; however, I applied at the address given, and wrote to Mr. Smith, who was staying at a large hotel at the West End. I must confess that my heart gave a jump when I received a note a couple of days later, asking me to call at the Cosmopole[4] at my earliest convenience.

---

1   Large park in central London, the location of major public events such as the Great Exhibition of 1851 as well as the promenades of fashionable society (Ayto et al.).

2   In England this was the original term for a "public library." The first public library built under the terms of the 1850 Public Libraries Act in England opened in 1857, but many more would follow, especially after the 1880s.

3   "A literary assistant, *esp.* one who takes dictation or copies text" (*OED*).

4   A likely fictional hotel.

I do not know, sir, what your experiences of life may have been, and so I cannot tell whether you have known such moments. A slight sickness, my heart beating rather more rapidly than usual, a choking in the throat, and a difficulty of utterance; such were my sensations as I walked to the Cosmopole. I had to mention the name twice before the hall porter could understand me, and as I went upstairs my hands were wet. I was a good deal struck by Mr. Smith's appearance; he looked younger than I did, and there was something mild and hesitating about his expression. He was reading when I came in, and he looked up when I gave my name. "My dear sir," he said, "I am really delighted to see you. I have read very carefully the letter you were good enough to send me. Am I to understand that this document is in your own handwriting?" He showed me the letter I had written, and I told him I was not so fortunate as to be able to keep a secretary myself. "Then, sir," he went on, "the post I advertised is at your service. You have no objection to travel, I presume?" As you may imagine, I closed pretty eagerly with the offer he made, and thus I entered the service of Mr. Smith. For the first few weeks I had no special duties; I had received a quarter's salary, and a handsome allowance was made me in lieu of board and lodging. One morning, however, when I called at the hotel according to instructions, my master informed me that I must hold myself in readiness for a sea-voyage, and, to spare unnecessary detail, in the course of a fortnight we had landed at New York. Mr. Smith told me that he was engaged on a work of a special nature, in the compilation of which some peculiar researches had to be made; in short, I was given to understand that we were to travel to the far West.

After about a week had been spent in New York we took our seats in the cars, and began a journey tedious beyond all conception. Day after day, and night after night, the great train rolled on, threading its way through cities the very names of which were strange to me, passing at slow speed over perilous viaducts, skirting mountain ranges and pine forests, and plunging into dense tracts of wood, where mile after mile and hour after hour the same monotonous growth of brushwood met the eye, and all along the continual clatter and rattle of the wheels upon the ill-laid lines made it difficult to hear the voices of our fellow-passengers. We were a heterogeneous and ever-changing company; often I woke up in the dead of night with the sudden grinding jar of the brakes, and looking out found that we had stopped in the shabby street of some frame-built town, lighted chiefly by the flaring windows of the saloon. A few rough-looking fellows would often come out to stare at the cars, and sometimes passengers got down, and sometimes there was a party of two or three waiting on the wooden sidewalk to get on board. Many of the passengers were English; humble households torn up from the moorings of a thousand years, and bound for some problematical paradise in the alkali desert or the Rockies. I heard the men talking to one another of the great profits to be made on the virgin soil of America, and two or three, who were mechanics, expatiated on the wonderful wages given to skilled labour on the railways and in the factories of the States. This talk usually fell dead after a few minutes, and I could see a sickness and dismay in the faces of these men as they looked at the ugly brush or at the desolate expanse of the prairie, dotted here and there with frame-houses, devoid of garden, or flowers or trees, standing all alone in what might have been a great grey sea frozen into stillness. Day after day the waving sky-line, and the desolation of a land without form or colour or variety, appalled the hearts of such of us as were Englishmen, and once in the night as I lay awake I heard a woman weeping and sobbing and asking what she had done to come to such a place. Her husband tried to comfort her in the broad speech of Gloucestershire, telling her the ground was so rich that one had only to plough it up and it would grow sunflowers of itself, but she cried for her mother and their old cottage and the beehives like a little child. The sadness of it all overwhelmed me, and I had no heart to think of other matters; the question of what Mr. Smith could have to do in such a country, and of what manner of literary research could be carried on in the wilderness, hardly troubled me. Now and again my situation struck me as peculiar; I had been engaged as a literary assistant at a handsome salary, and yet my master was still almost a stranger to me; sometimes he would come to where I was sitting in the cars and make a few banal remarks about the country, but for the most part of the journey he sat by himself, not speaking to any one, and so far as I could judge, deep in his thoughts. It was, I think, on the fifth day from New York when I received the intimation that we should shortly leave the cars; I had been watching some distant mountains which rose wild and savage before us, and I was wondering if there were human beings so unhappy as to speak of home in connection with those piles of lumbered rock, when Mr. Smith touched me lightly on the shoulder. "You will be glad to be done with the cars, I have no doubt, Mr. Wilkins," he said. "You were looking at the mountains, I think? Well, I hope we shall be there to-night. The train stops at Reading,[1] and I dare say we shall manage to find our way."

A few hours later the breaksman brought the tram to a standstill at the Reading depôt, and we got out. I noticed that the town, though of course built almost entirely of frame-houses, was larger and busier than any we had passed for the last two days. The depôt was crowded; and as the bell and whistle sounded, I saw that a number of persons were preparing to leave the cars, while an even greater number were waiting to get on board. Besides the passengers, there was a pretty dense crowd of people, some of whom had come to meet or to see off their friends and relatives, while others were mere loafers. Several of our English fellow-passengers got down at Reading, but the confusion was so great that they were lost to my sight almost immediately. Mr. Smith beckoned to me to follow him, and we were soon in the thick of the mass; and the continual ringing of bells, the hubbub of voices, the shrieking of whistles, and the hiss of escaping steam, confused my senses, and I wondered dimly, as I struggled after my employer, where we were going, and how we should be able to find our way through an unknown country. Mr. Smith had put on a wide-brimmed hat, which he had sloped over his eyes, and as all the men wore hats of the same pattern, it was with some difficulty that I distinguished him in the crowd. We got free at last, and he struck down a side street, and made one or two sharp turns to right and left. It was getting dusk, and we seemed to be passing through a shy portion of the town; there were few people about in the ill-lighted streets, and these few were men of the most unprepossessing pattern. Suddenly we stopped before a corner house. A man was standing at the door, apparently on the look-out for some one, and I noticed that he and Smith gave sharp glances one to the other.

"From NewYork City, I expect, mister?"

"From NewYork."

"All right; they 're ready, and you can have 'em when you choose. I know my orders, you see, and I mean to run this business through."

"Very well, Mr. Evans, that is what we want. Our money is good, you know. Bring them round."

I had stood silent, listening to this dialogue and wondering what it meant. Smith began to walk impatiently up and down the

---

1 Purportedly in Colorado, as indicated in the newspaper cutting Mr. Wilkins later provides as "proof" of the veracity of his tale.

street, and the man Evans was still standing at his door. He had given a sharp whistle, and I saw him looking me over in a quiet leisurely way, as if to make sure of my face for another time. I was thinking what all this could mean, when an ugly, slouching lad came up a side passage, leading two raw-boned horses.

"Get up, Mr. Wilkins, and be quick about it," said Smith; "we ought to be on our way."

We rode off together into the gathering darkness, and before long I looked back and saw the far plain behind us, with the lights of the town glimmering faintly; and in front rose the mountains. Smith guided his horse on the rough track as surely as if he had been riding along Piccadilly, and I followed him as well as I could. I was weary and exhausted, and scarcely took note of anything; I felt that the track was a gradual ascent, and here and there I saw great boulders by the road. The ride made but little impression on me. I have a faint recollection of passing through a dense black pine forest, where our horses had to pick their way among the rocks, and I remember the peculiar effect of the rarefied air as we kept still mounting higher and higher. I think I must have been half asleep for the latter half of the ride, and it was with a shock that I heard Smith saying—

"Here we are, Wilkins. This is Blue Rock Park. You will enjoy the view to-morrow. To-night we will have something to eat, and then go to bed."

A man came out of a rough-looking house and took the horses, and we found some fried steak and coarse whiskey awaiting us inside. I had come to a strange place. There were three rooms—the room in which we had supper, Smith's room, and my own. The deaf old man who did the work slept in a sort of shed, and when I woke up the next morning and walked out I found that the house stood in a sort of hollow amongst the mountains; the clumps of pines and some enormous bluish-grey rocks that stood here and there between the trees had given the place the name of Blue Rock Park. On every side the snow-covered mountains surrounded us, the breath of the air was as wine, and when I climbed the slope and looked down, I could see that, so far as any human fellowship was concerned, I might as well have been wrecked on some small island in mid-Pacific. The only trace of man I could see was the rough log-house where I had slept, and in my ignorance I did not know that there were similar houses within comparatively easy distance, as distance is reckoned in the Rockies. But at the moment, the utter, dreadful loneliness rushed upon me, and the thought of the great plain and the great sea that parted me from the world I knew caught me by the throat, and I wondered if I should die there in that mountain hollow. It was a terrible instant, and I have not yet forgotten it. Of course, I managed to conquer my horror; I said I should be all the stronger for the experience, and I made up my mind to make the best of everything. It was a rough life enough, and rough enough board and lodging. I was left entirely to myself. Smith I scarcely ever saw, nor did I know when he was in the house. I have often thought he was far away, and have been surprised to see him walking out of his room, locking the door behind him, and putting the key in his pocket; and on several occasions, when I fancied he was busy in his room, I have seen him come in with his boots covered with dust and dirt. So far as work went I enjoyed a complete sinecure; I had nothing to do but to walk about the valley, to eat, and to sleep. With one thing and another I grew accustomed to the life, and managed to make myself pretty comfortable, and by degrees I began to venture farther away from the house, and to explore the country. One day I had contrived to get into a neighbouring valley, and suddenly I came upon a group of men sawing timber. I went up to them, hoping that perhaps some of them might be Englishmen; at all events, they were human beings, and I should hear articulate speech; for the old man I have mentioned, besides being half blind and stone deaf, was wholly dumb so far as I was concerned. I was prepared to be welcomed in a rough and ready fashion, without much of the forms of politeness, but the grim glances and the short, gruff answers I received astonished me. I saw the men glancing oddly at each other; and one of them who had stopped work, began fingering a gun, and I was obliged to return on my path uttering curses on the fate which had brought me into a land where men were more brutish than the very brutes. The solitude of the life began to oppress me as with a nightmare, and a few days later I determined to walk to a kind of station some miles distant, where a rough inn was kept for the accommodation of hunters and tourists. English gentlemen occasionally stopped there for the night, and I thought I might perhaps fall in with some one of better manners than the inhabitants of the country. I found, as I had expected, a group of men lounging about the door of the log-house that served as a hotel, and as I came nearer I could see that heads were put together and looks interchanged, and when I walked up the six or seven trappers stared at me in stony ferocity, and with something of the disgust that one eyes a loathsome and venomous snake. I felt that I could bear it no longer, and I called out—

"Is there such a thing as an Englishman here, or any one with a little civilisation?"[1]

One of the men put his hand to his belt, but his neighbour checked him, and answered me—

"You'll find we've got some of the resources of civilisation before very long, mister, and I expect you'll not fancy them extremely. But, any way, there's an Englishman tarrying here, and I've no doubt he'll be glad to see you. There you are; that's Mr. D'Aubernoun."

A young man, dressed like an English country squire, came and stood at the door, and looked at me. One of the men pointed to me and said—

"That's the individual we were talking about last night. Thought you might like to have a look at him, squire, and here he is."

The young fellow's good-natured English face clouded over, and he glanced sternly at me, and turned away with a gesture of contempt and aversion.

"Sir," I cried, "I do not know what I have done to be treated in this manner. You are my fellow-countryman, and I expected some courtesy."

He gave me a black look and made as if he would go in, but he changed his mind and faced me.

"You are rather imprudent, I think, to behave in this manner. You must be counting on a forbearance which cannot last very long, which may last a very short time indeed. And let me tell you this, sir, you may call yourself an Englishman, and drag the name of England through the dirt, but you need not count on any English influence to help you. If I were you, I would not stay here much longer."

He went into the inn, and the men quietly watched my face as I stood there, wondering whether I was going mad. The woman of the house came out and stared at me as if I were a wild beast or a savage, and I turned to her, and spoke quietly—

---

1 Although "civilisation" referred broadly to "a general progress of knowledge, technique, social organization, and morality," the term was often aligned with specifically middle-class British views of progress that opposed savagery and civilization, and with British cultural values of self-restraint and rational control "over one's baser instincts" (Stocking 35). Wilkins's prejudicial assumption that Englishness implies civilization is repeatedly undermined both within this story and in the larger frame narrative.

"I am very hungry and thirsty. I have walked a long way. I have plenty of money. Will you give me something to eat and drink?"

"No, I won't," she said. "You had better quit this."

I crawled home like a wounded beast, and lay down on my bed. It was all a hopeless puzzle to me; I knew nothing but rage, and shame, and terror, and I suffered little more when I passed by a house in an adjacent valley, and some children who were playing outside ran from me shrieking. I was forced to walk to find some occupation; I should have died if I had sat down quietly in Blue Rock Park and looked all day at the mountains; but wherever I saw a human being I saw the same glance of hatred and aversion, and once as I was crossing a thick brake I heard a shot and the venomous hiss of a bullet close to my ear.

One day I heard a conversation which astounded me; I was sitting behind a rock resting, and two men came along the track and halted. One of them had got his feet entangled in some wild vines, and swore fiercely, but the other laughed, and said they were useful things sometimes.

"What the hell do you mean?"

"Oh, nothing much. But they're uncommon tough, these here vines, and sometimes rope is skerse and dear."

The man who had sworn chuckled at this, and I heard them sit down and light their pipes.

"Have you seen him lately?" asked the humourist.

"I sighted him the other day, but the darned bullet went high. He's got his master's luck I expect, sir, but it can't last much longer. You heard about him going to Jinks's and trying his brass, but the young Britisher downed him pretty considerable, I can tell you."

"What the devil is the meaning of it?"

"I don't know, but I believe it'll have to be finished, and done in the old style too. You know how they fix the niggers?"[1]

"Yes, sir, I've seen a little of that. A couple of gallons of kerosene'll cost a dollar at Brown's store, but I should say it's cheap anyway."

They moved off after this, and I lay still behind the rock, the sweat pouring down my face. I was so sick that I could barely

---

1 This racial slur, now considered highly offensive, registers the racism implicit in practices of mob violence and killings in the United States. Although many associate this kind of violence with the Southern states, it also took place in the West (the setting of the above story). For more on the history of racially motivated mob violence, see Pfeifer.

stand, and I walked home as slowly as an old man, leaning on my stick. I knew that the two men had been talking about me, and I knew that some terrible death was in store for me. That night I could not sleep; I tossed on the rough bed and tortured myself to find out the meaning of it all. At last, in the very dead of night, I rose from the bed and put on my clothes, and went out. I did not care where I went, but I felt that I must walk till I had tired myself out. It was a clear moonlight night, and in a couple of hours I found I was approaching a place of dismal reputation in the mountains, a deep cleft in the rocks, known as Black Gulf Cañon.[1] Many years before an unfortunate party of Englishmen and Englishwomen had camped here and had been surrounded by Indians. They were captured, outraged, and put to death with almost inconceivable tortures, and the roughest of the trappers or woodsmen gave the cañon a wide berth even in the daytime. As I crushed through the dense brushwood which grew above the cañon I heard voices; and wondering who could be in such a place at such a time, I went on, walking more carefully, and making as little noise as possible. There was a great tree growing on the very edge of the rocks, and I lay down and looked out from behind the trunk. Black Gulf Cañon was below me, the moonlight shining bright into its very depths from mid-heaven, and casting shadows as black as death from the pointed rock, and all the sheer rock on the other side, overhanging the cañon, was in darkness. At intervals a light veil obscured the moonlight, as a filmy cloud fleeted across the moon, and a bitter wind blew shrill across the gulf. I looked down, as I have said, and saw twenty men standing in a semicircle round a rock; I counted them one by one, and knew most of them. They were the very vilest of the vile, more vile than any den in London could show, and there was murder, and worse than murder, on the heads of not a few. Facing them and me stood Mr. Smith, with the rock before him, and on the rock was a great pair of scales, such, as are used in the stores. I heard his voice ringing down the cañon as I lay beside the tree, and my heart turned cold as I heard it.

"Life for gold," he cried, "a life for gold. The blood and the life of an enemy for every pound of gold."

A man stepped out and raised one hand, and with the other flung a bright lump of something into the pan of the scales, which clanged down, and Smith muttered something in his ear. Then he cried again—

---

1 A fictional place.

"Blood for gold, for a pound of gold, the life of an enemy. For every pound of gold upon the scales, a life."

One by one the men came forward, each lifting up his right hand; and the gold was weighed in the scales, and each time Smith leaned forward and spoke to each man in his ear. Then he cried again—

"Desire and lust for gold on the scales. For every pound of gold enjoyment of desire."

I saw the same thing happen as before; the uplifted hand and the metal weighed, and the mouth whispering, and black passion on every face.

Then, one by one, I saw the men again step up to Smith. A muttered conversation seemed to take place. I could see that Smith was explaining and directing, and I noticed that he gesticulated a little as one who points out the way, and once or twice he moved his hands quickly as if he would show that the path was clear and could not be missed. I kept my eyes so intently on his figure that I noted little else, and at last it was with a start that I realised that the cañon was empty. A moment before I thought I had seen the group of villainous faces, and the two standing, a little apart, by the rock; I had looked down a moment, and when I glanced again into the cañon there was no one there. In dumb terror I made my way home, and I fell asleep in an instant from exhaustion. No doubt I should have slept on for many hours, but when I woke up the sun was only rising, and the light shone in on my bed. I had started up from sleep with the sensation of having received a violent shock; and as I looked in confusion about me, I saw, to my amazement, that there were three men in the room. One of them had his hand on my shoulder and spoke to me—

"Come, mister, wake up. Your time's up now, I reckon, and the boys are waiting for you outside, and they're in a big hurry. Come on; you can put on your clothes; it's kind of chilly this morning."

I saw the other two men smiling sourly at each other, but I understood nothing. I simply pulled on my clothes and said I was ready.

"All right; come on, then. You go first, Nichols, and Jim and I will give the gentleman an arm."

They took me out into the sunlight, and then I understood the meaning of a dull murmur that had vaguely perplexed me while I was dressing. There were about two hundred men waiting outside, and some women too, and when they saw me there was a low muttering growl. I did not know what I had done, but that noise made my heart beat and the sweat come out on my face. I saw confusedly, as through a veil, the tumult and tossing of the crowd, discordant voices were speaking, and amongst all those faces there was not one glance of mercy, but a fury of lust that I did not understand. I found myself presently walking in a sort of procession up the slope of the valley, and on every side of me there were men with revolvers in their hands. Now and then a voice struck me, and I heard words and sentences of which I could form no connected story. But I understood that there was one sentence of execration; I heard scraps of stories that seemed strange and improbable. Some one was talking of men, lured by cunning devices from their homes and murdered with hideous tortures, found writhing like wounded snakes in dark and lonely places, only crying for some one to stab them to the heart, and so end their torments; and I heard another voice speaking of innocent girls who had vanished for a day or two, and then had come back and died, blushing red with shame even in the agonies of death. I wondered what it all meant, and what was to happen; but I was so weary that I walked on in a dream, scarcely longing for anything but sleep. At last we stopped. We had reached the summit of the hill overlooking Blue Rock Valley, and I saw that I was standing beneath a clump of trees where I had often sat. I was in the midst of a ring of armed men, and I saw that two or three men were very busy with piles of wood, while others were fingering a rope. Then there was a stir in the crowd, and a man was pushed forward. His hands and feet were tightly bound with cord; and though his face was unutterably villainous, I pitied him for the agony that worked his features and twisted his lips. I knew him; he was amongst those that had gathered round Smith in Black Gulf Cañon. In an instant he was unbound and stripped naked, and borne beneath one of the trees, and his neck encircled by a noose that went around the trunk. A hoarse voice gave some kind of order; there was a rush of feet, and the rope tightened; and there before me I saw the blackened face and the writhing limbs and the shameful agony of death. One after another half a dozen men, all of whom I had seen in the cañon the night before, were strangled before me, and their bodies were flung forth on the ground. Then there was a pause, and the man who had roused me a short while before came up to me, and said—

"Now, mister, it's your turn. We give you five minutes to cast up your accounts, and when that's clocked, by the living God, we will burn you alive at that tree."

It was then I awoke and understood. I cried out—

"Why, what have I done? Why should you hurt me? I am a harmless man; I never did you any wrong." I covered my face with my hands; it seemed so pitiful, and it was such a terrible death.

"What have I done?" I cried again. "You must take me for some other man. You cannot know me."

"You black-hearted devil," said the man at my side, "we know you well enough. There's not a man within thirty miles of this that won't curse Jack Smith when you are burning in hell."

"My name is not Smith," I said, with some hope left in me. "My name is Wilkins. I was Mr. Smith's secretary, but I knew nothing of him."

"Hark at the black liar," said the man. "Secretary be damned! You were clever enough, I dare say, to slink out at night and keep your face in the dark, but we've tracked you out at last. But your time's up. Come along."

I was dragged to the tree and bound to it with chains; and I saw the piles of wood heaped all about me, and shut my eyes. Then I felt myself drenched all over with some liquid, and looked again, and a woman grinned at me. She had just emptied a great can of petroleum over me and over the wood. A voice shouted, "Fire away!" and I fainted, and knew nothing more.

When I opened my eyes I was lying on a bed in a bare comfortless room. A doctor was holding some strong salts to my nostrils, and a gentleman standing by the bed, whom I afterwards found to be the sheriff, addressed me.

"Say, mister," he began, "you've had an uncommon narrow squeak for it. The boys were just about lighting up when I came along with the posse,[1] and I had as much as I could do to bring you off, I can tell you. And, mind you, I don't blame them; they had made up their minds, you see, that you were the head of the Black Gulf gang, and at first nothing I could say would persuade them you weren't Jack Smith. Luckily, a man from here named Evans, that came along with us, allowed he had seen you with Jack Smith, and that you were yourself. So we brought you along and gaoled you, but you can go if you like when you're through with this faint turn."

I got on the cars the next day, and in three weeks I was in London; again almost penniless. But from that time my fortune seemed to change; I made influential friends in all directions; bank directors courted my company, and editors positively

---

1 A term that here refers to the sheriff's police officers or, more likely, a group of men recruited to work with the sheriff.

flung themselves into my arms. I had only to choose my career, and after a while I determined that I was meant by nature for a life of comparative leisure. With an ease that seemed almost ridiculous, I obtained a well-paid position in connection with a prosperous political club. I have charming chambers in a central neighbourhood, close to the parks, the club chef exerts himself when I lunch or dine, and the rarest vintages in the cellar are always at my disposal. Yet, since my return to London, I have never known a day's security or peace; I tremble when I awake lest Smith should be standing at my bed, and every step I take seems to bring me nearer to the edge of the precipice. Smith, I knew, had escaped free from the raid of the Vigilantes, and I grew faint at the thought that he would in all probability return to London, and that suddenly and unprepared I should meet him face to face. Every morning as I left my house I would peer up and down the street, expecting to see that dreaded figure awaiting me; I have delayed at street-corners, my heart in my mouth, sickening at the thought that a few quick steps might bring us together; I could not bear to frequent the theatres or music-halls, lest by some bizarre chance he should prove to be my neighbour. Sometimes I have been forced, against my will, to walk out at night, and then in silent squares the shadows have made me shudder, and in the medley of meetings in the crowded thoroughfares I have said to myself, "It must come sooner or later; he will surely return to town, and I shall see him when I feel most secure." I scanned the newspapers for hint or intimation of approaching danger, and no small type nor report of trivial interest was allowed to pass unread. Especially I read and re-read the advertisement columns, but without result; months passed by and I was undisturbed till, though I felt far from safe, I no longer suffered from the intolerable oppression of instant and ever-present terror. This afternoon, as I was walking quietly along Oxford Street, I raised my eyes and looked across the road, and then at last I saw the man who had so long haunted my thoughts.

Mr. Wilkins finished his wine, and leant back in his chair, looking sadly at Dyson; and then, as if a thought struck him, fished out of an inner pocket a leather letter-case, and handed a newspaper cutting across the table.

Dyson glanced closely at the slip, and saw that it had been extracted from the columns of an evening paper. It ran as follows:—

WHOLESALE LYNCHING.
SHOCKING STORY.[1]

"A Dalziel[2] telegram from Reading (Colorado) states that advices received there from Blue Rock Park report a frightful instance of popular vengeance. For some time the neighbourhood has been terrorised by the crimes of a gang of desperadoes, who, under the cover of a carefully planned organisation, have perpetrated the most infamous cruelties on men and women. A Vigilance Committee was formed, and it was found that the leader of the gang was a person named Smith, living in Blue Rock Park. Action was taken, and six of the worst in the band were summarily strangled in the presence of two or three hundred men and women. Smith is said to have escaped."

"This is a terrible story," said Dyson; "I can well believe that your days and nights are haunted by such fearful scenes as you have described. But surely you have no need to fear Smith? He has much more cause to fear you. Consider: you have only to lay your information before the police, and a warrant would be immediately issued for his arrest. Besides, you will, I am sure, excuse me for what I am going to say."

"My dear sir," said Mr. Wilkins, "I hope you will speak to me with perfect freedom."

"Well, then, I must confess that my impression was that you were rather disappointed at not being able to stop the man before he drove off. I thought you seemed annoyed that you could not get across the street."

"Sir, I did not know what I was about. I caught sight of the man, but it was only for a moment, and the agony you witnessed was the agony of suspense. I was not perfectly certain of the face; and the horrible thought that Smith was again in London overwhelmed me. I shuddered at the idea of this incarnate fiend, whose soul is black with shocking crimes, mingling free and unobserved amongst the harmless crowds, meditating perhaps a new and more fearful cycle of infamies. I tell you, sir, that an awful being stalks through the streets, a being before whom the sunlight itself should blacken, and the summer air grow chill and dank. Such thoughts as these rushed upon me with the force of a whirlwind; I lost my senses."

---

1 The emphasis on sensationalism in the news was common then as now. For more on the history of lynching, see p. 78, note 1, above.
2 An American news agency.

"I see. I partly understand your feelings, but I would impress on you that you have nothing really to fear. Depend upon it, Smith will not molest you in any way. You must remember he himself has had a warning; and indeed, from the brief glance I had of him, he seemed to me to be a frightened-looking man. However, I see it is getting late, and if you will excuse me, Mr. Wilkins, I think I will be going. I dare say we shall often meet here."

Dyson walked off smartly, pondering the strange story chance had brought him, and finding on cool reflection that there was something a little strange in Mr. Wilkins's manner, for which not even so weird a catalogue of experiences could altogether account.

ADEVENTURE OF THE MISSING BROTHER

Mr. Charles Phillipps was, as has been hinted, a gentleman of pronounced scientific tastes. In his early days he had devoted himself with fond enthusiasm to the agreeable study of biology, and a brief monograph on the Embryology of the Microscopic Holothuria had formed his first contribution to the *belles lettres*.[1] Later he had somewhat relaxed the severity of his pursuits, and had dabbled in the more frivolous subjects of palæontology and ethnology;[2] he had a cabinet in his sitting-room whose drawers were stuffed with rude flint implements, and a charming fetish[3] from the South Seas was the dominant note in the decorative scheme of the apartment. Flattering himself with the title of materialist,[4] he was in truth one of the most credulous of men, but he required a marvel to be neatly draped in the robes of Science before he would give it any credit, and the wildest dreams took solid shape to him if only the nomenclature were severe and irreproachable. He laughed at the witch, but quailed before the powers of the hypnotist, lifting his eyebrows when Christianity

---

1 French for "fine letters," the term is typically used to refer to works of literature. Holothuria (sea cucumbers or sea slugs) refers to a genus of the phylum Echinodermata.

2 The study of human cultures, societies, and races; it incorporated studies of archaeology, physiology, history, and philology, among others, and is one of the bases of what is now anthropology.

3 The collecting of scientific specimens was common for amateurs of ethnology but also part of a broader Victorian museum movement that helped institutionalize the study of anthropology, with some private collections becoming part of major museum collections. See Introduction, pp. 26–34, for more details.

4 See p. 29, note 1, above.

was mentioned, but adoring protyle and the ether.[1] For the rest, he prided himself on a boundless scepticism; the average tale of wonder he heard with nothing but contempt, and he would certainly not have credited a word or syllable of Dyson's story of the pursuer and pursued unless the gold coin had been produced as visible and tangible evidence. As it was, he half suspected that Dyson had imposed on him; he knew his friend's disordered fancies, and his habit of conjuring up the marvellous to account for the entirely commonplace; and, on the whole, he was inclined to think that the so-called facts in the odd adventure had been gravely distorted in the telling. Since the evening on which he had listened to the tale he had paid Dyson a visit, and had delivered himself of some serious talk on the necessity of accurate observation, and the folly, as he put it, of using a kaleidoscope[2] instead of a telescope in the view of things, to which remarks his friend had listened with a smile that was extremely sardonic. "My dear fellow," Dyson had remarked at last, "you will allow me to tell you that I see your drift perfectly. However, you will be astonished to hear that I consider you to be the visionary, while I am a sober and serious spectator of human life. You have gone round the circle; and while you fancy yourself far in the golden land of new philosophies, you are in reality a dweller in metaphorical Clapham;[3] your scepticism has defeated itself and become a monstrous credulity; you are, in fact, in the position of the bat or owl, I forget which it was, who denied the existence of the sun at noonday,[4] and I shall be astonished if you do not one

---

1 Protyle refers to a hypothetical original form of matter from which all chemical elements derived. Ether is similarly hypothetical; it referred to a kind of universal medium that was employed to explain a wide range of phenomena since the beginning of the nineteenth century, including light, electricity, and electromagnetism. In Machen's time, ether was also employed in attempts to explain communication with the dead, telepathy, telekinesis, and other otherwise inexplicable psychical phenomena.

2 Perhaps alluding to a key influence on Decadent writers in France and Britain, poet Charles Baudelaire (1821–67), who famously defined the artist as "a kaleidoscope gifted with consciousness" in his essay "The Painter of Modern Life" (1863).

3 A district of southwest London. Perhaps a reference to the idiom "the man on the Clapham bus," used to refer to an ordinary or average individual (*OED*).

4 Dyson is likely referring to the fable "The Owl that Wrote a Book,"

day come to me full of contrition for your manifold intellectual errors, with a humble resolution to see things in their true light for the future." This tirade had left Mr. Phillipps unimpressed; he considered Dyson as hopeless, and he went home to gloat over some primitive stone implements that a friend had sent him from India. He found that his landlady, seeing them displayed in all their rude formlessness upon the table, had removed the collection to the dustbin, and had replaced it by lunch; and the afternoon was spent in malodorous research. Mrs. Brown, hearing these stones spoken of as very valuable knives, had called him in his hearing "poor Mr. Phillipps," and between rage and evil odours he spent a sorry afternoon. It was four o'clock before he had completed his work of rescue; and, overpowered with the flavours of decaying cabbage leaves, Phillipps felt that he must have a walk to gain an appetite for the evening meal. Unlike Dyson, he walked fast, with his eyes on the pavement, absorbed in his thoughts, and oblivious of the life around him; and he could not have told by what streets he had passed, when he suddenly lifted up his eyes and found himself in Leicester Square. The grass and flowers pleased him, and he welcomed the opportunity of resting for a few minutes, and glancing round, he saw a bench which had only one occupant, a lady, and as she was seated at one end, Phillipps took up a position at the other extremity, and began to pass in angry review the events of the afternoon. He had noticed as he came up to the bench that the person already there was neatly dressed, and to all appearance young; her face he could not see, as it was turned away in apparent contemplation of the shrubs, and, moreover shielded with her hand; but it would be doing wrong to Mr. Phillipps to imagine that his choice of a seat was dictated by any hopes of an affair of the heart; he had simply preferred the company of one lady to that of five dirty children, and having seated himself, was immersed directly in thoughts of his misfortunes. He had meditated changing his lodgings; but now, on a judicial review of the case in all its bearings, his calmer judgment told him that the race of landladies is like to the race of the leaves, and that there was but little to choose between them. He resolved, however, to talk to Mrs. Brown, the offender, very coolly and yet

---

in which an owl manages to convince other "night birds" (including a bat) that "the sun was not full of light, that the moon was in reality much more luminous, that past ages had made a mistake about it, and the world was quite in the dark on the subject."

severely, to point out the extreme indiscretion of her conduct, and to express a hope for better things in the future. With this decision registered in his mind, Phillipps was about to get up from the seat and move off, when he was intensely annoyed to hear a stifled sob, evidently from the lady, who still continued her contemplation of the shrubs and flower-beds. He clutched his stick desperately, and in a moment would have been in full retreat, when the lady turned her face towards him, and with a mute entreaty bespoke his attention. She was a young girl with a quaint and piquant rather than a beautiful face, and she was evidently in the bitterest distress. Mr. Phillipps sat down again, and cursed his chances heartily. The young lady looked at him with a pair of charming eyes of a shining hazel, which showed no trace of tears, though a handkerchief was in her hand; she bit her lip, and seemed to struggle with some overpowering grief, and her whole attitude was all beseeching and imploring. Phillipps sat on the edge of the bench gazing awkwardly at her, and wondering what was to come next, and she looked at him still without speaking.

"Well, madam," he said at last, "I understood from your gesture that you wished to speak to me. Is there anything I can do for you? Though, if you will pardon me, I cannot help saying that that seems highly improbable."

"Ah, sir," she said in a low, murmuring voice, "do not speak harshly to me. I am in sore straits, and I thought from your face that I could safely ask your sympathy, if not your help."

"Would you kindly tell me what is the matter?" said Phillipps. "Perhaps you would like some tea?"

"I knew I could not be mistaken," the lady replied. "That offer of refreshment bespeaks a generous mind. But tea, alas! is powerless to console me. If you will let me, I will endeavour to explain my trouble."

"I should be glad if you would."

"I will do so, and I will try and be brief, in spite of the numerous complications which have made me, young as I am, tremble before what seems the profound and terrible mystery of existence. Yet the grief which now racks my very soul is but too simple: I have lost my brother."

"Lost your brother! How on earth can that be?"

"I see I must trouble you with a few particulars. My brother, then, who is by some years my elder, is a tutor in a private school in the extreme north of London. The want of means deprived him of the advantages of a University education; and lacking the stamp of a degree, he could not hope for that position which his scholarship and his talents entitled him to claim. He was thus forced to accept the post of classical master at Dr. Saunderson's Highgate Academy for the sons of gentlemen, and he has performed his duties with perfect satisfaction to his principal for some years. My personal history need not trouble you; it will be enough if I tell you that for the last month I have been governess in a family residing at Tooting.[1] My brother and I have always cherished the warmest mutual affection; and though circumstances into which I need not enter have kept us apart for some time, yet we have never lost sight of one another. We made up our minds that unless one of us was absolutely unable to rise from a bed of sickness, we should never let a week pass by without meeting, and some time ago we chose this square as our rendezvous on account of its central position and its convenience of access. And indeed, after a week of distasteful toil, my brother felt little inclination for much walking, and we have often spent two or three hours on this bench, speaking of our prospects and of happier days, when we were children. In the early spring it was cold and chilly, still we enjoyed the short respite, and I think that we were often taken for a pair of lovers, as we sat close together, eagerly talking. Saturday after Saturday we have met each other here; and though the doctor told him it was madness, my brother would not allow the influenza to break the appointment. That was some time ago; last Saturday we had a long and happy afternoon, and separated more cheerfully than usual, feeling that the coming week would be bearable, and resolving that our next meeting should be if possible still more pleasant. I arrived here at the time agreed upon, four o'clock, and sat down and watched for my brother, expecting every moment to see him advancing towards me from that gate at the north side of the square. Five minutes passed by, and he had not arrived; I thought he must have missed his train, and the idea that our interview would be cut short by twenty minutes, or perhaps half an hour, saddened me; I had hoped we should be so happy together to-day. Suddenly, moved by I know not what impulse, I turned abruptly round, and how can I describe to you my astonishment when I saw my brother advancing slowly towards me from the southern side of the square, accompanied by another person. My first thought, I remember, had in it something of resentment that this man, whoever he was, should intrude himself into our meeting;

1 A district of southwest London.

I wondered who it could possibly be, for my brother had, I may say, no intimate friends. Then as I looked still at the advancing figures, another feeling took possession of me; it was a sensation of bristling fear, the fear of the child in the dark, unreasonable and unreasoning, but terrible, clutching at my heart as with the cold grip of a dead man's hands. Yet I overcame the feeling, and looked steadily at my brother, waiting for him to speak, and more closely at his companion. Then I noticed that this man was leading my brother rather than walking arm in arm with him; he was a tall man, dressed in quite ordinary fashion. He wore a high bowler hat, and, in spite of the warmth of the day, a plain black overcoat, tightly buttoned, and I noticed his trousers, of a quiet black and grey stripe. The face was commonplace too, and indeed I cannot recall any special features, or any trick of expression; for though I looked at him as he came near, curiously enough his face made no impression on me—it was as though I had seen a well-made mask. They passed in front of me, and to my unutterable astonishment I heard my brother's voice speaking to me, though his lips did not move, nor his eyes look into mine. It was a voice I cannot describe, though I knew it, but the words came to my ears as if mingled with plashing water and the sound of a shallow brook flowing amidst stones. I heard, then, the words, 'I cannot stay,' and for a moment the heavens and the earth seemed to rush together with the sound of thunder, and I was thrust forth from the world into a black void without beginning and without end. For, as my brother passed me, I saw the hand that held him by the arm, and seemed to guide him, and in one moment of horror I realised that it was as a formless thing that has mouldered for many years in the grave. The flesh was peeled in strips from the bones, and hung apart dry and granulated, and the fingers that encircled my brother's arm were all unshapen, claw-like things, and one was but a stump from which the end had rotted off. When I recovered my senses I saw the two passing out by that gate. I paused for a moment, and then with a rush as of fire to my heart I knew that no horror could stay me, but that I must follow my brother and save him, even though all hell rose up against me. I ran out, and looked up the pavement, and saw the two figures walking amidst the crowd. I ran across the road, and saw them turn up that side street, and I reached the corner a moment later. In vain I looked to right and left, for neither my brother nor his strange guardian was in sight; two elderly men were coming down arm-in-arm, and a telegraph boy was walking lustily along whistling.

I remained there a moment horror-struck, and then I bowed my head and returned to this seat, where you found me. Now, sir, do you wonder at my grief? Oh, tell me what has happened to my brother, or I feel I shall go mad!"

Mr. Phillipps, who had listened with exemplary patience to this tale, hesitated a moment before he spoke.

"My dear madam," he said at length, "you have known how to engage me in your service, not only as a man, but as a student of science. As a fellow-creature I pity you most profoundly; you must have suffered extremely from what you saw, or rather from what you fancied you saw. For, as a scientific observer, it is my duty to tell you the plain truth, which, indeed, besides being true, must also console you. Allow me to ask you then to describe your brother."

"Certainly," said the lady eagerly; "I can describe him accurately. My brother is a somewhat young-looking man; he is pale, has small black whiskers, and wears spectacles. He has rather a timid, almost a frightened expression, and looks about him nervously from side to side. Think, think! Surely you must have seen him. Perhaps you are an *habitué*[1] of this engaging quarter; you may have met him on some previous Saturday. I may have been mistaken in supposing that he turned up that side street; he may have gone on, and you may have passed each other. Oh, tell me, sir, whether you have not seen him!"

"I am afraid I do not keep a very sharp look-out when I am walking," said Phillipps, who would have passed his mother unnoticed; "but I am sure your description is admirable. And now will you describe the person, who, you say, held your brother by the arm?"

"I cannot do so. I told you, his face seemed devoid of expression or salient feature. It was like a mask."

"Exactly; you cannot describe what you have never seen. I need hardly point out to you the conclusion to be drawn; you have been the victim of an hallucination. You expected to see your brother, you were alarmed because you did not see him, and unconsciously, no doubt, your brain went to work, and finally you saw a mere projection of your own morbid thoughts—a vision of your absent brother, and a mere confusion of terrors incorporated in a figure which you can't describe. Of course your brother has been in some way prevented from coming to meet you as usual. I expect you will hear from him in a day or two."

1 An habitual visitor.

The lady looked seriously at Mr. Phillipps, and then for a second there seemed almost a twinkling as of mirth about her eyes, but her face clouded sadly at the dogmatic conclusions to which the scientist was led so irresistibly.

"Ah!" she said, "you do not know. I cannot doubt the evidence of my waking senses. Besides, perhaps I have had experiences even more terrible. I acknowledge the force of your arguments, but a woman has intuitions which never deceive her. Believe me, I am not hysterical; feel my pulse, it is quite regular."

She stretched out her hand with a dainty gesture, and a glance that enraptured Phillipps in spite of himself. The hand held out to him was soft and white and warm, and as, in some confusion, he placed his fingers on the purple vein, he felt profoundly touched by the spectacle of love and grief before him.

"No," he said, as he released her wrist, "as you say, you are evidently quite yourself. Still, you must be aware that living men do not possess dead hands. That sort of thing doesn't happen. It is, of course, barely possible that you did see your brother with another gentleman, and that important business prevented him from stopping. As for the wonderful hand, there may have been some deformity, a finger shot off by accident, or something of that sort."

The lady shook her head mournfully.

"I see you are a determined rationalist," she said. "Did you not hear me say that I have had experiences even more terrible? I too was once a sceptic, but after what I have known I can no longer affect to doubt."

"Madam," replied Mr. Phillipps, "no one shall make me deny my faith. I will never believe, nor will I pretend to believe, that two and two make five, nor will I on any pretences admit the existence of two-sided triangles."

"You are a little hasty," rejoined the lady. "But may I ask you if you ever heard the name of Professor Gregg, the authority on ethnology and kindred subjects?"

"I have done much more than merely hear of Professor Gregg," said Phillipps. "I always regarded him as one of our most acute and clear-headed observers; and his last publication, the *Textbook of Ethnology*, struck me as being quite admirable in its kind. Indeed, the book had but come into my hands when I heard of the terrible accident which cut short Gregg's career. He had, I think, taken a country house in the West of England for the summer, and is supposed to have fallen into a river. So far as I remember, his body was never recovered."

"Sir, I am sure that you are discreet. Your conversation seems to declare as much, and the very title of that little work of yours which you mentioned assures me that you are no empty trifler. In a word, I feel that I may depend on you. You appear to be under the impression that Professor Gregg is dead; I have no reason to believe that that is the case."

"What?" cried Phillipps, astonished and perturbed. "You do not hint that there was anything disgraceful? I cannot believe it. Gregg was a man of clearest character; his private life was one of great benevolence; and though I myself am free from delusions, I believe him to have been a sincere and devout Christian. Surely you cannot mean to insinuate that some disreputable history forced him to flee the country?"

"Again you are in a hurry," replied the lady. "I said nothing of all this. Briefly, then, I must tell you that Professor Gregg left his house one morning in full health both of mind and body. He never returned, but his watch and chain, a purse containing three sovereigns in gold, and some loose silver, with a ring that he wore habitually, were found three days later on a wild and savage hillside, many miles from the river. These articles were placed beside a limestone rock of fantastic form; they had been wrapped into a parcel with a kind of rough parchment which was secured with gut. The parcel was opened, and the inner side of the parchment bore an inscription done with some red substance; the characters were undecipherable, but seemed to be a corrupt cuneiform."[1]

"You interest me intensely," said Phillipps. "Would you mind continuing your story? The circumstance you have mentioned seems to me of the most inexplicable character, and I thirst for an elucidation."

The young lady seemed to meditate for a moment, and she then proceeded to relate the

NOVEL OF THE BLACK SEAL.

I must now give you some fuller particulars of my history. I am the daughter of a civil engineer, Steven Lally by name, who was so unfortunate as to die suddenly at the outset of his career, and before he had accumulated sufficient means to support his wife

---

1 Refers to "the characters of the ancient inscriptions of Persia, Assyria, etc., composed of wedge-shaped or arrow-headed elements; and hence to the inscriptions or records themselves" (*OED*). The fact that the cuneiform is corrupt would suggest that the people who produced it were primitive or degenerate.

and her two children. My mother contrived to keep the small household going on resources which must have been incredibly small; we lived in a remote country village, because most of the necessaries of life were cheaper than in a town, but even so we were brought up with the severest economy. My father was a clever and well-read man, and left behind him a small but select collection of books, containing the best Greek, Latin, and English classics, and these books were the only amusement we possessed. My brother, I remember, learnt Latin out of Descartes' *Meditationes*,[1] and I, in place of the little tales which children are usually told to read, had nothing more charming than a translation of the *Gesta Romanorum*.[2] We grew up thus, quiet and studious children, and in course of time my brother provided for himself in the manner I have mentioned. I continued to live at home; my poor mother had become an invalid, and demanded my continual care, and about two years ago she died after many months of painful illness. My situation was a terrible one; the shabby furniture barely sufficed to pay the debts I had been forced to contract, and the books I despatched to my brother, knowing how he would value them. I was absolutely alone; I was aware how poorly my brother was paid; and though I came up to London in the hope of finding employment, with the understanding that he would defray my expenses, I swore it should only be for a month, and that if I could not in that time find some work, I would starve rather than deprive him of the few miserable pounds he had laid by for his day of trouble. I took a little room in a distant suburb, the cheapest that I could find; I lived on bread and tea, and I spent my time in vain answering of advertisements, and vainer walks to addresses I had noted. Day followed on day, and week on week, and still I was unsuccessful, till at last the term I had appointed drew to a close, and I saw before me the grim prospect of slowly dying of starvation. My landlady was good-natured in her way; she knew the slenderness of my means, and I am sure that she would not have turned me out of doors; it remained for me then to go away, and to try and die in some quiet place. It was winter then, and a thick white fog gathered in the early part of the afternoon, becoming

---

1 *Meditations on First Philosophy* (published in Latin in 1641) by René Descartes (1596–1650).

2 *Gesta Romanorum* (*Deeds of the Romans*) is a collection of anecdotes and tales likely compiled in England in the fourteenth century. It was highly popular and influenced numerous writers including Geoffrey Chaucer (c. 1340–1400) and William Shakespeare (1564–1616).

more dense as the day wore on; it was a Sunday, I remember, and the people of the house were at chapel. At about three o'clock I crept out and walked away as quickly as I could, for I was weak from abstinence. The white mist wrapped all the streets in silence, and a hard frost had gathered thick upon the bare branches of the trees, and frost crystals glittered on the wooden fences, and on the cold, cruel ground beneath my feet. I walked on, turning to right and left in utter haphazard, without caring to look up at the names of the streets, and all that I remember of my walk on that Sunday afternoon seems but the broken fragments of an evil dream. In a confused vision I stumbled on, through roads half-town and half-country; grey fields melting into the cloudy world of mist on one side of me, and on the other comfortable villas with a glow of firelight flickering on the walls, but all unreal; red brick walls and lighted windows, vague trees, and glimmering country, gas-lamps beginning to star the white shadows, the vanishing perspectives of the railway line beneath high embankments, the green and red of the signal lamps,—all these were but momentary pictures flashed on my tired brain and senses numbed by hunger. Now and then I would hear a quick step ringing on the iron road, and men would pass me well wrapped up, walking fast for the sake of warmth, and no doubt eagerly foretasting the pleasures of a glowing hearth, with curtains tightly drawn about the frosted panes, and the welcomes of their friends; but as the early evening darkened and night approached, foot-passengers got fewer and fewer, and I passed through street after street alone. In the white silence I stumbled on, as desolate as if I trod the streets of a buried city; and as I grew more weak and exhausted, something of the horror of death was folding thickly round my heart. Suddenly, as I turned a corner, some one accosted me courteously beneath the lamp-post, and I heard a voice asking if I could kindly point the way to Avon Road. At the sudden shock of human accents I was prostrated, and my strength gave way; and I fell all huddled on the sidewalk, and wept and sobbed and laughed in violent hysteria. I had gone out prepared to die, and as I stepped across the threshold that had sheltered me, I consciously bade adieu to all hopes and all remembrances; the door clanged behind me with the noise of thunder, and I felt that an iron curtain had fallen on the brief passages of my life, that henceforth I was to walk a little way in a world of gloom and shadow; I entered on the stage of the first act of death. Then came my wandering in the mist, the whiteness wrapping all things, the void streets, and muffled silence, till when that voice spoke to me it was as if I had died and life returned to me. In a few minutes I was able to compose my feelings, and as I rose I saw that I was confronted by a middle-aged gentleman of specious appearance, neatly and correctly dressed. He looked at me with an expression of great pity, but before I could stammer out my ignorance of the neighbourhood, for indeed I had not the slightest notion of where I had wandered, he spoke.

"My dear madam," he said, "you seem in some terrible distress. You cannot think how you alarmed me. But may I inquire the nature of your trouble? I assure you that you can safely confide in me."

"You are very kind," I replied, "but I fear there is nothing to be done. My condition seems a hopeless one."

"Oh, nonsense, nonsense! You are too young to talk like that. Come, let us walk down here, and you must tell me your difficulty. Perhaps I may be able to help you."

There was something very soothing and persuasive in his manner, and as we walked together I gave him an outline of my story, and told of the despair that had oppressed me almost to death.

"You were wrong to give in so completely," he said, when I was silent. "A month is too short a time in which to feel one's way in London. London, let me tell you, Miss Lally, does not lie open and undefended; it is a fortified place, fossed and double-moated with curious intricacies. As must always happen in large towns, the conditions of life have become hugely artificial; no mere simple palisade is run up to oppose the man or woman who would take the place by storm, but serried lines of subtle contrivances, mines, and pitfalls which it needs a strange skill to overcome. You, in your simplicity, fancied you had only to shout for these walls to sink into nothingness, but the time is gone for such startling victories as these. Take courage; you will learn the secret of success before very long."

"Alas! sir," I replied, "I have no doubt your conclusions are correct, but at the present moment I seem to be in a fair way to die of starvation. You spoke of a secret; for heaven's sake tell it me, if you have any pity for my distress."

He laughed genially. "There lies the strangeness of it all. Those who know the secret cannot tell it if they would; it is positively as ineffable as the central doctrine of Freemasonry.[1] But I may say

---

1 One of the largest fraternal organizations in the world, whose origins likely date back to seventeenth- or eighteenth-century Britain but whose many legends claim its origins to be much older. Although

this, that you yourself have penetrated at least the outer husk of the mystery," and he laughed again.

"Pray do not jest with me," I said. "What have I done, *que sais-je?*[1] I am so far ignorant that I have not the slightest idea of how my next meal is to be provided."

"Excuse me. You ask what you have done? You have met me. Come, we will fence no longer. I see you have self-education, the only education which is not infinitely pernicious, and I am in want of a governess for my two children. I have been a widower for some years; my name is Gregg. I offer you the post I have named, and shall we say a salary of a hundred a year?"

I could only stutter out my thanks, and slipping a card with his address, and a bank-note by way of earnest into my hand, Mr. Gregg bade me good-bye, asking me to call in a day or two.

Such was my introduction to Professor Gregg, and can you wonder that the remembrance of despair and the cold blast that had blown from the gates of death upon me made me regard him as a second father? Before the close of the week I was installed in my new duties. The professor had leased an old brick manor-house in a western suburb of London, and here, surrounded by pleasant lawns and orchards, and soothed with the murmur of the ancient elms that rocked their boughs above the roof, the new chapter of my life began. Knowing as you do the nature of the professor's occupations, you will not be surprised to hear that the house teemed with books; and cabinets full of strange, and even hideous, objects filled every available nook in the vast low rooms. Gregg was a man whose one thought was for knowledge, and I too before long caught something of his enthusiasm, and strove to enter into his passion for research. In a few months I was perhaps more his secretary than the governess of the two children, and many a night I have sat at the desk in the glow of the shaded lamp while he, pacing up and down in the rich gloom of the firelight, dictated to me the substance of his *Textbook of Ethnology*. But amidst these more sober and accurate studies I always detected a something hidden, a longing and desire for some object to which he did not allude; and now and then he would break short in what he was saying and lapse into revery, intranced, as it seemed to me, by some distant prospect of adventurous discovery. The text-book was at last finished, and we began to receive proofs from the printers, which were intrusted to

---

Freemasonry is widely known, its inner workings have been, and remain, unknown to outsiders.

1 "What do I know?" (French).

me for a first reading, and then underwent the final revision of the professor. All the while his weariness of the actual business he was engaged on increased, and it was with the joyous laugh of a schoolboy when term is over that he one day handed me a copy of the book. "There," he said, "I have kept my word; I promised to write it, and it is done with. Now I shall be free to live for stranger things; I confess it, Miss Lally, I covet the renown of Columbus;[1] you will, I hope, see me play the part of an explorer."

"Surely," I said, "there is little left to explore. You have been born a few hundred years too late for that."

"I think you are wrong," he replied; "there are still, depend upon it, quaint, undiscovered countries and continents of strange extent. Ah, Miss Lally! believe me, we stand amidst sacraments and mysteries full of awe, and it doth not yet appear what we shall be. Life, believe me, is no simple thing, no mass of grey matter and congeries of veins and muscles to be laid naked by the surgeon's knife; man is the secret which I am about to explore, and before I can discover him I must cross over weltering seas indeed, and oceans and the mists of many thousand years. You know the myth of the lost Atlantis;[2] what if it be true, and I am destined to be called the discoverer of that wonderful land?"

I could see excitement boiling beneath his words, and in his face was the heat of the hunter; before me stood a man who believed himself summoned to tourney[3] with the unknown. A pang of joy possessed me when I reflected that I was to be in a way associated with him in the adventure, and I too burned with the lust of the chase, not pausing to consider that I knew not what we were to unshadow.

The next morning Professor Gregg took me into his inner study, where, ranged against the wall, stood a nest of pigeonholes, every drawer neatly labelled, and the results of years of toil classified in a few feet of space.

---

1 This reference to Italian explorer Christopher Columbus (1451–1506) suggests the alignment of Professor Gregg's project of (occult) knowledge with the imperial project of "discovering" "unknown" lands. See Introduction, p. 30, for more details.

2 A legendary place in the Atlantic Ocean (first mentioned by ancient Greek philosopher Plato); although assumed to be fictional, some believed it was real but that its ruins remained "lost" or hidden due to a possible historical cataclysm.

3 "To take part in a tourney; to contend or engage in a tournament" (*OED*).

"Here," he said, "is my life; here are all the facts which I have gathered together with so much pains, and yet it is all nothing. No, nothing to what I am about to attempt. Look at this"; and he took me to an old bureau, a piece fantastic and faded, which stood in a corner of the room. He unlocked the front and opened one of the drawers.

"A few scraps of paper," he went on, pointing to the drawer, "and a lump of black stone, rudely annotated with queer marks and scratches—that is all that drawer holds. Here you see is an old envelope with the dark red stamp of twenty years ago, but I have pencilled a few lines at the back; here is a sheet of manuscript, and here some cuttings from obscure local journals. And if you ask me the subject-matter of the collection, it will not seem extraordinary—a servant-girl at a farmhouse, who disappeared from her place and has never been heard of, a child supposed to have slipped down some old working[1] on the mountains, some queer scribbling on a limestone rock, a man murdered with a blow from a strange weapon; such is the scent I have to go upon. Yes, as you say, there is a ready explanation for all this; the girl may have run away to London, or Liverpool, or New York; the child may be at the bottom of the disused shaft; and the letters on the rock may be the idle whims of some vagrant. Yes, yes, I admit all that; but I know I hold the true key. Look!" and he held me out a slip of yellow paper.

Characters found inscribed on a limestone rock on the Grey Hills, I read, and then there was a word erased, presumably the name of a county, and a date some fifteen years back. Beneath was traced a number of uncouth characters, shaped somewhat like wedges or daggers, as strange and outlandish as the Hebrew alphabet.

"Now the seal," said Professor Gregg, and he handed me the black stone, a thing about two inches long, and something like an old-fashioned tobacco-stopper,[2] much enlarged.

I held it up to the light, and saw to my surprise the characters on the paper repeated on the seal.

"Yes," said the professor, "they are the same. And the marks on the limestone rock were made fifteen years ago, with some red substance. And the characters on the seal are four thousand years old at least. Perhaps much more."

"Is it a hoax?" I said.

---

1 An excavation where coal or some other mineral or metal was mined (*OED*).

2 "A contrivance for pressing down the tobacco in the bowl of a pipe while smoking" (*OED*).

"No, I anticipated that. I was not to be led to give my life to a practical joke. I have tested the matter very carefully. Only one person besides myself knows of the mere existence of that black seal. Besides, there are other reasons which I cannot enter into now."

"But what does it all mean?" I said. "I cannot understand to what conclusion all this leads."

"My dear Miss Lally, that is a question I would rather leave unanswered for some little time. Perhaps I shall never be able to say what secrets are held here in solution; a few vague hints, the outlines of village tragedies, a few marks done with red earth upon a rock, and an ancient seal. A queer set of data to go upon? Half a dozen pieces of evidence, and twenty years before even so much could be got together; and who knows what mirage or *terra incognita*[1] may be beyond all this? I look across deep waters, Miss Lally, and the land beyond may be but a haze after all. But still I believe it is not so, and a few months will show whether I am right or wrong."

He left me, and alone I endeavoured to fathom the mystery, wondering to what goal such eccentric odds and ends of evidence could lead. I myself am not wholly devoid of imagination, and I had reason to respect the professor's solidity of intellect; yet I saw in the contents of the drawer but the materials of fantasy, and vainly tried to conceive what theory could be founded on the fragments that had been placed before me. Indeed, I could discover in what I had heard and seen but the first chapter of an extravagant romance; and yet deep in my heart I burned with curiosity, and day after day I looked eagerly in Professor Gregg's face for some hint of what was to happen.

It was one evening after dinner that the word came.

"I hope you can make your preparations without much trouble," he said suddenly to me. "We shall be leaving here in a week's time."

"Really!" I said in astonishment. "Where are we going?"

"I have taken a country house in the west of England, not far from Caermaen,[2] a quiet little town, once a city, and the headquarters of a Roman legion. It is very dull there, but the country is pretty, and the air is wholesome."

I detected a glint in his eyes, and guessed that this sudden move had some relation to our conversation of a few days before.

---

1 "Unknown land" (Latin).

2 Likely fictional, but from its description it resembles Caerleon-on-Usk (and surrounding area), where Machen grew up and which he later described as a fairy land full of wonder that was the source of his writings. See Machen's *Far Off Things*.

"I shall just take a few books with me," said Professor Gregg, "that is all. Everything else will remain here for our return. I have got a holiday," he went on, smiling at me, "and I shan't be sorry to be quit for a time of my old bones and stones and rubbish. Do you know," he went on, "I have been grinding away at facts for thirty years; it is time for fancies."

The days passed quickly; I could see that the professor was all quivering with suppressed excitement, and I could scarce credit the eager appetence of his glance as we left the old manor house behind us and began our journey. We set out at midday, and it was in the dusk of the evening that we arrived at a little country station. I was tired and excited, and the drive through the lanes seems all a dream. First the deserted streets of a forgotten village, while I heard Professor Gregg's voice talking of the Augustan Legion[1] and the clash of arms, and all the tremendous pomp that followed the eagles;[2] then the broad river swimming to full tide with the last afterglow glimmering duskily in the yellow water, the wide meadows, and the cornfields whitening, and the deep lane winding on the slope between the hills and the water. At last we began to ascend, and the air grew rarer. I looked down and saw the pure white mist tracking the outline of the river like a shroud, and a vague and shadowy country; imaginations and fantasy of swelling hills and hanging woods, and half-shaped outlines of hills beyond, and in the distance the glare of the furnace fire on the mountain, growing by turns a pillar of shining flame and fading to a dull point of red. We were slowly mounting a carriage drive, and then there came to me the cool breath and the scent of the great wood that was above us; I seemed to wander in its deepest depths, and there was the sound of trickling water, the scent of the green leaves, and the breath of the summer night. The carriage stopped at last, and I could scarcely distinguish the form of the house as I waited a moment at the pillared porch. The rest of the evening seemed a dream of strange things bounded by the great silence of the wood and the valley and the river.

The next morning, when I awoke and looked out of the bow window of the big, old-fashioned bedroom, I saw under a grey sky a country that was still all mystery. The long, lovely valley, with the river winding in and out below, crossed in mid-vision by a mediæval bridge of vaulted and buttressed stone, the clear

---

1 Imperial army.

2 One of the "signa militaria" or military symbols or standards of the ancient Roman army (Yates 883).

presence of the rising ground beyond, and the woods that I had only seen in shadow the night before, seemed tinged with enchantment, and the soft breath of air that sighed in at the opened pane was like no other wind. I looked across the valley, and beyond, hill followed on hill as wave on wave, and here a faint blue pillar of smoke rose still in the morning air from the chimney of an ancient grey farmhouse, there was a rugged height crowned with dark firs, and in the distance I saw the white streak of a road that climbed and vanished into some unimagined country. But the boundary of all was a great wall of mountain, vast in the west, and ending like a fortress with a steep ascent and a domed tumulus clear against the sky.

I saw Professor Gregg walking up and down the terrace path below the windows, and it was evident that he was revelling in the sense of liberty, and the thought that he had for a while bidden good-bye to task-work. When I joined him there was exultation in his voice as he pointed out the sweep of valley and the river that wound beneath the lovely hills.

"Yes," he said, "it is a strangely beautiful country; and to me, at least, it seems full of mystery. You have not forgotten the drawer I showed you, Miss Lally? No; and you have guessed that I have come here not merely for the sake of the children and the fresh air?"

"I think I have guessed as much as that," I replied; "but you must remember I do not know the mere nature of your investigations; and as for the connection between the search and this wonderful valley, it is past my guessing."

He smiled queerly at me. "You must not think I am making a mystery for the sake of mystery," he said. "I do not speak out because, so far, there is nothing to be spoken, nothing definite, I mean, nothing that can be set down in hard black and white, as dull and sure and irreproachable as any blue-book.[1] And then I have another reason: Many years ago a chance paragraph in a newspaper caught my attention, and focussed in an instant the vagrant thoughts and half-formed fancies of many idle and speculative hours into a certain hypothesis. I saw at once that I was treading on a thin crust; my theory was wild and fantastic in the extreme, and I would not for any consideration have written a hint of it for publication. But I thought that in the company of scientific men like myself, men who knew the course of discovery, and were aware that the gas that blazes and flares in

---

1 Official British government reports, typically bound in blue.

the gin-palace[1] was once a wild hypothesis—I thought that with such men as these I might hazard my dream—let us say Atlantis, or the philosopher's stone,[2] or what you like—without danger of ridicule. I found I was grossly mistaken; my friends looked blankly at me and at one another, and I could see something of pity, and something also of insolent contempt, in the glances they exchanged. One of them called on me next day, and hinted that I must be suffering from overwork and brain exhaustion. 'In plain terms,' I said, 'you think I am going mad. I think not'; and I showed him out with some little appearance of heat. Since that day I vowed that I would never whisper the nature of my theory to any living soul; to no one but yourself have I ever shown the contents of that drawer. After all, I may be following a rainbow; I may have been misled by the play of coincidence; but as I stand here in this mystic hush and silence amidst the woods and wild hills, I am more than ever sure that I am hot on the scent. Come, it is time we went in."

To me in all this there was something both of wonder and excitement; I knew how in his ordinary work Professor Gregg moved step by step, testing every inch of the way, and never venturing on assertion without proof that was impregnable. Yet I divined more from his glance and the vehemence of his tone than from the spoken word, that he had in his every thought the vision of the almost incredible continually with him; and I, who was with some share of imagination no little of a sceptic, offended at a hint of the marvellous, could not help asking myself whether he was cherishing a monomania,[3] and barring out from this one subject all the scientific method of his other life.

Yet, with, this image of mystery haunting my thoughts, I surrendered wholly to the charm of the country. Above the faded house on the hillside began the great forest—a long, dark line seen from the opposing hills, stretching above the river for many a mile from north to south, and yielding in the north to even wilder country, barren and savage hills, and ragged

---

1 Refers to the history of the invention of gas lighting, which was once but a hard-to-believe hypothesis, though it would become part of everyday public places such as the "gin-palace" or public house.

2 From alchemy, a mythical substance believed to have the power to turn base metals into gold or silver and believed by some to also be capable of healing illnesses, providing eternal youth, and immortality (Bane).

3 An obsession.

common-land, a territory all strange and unvisited, and more unknown to Englishmen than the very heart of Africa. The space of a couple of steep fields alone separated the house from the wood, and the children were delighted to follow me up the long alleys of undergrowth, between smooth pleached walls of shining beech, to the highest point in the wood, whence one looked on one side across the river and the rise and fall of the country to the great western mountain wall, and on the other over the surge and dip of the myriad trees of the forest, over level meadows and the shining yellow sea to the faint coast beyond. I used to sit at this point on the warm sunlit turf which marked the track of the Roman Road, while the two children raced about hunting for the whinberries that grew here and there on the banks. Here beneath the deep blue sky and the great clouds rolling, like olden galleons with sails full-bellied, from the sea to the hills, as I listened to the whispered charm of the great and ancient wood, I lived solely for delight, and only remembered strange things when we would return to the house and find Professor Gregg either shut up in the little room he had made his study, or else pacing the terrace with the look, patient and enthusiastic, of the determined seeker.

One morning, some eight or nine days after our arrival, I looked out of my window and saw the whole landscape transmuted before me. The clouds had dipped low and hidden the mountain in the west; a southern wind was driving the rain in shifting pillars up the valley, and the little brooklet that burst the hill below the house now raged, a red torrent, down to the river. We were perforce obliged to keep snug within-doors; and when I had attended to my pupils, I sat down in the morning-room where the ruins of a library still encumbered an old-fashioned bookcase. I had inspected the shelves once or twice, but their contents had failed to attract me; volumes of eighteenth-century sermons, an old book on farriery,[1] a collection of *Poems* by 'persons of quality,' Prideaux's *Connection*, and an odd volume of Pope,[2] were the boundaries of the library, and there seemed little doubt that everything of interest or value had been

---

1 The practice of shoeing horses; early uses of the term also referred to more general veterinary care.

2 Humphrey Prideaux (1648–1724), author of *Old and New Testament Connected* (1716–18), a history of the Jews, still being reprinted in the mid-nineteenth century; Alexander Pope (1688–1744), English poet best known for his satirical poetry.

removed. Now, however, in desperation, I began to re-examine the musty sheepskin and calf bindings, and found, much to my delight, a fine old quarto printed by the Stephani, containing the three books of Pomponius Mela, *De Situ Orbis*, and other of the ancient geographers.[1] I knew enough of Latin to steer my way through an ordinary sentence, and I soon became absorbed in the odd mixture of fact and fancy—light shining on a little of the space of the world, and beyond, mist and shadow and awful forms. Glancing over the clear-printed pages, my attention was caught by the heading of a chapter in Solinus, and I read the words:—

"MIRA DE INTIMIS GENTIBUS LIBYAE, DE LAPIDE
HEXECONTALITHO,"

—"The wonders of the people that inhabit the inner parts of Libya, and of the stone called Sixtystone."

The odd title attracted me and I read on:—"Gens ista avia et secreta habitat, in montibus horrendis fœda mysteria celebrat. De hominibus nihil aliud illi præferunt quam figuram, ab humano ritu prorsus exulant, oderunt deum lucis. Stridunt potius quam loquuntur; vox absona nec sine horrore auditur. Lapide quodam gloriantur, quem Hexecontalithon vocant, dicunt enim hunc lapidem sexaginta notas ostendere. Cujus lapidis nomen secretum ineffabile colunt: quod Ixaxar."

"This folk," I translated to myself, "dwells in remote and secret places, and celebrates foul mysteries on savage hills. Nothing have they in common with men save the face, and the customs of humanity are wholly strange to them; and they hate the sun. They hiss rather than speak; their voices are harsh, and not to be heard without fear. They boast of a certain stone, which they call Sixtystone; for they say that it displays sixty characters. And this stone has a secret unspeakable name; which is Ixaxar."

---

1 Ancient Roman geographers Pomponius Mela (first century CE) and Gaius Julius Solinus (fourth century CE) wrote accounts of the world that included geographical, historical, and even mythological information. Mela's *De Situ Orbis* was first published in Latin in 1471 and translated into English in 1585. The passage Machen reproduces below from Solinus's *Collectanea rerum memorabilium* combines information from different paragraphs in the original text (see Josiffe for details), perhaps imitating his source text's "odd mixture of fact and fancy" noted by Miss Lally.

I laughed at the queer inconsequence of all this, and thought it fit for Sinbad the Sailor, or other of the supplementary Nights.[1] When I saw Professor Gregg in the course of the day, I told him of my find in the bookcase, and the fantastic rubbish I had been reading. To my surprise he looked up at me with an expression of great interest.

"That is really very curious," he said. "I have never thought it worth while to look into the old geographers, and I daresay I have missed a good deal. Ah, that is the passage, is it. It seems a shame to rob you of your entertainment, but I really think I must carry off the book."

The next day the professor called to me to come to the study. I found him sitting at a table in the full light of the window, scrutinising something very attentively with a magnifying-glass.

"Ah, Miss Lally," he began, "I want to use your eyes. This glass is pretty good, but not like my old one that I left in town. Would you mind examining the thing yourself, and telling me how many characters are cut on it?"

He handed me the object in his hand. I saw that it was the black seal he had shown me in London, and my heart began to beat with the thought that I was presently to know something. I took the seal, and, holding it up to the light, checked off the grotesque dagger-shaped characters one by one.

"I make sixty-two," I said at last.

"Sixty-two? Nonsense; it's impossible. Ah, I see what you have done, you have counted that and that," and he pointed to two marks which I had certainly taken as letters with the rest.

"Yes, yes," Professor Gregg went on, "but those are obvious

---

1 Sinbad or Sindbad the Sailor, a character who tells of his adventures; these tales were added to the *Arabian Nights* by translator and French Orientalist Antoine Galland (1646–1715), who is credited with introducing the tales into Europe with his early-eighteenth-century French translation of the *Arabian Nights*, but who is also known to have added to them stories not part of the fourteenth-century Syrian manuscript from which he worked. Of the numerous translations and adaptations of the tales available in English in the nineteenth century, one of the most well known was a translation by Sir Richard Francis Burton (1821–90), *The Book of a Thousand Nights and a Night* (1885), which was followed by *Supplemental Nights* (1886–88). For more on the complex history of the *Arabian Nights* tales and their relation to Machen's tales, see Introduction, pp. 37–40.

scratches, done accidentally; I saw that at once. Yes, then that's quite right. Thank you very much, Miss Lally."

I was going away, rather disappointed at my having been called in merely to count a number of marks on the black seal, when suddenly there flashed into my mind what I had read in the morning.

"But, Professor Gregg," I cried, breathless, "the seal, the seal. Why, it is the stone Hexecontalithos that Solinus writes of; it is Ixaxar."

"Yes," he said, "I suppose it is. Or it may be a mere coincidence. It never does to be too sure, you know, in these matters. Coincidence killed the professor."

I went away puzzled by what I had heard, and as much as ever at a loss to find the ruling clew in this maze of strange evidence. For three days the bad weather lasted, changing from driving rain to a dense mist, fine and dripping, and we seemed to be shut up in a white cloud that veiled all the world away from us. All the while Professor Gregg was darkling in his room, unwilling, it appeared, to dispense confidences or talk of any kind, and I heard him walking to and fro with a quick, impatient step, as if he were in some way wearied of inaction. The fourth morning was fine, and at breakfast the professor said briskly—

"We want some extra help about the house; a boy of fifteen or sixteen, you know. There are a lot of little odd jobs that take up the maids' time which a boy could do much better."

"The girls have not complained to me in any way," I replied. "Indeed, Anne said there was much less work than in London, owing to there being so little dust."

"Ah, yes, they are very good girls. But I think we shall do much better with a boy. In fact, that is what has been bothering me for the last two days."

"Bothering you?" I said in astonishment, for as a matter of fact the professor never took the slightest interest in the affairs of the house.

"Yes," he said, "the weather, you know. I really couldn't go out in that Scotch mist; I don't know the country very well, and I should have lost my way. But I am going to get the boy this morning."

"But how do you know there is such a boy as you want anywhere about?"

"Oh, I have no doubt as to that. I may have to walk a mile or two at the most, but I am sure to find just the boy I require."

I thought the professor was joking, but though his tone was airy enough there was something grim and set about his features that puzzled me. He got his stick, and stood at the door looking meditatively before him, and as I passed through the hall he called to me.

"By the way, Miss Lally, there was one thing I wanted to say to you. I daresay you may have heard that some of these country lads are not over bright; idiotic would be a harsh word to use, and they are usually called 'naturals,' or something of the kind. I hope you won't mind if the boy I am after should turn out not too keen-witted; he will be perfectly harmless, of course, and blacking boots doesn't need much mental effort."

With that he was gone, striding up the road that led to the wood, and I remained stupefied; and then for the first time my astonishment was mingled with a sudden note of terror, arising I knew not whence, and all unexplained even to myself, and yet I felt about my heart for an instant something of the chill of death, and that shapeless, formless dread of the unknown that is worse than death itself. I tried to find courage in the sweet air that blew up from the sea, and in the sunlight after rain, but the mystic woods seemed to darken around me; and the vision of the river coiling between the reeds, and the silver grey of the ancient bridge, fashioned in my mind symbols of vague dread, as the mind of a child fashions terror from things harmless and familiar.

Two hours later Professor Gregg returned. I met him as he came down the road, and asked quietly if he had been able to find a boy.

"Oh, yes," he answered; "I found one easily enough. His name is Jervase Cradock, and I expect he will make himself very useful. His father has been dead for many years, and the mother, whom I saw, seemed very glad at the prospect of a few shillings extra coming in on Saturday nights. As I expected, he is not too sharp, has fits at times, the mother said; but as he will not be trusted with the china, that doesn't much matter, does it? And he is not in any way dangerous, you know, merely a little weak."

"When is he coming?"

"To-morrow morning at eight o'clock. Anne will show him what he has to do, and how to do it. At first he will go home every night, but perhaps it may ultimately turn out more convenient for him to sleep here, and only go home for Sundays."

I found nothing to say to all this; Professor Gregg spoke in a quiet tone of matter-of-fact, as indeed was warranted by the circumstance; and yet I could not quell my sensation of astonishment at the whole affair. I knew that in reality no assistance was wanted in the housework, and the professor's prediction that the boy he was to engage might prove a little "simple," followed by so exact a fulfilment, struck me as bizarre in the extreme. The next morning I heard from the housemaid that the boy Cradock had come at eight, and that she had been trying to make him useful. "He doesn't seem quite all there, I don't think, miss," was her comment, and later in the day I saw him helping the old man who worked in the garden. He was a youth of about fourteen, with black hair and black eyes and an olive skin, and I saw at once from the curious vacancy of his expression that he was mentally weak. He touched his forehead awkwardly as I went by, and I heard him answering the gardener in a queer, harsh voice that caught my attention; it gave me the impression of some one speaking deep below under the earth, and there was a strange sibilance, like the hissing of the phonograph as the pointer travels over the cylinder. I heard that he seemed anxious to do what he could, and was quite docile and obedient, and Morgan the gardener, who knew his mother, assured me he was perfectly harmless. "He's always been a bit queer," he said, "and no wonder, after what his mother went through before he was born. I did know his father, Thomas Cradock, well, and a very fine workman he was too, indeed. He got something wrong with his lungs owing to working in the wet woods, and never got over it, and went off quite sudden like. And they do say as how Mrs. Cradock was quite off her head; anyhow, she was found by Mr. Hillyer, Ty Coch,[1] all crouched up on the Grey Hills, over there, crying and weeping like a lost soul. And Jervase, he was born about eight months afterwards, and as I was saying, he was a bit queer always; and they do say when he could scarcely walk he would frighten the other children into fits with the noises he would make."

A word in the story had stirred up some remembrance within me, and, vaguely curious, I asked the old man where the Grey Hills were.

"Up there," he said, with the same gesture he had used before; "you go past the Fox and Hounds, and through the forest, by the old ruins. It's a good five mile from here, and a strange sort of a place. The poorest soil between this and Monmouth, they do say, though it's good feed for sheep. Yes, it was a sad thing for poor Mrs. Cradock."

The old man turned to his work, and I strolled on down the

---

1 Place name, Welsh for "red house." Here and elsewhere, Machen suggests that Wales harbours ancient supernatural beings or "little people."

path between the espaliers, gnarled and gouty with age, thinking of the story I had heard, and groping for the point in it that had some key to my memory. In an instant it came before me; I had seen the phrase "Grey Hills" on the slip of yellowed paper that Professor Gregg had taken from the drawer in his cabinet. Again I was seized with pangs of mingled curiosity and fear; I remembered the strange characters copied from the limestone rock, and then again their identity with the inscription on the age-old seal, and the fantastic fables of the Latin geographer. I saw beyond doubt that, unless coincidence had set all the scene and disposed all these bizarre events with curious art, I was to be a spectator of things far removed from the usual and customary traffic and jostle of life. Professor Gregg I noted day by day; he was hot on his trail, growing lean with eagerness; and in the evenings, when the sun was swimming on the verge of the mountain, he would pace the terrace to and fro with his eyes on the ground, while the mist grew white in the valley, and the stillness of the evening brought far voices near, and the blue smoke rose a straight column from the diamond-shaped chimney of the grey farmhouse, just as I had seen it on the first morning. I have told you I was of sceptical habit; but though I understood little or nothing, I began to dread, vainly proposing to myself the iterated dogmas of science that all life is material, and that in the system of things there is no undiscovered land, even beyond the remotest stars, where the supernatural can find a footing. Yet there struck in on this the thought that matter is as really awful and unknown as spirit, that science itself but dallies on the threshold, scarcely gaining more than a glimpse of the wonders of the inner place.

There is one day that stands up from amidst the others as a grim red beacon, betokening evil to come. I was sitting on a bench in the garden, watching the boy Cradock weeding, when I was suddenly alarmed by a harsh and choking sound, like the cry of a wild beast in anguish, and I was unspeakably shocked to see the unfortunate lad standing in full view before me, his whole body quivering and shaking at short intervals as though shocks of electricity were passing through him, and his teeth grinding, and foam gathering on his lips, and his face all swollen and blackened to a hideous mask of humanity. I shrieked with terror, and Professor Gregg came running; and as I pointed to Cradock, the boy with one convulsive shudder fell face forward, and lay on the wet earth, his body writhing like a wounded blind-worm, and an inconceivable babble of sounds bursting and rattling and hissing from his lips. He seemed to pour forth an infamous jargon, with words, or what seemed words, that might have belonged to a tongue dead since untold ages, and buried deep beneath Nilotic mud, or in the inmost recesses of the Mexican forest. For a moment the thought passed through my mind, as my ears were still revolted with that infernal clamour, "Surely this is the very speech of hell,"[1] and then I cried out again and again, and ran away shuddering to my inmost soul. I had seen Professor Gregg's face as he stooped over the wretched boy and raised him, and I was appalled by the glow of exultation that shone on every lineament and feature. As I sat in my room with drawn blinds, and my eyes hidden in my hands, I heard heavy steps beneath, and I was told afterwards that Professor Gregg had carried Cradock to his study, and had locked the door. I heard voices murmur indistinctly, and I trembled to think of what might be passing within a few feet of where I sat; I longed to escape to the woods and sunshine, and yet I dreaded the sights that might confront me on the way; and at last, as I held the handle of the door nervously, I heard Professor Gregg's voice calling to me with a cheerful ring. "It's all right now, Miss Lally," he said. "The poor fellow has got over it, and I have been arranging for him to sleep here after to-morrow. Perhaps I may be able to do something for him."

"Yes," he said later, "it was a very painful sight, and I don't wonder you were alarmed. We may hope that good food will build him up a little, but I am afraid he will never be really cured," and he affected the dismal and conventional air with which one speaks of hopeless illness; and yet beneath it I detected the delight that leapt up rampant within him, and fought and struggled to find utterance. It was as if one glanced down on the even surface of the sea, clear and immobile, and saw beneath raging depths, and a storm of contending billows. It was indeed to me a torturing and offensive problem that this man, who had so bounteously rescued me from the sharpness of death, and showed himself in all the relations of life full of benevolence, and pity, and kindly forethought, should so manifestly be for once on the side of the demons, and take a ghastly pleasure in the torments of an afflicted fellow-creature. Apart, I struggled with the horned difficulty, and strove to find the solution; but without the hint of a clue, beset by mystery and contradiction, I saw nothing that might help me, and

---

1 Here again a corrupted language (much like the corrupted cuneiform found on the seal) suggests a possible connection between demons, "little people," and ancient races or "survivals." For more on the "little people," see Introduction, pp. 21 and 42.

began to wonder whether, after all, I had not escaped from the white mist of the suburb at too dear a rate. I hinted something of my thought to the professor; I said enough to let him know that I was in the most acute perplexity, but the moment after regretted what I had done, when I saw his face contort with a spasm of pain.

"My dear Miss Lally," he said, "you surely do not wish to leave us? No, no, you would not do it. You do not know how I rely on you; how confidently I go forward, assured that you are here to watch over my children. You, Miss Lally, are my rear-guard; for let me tell you that the business in which I am engaged is not wholly devoid of peril. You have not forgotten what I said the first morning here; my lips are shut by an old and firm resolve till they can open to utter no ingenious hypothesis or vague surmise but irrefragable fact, as certain as a demonstration in mathematics. Think over it, Miss Lally: not for a moment would I endeavor to keep you here against your own instincts, and yet I tell you frankly that I am persuaded that it is here, here amidst the woods, that your duty lies."

I was touched by the eloquence of his tone, and by the remembrance that the man, after all, had been my salvation, and I gave him my hand on a promise to serve him loyally and without question. A few days later the rector of our church—a little church, grey and severe and quaint, that hovered on the very banks of the river and watched the tides swim and return—came to see us, and Professor Gregg easily persuaded him to stay and share our dinner. Mr. Meyrick was a member of an antique family of squires, whose old manor-house stood amongst the hills some seven miles away, and thus rooted in the soil, the rector was a living store of all the old, fading customs and lore of the country. His manner, genial, with a deal of retired oddity, won on Professor Gregg; and towards the cheese, when a curious Burgundy had begun its incantations, the two men glowed like the wine, and talked of philology with the enthusiasm of a burgess over the peerage. The parson was expounding the pronunciation of the Welsh *ll*, and producing sounds like the gurgle of his native brooks, when Professor Gregg struck in.

"By the way," he said, "that was a very odd word I met with the other day; you know my boy, poor Jervase Cradock. Well, he has got the bad habit of talking to himself, and the day before yesterday I was walking in the garden here and heard him; he was evidently quite unconscious of my presence. A lot of what he said I couldn't make out, but one word struck me distinctly. It was such an odd sound, half-sibilant, half-guttural, and as quaint as those double *l*'s you have been demonstrating. I do not know whether I can give you an idea of the sound; 'Ishakshar' is perhaps as near as I can get; but the *k* ought to be a Greek *chi* or a Spanish *j*. Now what does it mean in Welsh?"

"In Welsh?" said the parson. "There is no such word in Welsh, nor any word remotely resembling it. I know the book-Welsh, as they call it, and the colloquial dialects as well as any man, but there's no word like that from Anglesea to Usk.[1] Besides, none of the Cradocks speak a word of Welsh; it's dying out about here."

"Really. You interest me extremely, Mr. Meyrick. I confess the word didn't strike me as having the Welsh ring. But I thought it might be some local corruption."

"No, I never heard such a word, or anything like it. Indeed," he added, smiling whimsically, "if it belongs to any language, I should say it must be that of the fairies—the Tylwydd Têg,[2] as we call them."

The talk went on to the discovery of a Roman villa in the neighbourhood; and soon after I left the room, and sat down apart to wonder at the drawing together of such strange clues of evidence. As the professor had spoken of the curious word, I had caught the glint of his eye upon me; and though the pronunciation he gave was grotesque in the extreme, I recognised the name of the stone of sixty characters mentioned by Solinus, the black seal shut up in some secret drawer of the study, stamped forever by a vanished race[3] with signs that no man could read, signs that might, for all

---

1 Anglesey, an island of North Wales, "which in the 1st century AD was a centre of Druid power and resistance to Roman invasion" (Knowles); place on the River Usk, Celtic river name. As noted in the Introduction, Machen was born in Caerleon-on-Usk (Gwent).

2 Fairies of Welsh folklore. In an article on "The Little People" (1923), Machen draws parallels among the Asiki (a group of African dwarfs), the Sidhe of Ireland, and the Tylweth Teg of Wales, claiming that these different beings nonetheless occupied a similar peculiar "borderland" between the natural and supernatural and that they share a common "substratum": in each case, they are "an aboriginal people of small stature overcome and sent into the dark by invaders" (46). In this and other of Machen's tales, these ancient aboriginal people continue as "survivals," not merely in fairy lore as some maintained but also in reality.

3 Although the race has vanished, it was believed either to be extinct or to have retreated (as with the little people) under the hills, emerging only to procreate.

I knew, be the veils of awful things done long ago, and forgotten before the hills were moulded into form.

When the next morning I came down, I found Professor Gregg pacing the terrace in his eternal walk.

"Look at that bridge," he said when he saw me; "observe the quaint and Gothic[1] design, the angles between the arches, and the silvery grey of the stone in the awe of the morning light. I confess it seems to me symbolic; it should illustrate a mystical allegory of the passage from one world to another."

"Professor Gregg," I said quietly, "it is time that I knew something of what has happened, and of what is to happen."

For the moment he put me off, but I returned again with the same question in the evening, and then Professor Gregg flamed with excitement. "Don't you understand yet?" he cried. "But I have told you a good deal; yes, and shown you a good deal; you have heard pretty nearly all that I have heard, and seen what I have seen; or at least," and his voice chilled as he spoke, "enough to make a good deal clear as noonday. The servants told you, I have no doubt, that the wretched boy Cradock had another seizure the night before last; he awoke me with cries in that voice you heard in the garden, and I went to him, and God forbid you should see what I saw that night. But all this is useless; my time here is drawing to a close; I must be back in town in three weeks, as I have a course of lectures to prepare, and need all my books about me. In a very few days it will be all over, and I shall no longer hint, and no longer be liable to ridicule as a madman and a quack. No, I shall speak plainly, and I shall be heard with such emotions as perhaps no other man has ever drawn from the breasts of his fellows."

He paused, and seemed to grow radiant with the joy of great and wonderful discovery.

"But all that is for the future, the near future certainly, but still the future," he went on at length. "There is something to be done yet; you will remember my telling you that my researches were not altogether devoid of peril? Yes, there is a certain amount of danger to be faced; I did not know how much when I spoke on the subject before, and to a certain extent I am still in the dark. But it will be a strange adventure, the last of all, the last demonstration in the chain."

He was walking up and down the room as he spoke, and

---

1 Gothic here refers to an architectural style associated with the medieval period.

I could hear in his voice the contending tones of exultation and despondence, or perhaps I should say awe, the awe of a man who goes forth on unknown waters, and I thought of his allusion to Columbus on the night he had laid his book before me. The evening was a little chilly, and a fire of logs had been lighted in the study where we were; the remittent flame and the glow on the walls reminded me of the old days. I was sitting silent in an arm-chair by the fire, wondering over all I had heard, and still vainly speculating as to the secret springs concealed from me under all the phantasmagoria I had witnessed, when I became suddenly aware of a sensation that change of some sort had been at work in the room, and that there was something unfamiliar in its aspect. For some time I looked about me, trying in vain to localise the alteration that I knew had been made; the table by the window, the chairs, the faded settee were all as I had known them. Suddenly, as a sought-for recollection flashes into the mind, I knew what was amiss. I was facing the professor's desk, which stood on the other side of the fire, and above the desk was a grimy looking bust of Pitt,[1] that I had never seen there before. And then I remembered the true position of this work of art; in the furthest corner by the door was an old cupboard, projecting into the room, and on the top of the cupboard, fifteen feet from the floor, the bust had been, and there, no doubt, it had delayed, accumulating dirt since the early years of the century.

I was utterly amazed, and sat silent still, in a confusion of thought. There was, so far as I knew, no such thing as a step-ladder in the house, for I had asked for one to make some alterations in the curtains of my room, and a tall man standing on a chair would have found it impossible to take down the bust. It had been placed not on the edge of the cupboard, but far back against the wall; and Professor Gregg was, if anything, under the average height.

"How on earth did you manage to get down Pitt?" I said at last.

The professor looked curiously at me, and seemed to hesitate a little.

"They must have found you a step-ladder, or perhaps the gardener brought in a short ladder from outside?"

"No, I have had no ladder of any kind. Now, Miss Lally," he went on with an awkward simulation of jest, "there is a little puzzle for you; a problem in the manner of the inimitable Holmes;[2]

---

1   English politician William Pitt, the elder (1708–78), or his son, also a politician (1759–1806).

2   Arthur Conan Doyle's famous detective character Sherlock Holmes had made his first appearance in *The Strand Magazine* in 1891.

there are the facts, plain and patent; summon your acuteness to the solution of the puzzle. For Heaven's sake," he cried with a breaking voice, "say no more about it! I tell you, I never touched the thing," and he went out of the room with horror manifest on his face, and his hand shook and jarred the door behind him.

I looked round the room in vague surprise, not at all realising what had happened, making vain and idle surmises by way of explanation, and wondering at the stirring of black waters by an idle word and the trivial change of an ornament. "This is some petty business, some whim on which I have jarred," I reflected; "the professor is perhaps scrupulous and superstitious over trifles, and my question may have outraged unacknowledged fears, as though one killed a spider or spilled the salt before the very eyes of a practical Scotchwoman."[1] I was immersed in these fond suspicions, and began to plume myself a little on my immunity from such empty fears, when the truth fell heavily as lead upon my heart, and I recognised with cold terror that some awful influence had been at work. The bust was simply inaccessible; without a ladder no one could have touched it.

I went out to the kitchen and spoke as quietly as I could to the housemaid.

"Who moved that bust from the top of the cupboard, Anne?" I said to her. "Professor Gregg says he has not touched it. Did you find an old step-ladder in one of the outhouses?"

The girl looked at me blankly.

"I never touched it," she said. "I found it where it is now the other morning when I dusted the room. I remember now, it was Wednesday morning, because it was the morning after Cradock was taken bad in the night. My room is next to his, you know, miss," the girl went on piteously, "and it was awful to hear how

---

1   Miss Lally speaks of these "unacknowledged fears" and their attendant superstitions (about killing spiders or spilling salt) as likely "survivals," or something inherited from earlier cultures—that is, as "processes, customs, opinions, and so forth, which have been carried on by force of habit into a new state of society different from that in which they had their original home, and they thus remain as proofs and examples of an older condition of culture out of which a newer has been evolved" (Tylor, *Primitive* 16). The implication is that Professor Gregg's obsession with the little people is based on his unacknowledged irrational fears that, as a modern man of science, he should have superseded. See p. 10, note 1, above and Appendix D1 for more on "survivals."

he cried and called out names that I couldn't understand. It made me feel all afraid; and then master came, and I heard him speak, and he took down Cradock to the study and gave him something."

"And you found that bust moved the next morning?"

"Yes, miss. There was a queer sort of a smell in the study when I came down and opened the windows; a bad smell it was, and I wondered what it could be. Do you know, miss, I went a long time ago to the Zoo in London with my cousin Thomas Barker, one afternoon that I had off, when I was at Mrs. Prince's in Stanhope Gate, and we went into the snake-house to see the snakes, and it was just the same sort of a smell; very sick it made me feel, I remember, and I got Barker to take me out. And it was just the same kind of a smell in the study, as I was saying, and I was wondering what it could be from, when I see that bust with Pitt cut in it, standing on the master's desk, and I thought to myself, Now who has done that, and how have they done it? And when I came to dust the things, I looked at the bust, and I saw a great mark on it where the dust was gone, for I don't think it can have been touched with a duster for years and years, and it wasn't like finger-marks, but a large patch like, broad and spread out. So I passed my hand over it, without thinking what I was doing, and where that patch was it was all sticky and slimy, as if a snail had crawled over it. Very strange, isn't it, miss? and I wonder who can have done it, and how that mess was made."

The well-meant gabble of the servant touched me to the quick; I lay down upon my bed, and bit my lip that I should not cry out loud in the sharp anguish of my terror and bewilderment. Indeed, I was almost mad with dread; I believe that if it had been daylight I should have fled hot foot, forgetting all courage and all the debt of gratitude that was due to Professor Gregg, not caring whether my fate were that I must starve slowly, so long as I might escape from the net of blind and panic fear that every day seemed to draw a little closer round me. If I knew, I thought, if I knew what there were to dread, I could guard against it; but here, in this lonely house, shut in on all sides by the olden woods and the vaulted hills, terror seems to spring inconsequent from every covert, and the flesh is aghast at the half-heard murmurs of horrible things. All in vain I strove to summon scepticism to my aid, and endeavoured by cool common-sense to buttress my belief in a world of natural order, for the air that blew in at the open window was a mystic breath, and in the darkness I felt the silence go heavy and sorrowful as a mass of requiem, and

I conjured images of strange shapes gathering fast amidst the reeds, beside the wash of the river.

In the morning, from the moment that I set foot in the break-fast-room, I felt that the unknown plot was drawing to a crisis; the professor's face was firm and set, and he seemed hardly to hear our voices when we spoke.

"I am going out for rather a long walk," he said when the meal was over. "You mustn't be expecting me, now, or thinking any-thing has happened if I don't turn up to dinner. I have been get-ting stupid lately, and I dare say a miniature walking tour will do me good. Perhaps I may even spend the night in some little inn, if I find any place that looks clean and comfortable."

I heard this, and knew by my experience of Professor Gregg's manner that it was no ordinary business or pleasure that impelled him. I knew not, nor even remotely guessed, where he was bound, nor had I the vaguest notion of his errand, but all the fear of the night before returned; and as he stood, smiling, on the terrace, ready to set out, I implored him to stay, and to forget all his dreams of the undiscovered continent.

"No, no, Miss Lally," he replied, still smiling, "it's too late now. *Vestigia nulla retrorsum*,[1] you know, is the device of all true explorers, though I hope it won't be literally true in my case. But, indeed, you are wrong to alarm yourself so; I look upon my little expedition as quite commonplace; no more exciting than a day with the geological hammers. There is a risk, of course, but so there is on the commonest excursion. I can afford to be jaunty; I am doing nothing so hazardous as 'Arry[2] does a hundred times over in the course of every Bank Holiday.[3] Well, then, you must look more cheerfully; and so good-bye till to-morrow at latest."

He walked briskly up the road, and I saw him open the gate that marks the entrance of the wood, and then he vanished in the gloom of the trees.

All the day passed heavily with a strange darkness in the air, and again I felt as if imprisoned amidst the ancient woods, shut in

---

1 Latin for "Never a step backward," an old heraldic motto indicating that Professor Gregg is compelled to move ahead with his explora-tions, though he hopes to be able to return. Here, as elsewhere, the project of knowledge is aligned with an imperial one. See Introduction, p. 30, for more details.

2 "(The type of) a boisterous or jovial young Cockney man" often used humorously or depreciatively (*OED*).

3 A weekday on which banks are closed, or a public holiday (*OED*).

an olden land of mystery and dread, and as if all was long ago and forgotten by the living outside. I hoped and dreaded; and when the dinner-hour came I waited, expecting to hear the professor's step in the hall, and his voice exulting at I knew not what triumph. I composed my face to welcome him gladly, but the night descended dark, and he did not come.

In the morning, when the maid knocked at my door, I called out to her, and asked if her master had returned; and when she replied that his bedroom stood open and empty, I felt the cold clasp of despair. Still, I fancied he might have discovered genial company, and would return for luncheon, or perhaps in the afternoon, and I took the children for a walk in the forest, and tried my best to play and laugh with them, and to shut out the thoughts of mystery and veiled terror. Hour after hour I waited, and my thoughts grew darker; again the night came and found me watching, and at last, as I was making much ado to finish my dinner, I heard steps outside and the sound of a man's voice.

The maid came in and looked oddly at me.

"Please, miss," she began, "Mr. Morgan the gardener wants to speak to you for a minute, if you didn't mind."

"Show him in, please," I answered, and I set my lips tight.

The old man came slowly into the room, and the servant shut the door behind him.

"Sit down, Mr. Morgan," I said; "what is it that you want to say to me?"

"Well, miss, Mr. Gregg he gave me something for you yesterday morning, just before he went off; and he told me particular not to hand it up before eight o'clock this evening exactly, if so be as he wasn't back again home before, and if he should come home before I was just to return it to him in his own hands. So, you see, as Mr. Gregg isn't here yet, I suppose I'd better give you the parcel directly."

He pulled out something from his pocket, and gave it to me, half rising. I took it silently, and seeing that Morgan seemed doubtful as to what he was to do next, I thanked him and bade him good-night, and he went out. I was left alone in the room with the parcel in my hand—a paper parcel neatly sealed and directed to me, with the instructions Morgan had quoted, all written in the professor's large loose hand. I broke the seals with a choking at my heart, and found an envelope inside, addressed also, but open, and I took the letter out.

"MY DEAR MISS LALLY," it began,—"To quote the old logic manual, the case of your reading this note is a case of my having made a blunder of some sort, and, I am afraid, a blunder that turns these lines into a farewell. It is practically certain that neither you nor anyone else will ever see me again. I have made my will with provision for this eventuality, and I hope you will consent to accept the small remembrance addressed to you, and my sincere thanks for the way in which you joined your fortunes to mine. The fate which has come upon me is desperate and terrible beyond the remotest dreams of man; but this fate you have a right to know—if you please. If you look in the left-hand drawer of my dressing-table, you will find the key of the escritoire,[1] properly labelled. In the well of the escritoire is a large envelope sealed and addressed to your name. I advise you to throw it forthwith into the fire; you will sleep better of nights if you do so. But if you must know the history of what has happened, it is all written down for you to read."

The signature was firmly written below, and again I turned the page and read out the words one by one, aghast and white to the lips, my hands cold as ice, and sickness choking me. The dead silence of the room, and the thought of the dark woods and hills closing me in on every side, oppressed me, helpless and without capacity, and not knowing where to turn for counsel. At last I resolved that though knowledge should haunt my whole life and all the days to come, I must know the meaning of the strange terrors that had so long tormented me, rising grey, dim, and awful, like the shadows in the wood at dusk. I carefully carried out Professor Gregg's directions, and not without reluctance broke the seal of the envelope, and spread out his manuscript before me. That manuscript I always carry with me, and I see that I cannot deny your unspoken request to read it. This, then, was what I read that night, sitting at the desk, with a shaded lamp beside me.

The young lady who called herself Miss Lally then proceeded to recite

The Statement of William Gregg, F.R.S.,[2] etc.

It is many years since the first glimmer of the theory which is now almost, if not quite, reduced to fact dawned first on my

---

1 French term referring to a writing desk.
2 Fellow of the Royal Society, a public institution founded in 1660 to promote scientific research and knowledge. In this case, FRS underlines Professor Gregg's authority as a scientific figure and is thus meant to lend credibility to his unbelievable account.

mind. A somewhat extensive course of miscellaneous and obsolete reading had done a good deal to prepare the way, and, later, when I became somewhat of a specialist, and immersed myself in the studies known as ethnological, I was now and then startled by facts that would not square with orthodox scientific opinion, and by discoveries that seemed to hint at something still hidden for all our research. More particularly I became convinced that much of the folk-lore of the world is but an exaggerated account of events that really happened, and I was especially drawn to consider the stories of the fairies, the good folk of the Celtic races. Here I thought I could detect the fringe of embroidery and exaggeration, the fantastic guise, the little people dressed in green and gold sporting in the flowers, and I thought I saw a distinct analogy between the name given to this race (supposed to be imaginary) and the description of their appearance and manners. Just as our remote ancestors called the dreaded beings "fair" and "good" precisely because they dreaded them, so they had dressed them up in charming forms, knowing the truth to be the very reverse. Literature, too, had gone early to work, and had lent a powerful hand in the transformation, so that the playful elves of Shakespeare are already far removed from the true original, and the real horror is disguised in a form of prankish mischief. But in the older tales, the stories that used to make men cross themselves as they sat round the burning logs, we tread a different stage; I saw a widely opposed spirit in certain histories of children and of men and women who vanished strangely from the earth. They would be seen by a peasant in the fields walking towards some green and rounded hillock, and seen no more on earth; and there are stories of mothers who have left a child quietly sleeping, with the cottage door rudely barred with a piece of wood, and have returned, not to find the plump and rosy little Saxon, but a thin and wizened creature, with sallow skin and black, piercing eyes, the child of another race. Then, again, there were myths darker still; the dread of witch and wizard, the lurid evil of the Sabbath, and the hint of demons who mingled with the daughters of men. And just as we have turned the terrible "fair folk" into a company of benignant, if freakish, elves, so we have hidden from us the black foulness of the witch and her companions under a popular *diablerie*[1] of old women and broomsticks and a comic cat with tail on end. So

---

1 Term of French origin meaning sorcery, witchcraft, or dealings with the devil (*OED*).

the Greeks called the hideous furies benevolent ladies, and thus the northern nations have followed their example. I pursued my investigations, stealing odd hours from other and more imperative labours, and I asked myself the question: Supposing these traditions to be true, who were the demons who are reported to have attended the Sabbaths? I need not say that I laid aside what I may call the supernatural hypothesis of the middle ages, and came to the conclusion that fairies and devils were of one and the same race and origin; invention, no doubt, and the Gothic fancy of old days, had done much in the way of exaggeration and distortion; yet I firmly believed that beneath all this imagery there was a black background of truth. As for some of the alleged wonders, I hesitated. While I should be very loth to receive any one specific instance of modern spiritualism as containing even a grain of the genuine, yet I was not wholly prepared to deny that human flesh may now and then, once perhaps in ten million cases, be the veil of powers which seem magical to us—powers which, so far from proceeding from the heights and leading men thither, are in reality survivals from the depths of being. The amœba and the snail have powers which we do not possess; and I thought it possible that the theory of reversion might explain many things which seem wholly inexplicable. Thus stood my position; I saw good reason to believe that much of the tradition, a vast deal of the earliest and uncorrupted tradition of the so-called fairies, represented solid fact, and I thought that the purely supernatural element in these traditions, was to be accounted for on the hypothesis that a race which had fallen out of the grand march of evolution might have retained, as a survival, certain powers which would be to us wholly miraculous. Such was my theory as it stood conceived in my mind; and working with this in view, I seemed to gather confirmation from every side, from the spoils of a tumulus or a barrow, from a local paper reporting an antiquarian meeting in the country, and from general literature of all kinds. Amongst other instances, I remember being struck by the phrase "articulate-speaking men" in Homer, as if the writer knew or had heard of men whose speech was so rude that it could hardly be termed articulate; and on my hypothesis of a race who had lagged far behind the rest, I could easily conceive that such a folk would speak a jargon but little removed from the inarticulate noises of brute beasts.

Thus I stood, satisfied that my conjecture was at all events not far removed from fact, when a chance paragraph in a small country print one day arrested my attention. It was a short account of what was to all appearance the usual sordid tragedy of the village—a young girl unaccountably missing, and evil rumour blatant and busy with her reputation. Yet I could read between the lines that all this scandal was purely hypothetical, and in all probability invented to account for what was in any other manner unaccountable. A flight to London or Liverpool, or an undiscovered body lying with a weight about its neck in the foul depths of a woodland pool, or perhaps murder—such were the theories of the wretched girl's neighbours. But as I idly scanned the paragraph, a flash of thought passed through me with the violence of an electric shock: what if the obscure and horrible race of the hills still survived, still remained haunting wild places and barren hills, and now and then repeating the evil of Gothic legend, unchanged and unchangeable as the Turanian Shelta, or the Basques of Spain.[1] I have said that the thought came with violence; and indeed I drew in my breath sharply, and clung with both hands to my elbow-chair, in a strange confusion of horror and elation. It was as if one of my *confrères*[2] of physical science, roaming in a quiet English wood, had been suddenly stricken aghast by the presence of the

---

1 Turanian Shelta appears to be an invention of Machen's. "Turanian" is a term applied to a group of languages of Asiatic origin and the peoples who speak them (*OED*). Notably, as Carole G. Silver explains, the term is also used by some nineteenth-century folkloric and anthropological euhemerist theories of the origins of the fairies. These theories posited that the fairies of folklore had actually existed and probably were members of a dark pygmy Turanian race with possibly Babylonian, Accadian, Iberian or other origins (47) and who were later displaced by the invading Celts. "Shelta" refers to a secret language spoken by Irish and Welsh tinkers and gypsies (Knowles). Machen, who was well aware of the euhemerist theories of the fairies and indeed plays on them in his stories featuring the "little people," appears to use the term "Turanian Shelta" to posit the existence of an enduring secret language spoken by small, dark aboriginal races and their descendants (what he refers to as the "little people"), the first people to inhabit Britain prior to the invasion of the Celts; in Machen's tales, these little people and their language persist into modernity. The "Basque of Spain" are an ethnic group living on both sides of the France-Spain border with a distinct language and culture that remained unchanged because of their relative isolation from their French and Spanish neighbours.

2 Colleagues or fellow professionals (French); in this case, fellow students or experts of physical science.

slimy and loathsome terror of the ichthyosaurus, the original of the stories of the awful worms killed by valorous knights, or had seen the sun darkened by the pterodactyl, the dragon of tradition. Yet as a resolute explorer of knowledge, the thought of such a discovery threw me into a passion of joy, and I cut out the slip from the paper and put it in a drawer in my old bureau, resolved that it should be but the first piece in a collection of the strangest significance. I sat long that evening dreaming of the conclusions I should establish, nor did cooler reflection at first dash my confidence. Yet as I began to put the case fairly, I saw that I might be building on an unstable foundation; the facts might possibly be in accordance with local opinion, and I regarded the affair with a mood of some reserve. Yet I resolved to remain perched on the look-out, and I hugged to myself the thought that I alone was watching and wakeful, while the great crowd of thinkers and searchers stood heedless and indifferent, perhaps letting the most prerogative facts pass by unnoticed.

Several years elapsed before I was enabled to add to the contents of the drawer; and the second find was in reality not a valuable one, for it was a mere repetition of the first, with only the variation of another and distant locality. Yet I gained something; for in the second case, as in the first, the tragedy took place in a desolate and lonely country, and so far my theory seemed justified. But the third piece was to me far more decisive. Again, amongst outland hills, far even from a main road of traffic, an old man was found done to death, and the instrument of execution was left beside him. Here, indeed, there was rumour and conjecture, for the deadly tool was a primitive stone axe, bound by gut to the wooden handle, and surmises the most extravagant and improbable were indulged in. Yet, as I thought with a kind of glee, the wildest conjectures went far astray; and I took the pains to enter into correspondence with the local doctor, who was called at the inquest. He, a man of some acuteness, was dumfounded. "It will not do to speak of these things in country places," he wrote to me; "but frankly, Professor Gregg, there is some hideous mystery here. I have obtained possession of the stone axe, and have been so curious as to test its powers. I took it into the back-garden of my house one Sunday afternoon when my family and the servants were all out, and there, sheltered by the poplar hedges, I made my experiments. I found the thing utterly unmanageable; whether there is some peculiar balance, some nice adjustment of weights, which require incessant practice, or whether an effectual blow can be struck only by a certain trick of the muscles, I do not know; but

I assure you that I went into the house with but a sorry opinion of my athletic capacities. It was like an inexperienced man trying 'putting the hammer';[1] the force exerted seemed to return on oneself, and I found myself hurled backwards with violence, while the axe fell harmless to the ground. On another occasion I tried the experiment with a clever woodman of the place; but this man, who had handled his axe for forty years, could do nothing with the stone implement, and missed every stroke most ludicrously. In short, if it were not so supremely absurd, I should say that for four thousand years no one on earth could have struck an effective blow with the tool that undoubtedly was used to murder the old man." This, as may be imagined, was to me rare news; and afterwards, when I heard the whole story, and learned that the unfortunate old man had babbled tales of what might be seen at night on a certain wild hillside, hinting at unheard-of wonders, and that he had been found cold one morning on the very hill in question, my exultation was extreme, for I felt I was leaving conjecture far behind me. But the next step was of still greater importance. I had possessed for many years an extraordinary stone seal—a piece of dull, black stone, two inches long from the handle to the stamp, and the stamping end a rough hexagon an inch and a quarter in diameter. Altogether, it presented the appearance of an enlarged tobacco-stopper[2] of an old-fashioned make. It had been sent to me by an agent in the east, who informed me that it had been found near the site of the ancient Babylon. But the characters engraved on the seal were to me an intolerable puzzle. Somewhat of the cuneiform pattern, there were yet striking differences, which I detected at the first glance, and all efforts to read the inscription on the hypothesis that the rules for deciphering the arrow-headed writing would apply proved futile. A riddle such as this stung my pride, and at odd moments I would take the Black Seal out of the cabinet, and scrutinise it with so much idle perseverance that every letter was familiar to my mind, and I could have drawn the inscription from memory without the slightest error. Judge, then, of my surprise when I one day received from a correspondent in the west of England a letter and an enclosure that positively left me thunderstruck. I saw carefully traced on a large piece of paper the very characters of the Black Seal, without alteration of any

---

1 Likely a reference to "throwing the hammer," an athletic contest in which participants attempt to throw a heavy hammer as far as possible (*OED*).

2 See p. 99, note 2, above.

kind, and above the inscription my friend had written: *Inscription found on a limestone rock on the Grey Hills, Monmouthshire.*[1] *Done in some red earth, and quite recent.* I turned to the letter. My friend wrote: "I send you the enclosed inscription with all due reserve. A shepherd who passed by the stone a week ago swears that there was then no mark of any kind. The characters, as I have noted, are formed by drawing some red earth over the stone, and are of an average height of one inch. They look to me like a kind of cuneiform character, a good deal altered, but this, of course, is impossible. It may be either a hoax, or more probably some scribble of the gypsies, who are plentiful enough in this wild country. They have, as you are aware, many hieroglyphics which they use in communicating with one another. I happened to visit the stone in question two days ago in connection with a rather painful incident which has occurred here."

As may be supposed, I wrote immediately to my friend, thanking him for the copy of the inscription, and asking him in a casual manner the history of the incident he mentioned. To be brief, I heard that a woman named Cradock, who had lost her husband a day before, had set out to communicate the sad news to a cousin who lived some five miles away. She took a short cut which led by the Grey Hills. Mrs. Cradock, who was then quite a young woman, never arrived at her relative's house. Late that night a farmer who had lost a couple of sheep, supposed to have wandered from the flock, was walking over the Grey Hills, with a lantern and his dog. His attention was attracted by a noise, which he described as a kind of wailing, mournful and pitiable to hear; and, guided by the sound, he found the unfortunate Mrs. Cradock crouched on the ground by the limestone rock, swaying her body to and fro, and lamenting and crying in so heart-rending a manner that the farmer was, as he says, at first obliged to stop his ears, or he would have run away. The woman allowed herself to be taken home, and a neighbour came to see to her necessities. All the night she never ceased her crying, mixing her lament with words of some unintelligible jargon, and when the doctor arrived he pronounced her insane. She lay on her bed for a week, now wailing, as people said, like one lost and damned for eternity, and now sunk in a heavy coma; it was thought that grief at the loss of her husband had unsettled her mind, and the medical man did not at one time expect her to live. I need not say that I was deeply interested in this story, and I made my friend write to me

---

1 Area in south Wales (Machen's birthplace).

at intervals with all the particulars of the case. I heard then that in the course of six weeks the woman gradually recovered the use of her faculties, and some months later she gave birth to a son, christened Jervase, who unhappily proved to be of weak intellect. Such were the facts known to the village; but to me, while I whitened at the suggested thought of the hideous enormities that had doubtless been committed, all this was nothing short of conviction, and I incautiously hazarded a hint of something like the truth to some scientific friends. The moment the words had left my lips I bitterly regretted having spoken, and thus given away the great secret of my life, but with a good deal of relief mixed with indignation I found my fears altogether misplaced, for my friends ridiculed me to my face, and I was regarded as a madman; and beneath a natural anger I chuckled to myself, feeling as secure amidst these blockheads, as if I had confided what I knew to the desert sands.

But now, knowing so much, I resolved I would know all, and I concentrated my efforts on the task of deciphering the inscription on the Black Seal. For many years I made this puzzle the sole object of my leisure moments; for the greater portion of my time was, of course, devoted to other duties, and it was only now and then that I could snatch a week of clear research. If I were to tell the full history of this curious investigation, this statement would be wearisome in the extreme, for it would contain simply the account of long and tedious failure. By what I knew already of ancient scripts I was well equipped for the chase, as I always termed it to myself. I had correspondents amongst all the scientific men in Europe, and, indeed, in the world, and I could not believe that in these days any character, however ancient and however perplexed, could long resist the search-light I should bring to bear upon it. Yet, in point of fact, it was fully fourteen years before I succeeded. With every year my professional duties increased, and my leisure became smaller. This no doubt retarded me a good deal; and yet, when I look back on those years, I am astonished at the vast scope of my investigation of the Black Seal. I made my bureau a centre, and from all the world and from all the ages I gathered transcripts of ancient writing. Nothing, I resolved, should pass me unawares, and the faintest hint should be welcomed and followed up. But as one covert after another was tried and proved empty of result, I began in the course of years to despair, and to wonder whether the Black Seal were the sole relic of some race that had vanished from the world and left no other trace of its existence—had perished, in fine, as Atlantis is said to have done, in some great cataclysm, its secrets perhaps drowned beneath the ocean or moulded into the heart of the hills. The thought chilled my warmth a little, and though I still persevered, it was no longer with the same certainty of faith. A chance came to the rescue. I was staying in a considerable town in the north of England, and took the opportunity of going over the very creditable museum that had for some time been established in the place. The curator was one of my correspondents; and, as we were looking through one of the mineral cases, my attention was struck by a specimen, a piece of black stone some four inches square, the appearance of which reminded me in a measure of the Black Seal. I took it up carelessly, and was turning it over in my hand, when I saw, to my astonishment, that the under side was inscribed. I said, quietly enough, to my friend the curator that the specimen interested me, and that I should be much obliged if he would allow me to take it with me to my hotel for a couple of days. He, of course, made no objection, and I hurried to my rooms and found that my first glance had not deceived me. There were two inscriptions; one in the regular cuneiform character, another in the character of the Black Seal, and I realised that my task was accomplished. I made an exact copy of the two inscriptions; and when I got to my London study, and had the Seal before me, I was able seriously to grapple with the great problem. The interpreting inscription on the museum specimen, though in itself curious enough, did not bear on my quest, but the transliteration made me master of the secret of the Black Seal. Conjecture, of course, had to enter into my calculations; there was here and there uncertainty about a particular ideograph, and one sign recurring again and again on the Seal baffled me for many successive nights. But at last the secret stood open before me in plain English, and I read the key of the awful transmutation of the hills. The last word was hardly written, when with fingers all trembling and unsteady I tore the scrap of paper into the minutest fragments, and saw them flame and blacken in the red hollow of the fire, and then I crushed the grey films that remained into finest powder. Never since then have I written those words; never will I write the phrases which tell me how man can be reduced to the slime from which he came, and be forced to put on the flesh of the reptile and the snake.[1] There

---

1 Here one of the meanings of "transmutation" of the novel's subtitle highlights its association with the theory of the "transmutation of species"—an important and controversial precursor to Darwin's theory of evolution first popularized in Britain through Robert Chambers's best-selling *Vestiges of the Natural History of Creation* (1844). The theory is grounded in materialist doctrines about "self-activating" (rather than divinely activated) matter (Secord xxiv). See also p. 22, notes 1 and 2.

was now but one thing remaining. I knew, but I desired to see, and I was after some time able to take a house in the neighbourhood of the Grey Hills, and not far from the cottage where Mrs. Cradock and her son Jervase resided. I need not go into a full and detailed account of the apparently inexplicable events which have occurred here, where I am writing this. I knew that I should find in Jervase Cradock something of the blood of the "Little People," and I found later that he had more than once encountered his kinsmen in lonely places in that lonely land. When I was summoned one day to the garden, and found him in a seizure speaking or hissing the ghastly jargon of the Black Seal, I am afraid that exultation prevailed over pity. I heard bursting from his lips the secrets of the underworld, and the word of dread, "Ishakshar," the signification of which I must be excused from giving.

But there is one incident I cannot pass over unnoticed. In the waste hollow of the night I awoke at the sound of those hissing syllables I knew so well; and on going to the wretched boy's room, I found him convulsed and foaming at the mouth, struggling on the bed as if he strove to escape the grasp of writhing demons. I took him down to my room and lit the lamp, while he lay twisting on the floor, calling on the power within his flesh to leave him. I saw his body swell and become distended as a bladder, while the face blackened before my eyes; and then at the crisis I did what was necessary according to the directions on the Seal, and putting all scruple on one side, I became a man of science, observant of what was passing. Yet the sight I had to witness was horrible, almost beyond the power of human conception and the most fearful fantasy. Something pushed out from the body there on the floor, and stretched forth, a slimy, wavering tentacle, across the room, and grasped the bust upon the cupboard, and laid it down on my desk.

When it was over, and I was left to walk up and down all the rest of the night, white and shuddering, with sweat pouring from my flesh, I vainly tried to reason with myself: I said, truly enough, that I had seen nothing really supernatural, that a snail pushing out his horns and drawing them in was but an instance on a smaller scale of what I had witnessed;[1] and yet horror broke

---

1 Machen states in his autobiography *Things Near and Far* that his idea for this story came from a theory put forth by physicist and member of the Society for Psychical Research, Sir Oliver Lodge (1851–1940), to explain moving objects in séances. Lodge claimed that the medium's body was capable of extending ectoplasmic pseudopodia. Upon reading the explanation, Machen imagined the pseudopodia *(continued)*

through all such reasonings and left me shattered and loathing myself for the share I had taken in the night's work.

There is little more to be said. I am going now to the final trial and encounter; for I have determined that there shall be nothing wanting, and I shall meet the "Little People" face to face. I shall have the Black Seal and the knowledge of its secrets to help me, and if I unhappily do not return from my journey, there is no need to conjure up here a picture of the awfulness of my fate.

Pausing a little at the end of Professor Gregg's statement, Miss Lally continued her tale in the following words:—

Such was the almost incredible story that the professor had left behind him. When I had finished reading it, it was late at night, but the next morning I took Morgan with me, and we proceeded to search the Grey Hills for some trace of the lost professor. I will not weary you with a description of the savage desolation of that tract of country, a tract of utterest loneliness, of bare green hills dotted over with grey limestone boulders, worn by the ravage of time into fantastic semblances of men and beasts. Finally, after many hours of weary searching, we found what I told you—the watch and chain, the purse, and the ring—wrapped in a piece of coarse parchment. When Morgan cut the gut that bound the parcel together, and I saw the professor's property, I burst into tears, but the sight of the dreaded characters of the Black Seal repeated on the parchment froze me to silent horror, and I think I understood for the first time the awful fate that had come upon my late employer.

I have only to add that Professor Gregg's lawyer treated my account of what had happened as a fairy tale,[1] and refused even to glance at the documents I laid before him. It was he who was responsible for the statement that appeared in the public press, to the effect that Professor Gregg had been drowned, and that his body must have been swept into the open sea.

---

as being like a snail's horns, which can extend and retreat into its head. For more information, see Introduction, p. 42.

1 The story is quite literally a "fairy tale" in that it is a story about survivals of "little people" incorrectly assumed to be an extinct race, but the use of the term "fairy tale" in this context also contrasts it with the truth value of science. Ironically, fairies were very much the subject of a variety of sciences at this time (see especially Silver), fairy-tales were used to explain science to children (see Keene), and science itself (as contemporary observers often noted) often appeared fairy-tale-like in its positing of, for example, ancient monsters (dinosaurs).

Miss Lally stopped speaking, and looked at Mr. Phillipps, with a glance of some inquiry. He, for his part, was sunken in a deep revery of thought; and when he looked up and saw the bustle of the evening gathering in the square, men and women hurrying to partake of dinner, and crowds already besetting the music-halls, all the hum and press of actual life seemed unreal and visionary, a dream in the morning after an awakening.

"I thank you," he said at last, "for your most interesting story; interesting to me, because I feel fully convinced of its exact truth."

"Sir," said the lady, with some energy of indignation, "you grieve and offend me. Do you think I should waste my time and yours by concocting fictions on a bench in Leicester Square?"

"Pardon me, Miss Lally, you have a little misunderstood me. Before you began I knew that whatever you told would be told in good faith, but your experiences have a far higher value than that of *bona fides*.[1] The most extraordinary circumstances in your account are perfect harmony with the very latest scientific theories. Professor Lodge would, I am sure, value a communication from you extremely; I was charmed from the first by his daring hypothesis in explanation of the wonders of Spiritualism[2] (so called), but your narrative puts the whole matter out of the range of mere hypothesis."

"Alas! sir, all this will not help me. You forget, I have lost my brother under the most startling and dreadful circumstances. Again, I ask you, did you not see him as you came here? His black whiskers, his spectacles, his timid glance to right and left; think, do not these particulars recall his face to your memory?"

---

1 Latin phrase for "good faith." Phillipps claims to believe that Miss Lally's story about Professor Gregg was told "in good faith" (without intending to deceive him), but he believes the story primarily because it appears consistent with "the very latest scientific theories," unlike Miss Lally's previous story about her missing brother.

2 Victorian spiritualism, popular in the second half of the nineteenth century, refers primarily to the belief that people could communicate with spirits of the dead through a medium. Séances often included spectacular elements that supposedly attested to the presence of spirits, including noises such as rappings and the unexpected movement of objects. Lodge's observations of a medium's body and his hypothesis about their abilities appeared in the *Proceedings of the Society for Psychical Research* in 1894, and Phillipps claims to have read them (as did Machen). On Lodge, see p. 42, above; for more on his hypotheses, see Raia.

"I am sorry to say I have never seen any one of the kind," said Phillipps, who had forgotten all about the missing brother. "But let me ask you a few questions. Did you notice whether Professor Gregg ..."

"Pardon me, sir, I have stayed too long. My employers will be expecting me. I thank you for your sympathy. Good-bye."

Before Mr. Phillipps had recovered from his amazement at this abrupt departure Miss Lally had disappeared from his gaze, passing into the crowd that now thronged the approaches to the Empire.[1] He walked home in a pensive frame of mind, and drank too much tea. At ten o'clock he had made his third brew, and had sketched out the outlines of a little work to be called *Protoplasmic Reversion*.[2]

INCIDENT OF THE PRIVATE BAR

Mr. Dyson often meditated at odd moments over the singular tale he had listened to at the Café de la Touraine. In the first place, he cherished a profound conviction that the words of truth were scattered with a too niggardly and sparing hand over the agreeable history of Mr. Smith and the Black Gulf Cañon; and secondly, there was the undeniable fact of the profound agitation of the narrator, and his gestures on the pavement, too violent to be simulated. The idea of a man going about London haunted by the fear of meeting a young man with spectacles struck Dyson as supremely ridiculous; he searched his memory for some precedent in romance, but without success; he paid visits at odd times to the little café, hoping to find Mr. Wilkins there; and he kept

---

1 The Empire Theatre opened in Leicester Square in 1884 but became popular only after it was redecorated and reopened in 1887 as the Empire Palace of Varieties, featuring a winning "combination of classical and trend-setting ballets with music hall turns" (Donohue 37). The area was "an internationally known pleasure ground" (4) featuring a variety of popular entertainment establishments (including the Alhambra music hall) that attracted large crowds.

2 "Protoplasm" was considered the "essence of life"; T.H. Huxley (1825–95) defined "protoplasm" as the "physical basis, or matter, of life," claiming that all living things from the "lowest" forms of animal and plant life to the highest all share a common *material* basis of life— that is, all forms of life were made of the same stuff, and that stuff was protoplasm. Notably, Phillipps's supposedly scientific treatise on the ways in which life forms can revert into earlier forms (what he calls "protoplasmic reversion") is inspired by a "fairy tale" or tale about survivals of ancient early peoples ("fairies").

a sharp watch on the great generation of the spectacled men, without much doubt that he would remember the face of the individual whom he had seen dart out of the aerated bread shop. All his peregrinations and researches, however, seemed to lead to nothing of value, and Dyson needed all his warm conviction of his innate detective powers and his strong scent for mystery to sustain him in his endeavours. In fact, he had two affairs on hand; and every day, as he passed through streets crowded or deserted, lurked in the obscure districts and watched at corners, he was more than surprised to find that the affair of the gold coin persistently avoided him, while the ingenious Wilkins, and the young man with spectacles whom he dreaded, seemed to have vanished from the pavements.

He was pondering these problems one evening in a house of call[1] in the Strand, and the obstinacy with which the persons he so ardently desired to meet hung back gave the modest tankard before him an additional touch of bitter. As it happened, he was alone in his compartment, and, without thinking, he uttered aloud the burden of his meditations. "How bizarre it all is!" he said, "a man walking the pavement with the dread of a timid-looking young man with spectacles continually hovering before his eyes. And there was some tremendous feeling at work, I could swear to that." Quick as thought, before he had finished the sentence, a head popped round the barrier, and was withdrawn again; and while Dyson was wondering what this could mean, the door of the compartment was swung open, and a smooth, clean-shaven, and smiling gentleman entered.

"You will excuse me, sir," he said politely, "for intruding on your thoughts, but you made a remark a minute ago."

"I did," said Dyson; "I have been puzzling over a foolish matter, and I thought aloud. As you heard what I said, and seem interested, perhaps you may be able to relieve my perplexity?"

"Indeed, I scarcely know; it is an odd coincidence. One has to be cautious. I suppose, sir, that you would have no repulsion in assisting the ends of justice."

"Justice," replied Dyson, "is a term of such wide meaning, that I too feel doubtful about giving an answer. But this place is not altogether fit for such a discussion; perhaps you would come to my rooms?"

"You are very kind; my name is Burton, but I am sorry to say I have not a card with me. Do you live near here?"

---

1 A public house.

"Within ten minutes' walk."

Mr. Burton took out his watch, and seemed to be making a rapid calculation.

"I have a train to catch," he said; "but after all, it is a late one. So if you don't mind, I think I will come with you. I am sure we should have a little talk together. We turn up here?"

The theatres were filling as they crossed the Strand; the street seemed alive with voices, and Dyson looked fondly about him. The glittering lines of gas-lamps, with here and there the blinding radiance of an electric light, the hansoms that flashed to and fro with ringing bells, the laden 'buses, and the eager hurrying east and west of the foot-passengers, made his most enchanting picture; and the graceful spire of St. Mary le Strand on the one hand, and the last flush of sunset on the other, were to him a cause of thanksgiving, as the gorse blossom to Linnæus.[1] Mr. Burton caught his look of fondness as they crossed the street.

"I see you can find the picturesque in London," he said. "To me this great town is as I see it is to you—the study and the love of life. Yet how few there are that can pierce the veils of apparent monotony and meanness! I have read in a paper, which is said to have the largest circulation in the world, a comparison between the aspects of London and Paris, a comparison which should be positively laureat, as the great masterpiece of fatuous stupidity. Conceive if you can a human being of ordinary intelligence preferring the Boulevards to our London streets; imagine a man calling for the wholesale destruction of our most charming city, in order that the dull uniformity of that whited sepulchre[2] called

---

1   The alignment here is between the beauty Dyson perceives in the modern city (with its gas-lamps, electric lights, and hustle and bustle) and the beauty Linnaeus supposedly perceived when he first saw the gorse blossom. The Decadent artist is here once again aligned with the scientist. Linnaeus (1707–78), a Swedish naturalist famous for his system of classification of living things, was the inspiration for the "global science of the surface" (McClintock 34), and Decadents who might be said to be artists of the surface would later be described as "botanizing on the sidewalk" (Benjamin, *Charles Baudelaire* 39). See Introduction, p. 29, for details.

2   Biblical allusion to Matthew 23:27: "Woe unto you, scribes and Pharisees, hypocrites! for ye are like unto whited sepulchres, which indeed appear beautiful outward, but are within full of dead men's bones, and of all uncleanness." Although the phrase is most often used to describe a hypocritical person (whose seemingly pleasant

Paris should be reproduced here in London. Is it not positively incredible?"

"My dear sir," said Dyson, regarding Burton with a good deal of interest, "I agree most heartily with your opinions, but I really cannot share your wonder. Have you heard how much George Eliot received for *Romola*?[1] Do you know what the circulation of *Robert Elsmere* was?[2] Do you read *Tit Bits* regularly?[3] To me, on the contrary, it is constant matter both for wonder and thanksgiving that London was not boulevardised twenty years ago. I praise that exquisite jagged skyline that stands up against the pale greens and fading blues and flushing clouds of sunset, but I wonder even more than I praise. As for St. Mary le Strand, its preservation is a miracle, nothing more or less.[4] A thing of exquisite beauty *versus*

---

outward appearance hides inner corruption), here the phrase is applied to Paris.

1 An 1862–63 novel by George Eliot (1819–80), pseudonym of Marian Evans. Dyson, who much like Machen, is drawn to literature of the marvelous, appears to share Machen's low opinion of George Eliot, one of the greatest Victorian realist writers, recognized as such both in her lifetime and since. For Machen (and Dyson), Eliot is overly concerned with the "materialistic or rationalistic" over the "spiritual or mystic" understandings of existence (*Hieroglyphics* 71–72).

2 Highly successful novel by Mary Augusta Ward, known as Mrs Humphry Ward (1851–1920). Dyson shares Machen's low regard for this work. Machen went so far as to suggest it was not literature (*Hieroglyphics* 134, 191).

3 *Tit-Bits* was a highly popular Victorian penny paper started by George Newnes (1851–1910) in 1881. Issued weekly, the periodical consisted of "a compilation of scraps from books, periodicals, and newspapers, and of contributions from readers" (Altick 363).

4 St. Mary Le Strand (built 1714–24) became the focus of some contemporary discussions about Strand improvements broadly discussed and debated in the popular press. In one account, "certain utilitarians" urged the London County Council to demolish the church and nearby houses to widen the street in an effort to improve traffic in this key thoroughfare. In response, "a considerable outcry was raised" by numerous people, including "the most distinguished persons in Art and Letters" (Horne 320). Discussions also mention that some suggested the street could be modeled on famous French streets such as the Rue de Rivoli in Paris, hence the reference to streets being "boulevardized" (made to look like large Parisian boulevards), a French term for "a broad street, promenade, or walk, planted with (*continued*)

four 'buses abreast! Really, the conclusion is too obvious. Didn't you read the letter of the man who proposed that the whole mysterious system, the immemorial plan of computing Easter, should be abolished off-hand, because he doesn't like his son having his holidays as early as March 25th? But shall we be going on?"

They had lingered at the corner of a street on the north side of the Strand, enjoying the contrasts and the glamour of the scene. Dyson pointed the way with a gesture, and they strolled up the comparatively deserted streets, slanting a little to the right, and thus arriving at Dyson's lodging on the verge of Bloomsbury. Mr. Burton took a comfortable arm-chair by the open window, while Dyson lit the candles and produced the whiskey and soda and cigarettes.

"They tell me these cigarettes are very good," he said; "but I know nothing about it myself. I hold at last that there is only one tobacco, and that is shag. I suppose I could not tempt you to try a pipeful?"

Mr. Burton smilingly refused the offer, and picked out a cigarette from the box. When he had smoked it half through, he said with some hesitation—

"It is really kind of you to have me here, Mr. Dyson; the fact is that the interests at issue are far too serious to be discussed in a bar, where, as you found for yourself, there may be listeners, voluntary or involuntary, on each side. I think the remark I heard you make was something about the oddity of an individual going about London in deadly fear of a young man with spectacles."

"Yes; that was it."

"Well, would you mind confiding to me the circumstances that gave rise to the reflection?"

"Not in the least. It was like this." And he ran over in brief outline the adventure in Oxford Street, dwelling on the violence of Mr. Wilkins's gestures, but wholly suppressing the tale told in the café. "He told me he lived in constant terror of meeting this man; and I left him when I thought he was cool enough to look after himself," said Dyson, ending his narrative.

"Really," said Mr. Burton. "And you actually saw this mysterious person."

---

rows of trees" (*OED*). Machen's frequent allusion to contemporary views and events expressed in the popular press at once speaks to Machen's own involvement as a writer for a wide range of periodicals and helps establish the characters' positions as critical of popular views of "the times."

"Yes."

"And could you describe him?"

"Well, he looked to me a youngish man, pale and nervous. He had small black side-whiskers, and wore rather large spectacles."

"But this is simply marvellous! You astonish me. For I must tell you that my interest in the matter is this. I'm not in the least in terror of meeting a dark young man with spectacles, but I shrewdly suspect a person of that description would much rather not meet me. And yet the account you give of the man tallies exactly. A nervous glance to right and left—is it not so? And, as you observed, he wears prominent spectacles, and has small black whiskers. There cannot be, surely, two people exactly identical— one a cause of terror, and the other, I should imagine, extremely anxious to get out of the way. But have you seen this man since?"

"No, I have not; and I have been looking out for him pretty keenly. But, of course, he may have left London, and England too, for the matter of that."

"Hardly, I think. Well, Mr. Dyson, it is only fair that I should explain my story, now that I have listened to yours. I must tell you, then, that I am an agent for curiosities and precious things of all kinds. An odd employment, isn't it? Of course, I wasn't brought up to the business; I gradually fell into it. I have always been fond of things queer and rare, and by the time I was twenty I had made half a dozen collections. It is not generally known how often farm-labourers come upon rarities; you would be astonished if I told you what I have seen turned up by the plough. I lived in the country in those days, and I used to buy anything the men on the farms brought me; and I had the queerest set of rubbish, as my friends called my collection. But that's how I got the scent of the business, which means everything; and, later on, it struck me that I might very well turn my knowledge to account and add to my income. Since those early days I have been in most quarters of the world, and some very valuable things have passed through my hands, and I have had to engage in difficult and delicate nego- tiations. You have possibly heard of the Khan opal—called in the East 'The Stone of a Thousand and One Colours'? Well, perhaps the conquest of that stone was my greatest achievement. I call it myself the stone of the thousand and one lies, for I assure you that I had to invent a cycle of folk-lore before the Rajah who owned it would consent to sell the thing. I subsidised wandering story-tell- ers, who told tales in which the opal played a frightful part; I hired a holy man—a great ascetic—to prophesy against the thing in the language of Eastern symbolism; in short, I frightened the Rajah out of his wits. So, you see, there is room for diplomacy in the traffic I am engaged in. I have to be ever on my guard, and I have often been sensible that unless I watched every step and weighed every word, my life would not last me much longer. Last April I became aware of the existence of a highly valuable antique gem; it was in southern Italy, and in the possession of persons who were ignorant of its real value. It has always been my experience that it is precisely the ignorant who are most difficult to deal with. I have met farmers who were under the impression that a shilling of George I. was a find of almost incalculable value; and all the defeats I have sustained have been at the hands of people of this description. Reflecting on these facts, I saw that the acquisition of the gem I have mentioned would be an affair demanding the nicest diplomacy; I might possibly have got it by offering a sum approaching its real value, but I need not point out to you that such a proceeding would be most unbusinesslike. Indeed, I doubt whether it would have been successful; for the cupidity of such persons is aroused by a sum which seems enormous, and the low cunning which serves them in place of intelligence immediately suggests that the object for which such an amount is offered must be worth at least double. Of course, when it is a matter of an ordinary curiosity—an old jug, a carved chest, or a queer brass lantern—one does not much care; the cupidity of the owner defeats its object; the collector laughs and goes away, for he is aware that such things are by no means unique. But this gem I fervently desired to possess; and as I did not see my way to giving more than a hundredth part of its value, I was conscious that all my, let us say, imaginative and diplomatic powers would have to be exerted. I am sorry to say that I came to the conclusion that I could not undertake to carry the matter through single-handed, and I determined to confide in my assistant, a young man named William Robbins, whom I judged to be by no means devoid of capacity. My idea was that Robbins should get himself up as a low-class dealer in precious stones; he could patter a little Italian, and would go to the town in question and manage to see the gem we were after, possibly by offering some trifling articles of jewellery for sale, but that I left to be decided. Then my work was to begin, but I will not trouble you with a tale told twice over. In due course, then, Robbins went off to Italy with an assortment of uncut stones and a few rings, and some jewellery I bought in Birmingham on purpose for his expedition. A week later I followed him, travelling leisurely, so that I was a fortnight later in arriving at our common destination. There was a decent hotel in the town, and on my inquiring of the landlord whether there were many strangers in the place, he told me very few; he had heard there was an Englishman staying in a small tavern, a pedlar, he said, who sold beautiful trinkets very cheaply, and wanted to buy old rubbish. For five or six days I took life leisurely, and I must say I enjoyed myself. It was part of my plan to make the people think I was an enormously rich man; and I knew that such items as the extravagance of my meals, and the price of every bottle of wine I drank, would not be suffered, as Sancho Panza[1] puts it, to rot in the landlord's breast. At the end of the week I was fortunate enough to make the acquaintance of Signor Melini, the owner of the gem I coveted, at the café, and with his ready hospitality, and my geniality, I was soon established as a friend of the house. On my third or fourth visit I managed to make the Italians talk about the English pedlar, who, they said, spoke a most detestable Italian. 'But that does not matter,' said the Signora Melini, 'for he has beautiful things, which he sells very very cheap.' 'I hope you may not find he has cheated you,' I said, 'for I must tell you that English people give these fellows a very wide berth. They usually make a great parade of the cheapness of their goods, which often turn out to be double the price of better articles in the shops.' They would not hear of this, and Signora Melini insisted on showing me the three rings and the bracelet she had bought of the pedlar. She told me the price she had paid; and after scrutinising the articles carefully, I had to confess that she had made a bargain, and indeed Robbins had sold her the things at about fifty per cent. below market value. I admired the trinkets as I gave them back to the lady, and I hinted that the pedlar must be a somewhat foolish specimen of his class. Two days later, as I was taking my vermouth at the café with Signor Melini, he led the conversation back to the pedlar, and mentioned casually that he had shown the man a little curiosity, for which he had made rather a handsome offer. 'My dear sir,' I said, 'I hope you will be careful. I told you that the travelling tradesman does not bear a very high reputation in England; and notwithstanding his apparent simplicity, this fellow may turn out to be an arrant cheat. May I ask you what is the nature of the curiosity you have shown him?' He told me it was a little thing, a pretty little stone with some figures cut on it: people said it was old. 'I should like to examine it,' I replied; 'as it happens I have seen a good deal of these gems. We have a fine collection of them

---

1 Fictional character in Miguel de Cervantes's *Don Quixote* (1605 and 1615) known for his witty comments.

in our Museum at London.' In due course I was shown the article, and I held the gem I so coveted between my fingers. I looked at it coolly, and put it down carelessly on the table. 'Would you mind telling me, Signor,' I said, 'how much my fellow-countryman offered you for this?' 'Well,' he said, 'my wife says the man must be mad; he said he would give me twenty lire[1] for it.'

"I looked at him quietly, and took up the gem and pretended to examine it in the light more carefully; I turned it over and over, and finally pulled out a magnifying glass from my pocket, and seemed to search every line in the cutting with minutest scrutiny. 'My dear sir,' I said at last, 'I am inclined to agree with Signora Melini. If this gem were genuine, it would be worth some money; but as it happens to be a rather bad forgery, it is not worth twenty centesimi.[2] It was sophisticated, I should imagine, some time in the last century, and by a very unskilful hand.' 'Then we had better get rid of it,' said Melini. 'I never thought it was worth anything myself. Of course, I am sorry for the pedlar, but one must let a man know his own trade. I shall tell him we will take the twenty lire.' 'Excuse me,' I said, 'the man wants a lesson. It would be a charity to give him one. Tell him that you will not take anything under eighty lire, and I shall be much surprised if he does not close with you at once.'

"A day or two later I heard that the English pedlar had gone away, after debasing the minds of the country people with Birmingham art jewellery; for I admit that the gold sleeve-links like kidney beans, the silver chains made apparently after the pattern of a dog-chain, and the initial brooches have always been heavy on my conscience. I cannot acquit myself of having indirectly contributed to debauch the taste of a simple folk; but I hope that the end I had in view may finally outbalance this heavy charge. Soon afterwards I paid a farewell visit at the Melinis, and the signor informed me with an oily chuckle that the plan I had suggested had been completely successful. I congratulated him on his bargain, and went away after expressing a wish that Heaven might send many such pedlars in his path.

"Nothing of interest occurred on my return journey. I had arranged that Robbins was to meet me at a certain place on a certain day, and I went to the appointment full of the coolest

---

1 Plural of "lira," the unit of Italian currency prior to the adoption of the euro. One lira was the equivalent of 100 "centesimi" (hundredths or cents).
2 Plural of "centesimo," Italian for "cent"; see previous note.

confidence; the gem had been conquered, and I had only to reap the fruits of victory. I am sorry to shake that trust in our common human nature which I am sure you possess, but I am compelled to tell you that up to the present date I have never set eyes on my man Robbins, or on the antique gem in his custody. I have found out that he actually arrived in London, for he was seen three days before my arrival in England by a pawnbroker of my acquaintance consuming his favourite beverage—four ale[1]—in the tavern where we met to-night. Since then he has not been heard of. I hope you will now pardon my curiosity as to the history and adventures of dark young men with spectacles. You will, I am sure, feel for me in my position; the savour of life has disappeared for me; it is a bitter thought that I have rescued one of the most perfect and exquisite specimens of antique art from the hands of ignorant, and indeed unscrupulous persons, only to deliver it into the keeping of a man who is evidently utterly devoid of the very elements of commercial morality."

"My dear sir," said Dyson, "you will allow me to compliment you on your style; your adventures have interested me exceedingly. But, forgive me, you just now used the word morality; would not some persons take exception to your own methods of business? I can conceive, myself, flaws of a moral kind being found in the very original conception you have described to me; I can imagine the Puritan shrinking in dismay from your scheme, pronouncing it unscrupulous—nay, dishonest."

Mr. Burton helped himself very frankly to some more whiskey.

"Your scruples entertain me," he said. "Perhaps you have not gone very deeply into these questions of ethics. I have been compelled to do so myself, just as I was forced to master a simple system of book-keeping. Without book-keeping, and still more without a system of ethics, it is impossible to conduct a business such as mine. But I assure you that I am often profoundly saddened as I pass through the crowded streets and watch the world at work by the thought of how few amongst all these hurrying individuals, black hatted, well dressed, educated we may presume sufficiently,—how few amongst them have any reasoned system of morality. Even you have not weighed the question; although you study life and affairs, and to a certain extent penetrate the veils and masks of the comedy of man, even you judge by empty conventions, and the false money which is allowed to pass current as sterling coin. Allow me to play the part of Socrates; I shall

---

1 "Ale sold at four-pence a quart" (*OED*).

teach you nothing that you do not know. I shall merely lay aside the wrappings of prejudice and bad logic, and show you the real image which you possess in your soul. Come then. Do you allow that happiness is anything?"

"Certainly," said Dyson.

"And happiness is desirable or undesirable?"

"Desirable, of course."

"And what shall we call the man who gives happiness? Is he not a philanthropist?"

"I think so."

"And such a person is praiseworthy, and the more praiseworthy in the proportion of the persons whom he makes happy?"

"By all means."

"So that he who makes a whole nation happy is praiseworthy in the extreme, and the action by which he gives happiness is the highest virtue?"

"It appears so, O Burton," said Dyson, who found something very exquisite in the character of his visitor.

"Quite so; you find the several conclusions inevitable. Well, apply them to the story I have told you. I conferred happiness on myself by obtaining (as I thought) possession of the gem; I conferred happiness on the Melinis by getting them eighty lire instead of an object for which they had not the slightest value, and I intended to confer happiness on the whole British nation by selling the thing to the British Museum, to say nothing of the happiness a profit of about nine thousand per cent. would have conferred on me. I assure you, I regard Robbins as an interferer with the cosmos and fair order of things. But that is nothing; you perceive that I am an apostle of the very highest morality; you have been forced to yield to argument."

"There certainly seems a great deal in what you advance," said Dyson. "I admit that I am a mere amateur of ethics, while you, as you say, have brought the most acute scrutiny to bear on these perplexed and doubtful questions. I can well understand your anxiety to meet the fallacious Robbins, and I congratulate myself on the chance which has made us acquainted. But you will pardon my seeming inhospitality; I see it is half-past eleven, and I think you mentioned a train."

"A thousand thanks, Mr. Dyson, I have just time, I see. I will look you up some evening if I may. Good night."

THE DECORATIVE IMAGINATION

In the course of a few weeks Dyson became accustomed, to the constant incursions of the ingenious Mr. Burton, who showed himself ready to drop in at all hours, not averse to refreshment, and a profound guide in the complicated questions of life. His visits at once terrified and delighted Dyson, who could no longer seat himself at his bureau secure from interruption while he embarked on literary undertakings, each one of which was to be a masterpiece. On the other hand, it was a vivid pleasure to be confronted with views so highly original; and if here and there Mr. Burton's reasonings seemed tinged with fallacy, yet Dyson freely yielded to the joy of strangeness, and never failed to give his visitor a frank and hearty welcome. Mr. Burton's first inquiry was always after the unprincipled Robbins, and he seemed to feel the stings of disappointment when Dyson told him that he had failed to meet this outrage on all morality, as Burton styled him, vowing that sooner or later he would take vengeance on such a shameless betrayal of trust.

One evening they had sat together for some time discussing the possibility of laying down for this present generation and our modern and intensely complicated order of society, some rules of social diplomacy, such as Lord Bacon gave to the courtiers of King James I. "It is a book to make," said Mr. Burton, "but who is there capable of making it? I tell you, people are longing for such a book; it would bring fortune to its publisher. Bacon's Essays are exquisite, but they have now no practical application; the modern strategist can find but little use in a treatise *De Re Militari*, written by a Florentine in the fifteenth century.[1] Scarcely more dissimilar are the social conditions of Bacon's time and our own; the rules that he lays down so exquisitely for the courtier and diplomatist of James the First's age will avail us little in the rough-and-tumble struggle of to-day. Life, I am afraid, has deteriorated; it gives little play for fine strokes such as formerly advanced men in the state. Except in such businesses as mine, where a chance does occur now and then, it has

---

1 Despite Mr. Burton's claims, both texts invoked by him are notable for their enduring influence. *Essays* (1597) by Francis Bacon (1561–1626) is among his best-known works, and *De re militari*, written in the fourth century (not the fifteenth, as Mr. Burton claims) by a Roman named Flavius Vegetius Renatus, was one of the most influential military manuals in the Western world, translated into numerous languages and still well known even in the nineteenth century.

all become, as I said, an affair of rough and tumble; men still desire to attain, it is true, but what is their *moyen de parvenir*?[1] A mere imitation—and not a gracious one—of the arts of the soap-vender and the proprietor of baking-powder. When I think of these things, my dear Dyson, I confess that I am tempted to despair of my century."

"You are too pessimistic, my dear fellow; you set up too high a standard. Certainly, I agree with you, that the times are decadent in many ways. I admit a general appearance of squalor; it needs much philosophy to extract the wonderful and the beautiful from the Cromwell Road or the Nonconformist conscience. Australian wines of fine Burgundy character, the novels alike of the old women and the new women, popular journalism,—these things, indeed, make for depression.[2] Yet we have our advantages: before us is unfolded the greatest spectacle the world has ever seen—the mystery of the innumerable, unending streets, the strange adventures that must infallibly arise from so complicated a press of interests. Nay, I will say that he who has stood in the ways of a suburb, and has seen them stretch before him all shining, void, and desolate at noonday, has not lived in vain. Such a sight is in reality more wonderful than any perspective of Bagdad or Grand Cairo. And, to set on one side the entertaining history

---

1 French for the "way to attain" or the "way to achieve," also the title of a satiric work in Rabelaisian style, *Moyen de parvenir* (1610) by Béroalde de Verville (1556–1626), which Machen translated. Machen's partial translation appeared as *The Way to Obtain* (1889) and a more complete version as *Fantastic Tales* (1890).

2 Dyson here lists a number of "ugly" signs of the "decadent" times, including Cromwell Road in South Kensington, the location of the Natural History Museum (built in the 1870s), which, together with other museums in the area, including the South Kensington Museum, the precursor to the Victoria and Albert Museum, was a well-known intellectual centre; Nonconformism, which referred to a wide range of religious denominations that challenged the Church of England as the representative church of Britain at this time; the Australian version of a French wine from the Burgundy region of France; "manly" New Women (much like the often effeminate Decadent "New Man"), emblematic of the time's "sexual anarchy," but as Elaine Showalter has pointed out, although both new women and Decadent men challenged their time's gender ideology, they were not allies (170); and the age's explosion of periodicals and popular journalism, to which Machen was a prolific contributor.

of the gem which you told me, surely you must have had many singular adventures in your own career?"

"Perhaps not so many as you would think; a good deal—the larger part—of my business has been as commonplace as linen-drapery. But, of course, things happen now and then. It is ten years since I have established my agency, and I suppose that a house- and estate-agent who had been in trade for an equal time could tell you some queer stories. But I must give you a sample of my experiences some night."

"Why not to-night?" said Dyson. "This evening seems to me admirably adapted for an odd chapter. Look out into the street; you can catch a view of it if you crane your neck from that chair of yours. Is it not charming? The double row of lamps growing closer in the distance, the hazy outline of the plane-tree in the square, and the lights of the hansoms swimming to and fro, gliding and vanishing; and above, the sky all clear and blue and shining. Come, let us have one of your *cent nouvelles nouvelles*."[1]

"My dear Dyson, I am delighted to amuse you." With these words Mr. Burton prefaced the

NOVEL OF THE IRON MAID.

I think the most extraordinary event which I can recall took place about five years ago. I was then still feeling my way; I had declared for business, and attended regularly at my office; but I had not succeeded in establishing a really profitable connection, and consequently I had a good deal of leisure time on my hands. I have never thought fit to trouble you with the details of my private life; they would be entirely devoid of interest. I must briefly say, however, that I had a numerous circle of acquaintance, and

---

1 A collection of licentious French tales written anonymously between 1456 and 1461. In 1884, Machen was commissioned to translate Marguerite de Navarre's (1492–1549) *Heptaméron* (1559), a collection of seventy-two tales, itself modelled on Boccaccio's fourteenth-century *Decameron* (as were the *Cent nouvelles nouvelles*) and possibly also drawing on the *Cent nouvelles nouvelles* (see, for example, De Ridder-Vignone). Although Machen's nearest and most obvious model for *The Three Impostors* is the Stevensons' *The Dynamiter* (see Appendix E1), he was likely influenced by multiple overlapping traditions of story cycles, perhaps most significantly the *Arabian Nights*. See Introduction, pp. 36–40, for details.

was never at a loss as to how to spend my evenings. I was so fortunate as to have friends in most of the ranks of the social order; there is nothing so unfortunate, to my mind, as a specialised circle, wherein a certain round of ideas is continually traversed and retraversed. I have always tried to find out new types and persons whose brains contained something fresh to me; one may chance to gain information even from the conversation of city men on an omnibus. Amongst my acquaintance I knew a young doctor, who lived in a far outlying suburb, and I used often to brave the intolerably slow railway journey to have the pleasure of listening to his talk. One night we conversed so eagerly together over our pipes and whiskey that the clock passed unnoticed; and when I glanced up, I realised with a shock that I had just five minutes in which to catch the last train. I made a dash for my hat and stick, jumped out of the house and down the steps, and tore at full speed up the street. It was no good, however; there was a shriek of the engine whistle, and I stood there at the station door and saw far on the long, dark line of the embankment a red light shine and vanish, and a porter came down and shut the door with a bang.

"How far to London?" I asked him.

"A good nine miles to Waterloo Bridge." And with that he went off.

Before me was the long suburban street, its dreary distance marked by rows of twinkling lamps, and the air was poisoned by the faint, sickly smell of burning bricks; it was not a cheerful prospect by any means, and I had to walk through nine miles of such streets, deserted as those of Pompeii.[1] I knew pretty well what direction to take, so I set out wearily, looking at the stretch of lamps vanishing in perspective; and as I walked, street after street branched off to right and left, some far-reaching, to distances that seemed endless, communicating with other systems of thoroughfare, and some mere protoplasmic streets, beginning in orderly fashion with serried two-storied houses, and ending suddenly in waste, and pits, and rubbish heaps, and fields whence the magic had departed. I have spoken of systems of thoroughfare, and I assure you that walking alone through these silent places I felt fantasy growing on me, and some glamour of the infinite. There was

---

1 An ancient Roman city buried (and thus uniquely well preserved) under ash and pumice following the catastrophic eruption of Mount Vesuvius in 79 CE; one of the best-known Roman cities explored by archaeologists.

here, I felt, an immensity as in the outer void of the universe; I passed from unknown to unknown, my way marked by lamps like stars, and on either band was an unknown world where myriads of men dwelt and slept, street leading into street, as it seemed to world's end. At first the road by which I was travelling was lined with houses of unutterable monotony, a wall of grey brick pierced by two stories of windows, drawn close to the very pavement; but by degrees I noticed an improvement, there were gardens, and these grew larger; the suburban builder began to allow himself a wider scope; and for a certain distance each flight of steps was guarded by twin lions of plaster, and scents of flowers prevailed over the fume of heated bricks. The road began to climb a hill, and looking up a side street I saw the half moon rise over plane-trees, and there on the other side was as if a white cloud had fallen, and the air around it was sweetened as with incense; it was a may-tree in full bloom. I pressed on stubbornly, listening for the wheels and the clatter of some belated hansom; but into that land of men who go to the city in the morning and return in the evening the hansom rarely enters, and I had resigned myself once more to the walk, when I suddenly became aware that some one was advancing to meet me along the sidewalk. The man was strolling rather aimlessly; and though the time and the place would have allowed an unconventional style of dress, he was vested in the ordinary frock coat, black tie, and silk hat of civilisation. We met each other under the lamp, and, as often happens in this great town, two casual passengers brought face to face found each in the other an acquaintance.

"Mr. Mathias, I think?" I said.

"Quite so. And you are Frank Burton. You know you are a man with a Christian name, so I won't apologise for my familiarity. But may I ask where you are going?"

I explained the situation to him, saying I had traversed a region as unknown to me as the darkest recesses of Africa. "I think I have only about five miles further," I concluded.

"Nonsense! you must come home with me. My house is close by; in fact, I was just taking my evening walk when we met. Come along; I dare say you will find a makeshift bed easier than a five-mile walk."

I let him take my arm and lead me along, though I was a good deal surprised at so much geniality from a man who was, after all, a mere casual club acquaintance. I suppose I had not spoken to Mr. Mathias half a dozen times; he was a man who would sit silent in an arm-chair for hours, neither reading nor smoking, but now and again moistening his lips with his tongue and smiling queerly to himself. I confess he had never attracted me, and on the whole I should have preferred to continue my walk. But he took my arm and led me up a side street, and stopped at a door in a high wall. We passed through the still, moonlit garden, beneath the black shadow of an old cedar, and into an old red-brick house with many gables. I was tired enough, and I sighed with relief as I let myself fall into a great leather arm-chair. You know the infernal grit with which they strew the sidewalk in those suburban districts; it makes walking a penance, and I felt my four-mile tramp had made me more weary than ten miles on an honest country road. I looked about the room with some curiosity; there was a shaded lamp, which threw a circle of brilliant light on a heap of papers lying on an old brass-bound secretaire[1] of the last century, but the room was all vague and shadowy, and I could only see that it was long and low, and that it was filled with indistinct objects which might be furniture. Mr. Mathias sat down in a second arm-chair, and looked about him with that odd smile of his. He was a queer-looking man, clean shaven, and white to the lips. I should think his age was something between fifty and sixty.

"Now I have got you here," he began, "I must inflict my hobby on you. You knew I was a collector? Oh yes, I have devoted many years to collecting curiosities, which I think are really curious. But we must have a better light."

He advanced into the middle of the room, and lit a lamp which hung from the ceiling; and as the bright light flashed round the wick, from every corner and space there seemed to start a horror. Great wooden frames, with complicated apparatus of ropes and pulleys, stood against the wall; a wheel of strange shape had a place beside a thing that looked like a gigantic gridiron; little tables glittered with bright steel instruments carelessly put down as if ready for use; a screw and vice loomed out, casting ugly shadows, and in another nook was a saw with cruel jagged teeth.

"Yes," said Mr. Mathias, "they are, as you suggest, instruments of torture—of torture and death. Some—many, I may say—have been used; a few are reproductions after ancient examples. Those knives were used for flaying; that frame is a rack, and a very fine specimen. Look at this; it comes from Venice. You see that sort of collar, something like a big horse-shoe? Well, the patient, let us call him, sat down quite comfortably, and the horse-shoe was neatly fitted round his neck. Then the two ends were joined with

1 Writing desk.

a silken band, and the executioner began to turn a handle connected with the band. The horse-shoe contracted very gradually as the band tightened, and the turning continued till the man was strangled. It all took place quietly, in one of those queer garrets under the leads. But these things are all European; the Orientals[1] are, of course, much more ingenious. These are the Chinese contrivances; you have heard of the 'heavy death'? It is my hobby, this sort of thing. Do you know, I often sit here, hour after hour, and meditate over the collection. I fancy I see the faces of the men who have suffered, faces lean with agony, and wet with sweats of death growing distinct out of the gloom, and I hear the echoes of their cries for mercy. But I must show you my latest acquisition. Come into the next room."

I followed Mr. Mathias out. The weariness of the walk, the late hour, and the strangeness of it all made me feel like a man in a dream; nothing would have surprised me very much. The second room was as the first, crowded with ghastly instruments; but beneath the lamp was a wooden platform, and a figure stood on it. It was a large statue of a naked woman, fashioned in green bronze, the arms were stretched out, and there was a smile on the lips; it might well have been intended for a Venus, and yet there was about the thing an evil and a deadly look.

Mr. Mathias looked at it complacently. "Quite a work of art, isn't it?" he said. "It's made of bronze, as you see, but it has long had the name of the Iron Maid. I got it from Germany, and it was only unpacked this afternoon; indeed, I have not yet had time to open the letter of advice. You see that very small knob between the breasts? Well, the victim was bound to the Maid, the knob was pressed, and the arms slowly tightened round the neck. You can imagine the result."

As Mr. Mathias talked, he patted the figure affectionately. I had turned away, for I sickened at the sight of the man and his

---

1 While the term "Oriental" is defined by the *OED* as "Originally: belonging to, occurring in, or characteristic of the countries or regions lying to the east of the Mediterranean, the ancient Roman Empire, or the early Christian world; of or relating to the Near, Middle, or Far East. Now: *esp.* of or relating to East Asia," it is not only a geographical marker in Machen's time but part of a broader "conceptual" process through which Europeans *located* "a distinction between self and other" (Ahmed 114). Machen employs the orientalist codes of his time, even if he also undermines them; see Introduction, pp. 38–40, for details.

loathsome treasure. There was a slight click, of which I took no notice; it was not much louder than the tick of a clock; and then I heard a sudden whirr, the noise of machinery in motion, and I faced round. I have never forgotten the hideous agony on Mathias's face as those relentless arms tightened about his neck; there was a wild struggle as of a beast in the toils, and then a shriek that ended in a choking groan. The whirring noise had suddenly changed into a heavy droning. I tore with all my might at the bronze arms, and strove to wrench them apart, but I could do nothing. The head had slowly bent down, and the green lips were on the lips of Mathias.

Of course, I had to attend at the inquest. The letter which had accompanied the figure was found unopened on the study table. The German firm of dealers cautioned their client to be most careful in touching the Iron Maid, as the machinery had been put in thorough working order.

For many revolving weeks Mr. Burton delighted Dyson by his agreeable conversation, diversified by anecdote, and interspersed with the narration of singular adventures. Finally, however, he vanished as suddenly as he had appeared, and on the occasion of his last visit he contrived to loot a copy of his namesake's *Anatomy*.[1] Dyson, considering this violent attack on the rights of property, and certain glaring inconsistencies in the talk of his late friend, arrived at the conclusion that his stories were fabulous, and that the Iron Maid only existed in the sphere of a decorative imagination.

THE RECLUSE OF BAYSWATER[2]

Amongst the many friends who were favoured with the occasional pleasure of Mr. Dyson's society was Mr. Edgar Russell, realist and obscure struggler, who occupied a small back room on the second floor of a house in Abingdon Grove, Notting Hill. Turning off from the main street, and walking a few paces onward, one was conscious of a certain calm, a drowsy peace, which made the feet inclined to loiter, and this was ever the atmosphere of Abingdon Grove. The houses stood a little back, with gardens where the lilac, and laburnum, and blood-red may blossomed gayly in their seasons, and there was a corner where

---

1 *The Anatomy of Melancholy* (1621), by English clergyman Robert Burton (1577–1640), explores a wide range of mental afflictions.

2 In the nineteenth century, a fashionable residential area in west London (Ayto et al.).

an older house in another street had managed to keep a back garden of real extent, a walled-in garden, whence there came a pleasant scent of greenness after the rains of early summer, where old elms held memories of the open fields, where there was yet sweet grass to walk on. The houses in Abingdon Grove belonged chiefly to the nondescript stucco period of thirty-five years ago, tolerably built, with passable accommodation for moderate incomes; they had largely passed into the state of lodgings, and cards bearing the inscription "Furnished Apartments" were not infrequent over the doors. Here, then, in a house of sufficiently good appearance, Mr. Russell had established himself; for he looked upon the traditional dirt and squalor of Grub Street[1] as a false and obsolete convention, and preferred, as he said, to live within sight of green leaves. Indeed, from his room one had a magnificent view of a long line of gardens, and a screen of poplars shut out the melancholy back premises of Wilton Street during the summer months. Mr. Russell lived chiefly on bread and tea, for his means were of the smallest; but when Dyson came to see him, he would send out the slavey[2] for six-ale,[3] and Dyson was always at liberty to smoke as much of his own tobacco as he pleased. The landlady had been so unfortunate as to have her drawing-room floor vacant for many months; a card had long proclaimed the void within; and Dyson, when he walked up the steps one evening in early autumn, had a sense that something was missing, and, looking at the fanlight, saw the appealing card had disappeared.

"You have let your first floor, have you?" he said, as he greeted Mr. Russell.

"Yes; it was taken about a fortnight ago by a lady."

"Indeed," said Dyson, always curious; "a young lady?"

"Yes; I believe so. She is a widow, and wears a thick crape veil. I have met her once or twice on the stairs and in the street; but I should not know her face."

"Well," said Dyson, when the beer had arrived, and the pipes

---

1   A term that originated in the eighteenth century and originally the name of a street in London, where, according to Samuel Johnson's *Dictionary* (1755), writers of "small histories, dictionaries, and temporary poems" lived; it came to be used (often by writers) to refer to writing produced commercially.

2   A servant or attendant.

3   "A mixture of one at fourpence a pot with one at eightpence a pot in equal proportions" (*OED*).

were in full blast, "and what have you been doing? Do you find the work getting any easier?"

"Alas!" said the young man, with an expression of great gloom, "the life is a purgatory, and all but a hell. I write, picking out my words, weighing and balancing the force of every syllable, calculating the minutest effects that language can produce, erasing and rewriting, and spending a whole evening over a page of manuscript. And then, in the morning, when I read what I have written—Well, there is nothing to be done but to throw it in the wastepaper basket, if the verso has been already written on, or to put it in the drawer if the other side happens to be clean. When I have written a phrase which undoubtedly embodies a happy turn of thought, I find it dressed up in feeble commonplace; and when the style is good, it serves only to conceal the baldness of superannuated fancies. I sweat over my work, Dyson—every finished line means so much agony. I envy the lot of the carpenter in the side street who has a craft which he understands. When he gets an order for a table he does not writhe with anguish; but if I were so unlucky as to get an order for a book, I think I should go mad."

"My dear fellow, you take it all too seriously. You should let the ink flow more readily. Above all, firmly believe, when you sit down to write, that you are an artist, and that whatever you are about is a masterpiece. Suppose ideas fail you, say, as I heard one of our most exquisite artists say, 'It's of no consequence; the ideas are all there, at the bottom of that box of cigarettes!' You, indeed, smoke tobacco, but the application is the same. Besides, you must have some happy moments; and these should be ample consolation."

"Perhaps you are right. But such moments are so few; and then there is the torture of a glorious conception matched with execution beneath the standard of the Family Story Paper. For instance, I was happy for two hours a night or two ago; I lay awake and saw visions. But then the morning!"

"What was your idea?"

"It seemed to me a splendid one: I thought of Balzac and the *Comédie Humaine*, of Zola and the Rougon-Macquart family.[1] It dawned upon me that I would write the history of a street. Every house should form a volume. I fixed upon the street, I saw each house, and read as clearly as in letters the physiology and psychology of each; the little byway stretched before me in its actual

---

1 Honoré de Balzac (1799–1850) and Émile Zola (1840–1902) wrote the multi-volume works Russell refers to. Balzac worked in the realist tradition, Zola in the naturalist tradition.

shape—a street that I know and have passed down a hundred times, with some twenty houses, prosperous and mean, and lilac bushes in purple blossom. And yet it was, at the same time, a symbol, a *via dolorosa*[1] of hopes cherished and disappointed, of years of monotonous existence without content or discontent, of tragedies and obscure sorrows; and on the door of one of those houses I saw the red stain of blood, and behind a window two shadows, blackened and faded, on the blind, as they swayed on tightened cords—the shadows of a man and a woman hanging in a vulgar gas-lit parlour. These were my fancies; but when pen touched paper they shrivelled and vanished away."

"Yes," said Dyson, "there is a lot in that. I envy you the pains of transmuting vision into reality, and, still more, I envy you the day when you will look at your bookshelf and see twenty goodly books upon the shelves—the series complete and done forever. Let me entreat you to have them bound in solid parchment, with gold lettering. It is the only real cover for a valiant book. When I look in at the windows of some choice shop, and see the bindings of Levant morocco,[2] with pretty tools and panellings, and your sweet contrasts of red and green, I say to myself, 'These are not books, but *bibelots*.'[3] A book bound so—a true book, mind you—is like a Gothic statue draped in brocade of Lyons."[4]

"Alas!" said Russell, "we need not discuss the binding—the books are not begun."

The talk went on as usual till eleven o'clock, when Dyson bade his friend good night. He knew the way downstairs, and walked

---

1 "A painful way/road" (Latin), a reference to the "way of the cross," the route Christ took on the way to his crucifixion, here used figuratively to refer to enduring very painful experiences.

2 A fine leather produced from Angora goats in the East (Levant).

3 A French term that encompasses a wide variety of objects, from trifles to priceless objects. As Janell Watson explains, "By the 1880s, the medieval French word *bibelot* (knick-knack), which in the fifteenth century designated miscellaneous household items of little value, is revived by the most elite among Parisian collectors to designate the objects most precious to them, even though the term is also used to refer to the cheapest industrial kitsch. The term is not only revived and reinvented during the nineteenth century, it is also associated with the century" (5).

4 A kind of rich fabric "with a pattern of raised figures, originally in gold or silver; in later use, any kind of stuff richly wrought or 'flowered' with a raised pattern," associated with the French city of Lyon (*OED*).

down by himself; but, greatly to his surprise, as he crossed the first-floor landing the door opened slightly, and a hand was stretched out, beckoning.

Dyson was not the man to hesitate under such circumstances. In a moment he saw himself involved in adventure; and, as he told himself, the Dysons had never disobeyed a lady's summons. Softly, then, with due regard for the lady's honour, he would have entered the room, when a low but clear voice spoke to him—

"Go downstairs and open the door and shut it again rather loudly. Then come up to me; and for Heaven's sake, walk softly."

Dyson obeyed her commands, not without some hesitation, for he was afraid of meeting the landlady or the maid on his return journey. But, walking like a cat, and making each step he trod on crack loudly, he flattered himself that he had escaped observation; and as he gained the top of the stairs the door opened wide before him, and he found himself in the lady's drawing-room, bowing awkwardly.

"Pray be seated, sir. Perhaps this chair will be the best; it was the favoured chair of my landlady's deceased husband. I would ask you to smoke, but the odour would betray me. I know my proceedings must seem to you unconventional; but I saw you arrive this evening, and I do not think you would refuse to help a woman who is so unfortunate as I am."

Mr. Dyson looked shyly at the young lady before him. She was dressed in deep mourning, but the piquant smiling face and charming hazel eyes ill accorded with the heavy garments and the mouldering surface of the crape.

"Madam," he said gallantly, "your instinct has served you well. We will not trouble, if you please, about the question of social conventions; the chivalrous gentleman knows nothing of such matters. I hope I may be privileged to serve you."

"You are very kind to me, but I knew it would be so. Alas! sir, I have had experience of life, and I am rarely mistaken. Yet man is too often so vile and so misjudging that I trembled even as I resolved to take this step, which, for all I knew, might prove to be both desperate and ruinous."

"With me you have nothing to fear," said Dyson. "I was nurtured in the faith of chivalry, and I have always endeavoured to remember the proud traditions of my race. Confide in me, then, and count upon my secrecy, and if it prove possible, you may rely on my help."

"Sir, I will not waste your time, which I am sure is valuable, by idle parleyings. Learn, then, that I am a fugitive, and in hiding here; I place myself in your power; you have but to describe my features, and I fall into the hands of my relentless enemy."

Mr. Dyson wondered for a passing instant how this could be, but he only renewed his promise of silence, repeating that he would be the embodied spirit of dark concealment.

"Good," said the lady, "the Oriental fervour[1] of your style is delightful. In the first place, I must disabuse your mind of the conviction that I am a widow. These gloomy vestments have been forced on me by strange circumstance; in plain language, I have deemed it expedient to go disguised. You have a friend, I think, in the house, Mr. Russell? He seems of a coy and retiring nature."

"Excuse me, madam," said Dyson, "he is not coy, but he is a realist; and perhaps you are aware that no Carthusian monk[2] can emulate the cloistral seclusion in which a realistic novelist loves to shroud himself. It is his way of observing human nature."

"Well, well," said the lady; "all this, though deeply interesting, is not germane to our affair. I must tell you my history."

With these words the young lady proceeded to relate the

NOVEL OF THE WHITE POWDER.

My name is Leicester; my father, Major General Wyn Leicester, a distinguished officer of artillery, succumbed five years ago to a complicated liver complaint acquired in the deadly climate of India. A year later my only brother, Francis, came home after an exceptionally brilliant career at the University, and settled down with the resolution of a hermit to master what has been well called the great legend of the law. He was a man who seemed to live in utter indifference to everything that is called pleasure; and though he was handsomer than most men, and could talk as merrily and wittily as if he were a mere vagabond, he avoided society, and shut himself up in a large room at the top of the house to make himself a lawyer. Ten hours a day of hard reading was at first his allotted portion; from the first light in the east to the late afternoon he remained shut up with his books, taking a hasty half-hour's lunch with me as if he grudged the wasting of the moments, and going out for a short walk when it began to grow dusk. I thought that such relentless application must be injurious, and tried to cajole him from the crabbed

---

1 See p. 149, note 1, on Orientalism.
2 A monk belonging to an order "founded in Dauphiné, by St. Bruno, in the year 1086, remarkable for the severity of their rule" (*OED*).

text-books, but his ardour seemed to grow rather than diminish, and his daily tale[1] of hours increased. I spoke to him seriously, suggesting some occasional relaxation, if it were but an idle afternoon with a harmless novel; but he laughed, and said that he read about feudal tenures[2] when he felt in need of amusement, and scoffed at the notion of theatres, or a month's fresh air. I confessed that he looked well, and seemed not to suffer from his labours, but I knew that such unnatural toil would take revenge at last, and I was not mistaken. A look of anxiety began to lurk about his eyes, and he seemed languid, and at last he avowed that he was no longer in perfect health; he was troubled, he said, with a sensation of dizziness, and awoke now and then of nights from fearful dreams, terrified and cold with icy sweats. "I am taking care of myself," he said, "so you must not trouble; I passed the whole of yesterday afternoon in idleness, leaning back in that comfortable chair you gave me, and scribbling nonsense on a sheet of paper. No, no; I will not overdo my work; I shall be well enough in a week or two, depend upon it."

Yet in spite of his assurances I could see that he grew no better, but rather worse; he would enter the drawing-room with a face all miserably wrinkled and despondent, and endeavour to look gayly when my eyes fell on him, and I thought such symptoms of evil omen, and was frightened sometimes at the nervous irritation of his movements, and at glances which I could not decipher. Much against his will, I prevailed on him to have medical advice, and with an ill grace he called in our old doctor.

Dr. Haberden cheered me after his examination of his patient. "There is nothing really much amiss," he said to me. "No doubt he reads too hard, and eats hastily, and then goes back again to his books in too great a hurry, and the natural consequence is some digestive trouble and a little mischief in the nervous system. But I think—I do indeed, Miss Leicester—that we shall be able to set this all right. I have written him a prescription which ought to do great things. So you have no cause for anxiety."

My brother insisted on having the prescription made up by a chemist in the neighbourhood; it was an odd, old-fashioned

---

1 Likely a typesetting error, as "tale" should read "tally."

2 A kind of land holding in medieval times based on a "reciprocal relationship between the granter of the land—such as a king or baron—and the holder or 'tenant' of the land—such as a knight or free person; the form of the land was known as a 'fief'" (Mitchell 251).

shop, devoid of the studied coquetry and calculated glitter that make so gay a show on the counters and shelves of the modern apothecary; but Francis liked the old chemist, and believed in the scrupulous purity of his drugs. The medicine was sent in due course, and I saw that my brother took it regularly after lunch and dinner. It was an innocent-looking white powder, of which a little was dissolved in a glass of cold water; I stirred it in, and it seemed to disappear, leaving the water clear and colourless. At first Francis seemed to benefit greatly; the weariness vanished from his face, and he became more cheerful than he had ever been since the time when he left school; he talked gayly of reforming himself, and avowed to me that he had wasted his time.

"I have given too many hours to law," he said, laughing; "I think you have saved me in the nick of time. Come, I shall be Lord Chancellor yet, but I must not forget life. You and I will have a holiday together before long; we will go to Paris and enjoy ourselves, and keep away from the Bibliothèque Nationale."[1]

I confessed myself delighted with the prospect.

"When shall we go?" I said. "I can start the day after to-morrow if you like."

"Ah! that is perhaps a little too soon; after all, I do not know London yet, and I suppose a man ought to give the pleasures of his own country the first choice. But we will go off together in a week or two, so try and furbish up your French. I only know law French myself, and I am afraid that wouldn't do."

We were just finishing dinner, and he quaffed off his medicine with a parade of carousal as if it had been wine from some choicest bin.

"Has it any particular taste?" I said.

"No; I should not know I was not drinking water," and he got up from his chair and began to pace up and down the room as if he were undecided as to what he should do next.

"Shall we have coffee in the drawing-room," I said; "or would you like to smoke?"

"No, I think I will take a turn; it seems a pleasant evening. Look at the afterglow; why, it is as if a great city were burning in flames, and down there between the dark houses it is raining blood fast, fast. Yes, I will go out; I may be in soon, but I shall take my key; so good night, dear, if I don't see you again."

The door slammed behind him, and I saw him walk lightly

---

1 National Library of France located in Paris.

down the street, swinging his malacca cane,[1] and I felt grateful to Dr. Haberden for such an improvement.

I believe my brother came home very late that night, but he was in a merry mood the next morning.

"I walked on without thinking where I was going," he said, "enjoying the freshness of the air, and livened by the crowds as I reached more frequented quarters. And then I met an old college friend, Orford, in the press of the pavement, and then—well, we enjoyed ourselves. I have felt what it is to be young and a man; I find I have blood in my veins, as other men have. I made an appointment with Orford for to-night; there will be a little party of us at the restaurant. Yes; I shall enjoy myself for a week or two, and hear the chimes at midnight, and then we will go for our little trip together."

Such was the transmutation of my brother's character that in a few days he became a lover of pleasure, a careless and merry idler of western pavements, a hunter out of snug restaurants, and a fine critic of fantastic dancing; he grew fat before my eyes, and said no more of Paris, for he had clearly found his paradise in London. I rejoiced, and yet wondered a little; for there was, I thought, something in his gaiety that indefinitely displeased me, though I could not have defined my feeling. But by degrees there came a change; he returned still in the cold hours of the morning, but I heard no more about his pleasures, and one morning as we sat at breakfast together I looked suddenly into his eyes and saw a stranger before me.

"O Francis!" I cried. "O Francis, Francis, what have you done?" and rending sobs cut the words short. I went weeping out of the room; for though I knew nothing, yet I knew all, and by some odd play of thought I remembered the evening when he first went abroad to prove his manhood, and the picture of the sunset sky glowed before me; the clouds like a city in burning flames, and the rain of blood. Yet I did battle with such thoughts, resolving that perhaps, after all, no great harm had been done, and in the evening at dinner I resolved to press him to fix a day for our holiday in Paris. We had talked easily enough, and my brother had just taken his medicine, which he had continued all the while. I was about to begin my topic, when the words forming in my mind vanished, and I wondered for a second what icy and intolerable weight oppressed my heart and suffocated me as with the unutterable horror of the coffin-lid nailed down on the living.

---

1 A cane or walking stick made from Malaysian palms (*OED*).

We had dined without candles; the room had slowly grown from twilight to gloom, and the walls and corners were indistinct in the shadow. But from where I sat I looked out into the street; and as I thought of what I would say to Francis, the sky began to flush and shine, as it had done on a well-remembered evening, and in the gap between two dark masses that were houses an awful pageantry of flame appeared—lurid whorls of writhed cloud, and utter depths burning, grey masses like the fume blown from a smoking city, and an evil glory blazing far above shot with tongues of more ardent fire, and below as if there were a deep pool of blood. I looked down to where my brother sat facing me, and the words were shaped on my lips, when I saw his hand resting on the table. Between the thumb and forefinger of the closed hand there was a mark, a small patch about the size of a sixpence, and somewhat of the colour of a bad bruise. Yet, by some sense I cannot define, I knew that what I saw was no bruise at all; oh! if human flesh could burn with flame, and if flame could be black as pitch, such was that before me. Without thought or fashioning of words grey horror shaped within me at the sight, and in an inner cell it was known to be a brand. For a moment the stained sky became dark as midnight, and when the light returned to me I was alone in the silent room, and soon after I heard my brother go out.

Late as it was, I put on my bonnet and went to Dr. Haberden, and in his great consulting room, ill lighted by a candle which the doctor brought in with him, with stammering lips, and a voice that would break in spite of my resolve, I told him all, from the day on which my brother began to take the medicine down to the dreadful thing I had seen scarcely half an hour before.

When I had done, the doctor looked at me for a minute with an expression of great pity on his face.

"My dear Miss Leicester," he said, "you have evidently been anxious about your brother; you have been worrying over him, I am sure. Come, now, is it not so?"

"I have certainly been anxious," I said. "For the last week or two I have not felt at ease."

"Quite so; you know, of course, what a queer thing the brain is?"

"I understand what you mean; but I was not deceived. I saw what I have told you with my own eyes."

"Yes, yes, of course. But your eyes had been staring at that very curious sunset we had to-night. That is the only explanation. You will see it in the proper light to-morrow, I am sure. But, remember, I am always ready to give any help that is in my power; do not scruple to come to me, or to send for me if you are in any distress."

I went away but little comforted, all confusion and terror and sorrow, not knowing where to turn. When my brother and I met the next day, I looked quickly at him, and noticed, with a sickening at heart, that the right hand, the hand on which I had clearly seen the patch as of a black fire, was wrapped up with a handkerchief.

"What is the matter with your hand, Francis?" I said in a steady voice.

"Nothing of consequence. I cut a finger last night, and it bled rather awkwardly. So I did it up roughly to the best of my ability."

"I will do it neatly for you, if you like."

"No, thank you, dear; this will answer very well. Suppose we have breakfast; I am quite hungry."

We sat down, and I watched him. He scarcely ate or drank at all, but tossed his meat to the dog when he thought my eyes were turned away; there was a look in his eyes that I had never yet seen, and the thought fled across my mind that it was a look that was scarcely human. I was firmly convinced that awful and incredible as was the thing I had seen the night before, yet it was no illusion, no glamour of bewildered sense, and in the course of the morning I went again to the doctor's house.

He shook his head with an air puzzled and incredulous, and seemed to reflect for a few minutes.

"And you say he still keeps up the medicine? But why? As I understand, all the symptoms he complained of have disappeared long ago; why should he go on taking the stuff when he is quite well. And, by the bye, where did he get it made up? At Sayce's? I never send any one there; the old man is getting careless. Suppose you come with me to the chemist's; I should like to have some talk with him."

We walked together to the shop; old Sayce knew Dr. Haberden, and was quite ready to give any information.

"You have been sending that in to Mr. Leicester for some weeks I think on my prescription," said the doctor, giving the old man a pencilled scrap of paper.

The chemist put on his great spectacles with trembling uncertainty, and held up the paper with a shaking hand.

"Oh, yes," he said, "I have very little of it left; it is rather an uncommon drug, and I have had it in stock some time. I must get in some more, if Mr. Leicester goes on with it."

"Kindly let me have a look at the stuff," said Haberden, and the chemist gave him a glass bottle. He took out the stopper and smelt the contents, and looked strangely at the old man. "Where did you get this?" he said, "and what is it? For one thing, Mr. Sayce, it is not what I prescribed. Yes, yes, I see the label is right enough, but I tell you this is not the drug."

"I have had it a long time," said the old man, in feeble terror; "I got it from Burbage's in the usual way. It is not prescribed often, and I have had it on the shelf for some years. You see there is very little left."

"You had better give it to me," said Haberden. "I am afraid something wrong has happened."

We went out of the shop in silence, the doctor carrying the bottle neatly wrapped in paper under his arm.

"Dr. Haberden," I said when we had walked a little way—"Dr. Haberden."

"Yes," he said, looking at me gloomily enough.

"I should like you to tell me what my brother has been taking twice a day for the last month or so."

"Frankly, Miss Leicester, I don't know. We will speak of this when we get to my house."

We walked on quickly without another word till we reached Dr. Haberden's. He asked me to sit down, and began pacing up and down the room, his face clouded over, as I could see, with no common fears.

"Well," he said at length, "this is all very strange; it is only natural that you should feel alarmed, and I must confess that my mind is far from easy. We will put aside, if you please, what you told me last night and this morning, but the fact remains that for the last few weeks Mr. Leicester has been impregnating his system with a drug which is completely unknown to me. I tell you, it is not what I ordered; and what that stuff in the bottle really is remains to be seen."

He undid the wrapper, and cautiously tilted a few grains of the white powder on to a piece of paper, and peered curiously at it.

"Yes," he said, "it is like the sulphate of quinine, as you say; it is flaky. But smell it."

He held the bottle to me, and I bent over it. It was a strange, sickly smell, vaporous and overpowering, like some strong anæsthetic.

"I shall have it analysed," said Haberden; "I have a friend who has devoted his whole life to chemistry as a science. Then we shall have something to go upon. No, no; say no more about that other matter; I cannot listen to that; and take my advice and think no more about it yourself."

That evening my brother did not go out as usual after dinner.

"I have had my fling," he said with a queer laugh, "and I must go back to my old ways. A little law will be quite a relaxation after so sharp a dose of pleasure," and he grinned to himself, and soon after went up to his room. His hand was still all bandaged.

Dr. Haberden called a few days later.

"I have no special news to give you," he said. "Chambers is out of town, so I know no more about that stuff than you do. But I should like to see Mr. Leicester if he is in."

"He is in his room," I said; "I will tell him you are here."

"No, no, I will go up to him; we will have a little quiet talk together. I dare say that we have made a good deal of fuss about very little; for, after all, whatever the white powder may be, it seems to have done him good."

The doctor went upstairs, and standing in the hall I heard his knock, and the opening and shutting of the door; and then I waited in the silent house for an hour, and the stillness grew more and more intense as the hands of the clock crept round. Then there sounded from above the noise of a door shut sharply, and the doctor was coming down the stairs. His footsteps crossed the hall, and there was a pause at the door; I drew a long, sick breath with difficulty, and saw my face white in a little mirror, and he came in and stood at the door. There was an unutterable horror shining in his eyes; he steadied himself by holding the back of a chair with one hand, and his lower lip trembled like a horse's, and he gulped and stammered unintelligible sounds before he spoke.

"I have seen that man," he began in a dry whisper. "I have been sitting in his presence for the last hour. My God! And I am alive and in my senses! I, who have dealt with death all my life, and have dabbled with the melting ruins of the earthly tabernacle.[1] But not this, oh! not this," and he covered his face with his hands as if to shut out the sight of something before him.

"Do not send for me again, Miss Leicester," he said with more composure. "I can do nothing in this house. Good-bye."

As I watched him totter down the steps, and along the pavement towards his house, it seemed to me that he had aged by ten years since the morning.

My brother remained in his room. He called out to me in a voice I hardly recognised that he was very busy, and would like his

---

1 The human body.

meals brought to his door and left there, and I gave the order to the servants. From that day it seemed as if the arbitrary conception we call time had been annihilated for me; I lived in an ever-present sense of horror, going through the routine of the house mechanically, and only speaking a few necessary words to the servants. Now and then I went out and paced the streets for an hour or two and came home again; but whether I were without or within, my spirit delayed before the closed door of the upper room, and, shuddering, waited for it to open. I have said that I scarcely reckoned time; but I suppose it must have been a fortnight after Dr. Haberden's visit that I came home from my stroll a little refreshed and lightened. The air was sweet and pleasant, and the hazy form of green leaves, floating cloudlike in the square, and the smell of blossoms, had charmed my senses, and I felt happier and walked more briskly. As I delayed a moment at the verge of the pavement, waiting for a van to pass by before crossing over to the house, I happened to look up at the windows, and instantly there was the rush and swirl of deep cold waters in my ears, and my heart leapt up, and fell down, down as into a deep hollow, and I was amazed with a dread and terror without form or shape. I stretched out a hand blindly through folds of thick darkness, from the black and shadowy valley, and held myself from falling, while the stones beneath my feet rocked and swayed and tilted, and the sense of solid things seemed to sink away from under me. I had glanced up at the window of my brother's study, and at that moment the blind was drawn aside, and something that had life stared out into the world. Nay, I cannot say I saw a face or any human likeness; a living thing, two eyes of burning flame glared at me, and they were in the midst of something as formless as my fear, the symbol and presence of all evil and all hideous corruption. I stood shuddering and quaking as with the grip of ague, sick with unspeakable agonies of fear and loathing, and for five minutes I could not summon force or motion to my limbs. When I was within the door, I ran up the stairs to my brother's room, and knocked.

"Francis, Francis," I cried, "for Heaven's sake, answer me. What is the horrible thing in your room? Cast it out, Francis; cast it from you!"

I heard a noise as of feet shuffling slowly and awkwardly, and a choking, gurgling sound, as if some one was struggling to find utterance, and then the noise of a voice, broken and stifled, and words that I could scarcely understand.

"There is nothing here," the voice said. "Pray do not disturb me. I am not very well to-day."

I turned away, horrified, and yet helpless. I could do nothing, and I wondered why Francis had lied to me, for I had seen the appearance beyond the glass too plainly to be deceived, though it was but the sight of a moment. And I sat still, conscious that there had been something else, something I had seen in the first flash of terror, before those burning eyes had looked at me. Suddenly I remembered; as I lifted my face the blind was being drawn back, and I had had an instant's glance of the thing that was moving it, and in my recollection I knew that a hideous image was engraved for ever on my brain. It was not a hand; there were no fingers that held the blind, but a black stump pushed it aside, the mouldering outline and the clumsy movement as of a beast's paw had glowed into my senses before the darkling waves of terror had overwhelmed me as I went down quick into the pit. My mind was aghast at the thought of this, and of the awful presence that dwelt with my brother in his room; I went to his door and cried to him again, but no answer came. That night one of the servants came up to me and told me in a whisper that for three days food had been regularly placed at the door and left untouched; the maid had knocked, but had received no answer; she had heard the noise of shuffling feet that I had noticed. Day after day went by, and still my brother's meals were brought to his door and left untouched; and though I knocked and called again and again, I could get no answer. The servants began to talk to me; it appeared they were as alarmed as I; the cook said that when my brother first shut himself up in his room she used to hear him come out at night and go about the house; and once, she said, the hall door had opened and closed again, but for several nights she had heard no sound. The climax came at last; it was in the dusk of the evening, and I was sitting in the darkening dreary room when a terrible shriek jarred and rang harshly out of the silence, and I heard a frightened scurry of feet dashing down the stairs. I waited, and the servant-maid staggered into the room and faced me, white and trembling.

"O Miss Helen!" she whispered; "oh! for the Lord's sake, Miss Helen, what has happened? Look at my hand, miss; look at that hand!"

I drew her to the window, and saw there was a black wet stain upon her hand.

"I do not understand you," I said. "Will you explain to me?"

"I was doing your room just now," she began. "I was turning down the bed-clothes, and all of a sudden there was something fell upon my hand, wet, and I looked up, and the ceiling was black and dripping on me."

I looked hard at her and bit my lip.

"Come with me," I said. "Bring your candle with you."

The room I slept in was beneath my brother's, and as I went in I felt I was trembling. I looked up at the ceiling, and saw a patch, all black and wet, and a dew of black drops upon it, and a pool of horrible liquor soaking into the white bed-clothes.

I ran upstairs, and knocked loudly.

"O Francis, Francis, my dear brother," I cried, "what has happened to you?"

And I listened. There was a sound of choking, and a noise like water bubbling and regurgitating, but nothing else, and I called louder, but no answer came.

In spite of what Dr. Haberden had said, I went to him; and with tears streaming down my cheeks I told him of all that had happened, and he listened to me with a face set hard and grim.

"For your father's sake," he said at last, "I will go with you, though I can do nothing."

We went out together; the streets were dark and silent, and heavy with heat and a drought of many weeks. I saw the doctor's face white under the gas-lamps, and when we reached the house his hand was shaking.

We did not hesitate, but went upstairs directly. I held the lamp, and he called out in a loud, determined voice—

"Mr. Leicester, do you hear me? I insist on seeing you. Answer me at once."

There was no answer, but we both heard that choking noise I have mentioned.

"Mr. Leicester, I am waiting for you. Open the door this instant, or I shall break it down." And he called a third time in a voice that rang and echoed from the walls—

"Mr. Leicester! For the last time I order you to open the door."

"Ah!" he said, after a pause of heavy silence, "we are wasting time here. Will you be so kind as to get me a poker, or something of the kind?"

I ran into a little room at the back where odd articles were kept, and found a heavy adze-like tool[1] that I thought might serve the doctor's purpose.

"Very good," he said, "that will do, I dare say. I give you notice, Mr. Leicester," he cried loudly at the keyhole, "that I am now about to break into your room."

---

1 An adze is an ancient axe-like tool (associated with the Stone Age) used primarily for cutting, notching, or shaping wood.

Then I heard the wrench of the adze, and the woodwork split and cracked under it; with a loud crash the door suddenly burst open, and for a moment we started back aghast at a fearful screaming cry, no human voice, but as the roar of a monster, that burst forth inarticulate and struck at us out of the darkness.

"Hold the lamp," said the doctor, and we went in and glanced quickly round the room. "There it is," said Dr. Haberden, drawing a quick breath; "look, in that corner."

I looked, and a pang of horror seized my heart as with a white-hot iron. There upon the floor was a dark and putrid mass, seething with corruption and hideous rottenness, neither liquid nor solid, but melting and changing before our eyes, and bubbling with unctuous oily bubbles like boiling pitch. And out of the midst of it shone two burning points like eyes, and I saw a writhing and stirring as of limbs, and something moved and lifted up that might have been an arm. The doctor took a step forward, raised the iron bar and struck at the burning points; he drove in the weapon, and struck again and again in a fury of loathing. At last the thing was quiet.

★ ★ ★

A week or two later, when I had to some extent recovered from the terrible shock, Dr. Haberden came to see me.

"I have sold my practice," he began, "and to-morrow I am sailing on a long voyage. I do not know whether I shall ever return to England; in all probability I shall buy a little land in California, and settle there for the remainder of my life. I have brought you this packet, which you may open and read when you feel able to do so. It contains the report of Dr. Chambers on what I submitted to him. Good-bye, Miss Leicester, good-bye."

When he was gone I opened the envelope; I could not wait, and proceeded to read the papers within. Here is the manuscript, and if you will allow me, I will read you the astounding story it contains.

"My dear Haberden," the letter began, "I have delayed inexcusably in answering your questions as to the white substance you sent me. To tell you the truth, I have hesitated for some time as to what course I should adopt, for there is a bigotry and an orthodox standard in physical science as in theology, and I knew that if I told you the truth I should offend rooted prejudices which I once held dear myself. However, I have determined to be plain with you, and first I must enter into a short personal explanation.

"You have known me, Haberden, for many years as a scientific man; you and I have often talked of our profession together, and discussed the hopeless gulf that opens before the feet of those who think to attain to truth by any means whatsoever except the beaten way of experiment and observation, in the sphere of material things. I remember the scorn with which you have spoken to me of men of science who have dabbled a little in the unseen, and have timidly hinted that perhaps the senses are not, after all, the eternal, impenetrable bounds of all knowledge, the everlasting walls beyond which no human being has ever passed. We have laughed together heartily, and I think justly, at the 'occult' follies of the day, disguised under various names—the mesmerisms, spiritualisms, materialisations, theosophies, all the rabble rant of imposture, with their machinery of poor tricks and feeble conjuring, the true back-parlour magic of shabby London streets. Yet, in spite of what I have said, I must confess to you that I am no materialist,[1] taking the word of course in its usual signification. It is now many years since I have convinced myself, convinced myself a sceptic remember, that the old iron-bound theory is utterly and entirely false. Perhaps this confession will not wound you so sharply as it would have done twenty years ago; for I think you cannot have failed to notice that for some time hypotheses have been advanced by men of pure science which are nothing less than transcendental, and I suspect that most modern chemists and biologists of repute would not hesitate to subscribe [to] the *dictum* of the old Schoolman, *Omnia exeunt in mysterium*,[2] which means, I take it, that every branch of human knowledge if traced up to its source and final principles vanishes into mystery. I need not trouble you now with a detailed account of the painful steps which led me to my conclusions; a few simple experiments suggested a doubt as to my then standpoint, and a train of thought that rose from circumstances comparatively trifling brought me far; my old conception of the universe has been swept away, and I stand in a world that seems as strange and awful to me as the endless waves of the ocean seen for the first time, shining, from a Peak in Darien.[3] Now I know that the walls of sense that

---

1 See p. 29, note 1.

2 "All things pass into mystery" (Latin). This phrase is engraved on the gravestone of Machen and his wife Dorothie Purefoy in Old Amersham cemetery (Valentine 133).

3 A reference to Keats's poem "On First Looking into Chapman's Homer," where the wonder of first reading George Chapman's translation of *Homer* is compared with the wonder likely felt by (*continued*)

seemed so impenetrable, that seemed to loom up above the heavens and to be founded below the depths, and to shut us in forevermore, are no such everlasting impassable barriers as we fancied, but thinnest and most airy veils that melt away before the seeker, and dissolve as the early mist of the morning about the brooks. I know that you never adopted the extreme materialistic position; you did not go about trying to prove a universal negative, for your logical sense withheld you from that crowning absurdity; but I am sure that you will find all that I am saying strange and repellent to your habits of thought. Yet, Haberden, what I tell you is the truth, nay, to adopt our common language, the sole and scientific truth, verified by experience; and the universe is verily more splendid and more awful than we used to dream. The whole universe, my friend, is a tremendous sacrament; a mystic, ineffable force and energy, veiled by an outward form of matter; and man, and the sun and the other stars, and the flower of the grass, and the crystal in the test-tube, are each and every one as spiritual, as material, and subject to an inner working.

"You will perhaps wonder, Haberden, whence all this tends; but I think a little thought will make it clear. You will understand that from such a standpoint the whole view of things is changed, and what we thought incredible and absurd may be possible enough. In short, we must look at legend and belief with other eyes, and be prepared to accept tales that had become mere fables. Indeed, this is no such great demand. After all, modern science will concede as much, in a hypocritical manner; you must not, it is true, believe in witchcraft, but you may credit hypnotism; ghosts are out of date, but there is a good deal to be said for the theory of telepathy. Give a superstition a Greek name, and believe in it, should almost be a proverb.

"So much for my personal explanation. You sent me, Haberden, a phial, stoppered and sealed, containing a small quantity of a flaky white powder, obtained from a chemist who has been dispensing it to one of your patients. I am not surprised to hear that this powder refused to yield any results to your analysis. It is a substance which was known to a few many hundred years ago, but which I never expected to have submitted to me from the shop of a modern

---

a *conquistador*, one of the first European colonizing explorers to see South America and the Pacific. Much like Professor Gregg's earlier reference to Columbus, the project of scientific knowledge is aligned with a colonial project, but here the "terra incognita" is not a foreign land but rather the occult figured as a foreign land.

apothecary. There seems no reason to doubt the truth of the man's tale; he no doubt got, as he says, the rather uncommon salt you prescribed from the wholesale chemist's; and it has probably remained on his shelf for twenty years, or perhaps longer. Here what we call chance and coincidence begin to work; during all these years the salt in the bottle was exposed to certain recurring variations of temperature, variations probably ranging from 40° to 80°. And, as it happens, such changes, recurring year after year at irregular intervals, and with varying degrees of intensity and duration, have constituted a process, and a process so complicated and so delicate, that I question whether modern scientific apparatus directed with the utmost precision could produce the same result. The white powder you sent me is something very different from the drug you prescribed; it is the powder from which the wine of the Sabbath, the *Vinum Sabbati*, was prepared. No doubt you have read of the Witches' Sabbath,[1] and have laughed at the tales which terrified our ancestors; the black cats, and the broomsticks, and dooms pronounced against some old woman's cow. Since I have known the truth I have often reflected that it is on the whole a happy thing that such burlesque as this is believed, for it serves to conceal much that it is better should not be known generally. However, if you care to read the appendix to Payne Knight's monograph,[2] you will find that the true Sabbath was something very different, though the writer

---

1 Dr. Chambers's report explaining the Witches' Sabbath refers specifically to Richard Payne Knight, implying it is a pagan ritual that perhaps stretches back to rituals associated with Pan and/or Bacchus.

2 The monograph by Richard Payne Knight (1751–1824), an amateur archeologist and antiquarian who was also a collector and a pagan, is likely the notorious *Worship of Priapus*, first published privately in 1786 for the Society of Dilettanti, a gentleman's club of enthusiasts interested especially in the artefacts and history of ancient Greece. The work, which includes a detailed description of the Witches' Sabbath, focuses on ancient forms of phallic worship and is accompanied by numerous plates depicting ancient artefacts associated with such worship. A new edition of the work appeared in 1865 and was reprinted in 1894. Some of its claims were incorporated into *The Symbolical Language of Ancient Art and Mythology, An Inquiry* (first published in 1818, but a new edition had recently appeared in 1892). Renewed interest in Knight's work at the end of the nineteenth century is likely due to the rise of neo-paganism and an interest in the history of religion and the comparative study of religions.

has very nicely refrained from printing all he knew. The secrets of the true Sabbath were the secrets of remote times surviving into the Middle Ages, secrets of an evil science which existed long before Aryan man entered Europe. Men and women, seduced from their homes on specious pretences, were met by beings well qualified to assume, as they did assume, the part of devils, and taken by their guides to some desolate and lonely place, known to the initiate by long tradition, and unknown to all else. Perhaps it was a cave in some bare and wind-swept hill, perhaps some inmost recess of a great forest, and there the Sabbath was held. There, in the blackest hour of night, the *Vinum Sabbati* was prepared, and this evil graal[1] was poured forth and offered to the neophytes, and they partook of an infernal sacrament; *sumentes calicem principis inferorum,*[2] as an old author well expresses it. And suddenly, each one that had drunk found himself attended by a companion, a shape of glamour and unearthly allurement, beckoning him apart, to share in joys more exquisite, more piercing than the thrill of any dream, to the consummation of the marriage of the Sabbath. It is hard to write of such things as these, and chiefly because that shape that allured with loveliness was no hallucination, but, awful as it is to express, the man himself. By the power of that Sabbath wine, a few grains of white powder thrown into a glass of water, the house of life was riven asunder and the human trinity dissolved, and the worm which never dies,[3] that which lies sleeping within us all, was made tangible and an external thing, and clothed with a garment of flesh. And then, in the hour of midnight, the primal fall was repeated and re-presented, and the awful thing veiled in the mythos of the Tree in the Garden was done anew. Such was the *nuptiæ Sabbati.*[4]

"I prefer to say no more; you, Haberden, know as well as I do that the most trivial laws of life are not to be broken with impunity; and for so terrible an act as this, in which the very inmost place of the temple was broken open and defiled, a terrible

---

1 Middle English variation of "grail," meaning a platter or cup (*OED*). The "evil graal" above is in contrast with the famous "Holy Grail" of Arthurian legend.
2 Latin phrase, likely invented by Machen, meaning "taking from the chalice of the prince of the shades below" (Jones, *Horror* 501–02).
3 The worm of corruption referred to in the Bible (as in, for example, Mark 9:48: "Where their worm dieth not, and the fire is not quenched").
4 The marriage of the Witches' Sabbath; in the ritual described above, humans "marry" devils.

vengeance followed. What began with corruption ended also with corruption."

Underneath is the following in Dr. Haberden's writing:—

"The whole of the above is unfortunately strictly and entirely true. Your brother confessed all to me on that morning when I saw him in his room. My attention was first attracted to the bandaged hand, and I forced him to show it me. What I saw made me, a medical man of many years standing, grow sick with loathing, and the story I was forced to listen to was infinitely more frightful than I could have believed possible. It has tempted me to doubt the Eternal Goodness which can permit nature to offer such hideous possibilities; and if you had not with your own eyes seen the end, I should have said to you—disbelieve it all. I have not, I think, many more weeks to live, but you are young, and may forget all this.

JOSEPH HABERDEN, M.D."

In the course of two or three months I heard that Dr. Haberden had died at sea shortly after the ship left England.

Miss Leicester ceased speaking, and looked pathetically at Dyson, who could not refrain from exhibiting some symptoms of uneasiness.

He stuttered out some broken phrases expressive of his deep interest in her extraordinary history, and then said with a better grace—

"But, pardon me, Miss Leicester, I understood you were in some difficulty. You were kind enough to ask me to assist you in some way."

"Ah," she said, "I had forgotten that; my own present trouble seems of such little consequence in comparison with what I have told you. But as you are so good to me, I will go on. You will scarcely believe it, but I found that certain persons suspected, or rather pretended to suspect, that I had murdered my brother. These persons were relatives of mine, and their motives were extremely sordid ones; but I actually found myself subject to the shameful indignity of being watched. Yes, sir, my steps were dogged when I went abroad, and at home I found myself exposed to constant if artful observation. With my high spirit this was more than I could brook, and I resolved to set my wits to work and elude the persons who were shadowing me. I was so fortunate as to succeed; I assumed this disguise, and for some time have lain snug and unsuspected. But of late I have reason to believe that the pursuer is on my track; unless I am greatly deceived, I saw yesterday the detective who is charged with the odious duty of observing my movements. You, sir, are watchful and keen-sighted; tell me, did you see any one lurking about this evening?"

"I hardly think so," said Dyson, "but perhaps you would give me some description of the detective in question."

"Certainly; he is a youngish man, dark, with dark whiskers. He has adopted spectacles of large size in the hope of disguising himself effectually, but he cannot disguise his uneasy manner, and the quick, nervous glances he casts to right and left."

This piece of description was the last straw for the unhappy Dyson, who was foaming with impatience to get out of the house, and would gladly have sworn eighteenth-century oaths, if propriety had not frowned on such a course.

"Excuse me, Miss Leicester," he said with cold politeness, "I cannot assist you."

"Ah," she said sadly, "I have offended you in some way. Tell me what I have done, and I will ask you to forgive me."

"You are mistaken," said Dyson, grabbing his hat, but speaking with some difficulty; "you have done nothing. But, as I say, I cannot help you. Perhaps," he added, with some tinge of sarcasm, "my friend Russell might be of service."

"Thank you," she replied; "I will try him," and the lady went off into a shriek of laughter, which filled up Mr. Dyson's cup of scandal and confusion.

He left the house shortly afterwards, and had the peculiar delight of a five-mile walk, through streets which slowly changed from black to grey, and from grey to shining passages of glory for the sun to brighten. Here and there he met or overtook strayed revellers, but he reflected that no one could have spent the night in a more futile fashion than himself; and when he reached his home he had made resolves for reformation. He decided that he would abjure all Milesian and Arabian methods[1] of entertainment, and subscribe to Mudie's[2] for a regular supply of mild and innocuous romance.

---

1 Milesian: pertaining to "an erotic short story of a type produced by ancient Greek and Roman novelists" (*OED*); Arabian: the method of *The Arabian Nights* (see Introduction, pp. 36–40).

2 Popular circulating library, started by Charles Edward Mudie (1818–90), that upheld strict Evangelical standards and offered only family-friendly fare (see Altick, esp. 295–96).

STRANGE OCCURRENCE IN CLERKENWELL[1]

Mr. Dyson had inhabited for some years a couple of rooms in a moderately quiet street in Bloomsbury, where, as he somewhat pompously expressed it, he held his finger on the pulse of life without being deafened with the thousand rumours of the main arteries of London. It was to him a source of peculiar, if esoteric, gratification that from the adjacent corner of Tottenham Court Road a hundred lines of omnibuses went to the four quarters of the town; he would dilate on the facilities for visiting Dalston, and dwell on the admirable line that knew extremest Ealing and the streets beyond Whitechapel. His rooms, which had been originally "furnished apartments," he had gradually purged of their more peccant parts; and though one would not find here the glowing splendours of his old chambers in the street off the Strand, there was something of severe grace about the appointments which did credit to his taste. The rugs were old, and of the true faded beauty; the etchings, nearly all of them proofs printed by the artist, made a good show with broad white margins and black frames, and there was no spurious black oak. Indeed, there was but little furniture of any kind: a plain and honest table, square and sturdy, stood in one corner; a seventeenth-century settle fronted the hearth; and two wooden elbow-chairs, and a bookshelf of the Empire made up the equipment, with an exception worthy of note. For Dyson cared for none of these things, his place was at his own bureau, a quaint old piece of lacquered-work, at which he would sit for hour after hour, with his back to the room, engaged in the desperate pursuit of literature, or, as he termed his profession, the chase of the phrase. The neat array of pigeon-holes and drawers teemed and overflowed with manuscript and note-books, the experiments and efforts of many years; and the inner well, a vast and cavernous receptacle, was stuffed with accumulated ideas. Dyson was a craftsman who loved all the detail and the technique of his work intensely; and if, as has been hinted, he deluded himself a little with the name of artist, yet his amusements were eminently harmless, and, so far as can be ascertained, he (or the publishers) had chosen the good part of not tiring the world with printed matter.

Here, then, Dyson would shut himself up with his fancies, experimenting with words, and striving, as his friend the

---

1 District in central London that in the nineteenth century had a "reputation as a centre for radical dissent" (Ayto et al.).

recluse of Bayswater strove, with the almost invincible problem of style, but always with a fine confidence, extremely different from the chronic depression of the realist. He had been almost continuously at work on some scheme that struck him as well-nigh magical in its possibilities since the night of his adventure with the ingenious tenant of the first floor in Abingdon Grove; and as he laid down the pen with a glow of triumph, he reflected that he had not viewed the streets for five days in succession. With all the enthusiasm of his accomplished labour still working in his brain, he put away his papers and went out, pacing the pavement at first in that rare mood of exultation which finds in every stone upon the way the possibilities of a masterpiece. It was growing late, and the autumn evening was drawing to a close amidst veils of haze and mist, and in the stilled air the voices, and the roaring traffic, and incessant feet seemed to Dyson like the noise upon the stage when all the house is silent. In the square the leaves rippled down as quick as summer rain, and the street beyond was beginning to flare with the lights in the butcher's shops and the vivid illumination of the green-grocer. It was a Saturday night, and the swarming populations of the slums were turning out in force; the battered women in rusty black had begun to paw the lumps of cagmag,[1] and others gloated over unwholesome cabbages, and there was a brisk demand for four-ale.[2] Dyson passed through these night-fires with some relief; he loved to meditate, but his thoughts were not as De Quincey's[3] after his dose; he cared not two straws whether onions were dear or cheap, and would not have exulted if meat had fallen to twopence a pound. Absorbed in the wilderness of the tale he had been writing, weighing nicely the points of plot and construction, relishing the recollection of this and that happy phrase, and dreading failure here and there, he left the rush and the whistle of the gas-flares behind him, and began to touch upon pavements more deserted.

---

1 Unwholesome or decaying meat (*OED*).

2 See p. 141, note 1, above.

3 Thomas De Quincey's (1785–1859) *Confessions of an English Opium-Eater* (1821), an autobiographical account of the author's early life and opium addiction. The specific part Dyson appears to be referring to here is the following: "If wages were a little higher or expected to be so, or the quartern loaf a little lower, or it was reported that onions and butter were expected to fall, I was glad; yet, if the contrary were true, I drew from opium some means of consoling myself" (98).

He had turned, without taking note, to the northward, and was passing through an ancient fallen street, where now notices of floors and offices to let hung out, but still about it there was the grace and the stiffness of the Age of Wigs—a broad roadway, a broad pavement, and on each side a grave line of houses with long and narrow windows flush with the walls, all of mellowed brickwork. Dyson walked with quick steps, as he resolved that short work must be made of a certain episode; but he was in that happy humour of invention, and another chapter rose in the inner chamber of his brain, and he dwelt on the circumstances he was to write down with curious pleasure. It was charming to have the quiet streets to walk in, and in his thought he made a whole district the cabinet of his studies, and vowed he would come again. Heedless of his course, he struck off to the east again, and soon found himself involved in a squalid network of grey two-storied houses, and then in the waste void and elements of brickwork, the passages and unmade roads behind great factory walls, encumbered with the refuse of the neighborhood, forlorn, ill-lighted, and desperate. A brief turn, and there rose before him the unexpected, a hill suddenly lifted from the level ground, its steep ascent marked by the lighted lamps, and eager as an explorer, Dyson found his way to the place, wondering where his crooked paths had brought him. Here all was again decorous, but hideous in the extreme. The builder, some one lost in the deep gloom of the early 'twenties, had conceived the idea of twin villas in grey brick, shaped in a manner to recall the outlines of the Parthenon,[1] each with its classic form broadly marked with raised bands of stucco. The name of the street was all strange, and for a further surprise the top of the hill was crowned with an irregular plot of grass and fading trees, called a square, and here again the Parthenon-motive had persisted. Beyond, the streets were curious, wild in their irregularities, here a row of sordid, dingy dwellings, dirty and disreputable in appearance, and there, without warning, stood a house, genteel and prim, with wire blinds and brazen knocker, as clean and trim as if it had been the doctor's house in some benighted little country town. These surprises and discoveries began to exhaust Dyson, and he hailed with delight the blazing windows of a public-house, and went in with the intention of testing the beverage provided for the dwellers in this region, as remote as Libya and Pamphylia

---

1 Ancient Greek temple to the goddess Athena, in Athens, emblematic of Greek architecture, here imitated by a nineteenth-century, presumably London-based, builder.

and the parts about Mesopotamia.[1] The babble of voices from within warned him that he was about to assist at the true parliament of the London workman, and he looked about him for that more retired entrance called private. When he had settled himself on an exiguous bench, and had ordered some beer, he began to listen to the jangling talk in the public bar beyond; it was a senseless argument, alternately furious and maudlin, with appeals to Bill and Tom, and mediæval survivals of speech,[2] words that Chaucer wrote belched out with zeal and relish, and the din of pots jerked down and coppers rapped smartly on the zinc counter made a thorough bass for it all. Dyson was calmly smoking his pipe between the sips of beer, when an indefinite-looking figure slid rather than walked into the compartment. The man started violently when he saw Dyson placidly sitting in the corner, and glanced keenly about him. He seemed to be on wires, controlled by some electric machine, for he almost bolted out of the door when the barman asked with what he could serve him, and his hand shivered as he took the glass. Dyson inspected him with a little curiosity. He was muffled up almost to the lips, and a soft felt hat was drawn down over his eyes; he looked as if he shrank from every glance, and a more raucous voice suddenly uplifted in the public bar seemed to find in him a sympathy that made him shake and quiver like a jelly. It was pitiable to see any one so thrilled with nervousness, and Dyson was about to address some trivial remark of casual inquiry to the man, when another person came into the compartment, and, laying a hand on his arm, muttered something in an undertone, and vanished as he came. But

---

1 As with earlier references to Africa, here a poor area of London is framed as foreign, remote both in place and time, compared with Pamphylia, an ancient area in what is now southern Turkey, whose name derives from the Greek for "all races," and Mesopotamia, sometimes called the "cradle of civilization," an ancient region (in what is now Iraq) where archaeologists discovered the remnants of the world's earliest cities and earliest forms of writing (cuneiform, mentioned previously).

2 As noted on p. 10, note 1, Machen employs the term "survivals" in much the same way as it was employed by E.B. Tylor, who used it to refer to "processes, customs, opinions, and so forth, which have been carried on by force of habit into a new state of society different from that in which they had their original home, and they thus remain as proofs and examples of an older condition of culture out of which a newer has been evolved" (Appendix D1, p. 232).

Dyson had recognised him as the smooth-tongued and smooth-shaven Burton, who had displayed so sumptuous a gift in lying; and yet he thought little of it, for his whole faculty of observation was absorbed in the lamentable and yet grotesque spectacle before him. At the first touch of the hand on his arm the unfortunate man had wheeled round as if spun on a pivot, and shrank back with a low, piteous cry, as if some dumb beast were caught in the toils. The blood fled away from the wretch's face, and the skin became grey as if a shadow of death had passed in the air and fallen on it, and Dyson caught a choking whisper—

"Mr. Davies! For God's sake, have pity on me, Mr. Davies. On my oath, I say—" and his voice sank to silence as he heard the message, and strove in vain to bite his lip, and summon up to his aid some tinge of manhood. He stood there a moment, wavering as the leaves of an aspen, and then he was gone out into the street, as Dyson thought silently, with his doom upon his head. He had not been gone a minute when it suddenly flashed into Dyson's mind that he knew the man; it was undoubtedly the young man with spectacles for whom so many ingenious persons were searching; the spectacles indeed were missing, but the pale face, the dark whiskers, and the timid glances were enough to identify him. Dyson saw at once that by a succession of hazards he had unawares hit upon the scent of some desperate conspiracy, wavering as the track of a loathsome snake in and out of the highways and byways of the London cosmos; the truth was instantly pictured before him, and he divined that all unconscious and unheeding he had been privileged to see the shadows of hidden forms, chasing and hurrying, and grasping and vanishing across the bright curtain of common life, soundless and silent, or only babbling fables and pretences. For him in an instant the jargoning of voices, the garish splendour, and all the vulgar tumult of the public-house became part of magic; for here before his eyes a scene in this grim mystery play had been enacted, and he had seen human flesh grow grey with a palsy of fear; the very hell of cowardice and terror had gaped wide within an arm's-breadth. In the midst of these reflections the barman came up and stared at him as if to hint that he had exhausted his right to take his ease, and Dyson bought another lease of the seat by an order for more beer. As he pondered the brief glimpse of tragedy, he recollected that with his first start of haunted fear the young man with whiskers had drawn his hand swiftly from his great coat pocket, and that he had heard something fall to the ground; and pretending to have dropped his pipe, Dyson began to grope in the corner, searching with his fingers. He touched something and drew it gently to him, and with one brief glance, as he put it quietly in his pocket, he saw it was a little old-fashioned notebook, bound in faded green morocco.

He drank down his beer at a gulp, and left the place, overjoyed at his fortunate discovery, and busy with conjecture as to the possible importance of the find. By turns he dreaded to find perhaps mere blank leaves, or the laboured follies of a betting-book, but the faded morocco cover seemed to promise better things, and hint at mysteries. He piloted himself with no little difficulty out of the sour and squalid quarter he had entered with a light heart, and emerging at Gray's Inn Road, struck off down Guilford Street, and hastened home, only anxious for a lighted candle and solitude.

Dyson sat down at his bureau, and placed the little book before him; it was an effort to open the leaves and dare disappointment. But in desperation at last he laid his finger between the pages at haphazard, and rejoiced to see a compact range of writing with a margin, and as it chanced, three words caught his glance and stood out apart from the mass. Dyson read

'the Gold Tiberius,'

and his face flushed with fortune and the lust of the hunter.

He turned at once to the first leaf of the pocket-book, and proceeded to read with rapt interest the

HISTORY OF THE YOUNG MAN WITH SPECTACLES.

From the filthy and obscure lodging, situated, I verily believe, in one of the foulest slums of Clerkenwell, I indite this history of a life which, daily threatened, cannot last for very much longer. Every day—nay, every hour, I know too well my enemies are drawing their nets closer about me; even now I am condemned to be a close prisoner in my squalid room, and I know that when I go out I shall go to my destruction. This history, if it chance to fall into good hands, may, perhaps, be of service in warning young men of the dangers and pitfalls that most surely must accompany any deviation from the ways of rectitude.

My name is Joseph Walters. When I came of age I found myself in possession of a small but sufficient income, and I determined that I would devote my life to scholarship. I do not mean the scholarship of these days; I had no intention of associating myself with men whose lives are spent in the unspeakably degrading occupation of "editing" classics, befouling the fair margins of the fairest books with idle and superfluous annotation, and doing their utmost to give a lasting disgust of all that is beautiful. An abbey church turned to the base use of a stable or a bakehouse is a sorry sight; but more pitiable still is a masterpiece spluttered over with the commentator's pen, and his hideous mark "cf."[1]

For my part, I chose the glorious career of scholar in its ancient sense; I longed to possess encyclopædic learning, to grow old amongst books, to distil day by day, and year after year, the inmost sweetness of all worthy writings. I was not rich enough to collect a library, and I was therefore forced to betake myself to the Reading-Room of the British Museum.[2]

O dim, far-lifted, and mighty dome, Mecca of many minds, mausoleum of many hopes, sad house where all desires fail! For there men enter in with hearts uplifted, and dreaming minds, seeing in those exalted stairs a ladder to fame, in that pompous portico the gate of knowledge, and going in, find but vain vanity, and all but in vain. There, when the long streets are ringing, is silence, there eternal twilight, and the odour of heaviness. But there the blood flows thin and cold, and the brain burns adust; there is the hunt of shadows, and the chase of embattled phantoms; a striving against ghosts, and a war that has no victory. O dome, tomb of the quick! surely in thy galleries, where no reverberant voice can call, sighs whisper ever, and mutterings of dead hopes; and there men's souls mount like moths towards the flame, and fall scorched and blackened beneath thee, O dim, far-lifted, and mighty dome!

Bitterly do I now regret the day when I took my place at a desk for the first time, and began my studies. I had not been an *habitué*[3] of the place for many months, when I became acquainted with a serene and benevolent gentleman, a man somewhat past

---

1 A note used to invite a reader to compare (from the Latin *confer*).

2 Built based on a design by Sydney Smirke (1798–1877), the Reading Room first opened in 1857. Inspired by the domed Pantheon in Rome, the 42.6-metre-diameter room sat in the central courtyard of the Museum building and became a world-famous attraction. The British Museum, of which the Reading Room became a part, had been founded in 1753 and opened in 1759; it contained treasures of art and science from all over the world, including some famous artefacts stolen by the British, such as the famous Rosetta Stone and the Elgin Marbles.

3 See p. 91, note 1.

middle age, who nearly always occupied a desk next to mine. In the Reading-Room it takes little to make an acquaintance, a casual offer of assistance, a hint as to the search in the catalogue, and the ordinary politeness of men who constantly sit near each other; it was thus I came to know the man calling himself Dr. Lipsius. By degrees I grew to look for his presence, and to miss him when he was away, as was sometimes the case, and so a friendship sprang up between us. His immense range of learning was placed freely at my service; he would often astonish me by the way in which he would sketch out in a few minutes the bibliography of a given subject, and before long I had confided to him my ambitions.

"Ah," he said, "you should have been a German. I was like that myself when I was a boy. It is a wonderful resolve, an infinite career. I will know all things; yes, it is a device indeed. But it means this—a life of labour without end, and a desire unsatisfied at last. The scholar has to die, and die saying, 'I know very little!'"

Gradually, by speeches such as these, Lipsius seduced me: he would praise the career, and at the same time hint that it was as hopeless as the search for the philosopher's stone, and so by artful suggestions, insinuated with infinite address, he by degrees succeeded in undermining all my principles. "After all," he used to say, "the greatest of all sciences, the key to all knowledge, is the science and art of pleasure. Rabelais[1] was perhaps the greatest of all the encyclopædic scholars; and he, as you know, wrote the most remarkable book that has ever been written. And what does he teach men in this book? Surely the joy of living. I need not remind you of the words, suppressed in most of the editions, the key of all the Rabelaisian mythology, of all the enigmas of his grand philosophy, *Vivez joyeux*.[2] There you have all his learning; his work is the institutes of pleasure as the fine art; the finest art there is; the art of all arts. Rabelais had all science, but he had all life too. And we have gone a long way since his time. You are enlightened, I think; you do not consider all the petty rules and by-laws that a corrupt society has made for its own selfish convenience as the immutable decrees of the eternal."

---

1 François Rabelais (1493–c. 1553), French humanist and satirist, author of a series of fictional works consisting of five novels that together would come to be known as *The Life of Gargantua and Pantagruel* (1532–64). Machen admired the series greatly, and Lipsius above refers to it as "the most remarkable book that has ever been written."

2 "Live joyfully" or "live in good cheer" (French).

Such were the doctrines that he preached; and it was by such insidious arguments, line upon line, here a little and there a little, that he at last succeeded in making me a man at war with the whole social system. I used to long for some opportunity to break the chains and to live a free life, to be my own rule and measure. I viewed existence with the eyes of a pagan,[1] and Lipsius understood to perfection the art of stimulating the natural inclinations of a young man hitherto a hermit. As I gazed up at the great dome I saw it flushed with the flames and colours of a world of enticement, unknown to me, my imagination played me a thousand wanton tricks, and the forbidden drew me as surely as a loadstone draws on iron. At last my resolution was taken, and I boldly asked Lipsius to be my guide.

He told me to leave the Museum at my usual hour, halfpast four, to walk slowly along the northern pavement of Great Russell Street, and to wait at the corner of the street till I was addressed, and then to obey in all things the instructions of the person who came up to me. I carried out these directions, and stood at the corner looking about me anxiously, my heart beating fast, and my breath coming in gasps. I waited there for some time, and had begun to fear I had been made the object of a joke, when I suddenly became conscious of a gentleman who was looking at me with evident amusement from the opposite pavement of Tottenham Court Road. He came over, and raising his hat, politely begged me to follow him, and I did so without a word, wondering where we were going, and what was to happen. I was taken to a house of quiet and respectable aspect in a street lying to the north of Oxford Street, and my guide rang the bell. A servant showed us into a large room, quietly furnished, on the ground floor. We sat there in silence for some time, and I noticed that the furniture, though unpretending, was extremely valuable. There

---

1 The revival of paganism (also called New Paganism or neo-paganism) at the British *fin de siècle* was strongly associated with Decadence, as Denis Denisoff has shown. Although the new paganism refers to a "loose agglomeration of religious phenomena" (433) that is not easily defined, for the Decadents it frequently involved "sensual nature worship" (442), "deindividuation" (441) or the surrendering of the self into a larger collective (as in the initiation of the man with spectacles), the abandoning of belief in Truth (associated with monotheistic religions) for the multiplicities of truths associated with a polytheistic religion (434), and rebellion against normative sexuality and modes of living. In Machen, paganism is often tinged with horror.

were large oak-presses, two book-cases of extreme elegance, and in one corner a carved chest which must have been mediæval. Presently Dr. Lipsius came in and welcomed me with his usual manner, and after some desultory conversation my guide left the room. Then an elderly man dropped in and began talking to Lipsius, and from their conversation I understood that my friend was a dealer in antiques; they spoke of the Hittite seal,[1] and of the prospects of further discoveries, and later, when two or three more persons had joined us, there was an argument as to the possibility of a systematic exploration of the pre-Celtic monuments in England.[2] I was, in fact, present at an archæological reception of an informal kind; and at nine o'clock, when the antiquaries were gone, I stared at Lipsius in a manner that showed I was puzzled, and sought an explanation.

"Now," he said, "we will go upstairs."

As we passed up the stairs, Lipsius lighting the way with a hand-lamp, I heard the sound of a jarring lock and bolts and bars shot on at the front door. My guide drew back a baize door and we went down a passage, and I began to hear odd sounds, a noise of curious mirth; then he pushed me through a second door, and my initiation began. I cannot write down what I witnessed that night; I cannot bear to recall what went on in those secret rooms fast shuttered and curtained so that no light should escape into the quiet street; they gave me red wine to drink, and a woman told me as I sipped it that it was wine of the Red Jar that Avallaunius had made.[3] Another asked me how I liked the

---

1 Artefact associated with the Hittite empire established between 1400 and 1200 BCE in the ancient Middle East that once covered parts of what are today Turkey and Syria. Victorian interest in the Hittites was spurred by the discovery of ancient seals that contained different forms of writing (hieroglyph and cuneiform).

2 The interest in prehistoric monuments (such as the well-known Stonehenge) signals an interest in the ancient races that first inhabited Britain, what Machen calls the "little people." See Introduction, p. 21, for more information.

3 Avallaunius is a name likely invented by Machen that Romanizes Avalon, "the capital of King Arthur's Court of faerie and enchantment" (Machen, *Notes and Queries*) and links it to earlier ancient Roman pagan rituals; here it refers to an ancient wine of pagan rituals that is being recreated by the secret society into which the man with spectacles is being initiated, and it marks the kind of historical layering or simultaneity that Machen explores

wine of the Fauns,[1] and I heard a dozen fantastic names, while the stuff boiled in my veins, and stirred, I think, something that had slept within me from the moment I was born. It seemed as if my self-consciousness deserted me; I was no longer a thinking agent, but at once subject and object; I mingled in the horrible sport, and watched the mystery of the Greek groves and fountains enacted before me, saw the reeling dance and heard the music calling as I sat beside my mate, and yet I was outside it all, and viewed my own part an idle spectator. Thus with strange rites they made me drink the cup, and when I woke up in the morning I was one of them, and had sworn to be faithful. At first I was shown the enticing side of things; I was bidden to enjoy myself and care for nothing but pleasure, and Lipsius himself indicated to me as the acutest enjoyment the spectacle of the terrors of the unfortunate persons who were from time to time decoyed into the evil house. But after a time it was pointed out to me that I must take my share in the work, and so I found myself compelled to be in my turn a seducer; and thus it is on my conscience that I have led many to the depths of the pit.

One day Lipsius summoned me to his private room, and told me that he had a difficult task to give me. He unlocked a drawer and gave me a sheet of type-written paper, and bade me read it. It was without place, or date, or signature, and ran as follows:—

Mr. James Headley, F.S.A., will receive from his agent in Armenia, on the 12th inst., a unique coin, the gold Tiberius. It bears on the reverse a faun with the legend VICTORIA. It is believed that this coin is of immense value. Mr. Headley will come up to town to show the coin to his friend, Professor Memys, of Chenies Street, Oxford Street, on some date between the 13th and the 18th.

Dr. Lipsius chuckled at my face of blank surprise when I laid down this singular communication.

"You will have a good chance of showing your discretion," he said. "This is not a common case; it requires great management

---

repeatedly. Avallaunius appears in at least two other Machen works, *The Great God Pan* (1894) and *The Hill of Dreams* (1907). It was also the name of the first journal of the Arthur Machen Society (1987–97).

1 See p. 63, note 1.

and infinite tact. I am sure I wish I had a Panurge[1] in my service, but we will see what you can do."

"But is it not a joke?" I asked him. "How can you know—or rather, how can this correspondent of yours know—that a coin has been despatched from Armenia to Mr. Headley? And how is it possible to fix the period in which Mr. Headley will take it into his head to come up to town? It seems to me a lot of guess work."

"My dear Mr. Walters," he replied, "we do not deal in guess work here. It would bore you if I went into all these little details, the cogs and wheels, if I may say so, which move the machine. Don't you think it is much more amusing to sit in front of the house and be astonished than to be behind the scenes and see the mechanism? Better tremble at the thunder, believe me, than see the man rolling the cannon ball. But, after all, you needn't bother about the how and why; you have your share to do. Of course, I shall give you full instructions, but a great deal depends on the way the thing is carried out. I have often heard very young men maintain that style is everything in literature, and I can assure you that the same maxim holds good in our far more delicate profession. With us style is absolutely everything,[2] and that is why we have friends like yourself."

I went away in some perturbation; he had no doubt designedly left everything in mystery, and I did not know what part I should have to play. Though I had assisted at scenes of hideous revelry, I was not yet dead to all echo of human feeling, and I trembled lest I should receive the order to be Mr. Headley's executioner.

A week later, it was on the sixteenth of the month, Dr. Lipsius made me a sign to come into his room.

"It is for to-night," he began. "Please to attend carefully to what I am going to say, Mr. Walters, and on peril of your life, for it is a dangerous matter,—on peril of your life, I say, follow these instructions to the letter. You understand? Well, to-night at about half-past seven, you will stroll quietly up the Hampstead Road till you come to Vincent Street. Turn down here and walk along, taking the third turning to your right, which is Lambert Terrace. Then follow the terrace, cross the road, and go along

---

1 A trickster-figure character in Rabelais's *Pantagruel* and subsequent books.

2 Reference to the mechanism or "special effects" behind the scenes at the theatre or music hall. Lipsius and his crew clearly align themselves with performance and the cult of artifice. For more on the cult of artifice, see Introduction, pp. 18–26, and Appendix C.

Hertford Street, and so into Lillington Square. The second turning you will come to in the square is called Sheen Street; but in reality it is more a passage between blank walls than a street. Whatever you do, take care to be at the corner of this street at eight o'clock precisely. You will walk along it, and just at the bend, where you lose sight of the square, you will find an old gentleman with white beard and whiskers. He will in all probability be abusing a cabman for having brought him to Sheen Street instead of Chenies Street. You will go up to him quietly and offer your services; he will tell you where he wants to go, and you will be so courteous as to offer to show him the way. I may say that Professor Memys moved into Chenies Street a month ago; thus Mr. Headley has never been to see him there, and, moreover, he is very short-sighted, and knows little of the topography of London. Indeed, he has quite lived the life of a learned hermit at Audley Hall.

"Well, need I say more to a man of your intelligence? You will bring him to this house, he will ring the bell, and a servant in quiet livery will let him in. Then your work will be done, and I am sure done well. You will leave Mr. Headley at the door, and simply continue your walk, and I shall hope to see you the next day. I really don't think there is anything more I can tell you."

These minute instructions I took care to carry out to the letter. I confess that I walked up the Tottenham Court Road by no means blindly, but with an uneasy sense that I was coming to a decisive point in my life. The noise and rumour of the crowded pavements were to me but dumb-show; I revolved again and again in ceaseless iteration the task that had been laid on me, and I questioned myself as to the possible results. As I got near the point of turning, I asked myself whether danger were not about my steps; the cold thought struck me that I was suspected and observed, and every chance foot-passenger who gave me a second glance seemed to me an officer of police. My time was running out, the sky had darkened, and I hesitated, half resolved to go no farther, but to abandon Lipsius and his friends forever. I had almost determined to take this course, when the conviction suddenly came to me that the whole thing was a gigantic joke, a fabrication of rank improbability. Who could have procured the information about the Armenian agent? I asked myself. By what means could Lipsius have known the particular day and the very train that Mr. Headley was to take? how engage him to enter one special cab amongst the dozens waiting at Paddington? I vowed it a mere Milesian tale,[1] and went forward merrily, turned down Vincent Street, and threaded out the route that Lipsius had so carefully impressed upon me. The various streets he had named were all places of silence and an oppressive cheap gentility; it was dark, and I felt alone in the musty squares and crescents, where people pattered by at intervals, and the shadows were growing blacker. I entered Sheen Street, and found it, as Lipsius had said, more a passage than a street; it was a byway, on one side a low wall and neglected gardens, and grim backs of a line of houses, and on the other a timberyard. I turned the corner, and lost sight of the square, and then, to my astonishment, I saw the scene of which I had been told. A hansom cab had come to a stop beside the pavement, and an old man, carrying a handbag, was fiercely abusing the cabman, who sat on his perch the image of bewilderment.

"Yes, but I'm sure you said Sheen Street, and that's where I brought you," I heard him saying as I came up, and the old gentleman boiled in a fury, and threatened police and suits at law.

The sight gave me a shock, and in an instant I resolved to go through with it. I strolled on, and without noticing the cabman, lifted my hat politely to old Mr. Headley.

"Pardon me, sir," I said, "but is there any difficulty? I see you are a traveller; perhaps the cabman has made a mistake. Can I direct you?"

The old fellow turned to me, and I noticed that he snarled and showed his teeth like an ill-tempered cur as he spoke.

"This drunken fool has brought me here," he said. "I told him to drive to Chenies Street, and he brings me to this infernal place. I won't pay him a farthing, and I meant to have given him a handsome sum. I am going to call for the police and give him in charge."

At this threat the cabman seemed to take alarm; he glanced round, as if to make sure that no policeman was in sight, and drove off grumbling loudly, and Mr. Headley grinned savagely with satisfaction at having saved his fare, and put back one and sixpence into his pocket, the "handsome sum" the cabman had lost.

"My dear sir," I said, "I am afraid this piece of stupidity has annoyed you a great deal. It is a long way to Chenies Street, and you will have some difficulty in finding the place unless you know London pretty well."

---

1 See p. 172, note 1.

"I know it very little," he replied. "I never come up except on important business, and I've never been to Chenies Street in my life."

"Really? I should be happy to show you the way. I have been for a stroll, and it will not at all inconvenience me to take you to your destination."

"I want to go to Professor Memys, at number 15. It's most annoying to me; I'm short-sighted, and I can never make out the numbers on the doors."

"This way if you please," I said, and we set out.

I did not find Mr. Headley an agreeable man; indeed, he grumbled the whole way. He informed me of his name, and I took care to say, "The well-known antiquary?" and thenceforth I was compelled to listen to the history of his complicated squabbles with publishers, who had treated him, as he said, disgracefully; the man was a chapter in the Irritability of Authors. He told me that he had been on the point of making the fortune of several firms, but had been compelled to abandon the design owing to their rank ingratitude. Besides these ancient histories of wrong, and the more recent misadventure of the cabman, he had another grievous complaint to make. As he came along in the train, he had been sharpening a pencil, and the sudden jolt of the engine as it drew up at a station had driven the penknife against his face, inflicting a small triangular wound just on the cheek-bone, which he showed me. He denounced the railway company, heaped imprecations on the head of the driver, and talked of claiming damages. Thus he grumbled all the way, not noticing in the least where he was going; and so unamiable did his conduct appear to me, that I began to enjoy the trick I was playing on him.

Nevertheless, my heart beat a little faster as we turned into the street where Lipsius was waiting. A thousand accidents, I thought, might happen; some chance might bring one of Headley's friends to meet us; perhaps, though he knew not Chenies Street, he might know the street where I was taking him; in spite of his short-sight he might possibly make out the number; or, in a sudden fit of suspicion, he might make an inquiry of the policeman at the corner. Thus every step upon the pavement, as we drew nearer to the goal, was to me a pang and a terror, and every approaching passenger carried a certain threat of danger. I gulped down my excitement with an effort, and made shift to say pretty quietly—

"Number 15, I think you said? That is the third house from this. If you will allow me I will leave you now; I have been delayed a little, and my way lies on the other side of Tottenham Court Road."

He snarled out some kind of thanks, and I turned my back and walked swiftly in the opposite direction. A minute or two later I looked round, and saw Mr. Headley standing on the doorstep, and then the door opened and he went in. For my part, I gave a sigh of relief; I hastened to get away from the neighbourhood, and endeavoured to enjoy myself in merry company.

The whole of the next day I kept away from Lipsius. I felt anxious, but I did not know what had happened, or what was happening, and a reasonable regard for my own safety told me that I should do well to remain quietly at home. My curiosity, however, to learn the end of the odd drama in which I had played a part stung me to the quick, and late in the evening I made up my mind to go and see how events had turned out. Lipsius nodded when I came in, and asked me if I could give him five minutes' talk. We went into his room, and he began to walk up and down, and I sat waiting for him to speak.

"My dear Mr. Walters," he said at length, "I congratulate you warmly; your work was done in the most thorough and artistic manner. You will go far. Look."

He went to his escritoire and pressed a secret spring; a drawer flew out, and he laid something on the table. It was a gold coin; I took it up and examined it eagerly, and read the legend about the figure of the faun.

"Victoria," I said, smiling.

"Yes; it was a great capture, which we owe to you. I had great difficulty in persuading Mr. Headley that a little mistake had been made; that was how I put it. He was very disagreeable, and indeed ungentlemanly, about it; didn't he strike you as a very cross old man?"

I held the coin, admiring the choice and rare design, clear cut as if from the mint; and I thought the fine gold glowed and burned like a lamp.

"And what finally became of Mr. Headley?" I said at last.

Lipsius smiled, and shrugged his shoulders.

"What on earth does it matter?" he said. "He might be here, or there, or anywhere; but what possible consequence could it be? Besides, your question rather surprises me; you are an intelligent man, Mr. Walters. Just think it over, and I'm sure you won't repeat the question."

"My dear sir," I said, "I hardly think you are treating me fairly. You have paid me some handsome compliments on my share in the capture, and I naturally wish to know how the matter ended. From what I saw of Mr. Headley, I should think you must have had some difficulty with him."

He gave me no answer for the moment, but began again to walk up and down the room, apparently absorbed in thought.

"Well," he said at last, "I suppose there is something in what you say. We are certainly indebted to you. I have said that I have a high opinion of your intelligence, Mr. Walters. Just look here, will you."

He opened a door communicating with another room, and pointed.

There was a great box lying on the floor, a queer, coffin-shaped thing. I looked at it, and saw it was a mummy case, like those in the British Museum, vividly painted in the brilliant Egyptian colours, with I knew not what proclamation of dignity or hopes of life immortal. The mummy swathed about in the robes of death was lying within, and the face had been uncovered.

"You are going to send this away?" I said, forgetting the question I had put.

"Yes; I have an order from a local museum. Look a little more closely, Mr. Walters."

Puzzled by his manner, I peered into the face, while he held up the lamp. The flesh was black with the passing of the centuries; but as I looked I saw upon the right cheek-bone a small triangular scar, and the secret of the mummy flashed upon me: I was looking at the dead body of the man whom I had decoyed into that house.

There was no thought or design of action in my mind.[1] I held the accursed coin in my hand, burning me with a foretaste of hell, and I fled as I would have fled from pestilence and death, and dashed into the street in blind horror, not knowing where I went. I felt the gold coin grasped in my clenched fist, and throwing it away, I knew not where, and ran on and on through by-streets and dark ways, till at last I issued out into a crowded thoroughfare and checked myself. Then as consciousness returned I realized my instant peril, and understood what would happen if I fell into the hands of Lipsius. I knew that I had put forth my finger to thwart a relentless mechanism rather than a man. My recent adventure with the unfortunate Mr. Headley had taught me that Lipsius had agents

---

1 The man with spectacles acts seemingly without agency (in contrast with the apparent agency of the coin), but in keeping with his pagan initiation into the secret society in which he feels that he is "no longer a thinking agent, but at once subject and object."

in all quarters; and I foresaw that if I fell into his hands, he would remain true to his doctrine of style, and cause me to die a death of some horrible and ingenious torture. I bent my whole mind to the task of outwitting him and his emissaries, three of whom I knew to have proved their ability for tracking down persons who for various reasons preferred to remain obscure. These servants of Lipsius were two men and a woman, and the woman was incomparably the most subtle and the most deadly. Yet I considered that I too had some portion of craft, and I took my resolve. Since then I have matched myself day by day and hour by hour against the ingenuity of Lipsius and his myrmidons.[1] For a time I was successful; though they beat furiously after me in the covert of London, I remained *perdu*,[2] and watched with some amusement their frantic efforts to recover the scent lost in two or three minutes. Every lure and wile was put forth to entice me from my hiding-place; I was informed by the medium of the public prints that what I had taken had been recovered, and meetings were proposed in which I might hope to gain a great deal without the slightest risk. I laughed at their endeavours, and began a little to despise the organisation I had so dreaded, and ventured more abroad. Not once or twice, but several times, I recognised the two men who were charged with my capture, and I succeeded in eluding them easily at close quarters; and a little hastily I decided that I had nothing to dread, and that my craft was greater than theirs. But in the meanwhile, while I congratulated myself on my cunning, the third of Lipsius's emissaries was weaving her nets; and in an evil hour I paid a visit to an old friend, a literary man named Russell, who lived in a quiet street in Bayswater. The woman, as I found out too late, a day or two ago, occupied rooms in the same house, and I was followed and tracked down. Too late, as I have said, I recognised that I had made a fatal mistake, and that I was besieged. Sooner or later I shall find myself in the power of an enemy without pity; and so surely as I leave this house I shall go to receive doom. I hardly dare to guess how it will at last fall upon me; my imagination, always a vivid one, paints to me appalling pictures of the unspeakable torture which I shall probably endure; and I know that I shall die with Lipsius standing near and gloating over the refinements of my suffering and my shame.

Hours, nay minutes, have become very precious to me. I sometimes pause in the midst of anticipating my tortures, to wonder whether even now I cannot hit upon some supreme stroke, some

---

1 Lipsius's gang of "hired ruffian[s]" (*OED*).
2 "Lost" (French).

design of infinite subtlety, to free myself from the toils. But I find that the faculty of combination has left me; I am as the scholar in the old myth,[1] deserted by the power which has helped me hitherto. I do not know when the supreme moment will come, but sooner or later it is inevitable; before long I shall receive sentence, and from the sentence to execution will not be long.

★★★

I cannot remain here a prisoner any longer. I shall go out to-night when the streets are full of crowds and clamours, and make a last effort to escape.

★★★

It was with profound astonishment that Dyson closed the little book, and thought of the strange series of incidents which had brought him into touch with the plots and counterplots connected with the Gold Tiberius. He had bestowed the coin carefully away, and he shuddered at the bare possibility of its place of deposit becoming known to the evil band who seemed to possess such extraordinary sources of information.

It had grown late while he read, and he put the pocket-book away, hoping with all his heart that the unhappy Walters might even at the eleventh hour escape the doom he dreaded.

ADVENTURE OF THE DESERTED RESIDENCE

"A wonderful story, as you say, an extraordinary sequence and play of coincidence. I confess that your expressions when you first showed me the Gold Tiberius were not exaggerated. But do you think that Walters has really some fearful fate to dread?"

"I cannot say. Who can presume to predict events when life itself puts on the robe of coincidence and plays at drama? Perhaps we have not yet reached the last chapter in the queer story.[2] But, look,

---

1 The young man with spectacles compares himself with the legendary Faust, who made a pact with the devil to enjoy powers that would give him unlimited access to knowledge and pleasure for a brief time in exchange for his soul. Having served for a time his ambition to know everything, the man with spectacles must now pay the price.

2 One of several references to the theatricality and artifice of everyday life. The text's self-referentiality is most explicit in this final scene, given its resonance with the Prologue. See Introduction, pp. 18–26, for details.

we are drawing near to the verge of London; there are gaps, you see, in the serried ranks of brick, and a vision of green fields beyond."

Dyson had persuaded the ingenious Mr. Phillipps to accompany him on one of those aimless walks to which he was himself so addicted. Starting from the very heart of London, they had made their way westward through the stony avenues, and were now just emerging from the red lines of an extreme suburb, and presently the half-finished road ended, a quiet lane began, and they were beneath the shade of elm-trees. The yellow autumn sunlight that had lit up the bare distance of the suburban street now filtered down through the boughs of the trees and shone on the glowing carpet of fallen leaves, and the pools of rain glittered and shot back the gleam of light. Over all the broad pastures there was peace and the happy rest of autumn before the great winds begin, and afar off London lay all vague and immense amidst the veiling mist; here and there a distant window catching the sun and kindling with fire, and a spire gleaming high, and below the streets in shadow, and the turmoil of life. Dyson and Phillipps walked on in silence beneath the high hedges, till at a turn of the lane they saw a mouldering and ancient gate standing open, and the prospect of a house at the end of a moss-grown carriage drive.

"There is a survival for you," said Dyson; "it has come to its last days, I imagine. Look how the laurels have grown gaunt and weedy, and black and bare beneath; look at the house, covered with yellow wash, and patched with green damp. Why, the very notice-board, which informs all and singular that the place is to be let, has cracked and half fallen."

"Suppose we go in and see it," said Phillipps; "I don't think there is anybody about."

They turned up the drive, and walked slowly towards this remnant of old days. It was a large, straggling house, with curved wings at either end, and behind a series of irregular roofs and projections, showing that the place had been added to at divers dates; the two wings were roofed in cupola fashion, and at one side, as they came nearer, they could see a stableyard, and a clock turret with a bell, and the dark masses of gloomy cedars. Amidst all the lineaments of dissolution there was but one note of contrast: the sun was setting beyond the elm-trees, and all the west and the south were in flames; on the upper windows of the house the glow shone reflected, and it seemed as if blood and fire were mingled. Before the yellow front of the mansion, stained, as Dyson had remarked, with gangrenous patches, green and blackening, stretched what once had been, no doubt, a well-kept lawn, but it was now rough and ragged, and nettles and great docks, and all manner of coarse weeds, struggled in the places of the flower-beds. The urns had fallen from their pillars beside the walk, and lay broken in shards upon the ground, and everywhere from grass-plot and path a fungoid growth had sprung up and multiplied, and lay dank and slimy like a festering sore upon the earth. In the middle of the rank grass of the lawn was a desolate fountain; the rim of the basin was crumbling and pulverised with decay, and within the water stood stagnant, with green scum for the lilies that had once bloomed there; rust had eaten into the bronze flesh of the Triton[1] that stood in the middle, and the conch-shell he held was broken.

"Here," said Dyson, "one might moralise over decay and death. Here all the stage is decked out with the symbols of dissolution; the cedarn gloom and twilight hangs heavy around us, and everywhere within the pale dankness has found a harbour, and the very air is changed and brought to accord with the scene. To me, I confess, this deserted house is as moral as a graveyard, and I find something sublime in that lonely Triton, deserted in the midst of his water-pool. He is the last of the gods; they have left him, and he remembers the sound of water falling on water, and the days that were sweet."

"I like your reflections extremely," said Phillipps, "but I may mention that the door of the house is open."

"Let us go in, then."

The door was just ajar, and they passed into the mouldy hall and looked in at a room on one side. It was a large room, going far back, and the rich, old, red flock paper was peeling from the walls in long strips, and blackened with vague patches of rising damp; the ancient clay, the dank reeking earth rising up again, and subduing all the work of men's hands after the conquest of many years. The floor was thick with the dust of decay, and the painted ceiling fading from all gay colours and light fancies of cupids in a career, and disfigured with sores of dampness, seemed transmuted[2] into other work. No longer the amorini[3] chased one

---

1 See p. 56, note 1, above.

2 One of the final uses of the term "transmutations" (the novel's subtitle), here referring to the transformation of art disfigured in time and aligned with "matter so slowly and surely transformed" as in processes of decay.

3 A term that derives from the Italian diminutive form of "amore" or love, used here to refer to Cupid-like figures that Dyson finds painted on the ceiling.

another pleasantly, with limbs that sought not to advance, and hands that merely simulated the act of grasping at the wreathed flowers; but it appeared some savage burlesque of the old careless world and of its cherished conventions, and the dance of the Loves had become a Dance of Death; black pustules and festering sores swelled and clustered on fair limbs and smiling faces showed corruption, and the fairy blood had boiled with the germs of foul disease; it was a parable of the leaven[1] working, and worms devouring for a banquet the heart of the rose.

Strangely, under the painted ceiling, against the decaying walls, two old chairs still stood alone, the sole furniture of the empty place. High-backed, with curving arms and twisted legs, covered with faded gold leaf, and upholstered in tattered damask, they too were a part of the symbolism, and struck Dyson with surprise. "What have we here?" he said. "Who has sat in these chairs? Who, clad in peach-bloom satin, with lace ruffles and diamond buckles, all golden, a conté fleurettes[2] to his companion? Phillipps, we are in another age. I wish I had some snuff to offer you, but failing that, I beg to offer you a seat, and we will sit and smoke tobacco. A horrid practice, but I am no pedant."

They sat down on the queer old chairs, and looked out of the dim and grimy panes to the ruined lawn, and the fallen urns, and the deserted Triton.

Presently Dyson ceased his imitation of eighteenth-century airs; he no longer pulled forward imaginary ruffles, or tapped a ghostly snuff-box.

"It's a foolish fancy," he said, at last; "but I keep thinking I hear a noise like some one groaning. Listen; no, I can't hear it now. There it is again! Did you notice it, Phillipps?"

---

1 Reference to the Parable of the Leaven (Matthew 13:33 and Luke 13:20–21), in which the growth of the Kingdom of God is compared to what happens when a relatively small amount of "leaven" (a fermentation agent) is added to a much larger amount of flour, transforming it into dough. Here it is used against the grain to indicate how the small, slow changes of processes of corruption can destroy things wholesale.

2 French phrase referring to the act of whispering sweet nothings. Notably, Dyson feels they have been transported to a different time in the presence of ruins of an earlier time, much like Machen did when he walked in his native land: "I remember that these footpaths gave me a singular impression of travelling in time—backwards, not forwards, as in Mr. Wells's enchantment" (*Far Off Things* 150); the reference is to *The Time Machine* (1895) by English writer H.G. Wells (1866–1946).

"No, I can't say I heard anything. But I believe that old places like this are like shells from the shore, ever echoing with noises. The old beams, mouldering piecemeal, yield a little and groan; and such a house as this I can fancy all resonant at night with voices, the voices of matter so slowly and so surely transformed into other shapes, the voice of the worm that gnaws at last the very heart of the oak, the voice of stone grinding on stone, and the voice of the conquest of Time."

They sat still in the old arm-chairs, and grew graver in the musty ancient air, the air of a hundred years ago.

"I don't like the place," said Phillipps, after a long pause. "To me it seems as if there were a sickly, unwholesome smell about it, a smell of something burning."

"You are right; there is an evil odour here. I wonder what it is. Hark! Did you hear that?"

A hollow sound, a noise of infinite sadness and infinite pain, broke in upon the silence, and the two men looked fearfully at one another, horror, and the sense of unknown things, glimmering in their eyes.

"Come," said Dyson, "we must see into this," and they went into the hall and listened in the silence.

"Do you know," said Phillipps, "it seems absurd, but I could almost fancy that the smell is that of burning flesh."

They went up the hollow-sounding stairs, and the odour became thick and noisome, stifling the breath, and a vapour, sickening as the smell of the chamber of death, choked them. A door was open, and they entered the large upper room, and clung hard to one another, shuddering at the sight they saw.

A naked man was lying on the floor, his arms and legs stretched wide apart, and bound to pegs that had been hammered into the boards. The body was torn and mutilated in the most hideous fashion, scarred with the marks of red-hot irons, a shameful ruin of the human shape. But upon the middle of the body a fire of coals was smouldering; the flesh had been burnt through. The man was dead, but the smoke of his torment mounted still, a black vapour.

"The young man with spectacles," said Mr. Dyson.

THE END.

Appendix A: John Lane's Keynotes Series and Beyond

[As discussed in the Introduction, the initial reception of Machen's *The Three Impostors* is intimately tied to its place in John Lane's Keynotes series—a series considered in its own time as "daringly original." The series was distinguished by featuring mostly new works by new authors, by its material qualities (unique typography, high-quality paper, accompanying Aubrey Beardsley [1872–98] designs), and by its association with the Decadent, avant-garde periodical *The Yellow Book*. *The Three Impostors* was not only a beautiful book of the kind prized by collectors; it also made the book as crafted and collectible object an explicit part of its content. Below are some selected Beardsley designs (selected Keynotes and *Yellow Book* covers as well as an image from *Salomé* featuring "little people") and designs by S.H. Sime (1865–1941; an illustrator heavily influenced by Beardsley and best known for his illustrations for works of fantasy) from the first reprinting of *The Three Impostors* and his "Sime Zoology" of fantastic "Beasts that Might Have Been" (from *The Sketch*, 1905). These images show how visual (not just literary) traditions link Decadence with modern genres of horror, supernatural, and the weird.]

1. Illustrations by Aubrey Beardsley from John Lane's Keynotes Series

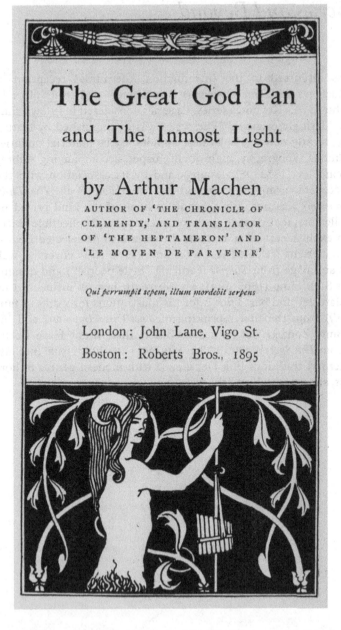

a. Cover image from *The Great God Pan* (1895) (second edition)

The Three Impostors
or The Transmutations

by Arthur Machen

TRANSLATOR OF 'L'HEPTAMERON' AND
'LE MOYEN DE PARVENIR'; AUTHOR
OF 'THE CHRONICLE OF CLEMENDY'
AND 'THE GREAT GOD PAN'

London: John Lane, Vigo St.
Boston: Roberts Bros., 1895

b. Cover image from *The Three Impostors* (1895)

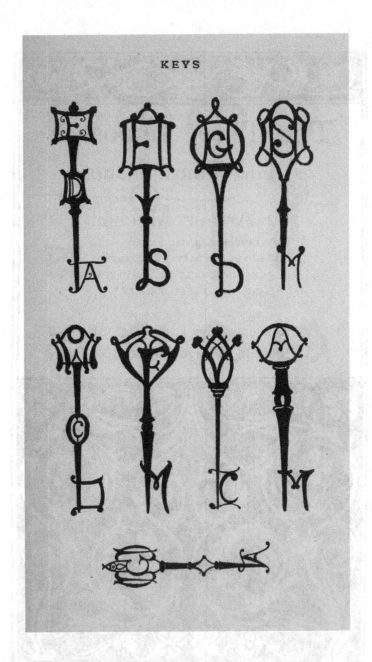

c. Keys, part 1 (1896). The right-most key in the second row is
Arthur Machen's key, containing his initials and appearing in
The Three Impostors. *The Great God Pan* featured a different key
not pictured here.

KEYS

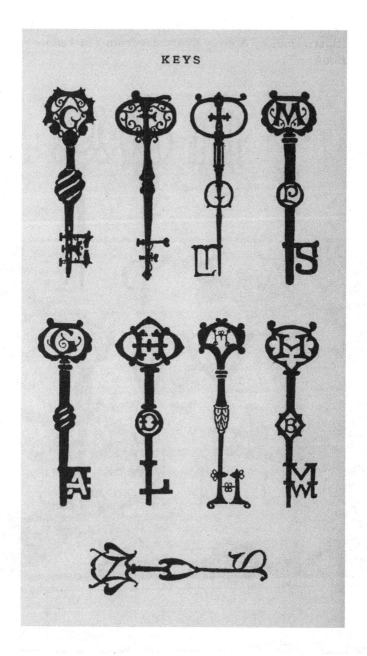

d. Keys, part 2 (1896)

2. Illustrations by Aubrey Beardsley from *The Yellow Book*

a. Front cover of *The Yellow Book* (April 1894)

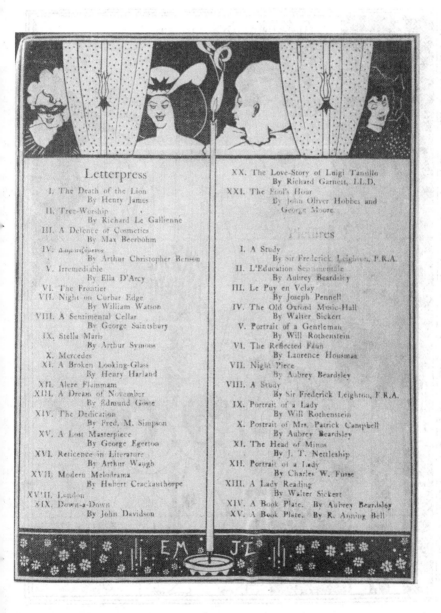

b. Back cover of *The Yellow Book* (April 1894)

3. Illustration featuring "little people" by Aubrey Beardsley for *Salomé* (1894)

4. Designs by S.H. Sime for *House of Souls* (1906)

a. Front cover

b. Spine

5. "The Sime Zoology," designs by S.H. Sime, *The Sketch* (8 March 1905)

THE SIME ZOOLOGY: BEASTS THAT MIGHT HAVE BEEN.—VII-X.

DRAWN BY S. H. SIME.

THE THREE-LEGGED BLARM.

THE MOONIJIM.

THE SEEKIM.

THE FLERNIKORN.

Appendix B: Reviews of The Three Impostors

[Reviews of Machen's *Three Impostors* were mixed, and although many reviewers note the similarities between *The Three Impostors* and Machen's earlier *The Great God Pan*, the later work would not garner the success of the previous work in part because it was published at a time when Victorian readers were much less open (or much less likely to openly admit their attraction) to "unhealthy" literature. For someone like Harry Quilter (whose review of Machen's *The Great God Pan* is excerpted below, B9), *The Three Impostors* was surely yet another unequivocally "abominable story" (*Quilter* 761), but most reviewers tended to notice the strengths of *The Three Impostors* (its style, its ability to "curdle" readers' blood, etc.) even as they deplored its weaknesses (its horrors go too far or at times remain unconvincing). Some reviewers align Machen with Poe (B3, B5, and B8), but nearly all reviews recognize *The Three Impostors* as imitating Stevenson's highly popular *The Dynamiter*, though most suggest that Machen's is a less successful, derivative work. In some ways, then, *The Three Impostors* was received in the shadows of other works and of the Wilde trials, even though in the longer term it would help establish Machen as a foundational figure of weird, occult, and even science fiction.[1]]

1. "The Three Impostors," *The Bookman* (January 1896), p. 131

The horrible is sweet to the taste of Mr. Machen. He plays with it a little frivolously at times, but now and then it does seriously take hold of him, and on some of these occasions it impresses us. A curious medley is this book of the sensational, the trivial, and the occult. Written on an old plan, some idea of its design and tone may be gathered from thinking of Stevenson's

---

1   See Appendix B6 below for an instance in which Machen's *The Great God Pan* is linked to a trend of incorporating science into fiction; even though this review focuses on *The Great God Pan*, arguably *The Three Impostors* adds to that trend.

"Dynamiters," with the sprightliness and fun, but not the frivolity, left out, and with dark occult sin substituted for the grotesque. Every now and again we are struck with admiration of the picturesque and suggestive writing, and sometimes we think the same overweights [sic] what had been a better story if more plainly and briskly told. We thought for a time that Mr. Machen was fooling us with his horrible hints. (We had forgotten the contents of the prologue.) The hunt of the gold Tiberius, the ingenious imaginations of the three impostors, we had thought might end farcically. Perhaps his learning in the black arts would so have been wasted, but we wish he had some restraining qualities that would keep him from writing such horrors as those in his last chapter.

2. From "The Three Impostors," *Saturday Review* (11 January 1896), pp. 48–49

Mr. Machen is an unfortunate man. He has determined to be weird, horrible, and as outspoken as his courage permits in an age which is noisily resolved to be "'ealthy" to the pitch of blatancy. His particular obsession is a kind of infernal matrimonial agency, and the begetting of human-diabolical mules. He has already skirted the matter in his previous book, the "Great God Pan," and here we find it well to the fore again. This time, however, it simply supplies one of a group of incoherent stories held together in a frame of wooden narrative about a young man with spectacles. [...] Mr. Machen has one simple expedient whereby he seeks to develop his effects. He piles them up very high, and makes his characters horror-struck at them. [...]

But it fails altogether to affect the reader as it is meant to do. It fails mainly because Mr. Machen has not mastered the necessary trick of commonplace detail which renders horrors convincing, and because he lacks even the most rudimentary conception of how to individualize characters. The framework of the book is evidently imitated from Mr. Stevenson's "New Arabian Nights," a humorous form quite unsuited, of course, to realistic horror. Mr. Machen writes with care and a certain whimsical choice of words, so that his style is at least distinctive.

3. From *The Speaker* (21 December 1895), pp. 679–80

Those persons who may chance to have read "The Great God Pan" will be prepared to find in its author's latest production, "The Three Impostors," a volume of unwholesome imaginings. In this expectation they will not be disappointed, for the book is no whit inferior to its precursor in weird gruesomeness and hideous suggestion. Mr. Machen is an artist in the horrible, possessing a peculiar talent for curdling the blood of his readers by means of veiled terrors and mysterious hints of abnormal atrocities, too appalling to be plainly stated. Nothing more uncanny than this tale of devilish malice and monstrous intrigue was ever imagined, even by such a master of his art as Edgar Poe. It is wholly unpleasant and unedifying, but all the same it is distinctly thrilling, and exercises over the reader that morbid fascination that belongs to this class of fiction. The plot is a very involved one, but its intricacies are unravelled with skilled adroitness, while the breathless interest which the author so cunningly arouses in the first pages remains unabated, and even intensified, right up to the close. [...] [The three impostors'] conspiracy against the harmless "young man in spectacles" who finally falls prey to their fiendish cruelty, malignant hate, an untiring lust for vengeance, is set forth with startling vividness in a series of interwoven adventures which savour strongly of 'The Arabian Nights.' Mr. Machen's aim is palpably that of producing upon his readers an effect of vague, inexplicable terror, and no better means to that end could have been devised than that which he has here employed, the very reticence of his method only serving to heighten the impression of nameless horror. [...] The book is by no means one we should care to recommend to young or nervous persons; but anyone who relishes horrors, and can safely defy nightmare, will assuredly find in "The Three Impostors" a work of fiction as ghastly and "creepy" as the perversity of man could desire.

4. Percy Addleshaw, "The Three Impostors," *Academy* (7 December 1895), p. 482

Mr. Machen has written a striking, clever, gruesome book. It owes something in its plan to Stevenson's *Dynamiter*, which is a pity; for, truth to tell, the various parts are but loosely knit together, and the author is strong enough to form a method of his own. When he follows no model, but gives his fancy and imagination free play, the result is capital. Throughout, save in a page or two, he manages to avoid being disgusting, a rare feat given some of the descriptions he attempts; his horrors are ideally terrifying, and of a truly original habit.

5. "New Novels," *Graphic* (8 February 1896), pp. 180–81

If the prologue to Mr. Machen's volume (John Lane) fails to excite an eager appetite for the rest in the case of a single reader, however satiated with mysteries and experienced in disappointments, we shall be exceedingly surprised. And even if he closes the book with an exclamation of "What nonsense!"—or even of something stronger—by way of *finis*, he will still have to confess that he could not possibly have laid the nonsense down. Yet the feast of unreason will not wholly have been one of pleasure. An almost more than human omnivorousness is required for anything that can be called pleasure in the perusal of "The Novel of the White Powder." Had it been written by Poe, its inspiration would certainly have been called genius. Mr. Machen ought, in justice, to have the benefit of that certainty. Moreover, in common with the rest of his work, it gains immensely in effect by his hard, cold, almost arid, method of narration, which is the exact opposite of what is termed word-painting. Nevertheless, it is fortunate that his particular form of genius—to accept the word boldly—is rare, and that genius, as a rule, prefers to discover beauty in types to the invention of impossible horrors. "The Three Impostors," however, is not wholly in this vein. Its undercurrent of humour is seldom quite out of sight, and is by no means always cynically grim. And readers who notice and appreciate the grains of suggestion in the author's 'chaff' concerning the revival of superstition by a scientific age may forget to exclaim, "What nonsense!" after all.

6. From "Science in Fiction," *Leeds Mercury Weekly Supplement* (26 January 1895), p. 4

It was, perhaps, inevitable that modern fiction should become scientific, or at any rate concern itself very considerably with scientific problems; and for that reason no habitual reader of contemporary novels feels himself at all surprised to find his attention invited to the discussion of phenomena which were formerly only treated in medical text-books. [...] Once upon a time the novelist's field of action was a decidedly narrow one. [...] At the time it was possible to boast that we had in England no represen-tatives of the morbidly analytical school which was beginning to revolutionise literature in France. [...] But within late years the reproach of undue limitation has been almost wholly removed from English fiction. The English novelist now-a-days either uses fiction for the purposes of explaining theories, or uses theo-ries as pegs whereon to hang fiction. [...]

If it were possible to exact a stern obedience to those unwritten laws which may be classed under the general term of "the fitness of things," it would be wise, we think, to rule henceforth that only scientific men should write scientific novels. Between mere imag-ination and scientific fact there is a gulf fixed which only extreme youth and brilliant audacity of genius dare to attempt bridging. If such a combination bridges the gulf the result is not altogether satisfactory, for the scientific man scoffs at it, and the imaginative man is not content. There is an object lesson to the point in one of the new "Keynotes" series—Mr. Arthur Machen's clever book, "The Great God Pan and The Inmost Light." Both of these sto-ries have to do with an operation on the brain [...] Science has not yet shown us that you can touch the fine tissue of a man's brain and release a devil that takes shape, or that any potion or pow-der will enable a human being to assume another man's aspect and fleshly covering [as in Stevenson's "Strange Case of Dr Jekyll and Mr Hyde" mentioned in relation to Machen in this piece]. That is just where imagination and science do not blend, and it is also why the scientific novel is best and safest, and, let us add, most entertaining when it comes from professed scientists like Dr. Conan Doyle. The average novelist, when he turns from invention to science, is apt to betray misty ideas as to treatment and symp-toms, but the man who knows medicine as intimately as literature combines both with a success that commands respect from the high-priests of both.

7. From "New Novels," *Athenæum* (1 February 1896), p. 146

Just as Mr. Machen's earlier book was compared by most of his reviewers to Stevenson's "Dr. Jekyll and Mr. Hyde," so his lat-est venture irresistibly challenges comparisons, both in method and style, with the same author's "New Arabian Nights." There is, however, this great distinction between the two writers, that whereas Stevenson's fantasies were often illumined with playful-ness and even gaiety, Mr. Machen is hardly ever diverted from his unwearied quest for the uncanny, the gruesome, and—in the classical sense—the obscene. [...] The result is never agreeable, occasionally disgusting, but seldom really blood-curdling, since in the last resort Mr. Machen generally takes refuge in a copious use of such words as "unutterable," "hideous," "loathsome," "appalling," and so on. Still these chapters present undeniable evidence of a sombre imagination, considerable descriptive power, and a keen sense of the mystery and picturesqueness of London.

8. H.D. Traill, "The World of Letters," *Graphic* (1 February 1896), p. 128

Among the many followers of Mr. Stevenson in the style of the "New Arabian Nights" there is, perhaps, no one who has been more successful in catching the manner of the master, and, what is more important still, of their common model, than Mr. Arthur Machen. The essential constituents of that manner are its gravity and its *naïveté*, and, of course, the quaint humour, even apparently conscious of itself, that results of the combinations. The English romancer who would imitate the Oriental fabulist must acquire the art of fitting his marvelous incidents into a framework of everyday life as naturally as though they belonged to it, and to clothe the most fantastic and extravagant *propos*[1] in the language in which men would exchange ideas with each other in the smoking-room or the railway-carriage. To do this gracefully and humourously requires not only a delicate sense of style, but a considerable command of it, and this Mr. Machen undoubtedly possesses. To read him at his best is to be more than faintly reminded of "The Rajah's Diamond."[2]

But it is a pity, I think, that he does not confine himself to the marvellous pure and simple, and eschew the gruesome—that he should not be content with following in the footsteps of Stevenson instead of entering into competition with Poe. For Mr. Machen, though he has, it must be admitted, an occasional inspiration of "the creepy," is too anxious to produce "goose-flesh" in the readers, and in his desire to do so he is apt to seek his efforts in what I cannot but consider an "unsportsmanlike" fashion. For instance, he is too much addicted to the artifice of describing by telling you

---

1 A term borrowed from French meaning proposition (*OED*).

2 A story cycle by Robert Louis Stevenson that first appeared in *London* magazine in 1878 but was later published in book form as part of *New Arabian Nights* (1882).

that things are indescribable. This is a device which, though perhaps not absolutely illegitimate, ought obviously to be very sparingly used; but in "The Three Impostors" (Lane), as even more conspicuously in Mr. Machen's earlier volume in the same series, "The Great God Pan," it is employed to an extent which is almost provocative of parody. A writer must, of course, leave something to our imagination; but when we are continually meeting with creatures too hideous to be portrayed in human language, who utter words too awful to be repeated, and take part in orgies so abominable and revolting that they must forever remain nameless, even the most indulgent reader may reasonably begin to feel that he is getting rather short measure for his money.

9. From Harry Quilter, "The Gospel of Intensity," *Contemporary Review*, vol. 67 (June 1895), pp. 761–82

"The Great God Pan" is, I have no hesitation in saying, a perfectly abominable story, in which the author has spared no endeavour to suggest loathsomeness and horror which he describes as beyond the reach of words. [...]

Surely it is strange that a book [...] should be praised and recommended for its very vices, for its horror and bestiality, by respectable newspapers. Yet here they are all apparently delighted with what the *Telegraph* calls these "blood-chilling masterpieces." Who can blame the poor chap whose imagination has here run riot, if he considers himself, and is considered by his friends for the future, as a very clever fellow, the pioneer of a new class of literature? Who can blame young writers if, seeing such things win praise and success, they follow in his footsteps, and endeavour to surpass him in his own strain? Who can wonder even at the nasty little naked figure of dubious sex and humanity with which Mr. Aubrey Beardsley has prefaced the story—in all truth a most fitting introduction. [...]

[...] Mr. Beardsley is a young man of decided and original ability, but I do not think there can be any two opinions as to the use he has made of his genius. There is, to the present writer, something absolutely repulsive in this artist's renderings of humanity, and in the general savour of his compositions. [...] I dare express it no more definitely, than by saying that however unnatural, extravagant, and morbid are the stories and the poems of the modern decadence [...] there is not one of them which is more perverted in what it says and suggests than these grotesques, in which the types of manhood and womanhood are, as it were, mingled together, and result in a monstrous sexless amalgam, miserable, morbid, dreary, and unnatural. [...] And since it is beyond doubt that this art has been made the handmaid of a very morbid species of literature, and has in that service achieved great success and emolument, it is essential that all those who attempt to point out the demoralising effect of the fiction and poetry in question, should point out also this artistic connection.

Appendix C: The Cult of Artifice and the "Modern Craze" for Collecting

[Although Machen would later claim to have had nothing to do with 1890s Decadence, *The Three Impostors*, which features a Decadent writer as one of its protagonists, frequently plays with Decadent concerns and themes. Perhaps foremost among these is its obsession with artifice, artificial things, and collecting. In this appendix, excerpts from Decadent poet and critic Arthur Symons (1865–1945) and physician and writer Havelock Ellis (1859–1939) provide some definitions of Decadence from some of Machen's contemporaries, while other excerpts by satirical writer Max Beerbohm (1872–1956) and Symons provide instances of the "cult of artifice." An excerpt from one of the most infamous Decadent novels, Oscar Wilde's *The Picture of Dorian Gray*, showcases how this obsession with artifice expressed itself through collecting and resulted in the use of lists that stretch the bounds of narrative, as things come to take up an unusual amount of Decadent protagonists' attention and an unusual amount of space in Decadent narratives. Lastly, selected *Punch* cartoons poke fun at "chinamania" and its intersection with Aestheticism and Oscar Wilde (1854–1900), who famously quipped, "I find it harder and harder every day to live up to my blue china" (qtd. in Ellmann 43).[1]]

1. From Arthur Symons, "The Decadent Movement in Literature," *Harper's New Monthly Magazine*, vol. 87, no. 522 (1893), pp. 858–67

The latest movement in European literature has been called by many names, none of them quite exact or comprehensive— Decadence, Symbolism, Impressionism, for instance. It is easy to dispute over words, and we shall find that Verlaine objects to being called a Decadent, Maeterlinck to being called a Symbolist, Huysmans to being called an Impressionist. These terms, as it happens, have been adopted as the badge of little separate

---

1 For more on the relationship between chinamania and Aestheticism and Decadence, see Anderson.

cliques, noisy, brainsick young people who haunt the brasseries of the Boulevard Saint-Michel, and exhaust their ingenuities in theorizing over the works they cannot write. But, taken frankly as epithets which express their own meaning, both Impressionism and Symbolism[1] convey some notion of that new kind of literature which is perhaps more broadly characterized by the word Decadence. The most representative literature of the day—the writing which appeals to, which has done so much to form, the younger generation—is certainly not classic, nor has it any relation with that old antithesis of the Classic, the Romantic. After a fashion it is no doubt a decadence; it has all the qualities that mark the end of great periods, the qualities that we find in the Greek, the Latin, decadence: an intense self-consciousness, a restless curiosity in research, an over-subtilizing refinement upon refinement, a spiritual and moral perversity. If what we call the classic is indeed the supreme art—those qualities of perfect simplicity, perfect sanity, perfect proportion, the supreme qualities—then this representative literature of to-day, interesting, beautiful, novel as it is, is really a new and beautiful and interesting disease.

Healthy we cannot call it, and healthy it does not wish to be considered. The Goncourts,[2] in their prefaces, in their *Journal*,

---

1 Like so many critics then and since, Symons here registers the difficulty of defining Decadence, noting in this case its possible relation to Impressionism and Symbolism. Impressionism in literature refers to a tendency to focus on subjective and transient experiences and can be found in late-nineteenth-century prose fiction, poetry, and even criticism such as that of Walter Pater (1839–94). By Symbolism, Symons is here referring to the works of a group of French poets of the 1870–90s that "aimed for a poetry of suggestion rather than of direct statement, evoking subjective moods through the use of private symbols, while avoiding the description of external reality or the expression of opinion" (Baldick). Interestingly, Symons would later publish a work on *The Symbolist Movement in Literature* (1899) in which (likely because of the aftermath of the Wilde trials) he claimed that Decadence was "half a mock-interlude" that "diverted the attention of critics while something more serious was in preparation" (7).

2 Brothers Edmond (1822–96) and Jules (1830–70) de Goncourt, French novelists and critics most often associated with naturalism or a kind of realism that examined humans as "passive victims of natural forces and social environment" (Baldick).

are always insisting on their own pet malady, *la névrose*.[1] It is in their work, too, that Huysmans notes with delight "*le style tacheté et faisandé*"—high-flavored and spotted with corruption—which he himself possesses in the highest degree. "Having desire without light, curiosity without wisdom, seeking God by strange ways, by ways traced by the hands of men; offering rash incense upon high places to an unknown God, who is the God of darkness"—that is how Ernest Hello, in one of his apocalyptic moments, characterizes the nineteenth century. And this unreason of the soul—of which Hello himself is so curious a victim—this unstable equilibrium, which has overbalanced so many brilliant intelligences into one form or another of spiritual confusion, is but another form of the *maladie fin de siècle*. For its very disease of form, this literature is certainly typical of a civilization grown over-luxurious, over-inquiring, too languid for the relief of action, too uncertain for any emphasis in opinion or in conduct. It reflects all the moods, all the manners, of a sophisticated society; its very artificiality is a way of being true to nature: simplicity, sanity, proportion—the classic qualities—how much do we possess them in our life, our surroundings, that we should look to find them in our literature—so evidently the literature of a decadence? [...]

[...] Joris Karl Huysmans[2] demands a prominent place in any record of the Decadent movement. His work, like that of the Goncourts, is largely determined by the *maladie fin de siècle*—the diseased nerves that, in his case, have given a curious personal quality of pessimism to his outlook on the world, his view of life. Part of his work—*Marthe, Les Sœurs Vatard, En Ménage, À Vau-l'Eau*—is a minute and searching study of the minor discomforts, the commonplace miseries of life, as seen by a peevishly disordered vision, delighting, for its own self-torture, in the insistent contemplation of human stupidity, of the sordid in existence. Yet these books do but lead up to the unique masterpiece, the astonishing caprice of *À Rebours*,[3] in which he has concentrated all that is delicately depraved, all that is beautifully, curiously poisonous, in modern art. *À Rebours* is the history of a typical Decadent—a study, indeed, after a real man, but a study that seizes the type

---

1 Neurosis (French).
2 French novelist (1848–1907) associated with both naturalism and famously with Decadence (see pp. 28–29 above).
3 For Symons (and many others then and since), this novel is an exemplary Decadent novel that helped define the Decadent type. See p. 28, note 2, above and Introduction, pp. 28–29.

rather than the personality. In the sensations and ideas of Des Esseintes we see the sensations and ideas of the effeminate, over-civilized, deliberately abnormal creature who is the last product of our society: partly the father, partly the offspring, of the perverse art that he adores. Des Esseintes creates for his solace, in the wilderness of a barren and profoundly uncomfortable world, an artificial paradise. [...] He delights in the beauty of strange, unnatural flowers, in the melodic combinations of scents, in the imagined harmonies of the sense of taste. And at last, exhausted by these spiritual and sensory debauches in the delights of the artificial, he is left (as we close the book) with a brief, doubtful choice before him—madness or death, or else a return to nature, to the normal life.

Since *À Rebours*, M. Huysmans has written one other remarkable book, *Là-Bas*, a study in the hysteria and mystical corruption of contemporary Black Magic. But it is on that one exceptional achievement, *À Rebours*, that his fame will rest; it is there that he has expressed not merely himself, but an epoch. [...]

2. From Havelock Ellis, "A Note on Paul Bourget," *Views and Reviews: A Selection of Uncollected Articles by Havelock Ellis, First Series: 1884–1919* (Desmond Harmsworth, 1932), pp. 51–52

["...] A society should be like an organism. Like an organism, in fact, it may be resolved into a federation of smaller organisms, which may themselves be resolved into a federation of cells. The individual is the social cell. In order that the organism should perform its functions with energy it is necessary that the organisms composing it should perform their functions with energy, but with a subordinated energy, and in order that these lesser organisms should themselves perform their functions with energy, it is necessary that the cells comprising them should perform their functions with energy, but with a subordinated energy. If the energy of the cells becomes independent, the lesser organisms will likewise cease to subordinate their energy to the total energy and the anarchy which is established constitutes the *decadence* of the whole. The social organism does not escape this law and enters into decadence as soon as the individual life becomes exaggerated beneath the influence of acquired well-being, and of heredity. A similar law governs the development and decadence of that other organism which we call language. A style of decadence is one in which the unity of the book is decomposed to give place to the independence of the page, in which the page is decomposed to give place to the independence of the phrase, and the phrase to give place to the independence of the word." A decadent style, in short, is an anarchistic style in which everything is sacrificed to the development of the individual parts.

3. From Arthur Symons, "An Apology for Puppets," *Saturday Review*, vol. 84, no. 2177 (17 July 1897), pp. 55–56

[...] The living actor, even when he condescends to subordinate himself to the requirements of pantomime, has always what he is proud to call his temperament; in other words, so much personal caprice, which for the most part means wilful misunderstanding; and in seeing his acting you have to consider this intrusive little personality of his as well as the author's. The marionette may be relied upon. He will respond to an indication without reserve or revolt; an error on his part (we are all human) will certainly be the fault of the author; he can be trained to perfection. As he is painted, so will he smile; as the wires lift or lower his hands, so will his gestures be; and he will dance when his legs are set in motion.

Seen at a distance, the puppets cease to be an amusing piece of mechanism, imitating real people; there is no difference. I protest that the Knight who came in with his plumed hat, his shining sword, and flung back his long cloak with so fine a sweep of the arm, was exactly the same to me as if he had been a living actor dressed in the same clothes, and imitating the gesture of a knight; and that the contrast of what was real (as we say) under the fiction appears to me less ironical in the former than in the latter. We have to allow (you will admit) at least as much to the beneficent heightening of travesty, if we have ever seen the living actor in the morning, not yet shaved, standing at the bar, his hat on one side, his mouth spreading in that abandonment to laughter which has become, from the necessity of his profession, a natural trick; oh, much more, I think, than if we merely come upon an always decorative, never an obtrusive, costumed figure, leaning against the wall, nonchalantly enough, in a corner of the coulisses.

To sharpen our sense of what is illusive in the illusion of the puppets, let us sit not too far from the stage. Choosing our place carefully, we shall have the satisfaction of always seeing the wires at their work, while I think we shall lose nothing of what is most savorous in the feast of the illusion. There is not indeed the appeal to the senses of the first row of the stalls at a ballet of living dancers. But is not that a trifle too obvious a sentiment for the true artist in artificial things? Why leave the ball-room? It is not nature that one looks for on the stage in this kind of spectacle, and our excitement in watching it should remain purely intellectual. If you prefer that other kind of illusion go a little further away, and I assure you you will find it quite easy to fall in love with a marionette. I have seen the most adorable heads, with real hair too, among the wooden dancers of a theatre of puppets; faces which might easily, with but a little of that good-will which goes to all falling in love, seem the answer to a particular dream, making all other faces in the world but spoilt copies of this inspired piece of painted wood. [...]

4. From Max Beerbohm, "A Defence of Cosmetics," *The Yellow Book*, vol. 1 (Elkin Matthews and John Lane, April 1894), pp. 65–82

NAY but it is useless to protest. Artifice must queen it once more in the town, and so, if there be any whose hearts chafe at her return, let them not say, "We have come into evil times," and be all for resistance, reformation or angry cavilling. For did the king's sceptre send the sea retrograde, or the wand of the sorcerer avail to turn the sun from its old course? And what man or what number of men ever stayed that reiterated process by which the cities of this world grow, are very strong, fail and grow again? Indeed, indeed, there is charm in every period, and only fools and flutterpates do not seek reverently for what is charming in their own day. No martyrdom, however fine, nor satire, however splendidly bitter, has changed by a little tittle the known tendency of things. It is the times that can perfect us, not we the times, and so let all of us wisely acquiesce. Like the little wired marionettes, let us acquiesce in the dance.

For behold! The Victorian era comes to its end and the day of *sancta simplicitas*[1] is quite ended. The old signs are here and the portents to warn the seer of life that we are ripe for a new epoch of artifice. Are not men rattling the dice-box and ladies dipping their fingers in the rouge-pots? At Rome, in the keenest time of her degringolade,[2] when there was gambling even in the holy temples,

---

1 Holy simplicity (Latin).
2 Dégringolade or "A rapid descent; deterioration, decadence; change from bad to worse" (*OED*).

great ladies (does not Lucian tell us?) did not scruple to squander all they had upon unguents from Arabia. [...]

5. From Oscar Wilde, *The Picture of Dorian Gray* (Ward, Lock and Co., 1891), pp. 189–208

Chapter 11

For years, Dorian Gray could not free himself from the influence of this book.[1] Or perhaps it would be more accurate to say that he never sought to free himself from it. He procured from Paris no less than nine large-paper copies of the first edition, and had them bound in different colours, so that they might suit his various moods and the changing fancies of a nature over which he seemed, at times, to have almost entirely lost control. The hero, the wonderful young Parisian in whom the romantic and the scientific temperaments were so strangely blended, became to him a kind of prefiguring type of himself. And, indeed, the whole book seemed to him to contain the story of his own life, written before he had lived it. [...]

[...] He knew that the senses, no less than the soul, have their spiritual mysteries to reveal.

And so he would now study perfumes and the secrets of their manufacture, distilling heavily scented oils and burning odorous gums from the East. He saw that there was no mood of the mind that had not its counterpart in the sensuous life, and set himself to discover their true relations, wondering what there was in frankincense that made one mystical, and in ambergris that stirred one's passions, and in violets that woke the memory of dead romances, and in musk that troubled the brain, and in champak that stained the imagination; and seeking often to elaborate a real psychology of perfumes, and to estimate the several influences of sweet-smelling roots and scented, pollen-laden flowers; of aromatic balms and of dark and fragrant woods; of spikenard, that sickens; of hovenia, that makes men mad; and of aloes, that are said to be able to expel melancholy from the soul.

At another time he devoted himself entirely to music, and in a long latticed room, with a vermilion-and-gold ceiling and walls of olive-green lacquer, he used to give curious concerts in which mad gipsies tore wild music from little zithers, or grave, yellow-shawled Tunisians plucked at the strained strings of monstrous lutes, while

---

1 See Introduction, pp. 28–29.

grinning Negroes beat monotonously upon copper drums and, crouching upon scarlet mats, slim turbaned Indians blew through long pipes of reed or brass and charmed—or feigned to charm—great hooded snakes and horrible horned adders. The harsh intervals and shrill discords of barbaric music stirred him at times when Schubert's grace, and Chopin's beautiful sorrows, and the mighty harmonies of Beethoven himself, fell unheeded on his ear. He collected together from all parts of the world the strangest instruments that could be found, either in the tombs of dead nations or among the few savage tribes that have survived contact with Western civilizations, and loved to touch and try them. He had the mysterious *juruparis* of the Rio Negro Indians, that women are not allowed to look at and that even youths may not see till they have been subjected to fasting and scourging, and the earthen jars of the Peruvians that have the shrill cries of birds, and flutes of human bones such as Alfonso de Ovalle heard in Chile, and the sonorous green jaspers that are found near Cuzco and give forth a note of singular sweetness. He had painted gourds filled with pebbles that rattled when they were shaken; the long *clarin* of the Mexicans, into which the performer does not blow, but through which he inhales the air; the harsh *ture* of the Amazon tribes, that is sounded by the sentinels who sit all day long in high trees, and can be heard, it is said, at a distance of three leagues; the *teponaztli*, that has two vibrating tongues of wood and is beaten with sticks that are smeared with an elastic gum obtained from the milky juice of plants; the *yotl*-bells of the Aztecs, that are hung in clusters like grapes; and a huge cylindrical drum, covered with the skins of great serpents, like the one that Bernal Diaz[1] saw when he went with Cortes into the Mexican temple, and of whose doleful sound he has left us so vivid a description. The fantastic character of these instruments fascinated him, and he felt a curious delight in the thought that art, like Nature, has her monsters, things of bestial shape and with hideous voices. Yet, after some time, he wearied of them, and would sit in his box at the opera, either alone or with Lord Henry, listening in rapt pleasure to "Tannhauser"[2] and seeing in the prelude to that great work of art a presentation of the tragedy of his own soul.

---

1 Bernal Díaz Del Castillo (c. 1490s–1584) participated in and wrote an influential account of the conquest of the Aztec Empire. Dorian's collection here and elsewhere aligns it with colonial acquisitiveness. See Introduction, pp. 26–29.

2 1845 opera by Richard Wagner (1813–83).

On one occasion he took up the study of jewels, and appeared at a costume ball as Anne de Joyeuse, Admiral of France, in a dress covered with five hundred and sixty pearls. This taste enthralled him for years, and, indeed, may be said never to have left him. He would often spend a whole day settling and resettling in their cases the various stones that he had collected, such as the olive-green chrysoberyl that turns red by lamplight, the cymophane with its wirelike line of silver, the pistachio-coloured peridot, rose-pink and wine-yellow topazes, carbuncles of fiery scarlet with tremulous, four-rayed stars, flame-red cinnamon-stones, orange and violet spinels, and amethysts with their alternate layers of ruby and sapphire. He loved the red gold of the sunstone, and the moonstone's pearly whiteness, and the broken rainbow of the milky opal. He procured from Amsterdam three emeralds of extraordinary size and richness of colour, and had a turquoise *de la vieille roche* that was the envy of all the connoisseurs.

He discovered wonderful stories, also, about jewels. [...]

Then he turned his attention to embroideries and to the tapestries that performed the office of frescoes in the chill rooms of the northern nations of Europe. As he investigated the subject—and he always had an extraordinary faculty of becoming absolutely absorbed for the moment in whatever he took up—he was almost saddened by the reflection of the ruin that time brought on beautiful and wonderful things. He, at any rate, had escaped that. Summer followed summer, and the yellow jonquils bloomed and died many times, and nights of horror repeated the story of their shame, but he was unchanged. No winter marred his face or stained his flowerlike bloom. How different it was with material things! Where had they passed to? Where was the great crocus-coloured robe, on which the gods fought against the giants, that had been worked by brown girls for the pleasure of Athena? Where the huge velarium that Nero had stretched across the Colosseum at Rome, that Titan sail of purple on which was represented the starry sky, and Apollo driving a chariot drawn by white, gilt-reined steeds? He longed to see the curious table-napkins wrought for the Priest of the Sun, on which were displayed all the dainties and viands that could be wanted for a feast; the mortuary cloth of King Chilperic, with its three hundred golden bees; the fantastic robes that excited the indignation of the Bishop of Pontus and were figured with "lions, panthers, bears, dogs, forests, rocks, hunters—all, in fact, that a painter can copy from nature"; and the coat that Charles of Orleans once wore, on the sleeves of which were embroidered the verses of a song beginning "*Madame, je suis tout joyeux,*" the musical accompaniment of the words being wrought in gold thread, and each note, of square shape in those days, formed with four pearls. He read of the room that was prepared at the palace at Rheims for the use of Queen Joan of Burgundy and was decorated with "thirteen hundred and twenty-one parrots, made in broidery, and blazoned with the king's arms, and five hundred and sixty-one butterflies, whose wings were similarly ornamented with the arms of the queen, the whole worked in gold." Catherine de Medicis had a mourning-bed made for her of black velvet powdered with crescents and suns. Its curtains were of damask, with leafy wreaths and garlands, figured upon a gold and silver ground, and fringed along the edges with broideries of pearls, and it stood in a room hung with rows of the queen's devices in cut black velvet upon cloth of silver. Louis XIV had gold embroidered caryatides fifteen feet high in his apartment. The state bed of Sobieski, King of Poland, was made of Smyrna gold brocade embroidered in turquoises with verses from the Koran. Its supports were of silver gilt, beautifully chased, and profusely set with enamelled and jewelled medallions. It had been taken from the Turkish camp before Vienna, and the standard of Mohammed had stood beneath the tremulous gilt of its canopy.

And so, for a whole year, he sought to accumulate the most exquisite specimens that he could find of textile and embroidered work, getting the dainty Delhi muslins, finely wrought with gold-thread palmates and stitched over with iridescent beetles' wings; the Dacca gauzes, that from their transparency are known in the East as "woven air," and "running water," and "evening dew"; strange figured cloths from Java; elaborate yellow Chinese hangings; books bound in tawny satins or fair blue silks and wrought with *fleurs-de-lis*, birds and images; veils of *lacis* worked in Hungary point; Sicilian brocades and stiff Spanish velvets; Georgian work, with its gilt coins, and Japanese *Foukousas*, with their green-toned golds and their marvellously plumaged birds.

He had a special passion, also, for ecclesiastical vestments, as indeed he had for everything connected with the service of the Church. In the long cedar chests that lined the west gallery of his house, he had stored away many rare and beautiful specimens of what is really the raiment of the Bride of Christ, who must wear purple and jewels and fine linen that she may hide the pallid macerated body that is worn by the suffering that she seeks for and wounded by self-inflicted pain. He possessed a gorgeous cope of crimson silk and gold-thread damask, figured with a repeating pattern of golden pomegranates set in six-petalled formal blossoms, beyond which on either side was the pine-apple device wrought in seed-pearls. The orphreys were divided into panels representing scenes from the life of the Virgin, and the coronation of the Virgin was figured in coloured silks upon the hood. This was Italian work of the fifteenth century. Another cope was of green velvet, embroidered with heart-shaped groups of acanthus-leaves, from which spread long-stemmed white blossoms, the details of which were picked out with silver thread and coloured crystals. The morse bore a seraph's head in gold-thread raised work. The orphreys were woven in a diaper of red and gold silk, and were starred with medallions of many saints and martyrs, among whom was St. Sebastian. He had chasubles, also, of amber-coloured silk, and blue silk and gold brocade, and yellow silk damask and cloth of gold, figured with representations of the Passion and Crucifixion of Christ, and embroidered with lions and peacocks and other emblems; dalmatics of white satin and pink silk damask, decorated with tulips and dolphins and *fleurs-de-lis*; altar frontals of crimson velvet and blue linen; and many corporals, chalice-veils, and sudaria. In the mystic offices to which such things were put, there was something that quickened his imagination.

For these treasures, and everything that he collected in his lovely house, were to be to him means of forgetfulness, modes by which he could escape, for a season, from the fear that seemed to him at times to be almost too great to be borne. [...]

6. Selected *Punch* Cartoons

a. "Acute Chinamania" (17 December 1874)

CHRONIC CHINAMANIA (INCURABLE).

Pata Æthelried. "THIS IS THE CREAM OF MY COLLECTION, LADIES AND GENTLEMEN. IT IS QUITE UNIQUE. IT WAS MADE BY THE FALLOWBROOK POTTERY THAT WAS STARTED IN 1870. IT TOOK THEM THREE YEARS TO PRODUCE THIS PLATE. THIS ONLY ONE, AND THEN—AND THEN— *Ruddy Philistine.* "AND THEN THEY SHUT UP, I SUPPOSE?" *Pata Æthelried.* "EH—YES!" *Ruddy Philistine.* "AND I DON'T WONDER!!!"

b. "Chronic Chinamania" (17 December 1874)

THE SIX-MARK TEA-POT.

Æsthetic Bridegroom. "IT IS QUITE CONSUMMATE, IS IT NOT ?"
Intense Bride. "IT IS, INDEED ! OH, ALGERNON, LET US LIVE UP TO IT !"

BY SPECIAL PHOTOPHONE.

(Ray-reported from Olympus.)

Mercury. "Nothing new under the sun," eh, Phœbus? What do you think of *this* ?

Phœbus (screwing up his treble string). Pooh! Mole-eyed mortals overlook a plain fact for a few thousand years, and then, accidentally stumbling over it, crow loudly about "progress" and "novelty." A snail, slowly and slimily trailing over a garden, blundered unwittingly against a strawberry. "Heavens! how clever am I!" cried the snail. You can make the application for yourself.

Mercury. Well, I know Prometheus is getting proud of his *protégés.* And I say, Phœbus, aren't they just making use of *you* ?

Venus. Disgusting! The preposterous *parvenu*, Man, is getting *too* impertinent. First he makes you take portraits of terrestrial tag-rag, from professional beauties to *endimanché* pork-butchers; now, forsooth, you're to carry messages for traders and those solemn idiots called—what is it—diplomatics ?

Mercury. Diplomatists, my dear Goddess. You are confounding deliberate burlesque

with that which is unconscious. The latter is far the funnier.

Venus (crushing an unoffending amaranth blossom with a rosy but restless foot). To *you*, cynic, not to me. Too heavy! I can stand OFFENBACH's *soufflée,* but not BISMARCK's "stodge," or GLADSTONE's Cabinet-pudding. But, Phœbus, *très cher,* why do you let the mannikins make a sort of tenth-rate Mercury of you ? Why don't you serve them as Jupiter did that forward minx Semele ?

Phœbus (twangling the air of "I am an Artless Thing"). Humph! It amuses them, and doesn't hurt me, you know.

(Sings.) Let EDISON and BELL
Do as they will, badly or well,
    I am a genial God!
    I am a genial God!
     Ma foi! le jeu ne vaut
  Pas la chandelle, pas la chandelle,
Although "tapping" Phœbus *de omnibus rebus*
    Perchance seem odd.
   Man's proud of his Photophone ;
  Let the poor little midget alone.
To coil and reflector I'm not an objector—
    I am such a genial God !

Mercury. Doubtless. But that's hardly the prevailing opinion among your "midgets" just at present. On the contrary, they think you get less and less genial every season — in London at least, where indeed they see little of you in the summer (?), and nothing at all in the winter.

Phœbus. Bah! The latter loss at least is mainly the fools' own fault. "Against dulness"—especially in the form of London fog—"even the Gods fight in vain !" Let Prometheus's latter-day pet, Science, teach them to make a better use of their stolen fire and banish darkness as well as utilise light.

Venus. Pooh! Men are born *Cimmerii,* all of them, and fog is their native element, *ne'est-ce pas ?* I once saw a London "Beauty" in November, with red eyes and a smut on her nose! Eugh !

[Rubs her own tenderly tip-tilted organ in unconscious sympathy.

Phœbus. Well, if the Cockneys don't soon set themselves seriously to the task of banishing the Smoke Fiend, *I* shall not be of much more service to them.

Mercury. They may light, they may lighten the town as they will,
    But the pea-soupy fog-pall will hang o'er it still.

Phœbus. Precisely. (Sings.)

I really don't desire
Their stolen fire should light their pyre,
    I am a genial God, &c.
  But 'neath the yoke of smoke
If they will choke—nor Science invoke,
It's no use to halloo for help to Apollo,
    Or ask Jove's nod.
  I'm willing quite my light
Should carry their messages right,
If they only won't clog up its pathway with fog—
    I *am* such a genial God !

BY JOB TROTTER'S BROTHER.

WHEN is it possible to mistake a horse for a hypocrite ?
    When you take him for a canter.

c. "The Six-Mark Tea-Pot" (30 October 1880)

WHAT IT HAS COME TO.

Mrs. Muggles. "WELL, DOCTOR, I DON'T KNOW AS WHAT'S THE MATTER WITH MARIER SINCE SHE COME FROM HER LAST STERWATION IN LUNNON. THERE SHE SITS ALL DAY A-STARING AT AN OLD CHINEY DISH, WHICH SHE CALLS A-GOING IN FOR *ATHLETICS!*"   [*Of course Mrs. M. meant "Æsthetics."*]

HIGH ART BELOW-STAIRS.

JOHN SMAULKER JUNIOR STARTS A SOCIETY.

MY DEAR MARY,

I SAID in my last that I would tell you all about the formashun of our new Society for bringing Beauty ome to the Pantry. I now perceed to do so.

We met, a round duzzen hof us, in the Suvvinks All at Peacocke Pleasaunce. Bein woted into the Chair—a reglar Chippingdale, my dear!—unanermous, I opened the perceedings with the following perryration.

"Frends and feller Suvvinks! (*Murmurs.*) Percisely! Them murmurs does you hall credit, and likeways gives me my kew. The word 'Suvvink' is hindeed hindiwidgious. ('*Ear! ear!*') Suvvice is simply Slavery—('*Quet so! quet so!*')—hunless helewated by Art into washup. (*Applause.*) Then the most meanyul horfis bekums a Kult, and *that* is the true *raisin date* of Kultchaw in the Kitching. (*Garsps of approval from Cook, who is a martyr to tightlacing in the oly kors of the Konsummit.*) It is igh time that those who live below-stairs should learn to Exist Beautifully, which can honly be done by leading a life wich is innardly hintense and hexternully dekkerative. At presink that is honly posserble to a limited hextent. Livrys all round is not what they should be. A trooly dekkerative footman is a rare objeck, and the distrybution of buttings on a page boy's jacket is a evvy haffliction to the heasthetick heye. ('*Ear! ear!*' *from pore young* MIGGLES, *who showed a dispersition to wrop hisself from view in a sage-green curling.*) Neither is the fizzikal surroundings of the suvvinks' quarters kondoocive to the free development of the Hutter. (*Groans.*) I know some sensitive soles—(*and ere I was a thinkin of you,* MARY, *dear*)—whose lives is made a burding to them along of the Philistian hobtuseness of their hemployers. Secret love of the Lily, or privit kontemplation of fragments of Blue Crockery, is not enuff. Aving to sweep a huneasthetick carpet, dust Philistian furniture, or lay hout a dinner wiolating all the most sacred cannons of Igh Art, is triles to wich no suvvink should be subjeck. ('*Ear! ear!*' *from* MELINDER JANE, *who, in her hextaticy of approval, somehow got her skirts in a tangle, and ad to be carefully unknutted, like a badly-tied parsel, by our Konsummit Cook.*) The hobjeck of the Twirl Society," I perceeded, "is, as you know, to bring Beauty ome to the Basement,—

in which there will then be no abasement wot somever. ('*Ear! ear!*' *all round, and '*Isn't he too tooly too?*' from* MELINDER JANE.) I kommend it artily to your pattrennage and support."

This speech were received with applause at once numerous and emphatick, and I were elected, *nem. kon.*, perpetual presidenk and poick-loreate in hordinary to the New Socierty—the latter in konsekens of my well known love of the Mews. One pussing presenk, hindeed, a six foot footman, with the most wulgarly wigorous wiskers, and carves of puffeckly revolting protubbyrance, said that the Hintense, so fur as he hunderstood it, seemed a bit bilious, not to say eppyleptic, and that limp spines, spindle shanks, and bamboo fingers were not *his* hidea of flunkey "form." He likeways remarked that the "fads" of Swell Society didn't suit the Suvvinks' All, any more than the labourer's Cottage, and that if Beauty hinterdooced erself to *his* Ome, looking as lanky and oller eyed as Miss HORIANNER LOWDER, he should feel it a Christian duty to wrop her up warm and take her straight to the Brompton Ospittle. These Philistian sentiments was met with a gashly groan all round, and MELINDER JANE, who wos got up in a spideresk kostume, like a Nockturn in drab and dust colour, struck a dekkerative hattitood of seeh Medoosa like wo, that Wiskers seemed stone-struck, and backing out backwards, well nigh broke his back down the airey steps.

This hobnoxhus hobstructive bein thus cumfably disposed of, we perceeded in our oly work as reposefully as a kumpunny of Mister BURN JONES's hangels. As poick-loreate I were requested to write a sort of Inoggerel Hode, and since then I ave bin day and night in the throws of compogition to that hextent that my timpynum as become inserverble to the bells, I presented Mr. MOLDWARP's card to Miss HORIANNER on a soup-plate, and akshally anded that kollerick Cayting Stoo a peacock's feather when he asked for his unting krop. I believe if he *could* ave knocked me down with a feather he'd a done it there and then, seeh is the unsympathetiek hattitood of the Philistian mind towards the habsorbed hintensity of the Hutter! Owsomever the poick in me as riz superior to the slings and arrers of rampageous thingummy, and my labouring Mews has give buth to somethink Distinctly Quite, though to the wulgar hintelligence possibly not quite distinct. The Pome is called "Pan in the Pantry," and is treated paregorically. In my nex I shall ave the pleshure of persenting it to you, my dear gurl, and of giving you some account of its reception by our seleck little Igh Art Suckle at Peacocke Pleasaunce. Hever your own,

JOHN SMAULKER JEWNIOR.

MOORE MODERNISED.

For the Use of Contemporary Society.

SONG FOR A HIGH-ART HOSTESS.

AIR—"*Come rest on this bosom, my own stricken dear.*"

COME, rest on this gridiron, my own dear æsthete,
Though the herd may contemn, 'tis a true High-Art seat:
These, these the contours that Art yearns to create,
A leg that is spindly, a back that is straight.

Oh, where is the taste that is worthy the name
Loves not the stiff lines of this cast-iron frame?
I know not, I ask not if ease they impart,
I but know they are true to the canons of Art.

Do they call it all corners? They know not the bliss
Of the angular style in a seat such as this.
In furnishing, firmly High Art I'll pursue,
And I'll crouch on my gridiron couch till all's blue.

"Budget" and "Mum."

EVERYBODY, of course, has been ready with their quotation from *The Merry Wives, à propos* of Mr. GLADSTONE's "Budget" and "Mum." It occurs in a dialogue between *Slender* and *Shallow.* It is *Slender's* "Budget" and "Mum," and it is a shallow objection that is made to it.

---

d. "What It Has Come to" (16 April 1881)
d. "What It Has Come to" (16 April 1881)

Appendix D: Reading Material Cultures

[The following works highlight how the emerging science of anthropology practised a kind of reading of material objects as signs of evolutionary development, as in E.B. Tylor's discussion of primitive cultures (in *Primitive Culture*, excerpts of which are reproduced below). Excerpts from Max Nordau's *Degeneration* show how he "reads" objects and object practices such as the collecting of *bric-à-brac* as "symptoms" or tell-tale signs of degeneration. While Decadent authors and protagonists often fashioned themselves as counter-cultural, their obsession with collecting, especially of "exotic" things, aligns with hegemonic imperial sentiments and practices as well as with the emergence of specimen-based sciences (themselves also implicated in hegemonic imperial sentiments and practices).]

1. From E.B. Tylor, *Primitive Culture: Researches into the Development of Mythology, Philosophy, Religion, Art and Custom*, vol. 1 (John Murray, 1871)

Chapter I: "The Science of Culture"

Culture or Civilization, taken in its wide ethnographic sense, is that complex whole which includes knowledge, belief, art, morals, law, custom, and any other capabilities and habits acquired by man as a member of society. The condition of culture among the various societies of mankind, in so far as it is capable of being investigated on general principles, is a subject apt for the study of laws of human thought and action. On the one hand, the uniformity which so largely pervades civilization may be ascribed, in great measure, to the uniform action of uniform causes; while on the other hand its various grades may be regarded as stages of development or evolution, each the outcome of previous history, and about to do its proper part in shaping the history of the future. To the investigation of these two great principles in several departments of ethnography, with especial consideration of the civilization of the lower tribes as related to the civilization of the higher nations, the present volumes are devoted.(1) [...]

A first step in the study of civilization is to dissect it into details, and to classify these in their proper groups. Thus, in examining weapons, they are to be classed under spear, club, sling, bow and arrow, and so forth; among textile arts are to be ranged matting, netting, and several grades of making and weaving threads; myths are divided under such headings as myths of sunrise and sunset, eclipse-myths, earthquake-myths, local myths which account for the names of places by some fanciful tale, eponymic myths which account for the parentage of a tribe by turning its name into the name of an imaginary ancestor; under rites and ceremonies occur such practices as the various kinds of sacrifice to the ghosts of the dead and to other spiritual beings, the turning to the east in worship, the purification of ceremonial or moral uncleanness by means of water or fire. Such are a few miscellaneous examples from a list of hundreds, and the ethnographer's business is to classify such details with a view to making out their distribution in geography and history, and the relations which exist among them. What this task is like, may be almost perfectly illustrated by comparing these details of culture with the species of plants and animals as studied by the naturalist. To the ethnographer, the bow and arrow is a species, the habit of flattening children's skulls is a species, the practice of reckoning numbers by tens is a species. The geographical distribution of these things, and their transmission from region to region, have to be studied as the naturalist studies the geography of his botanical and zoological species. Just as certain plants and animals are peculiar to certain districts, so it is with such instruments [...]. Just as the catalogue of all the species of plants and animals of a district represents its Flora and Fauna, so the list of all the items of the general life of a people represent that whole which we call its culture. And just as distant regions so often produce vegetables and animals which are analogous, though by no means identical, so it is with the details of the civilization of their inhabitants. (7–8) [...]

Among evidence aiding us to trace the course which the civilization of the world has actually followed, is that great class of facts to denote which I have found it convenient to introduce the term "survivals." These are processes, customs, opinions, and so forth, which have been carried on by force of habit into a new state of society different from that in which they had their original home, and they thus remain as proofs and examples of an older condition of culture out of which a newer has been evolved. Thus, I know an old Somersetshire woman whose hand-loom dates from the time before the introduction of the "flying shuttle," which new-fangled appliance she has never even learnt to use, and I have seen her throw her shuttle from hand to hand in true classic fashion; this old woman is not a century behind her times, but she is a case of survival. Such examples often lead us back to the habits of hundreds and even thousands of years ago. The ordeal of the Key and Bible, still in use, is a survival; the Midsummer bonfire is a survival; the Breton peasants 'All Souls' supper for the spirits of the dead is a survival. The simple keeping up of ancient habits is only one part of the transition from old into new and changing times. The serious business of ancient society may be seen to sink into the sport of later generations, and its serious belief to linger on in nursery folk-lore, while superseded habits of old-world life may be modified into new-world forms still powerful for good and evil. Sometimes old thoughts and practices will burst out afresh, to the amazement of a world that thought them long since dead or dying; here survival passes into revival, as has lately happened in so remarkable a way in the history of modern spiritualism, a subject full of instruction from the ethnographer's point of view. The study of the principles of survival has, indeed, no small practical importance, for most of what we call superstition is included within survival, and in this way lies open to the attack of its deadliest enemy, a reasonable explanation. Insignificant, moreover, as multitudes of the facts of survival are in themselves, their study is so effective for tracing the course of the historical development through which alone it is possible to understand their meaning, that it becomes a vital point of ethnographic research to gain the clearest possible insight into their nature. This importance must justify the detail here devoted to an examination of survival, on the evidence of such games, popular sayings, customs, superstitions, and the like, as may serve well to bring into view the manner of its operation.

Progress, degradation, survival, revival, modification, are all modes of the connexion that binds together the complex network of civilization. It needs but a glance into the trivial details of our own daily life to set us thinking how far we are really its originators, and how far but the transmitters and modifiers of the results of long past ages. Looking round the rooms we live in, we may try here how far he who only knows his own time can be capable of rightly comprehending even that. Here is the honeysuckle of Assyria, there the fleur-de-lis of Anjou, a cornice with a Greek border runs round the ceiling, the style of Louis XIV. and its parent the Renaissance share the looking-glass between them. Transformed, shifted, or mutilated, such elements of art still carry their history plainly stamped upon them; and if the history yet farther behind is less easy to read, we are not to say that because we cannot clearly discern it there is therefore no history there. [...] (14–16)

Chapter II: "The Development of Culture"

In taking up the problem of the development of culture as a branch of ethnological research, a first proceeding is to obtain a means of measurement. Seeking something like a definite line along which to reckon progression and retrogression in civilization, we may apparently find it best in the classification of real tribes and nations, past and present. Civilization actually existing among mankind in different grades, we are enabled to estimate and compare it by positive examples. The educated world of Europe and America practically settles a standard by simply placing its own nations at one end of the social series and savage tribes at the other, arranging the rest of mankind between these limits according as they correspond more closely to savage or to cultured life. The principal criteria of classification are the absence or presence, high or low development, of the industrial arts, especially metal-working, manufacture of implements and vessels, agriculture, architecture, &c, the extent of scientific knowledge, the definiteness of moral principles, the condition of religious belief and ceremony, the degree of social and political organization, and so forth. Thus, on the definite basis of compared facts, ethnographers are able to set up at least a rough scale of civilization. (23–24) [...]

By long experience of the course of human society, the principle of development in culture has become so ingrained in our philosophy that ethnologists, of whatever school, hardly doubt but that, whether by progress or degradation, savagery and civilization are connected as lower and higher stages of one formation. As such, then, two principal theories claim to account for their relation. As to the first hypothesis, which takes savage life as in some sort representing an early human state whence higher states were, in time, developed, it has to be noticed that advocates of this progression-theory are apt to look back toward yet lower original conditions of mankind. It has been truly remarked that the modern naturalist's doctrine of progressive development has encouraged a train of thought singularly accordant with the Epicurean theory of man's early existence on earth, in a condition not far removed from that of the lower animals. On such a view, savage life itself would be a far advanced condition. If the advance of culture be regarded as taking place along one general line, then existing savagery stands directly intermediate between animal and civilized life; if along different lines, then savagery and civilization may be considered as, at least, indirectly connected through their common origin. The method and evidence here employed are not, however, suitable for the discussion of this remoter part of the problem of civilization. Nor is it necessary to enquire how, under this or any other theory, the savage state first came to be on earth. It is enough that, by some means or other, it has actually come into existence; and so far as it may serve as a guide in inferring an early condition of the human race at large, so far the argument takes the very practicable shape of a discussion turning rather on actual than imaginary states of society. The second hypothesis, which regards higher culture as original, and the savage condition as produced from it by a course of degeneration, at once cuts the hard knot of the origin of culture. It takes for granted a supernatural interference [...]. It may be incidentally remarked, however, that the doctrine of original civilization bestowed on man by divine intervention, by no means necessarily involves the view that this original civilization was at a high level. Its advocates are free to choose their starting-point of culture above, at, or below the savage condition, as may on the evidence seem to them most reasonable.

The two theories which thus account for the relation of savage to cultured life may be contrasted according to their main character, as the progression-theory and the degradation-theory. Yet of course the progression-theory recognizes degradation, and the degradation-theory recognizes progression, as powerful influences in the course of culture. Under proper limitations the principles of both theories are conformable to historical knowledge, which shows us, on the one hand, that the state of the higher nations was reached by progression from a lower state, and, on the other hand, that culture gained by progression may be lost by degradation. If in this enquiry we should be obliged to end in the dark, at any rate we need not begin there. History, taken as our guide in explaining the different stages of civilization, offers a theory based on actual experience. This is a development-theory, in which both advance and relapse have their acknowledged places. But so far as history is to be our criterion, progression is primary and degradation secondary; culture must be gained before it can be lost. Moreover, in striking a balance between the effects of forward and backward movement in civilization, it must be borne in mind how powerfully the diffusion of culture acts in preserving the results of progress from the attacks of degeneration. A progressive movement in culture spreads, and becomes independent of the fate of its originators. What is produced in some limited district is diffused over a wider and wider area, where the process of effectual "stamping out" becomes more and more difficult. Thus it is even possible for the habits and inventions of races long extinct to remain as the common property of surviving nations; and the destructive actions which make such havoc with the civilizations of particular districts fail to destroy the civilization of the world. (33–35) [...]

The master-key to the investigation of man's primæval condition is held by Prehistoric Archaeology. This key is the evidence of the Stone Age, proving that men of remotely ancient ages were in the savage state. Ever since the long-delayed recognition of M. Boucher de Perthes' discoveries (1841 and onward) of the flint implements in the Drift gravels of the Somme Valley, evidence has been accumulating over a wide European area to show that the ruder Stone Age, represented by implements of the Palæolithic or Drift type, prevailed among savage tribes of the Quaternary period, the contemporaries of the mammoth and the woolly rhinoceros, in ages for which Geology asserts an antiquity far more remote than History can avail to substantiate for the human race. Mr. John Frere had already written in 1797 respecting such flint instruments discovered at Hoxne in Suffolk. "The situation in which these weapons were found may tempt us to refer them to a very remote period indeed, even beyond that of the present world."[1] The vast lapse of time through which the history of London has represented the history of human civilization, is to my mind one of the most suggestive facts disclosed by archæology. The antiquary, excavating but a few yards deep, may descend from the debris representing our modern life, to relics of the art and science of the Middle Ages, to signs of Norman, Saxon, Romano-British times, to traces of the higher Stone Age. And on his way from Temple Bar to the Great Northern Station he passes near the spot ("opposite to black Mary's, near Grayes inn lane") where a drift implement of black flint was found with the skeleton of an elephant by Mr. Conyers, about a century and a half ago, the relics side by side with the London mammoth and the London savage.[2] In the gravel-beds of Europe, the laterite of India, and

---

1 [Tylor's note:] Frere, in 'Archæologia,' 1800.
2 [Tylor's note:] J. Evans, in 'Archæologia,' 1861; Lubbock, 'Prehistoric Times,' 2nd ed., p. 335.

other more superficial localities, where relics of the Palæolithic Age are found, what principally testifies to man's condition is the extreme rudeness of his stone implements, and the absence of even edge-grinding. (52–53)

Chapter III: "Survival in Culture"

When a custom, an art, or an opinion is fairly started in the world, disturbing influences may long affect it so slightly that it may keep its course from generation to generation, as a stream once settled in its bed will flow on for ages. This is mere permanence of culture; and the special wonder about it is that the change and revolution of human affairs should have left so many of its feeblest rivulets to run so long. [...]

Now there are thousands of cases of this kind which have become, so to speak, landmarks in the course of culture. When in the process of time there has come general change in the condition of a people, it is usual, notwithstanding, to find much that manifestly had not its origin in the new state of things, but has simply lasted on into it. On the strength of these survivals, it becomes possible to declare that the civilization of the people they are observed among must have been derived from an earlier state, in which the proper home and meaning of these things are to be found; and thus collections of such facts are to be worked as mines of historic knowledge. In dealing with such materials, experience of what actually happens is the main guide, and direct history has to teach us, first and foremost, how old habits hold their ground in the midst of a new culture which certainly would never have brought them in, but on the contrary presses hard to thrust them out. (63–64) [...]

Chapter IV: "Survival in Culture (continued)"

In examining the survival of opinions in the midst of conditions of society becoming gradually estranged from them, and tending at last to suppress them altogether, much may be learnt from the history of one of the most pernicious delusions that ever vexed mankind, the belief in Magic. Looking at Occult Science from this ethnographic point of view, I shall instance some of its branches as illustrating the course of intellectual culture. Its place in history is briefly this. It belongs in its main principle to the lowest known stages of civilization, and the lower races, who have not partaken largely of the education of the world, still maintain it in vigour. From this level it may be traced upward, much of the savage art holding its place substantially unchanged, and many new practices being in course of time developed, while both the older and newer developments have lasted on more or less among modern cultured nations. But during the ages in which progressive races have been learning to submit their opinions to closer and closer experimental tests, occult science has been breaking down into the condition of a survival, in which state we mostly find it among ourselves.

The modern educated world, rejecting occult science as a contemptible superstition, has practically committed itself to the opinion that magic belongs to a lower level of civilization. It is very instructive to find the soundness of this judgment undesignedly confirmed by nations whose education has not advanced far enough to destroy their belief in the craft itself. In some cases, indeed, the reputation of a race as sorcerers may depend on their actually putting forward supernatural pretensions, or merely on their being isolated and mysterious people. (101–02) [...]

The principal key to the understanding of Occult Science is to consider it as based on the Association of Ideas, a faculty which lies at the very foundation of human reason, but in no small degree of human unreason also. Man, as yet in a low intellectual condition, having come to associate in thought those things which he found by experience to be connected in fact, proceeded erroneously to invert this action, and to conclude that association in thought must involve similar connexion in reality. He thus attempted to discover, to foretell, and to cause events by means of processes which we can now see to have only an ideal significance. By a vast mass of evidence from savage, barbaric, and civilized life, magic arts which have resulted from thus mistaking an ideal for a real connexion, may be clearly traced from the lower culture which they are of, to the higher culture which they are in. (104–05) [...]

Throughout the whole of this varied investigation, whether of the dwindling survival of old culture, or of its bursting forth afresh in active revival, it may perhaps be complained that its illustrations should be so much among things worn out, worthless, frivolous, or even bad with downright harmful folly. It is in fact so, and I have taken up this course of argument with full knowledge and intent. For, indeed, we have in such enquiries continual reason to be thankful for fools. It is quite wonderful, even if we hardly go below the surface of the subject, to see how large a share stupidity and unpractical conservatism and dogged superstition have had in preserving for us traces of the history of our race, which practical utilitarianism would have remorselessly swept away. The savage is firmly, obstinately conservative. No man appeals with more unhesitating confidence to the great precedent-makers of the past; the wisdom of his ancestors can control against the most obvious evidence his own opinions and actions.

The nobler tendency of advancing culture, and above all of scientific culture, is to honour the dead without grovelling before them, to profit by the past without sacrificing the present to it. Yet even the modern civilized world has but half learnt this lesson, and an unprejudiced survey may lead us to judge how many of our ideas and customs exist rather by being old than by being good. (142)

Chapter XI: "Animism"

[...] Certain high savage races distinctly hold, and a large proportion of other savage and barbarian races make a more or less close approach to, a theory of separable and surviving souls or spirits belonging to stocks and stones, weapons, boats, food, clothes, ornaments, and other objects which to us are not merely soulless but lifeless.

Yet, strange as such a notion may seem to us at first sight, if we place ourselves by an effort in the intellectual position of an uncultured tribe, and examine the theory of object-souls from their point of view, we shall hardly pronounce it irrational. In discussing the origin of myth, some account has been already given of the primitive stage of thought in which personality and life are ascribed not to men and beasts only, but to things. It has been shown how what we call inanimate objects—rivers, stones, trees, weapons, and so forth—are treated as living intelligent beings, talked to, propitiated, punished for the harm they do. Auguste Comte[1] has even ventured to bring such a state of thought under terms of strict definition in his conception of the primary mental condition of mankind—a state of "pure fetishism, constantly characterized by the free and direct exercise of our primitive tendency to conceive all external bodies soever, natural or artificial, as animated by a life essentially analogous to our own, with

---

1   French philosopher (1798–1857) who proposed that human intellectual development progressed through stages: the theological, the metaphysical, and culminating in positivism or the belief in empirically verifiable phenomena.

mere differences of intensity."[1] Our comprehension of the lower stages of mental culture depends much on the thoroughness with which we can appreciate this primitive, childlike conception, and in this our best guide may be the memory of our own childish days. He who recollects when there was still personality to him in posts and sticks, chairs and toys, may well understand how the infant philosophy of mankind could extend the notion of vitality to what modern science only recognises as lifeless things; thus one main part of the lower animistic doctrine as to souls of objects is accounted for. The doctrine requires for its full conception of a soul not only life, but also a phantom or apparitional spirit; this development, however, follows without difficulty, for the evidence of dreams and visions applies to the spirits of objects in much the same manner as to human ghosts. Everyone who has seen visions while light-headed in fever, everyone who has ever dreamt a dream, has seen the phantoms of objects as well as of persons. How then can we charge the savage with far-fetched absurdity for taking into his philosophy and religion an opinion which rests on the very evidence of his senses? The notion is implicitly recognised in his accounts of ghosts which do not come naked, but clothed and even armed; of course there must be spirits of garments and weapons, seeing that the spirits of men come bearing them. It will indeed place savage philosophy in no unfavourable light, if we compare this extreme animistic development of it with the popular opinion still surviving in civilized countries, as to ghosts and the nature of the human soul as connected with them. When the ghost of Hamlet's father appeared armed cap-a-pe,

"Such was the very armour he had on
When he the ambitious Norway combated."

And thus it is a habitual feature of the ghost-stories of the civilized, as of the savage world, that the ghost comes dressed, and even dressed in well-known clothing worn in life. Hearing as well as sight testifies to the phantoms of objects: the clanking of ghostly chains and the rustling of ghostly dresses are described in the literature of apparitions. Now by the savage theory, according to which the ghost and his clothes are alike real and objective, and by the modern scientific theory, according to which both ghost and garment are alike imaginary and subjective, the facts of apparitions are rationally met. But the modern

---

1 [Tylor's note:] Comte, 'Philosophie Positive,' vol. v., p. 30.

vulgar who ignore or repudiate the notion of ghosts of things, while retaining the notion of ghosts of persons, have fallen into a hybrid state of opinion which has neither the logic of the savage nor of the civilized philosopher. [...] (430–32)

2. From E.B. Tylor, "On the Tasmanians as Representatives of Palæolithic Man," *Journal of the Archeological Institute of Great Britain and Ireland*, vol. 23, 1894, pp. 141–52

[...] The question which suggests itself on first inspection of this collection of Tasmanian implements, is how with such poor tools even the rude native crafts could be carried on. It must be noticed, however, that they are for practical purposes somewhat better than they look, being indeed made with great care and skill in getting the edges straight and the grip firm. Fortunately also there are a few passages which show how they were actually used. It seems wonderful that with one of the disc-shaped notching-stones the natives should so quickly have made the notches for climbing the gum-trees, till we notice Mr. Thirkell's remark that they would "chip the bark downwards and make a notch for the big toe," which shows that they did not hack out a piece of the bark, but merely split it in the direction of the fibre, forcing the cut open with the toe till it could rest there. The following, remark by Mr. Rollings shows how cutting was done. "The knives when used for skinning kangaroos, &c., were held by the fore-finger and thumb, and the arm, being extended, was drawn rapidly toward the body. The carcase was afterwards cut up, and the knife was held in the same way. In cutting their hair, one stone was held under the hair, another stone being used above, and by this means the hair was cut, or rather, by repeated nickings, came off."

From the foregoing evidence it appears that the Tasmanians, up to the time of the British colonization in the present century, habitually used stone implements shaped and edged by chipping, not ground or polished. These belong, notwithstanding their modern date, to the order of the very ancient "palæolithic" implements of the Drift and Cave Periods, from which the later implements of the "neolithic" order are distinguished by greater variety of form and skill of finish, and especially by the presence of grinding or polishing. The comparison of the Tasmanian stone implements with those of the ancient world impresses on us the fact that the rude modern savage was content to use a few forms of implement for all purposes of cutting, chopping, &c., these being flakes as struck off the stone, and such flakes or even chance fragments trimmed and brought to a cutting edge by striking off chips along the edge of one surface only, whether completely or partly round. Such tools are known to the Stone Age of the Old World. [...] If it may be taken that the information from Tasmania is conclusive in this respect, it will appear that the savages there, within this century so miserably erased from the catalogue of the human race, were representatives of stone age development, a stage lower than that of the Quaternary period. Even should specimens of higher order be found in Tasmania, they will leave untouched the conclusion now established by abundant evidence, that during the present century the natives habitually made and used for the ordinary purposes of life stone implements of a low palæolithic kind. [...]

Of degeneration in culture as accounting for the low state of implement-making in Tasmania, there is at present no evidence, nor is it easy to imagine their rude tools as the successors of higher ancestral forms. Had they had even the hatchet of their Australian neighbours, sharpened by rubbing its edge on a gritstone, and bound into a withe or cemented to a stick, it is hardly conceivable that they should have abandoned such a tool for a rudely-sharpened cutting stone gripped in the hand; they would have lost more time and pains in the first day than would have sufficed to replace the better implement. Such carelessness would not indeed agree with the careful and patient skill which they, like other savages, gave to finishing their rude implements to the most serviceable point, in which they would spend hours and even days, regardless of trouble. The well-known readiness with which they took to European tools, shows an appreciation of labour-saving which contrasts strongly with the idea that at any time, possessing ground stone hatchets with handles, they abandoned them for chipped stones grasped in the hand. It seems more likely to consider that in their remote corner of the globe they may have gone on little changed from early ages, so as to have remained to our day living representatives of the early Stone Age, left behind in industrial development. [...]

3. From Max Nordau, *Degeneration* (William Heinemann, 1898), pp. 1–15

"The Dusk of Nations"

Fin-de-siècle is a name covering both what is characteristic of many modern phenomena, and also the underlying mood which in them finds expression. [...] *Fin-de-siècle* is French, for it was in France that the mental state so entitled was first consciously realized. The word has flown from one hemisphere to the other, and found its way into all civilized languages. A proof this that the need of it existed. The *fin-de-siècle* state of mind is to-day everywhere to be met with; nevertheless, it is in many cases a mere imitation of a foreign fashion gaining vogue, and not an organic evolution. It is in the land of its birth that it appears in its most genuine form, and Paris is the right place in which to observe its manifold expressions. [...]
[...] The disposition of the times is curiously confused, a compound of feverish restlessness and blunted discouragement, of fearful presage and hang-dog renunciation. The prevalent feeling is that of imminent perdition and extinction. *Fin-de-siècle* is at once a confession and a complaint. [...] In our days there have arisen in more highly-developed minds vague qualms of a Dusk of the Nations, in which all suns and all stars are gradually waning, and mankind with all its institutions and creations is perishing in the midst of a dying world. [...]

"The Symptoms" [After examining, in great detail, the unnatural hairstyles, discordant modes of dress or costume and accessories worn by degenerate women, children, and men, Nordau examines the contents of their homes, including a long list of collected things as "symptoms" of degeneration.]

[...] Let us follow these folk in masquerade and with heads in character to their dwellings. Here are at once stage properties and lumber-rooms, rag-shops and museums. The study of the master of the house is a Gothic hall of chivalry, with cuirasses, shields and crusading banners on the walls; or the shop of an Oriental bazaar with Kurd carpets, Bedouin chests, Circassian narghilehs and Indian lacquered caskets. By the mirror on the mantelpiece are fierce or funny Japanese masks. Between the windows are staring trophies of swords, daggers, clubs and old wheel-trigger pistols. Daylight filters in through painted glass, where lean saints kneel in rapture. In the drawing-room the walls are either hung with worm-eaten Gobelin tapestry, discoloured by the sun of two centuries (or it may be by a deftly mixed chemical bath), or covered with Morris draperies, on which strange birds flit amongst crazily ramping branches, and blowzy flowers coquet with vain butterflies. Amongst armchairs and padded seats, such as the cockered bodies of our contemporaries know and expect, there are Renaissance stools, the heart or shell-shaped bottoms of which would attract none but the toughened hide of a rough hero of the jousting lists. Startling is the effect of a gilt-painted couch between buhl-work cabinets and a puckered Chinese table, next an inlaid writing-table of graceful rococo. On all the tables and in all the cabinets is a display of antiquities or articles of vertù, big or small, and for the most part warranted not genuine; a figure of Tanagra near a broken jade snuff-box, a Limoges plate beside a long-necked Persian waterpot of brass, a *bonbonnière* between a breviary bound in carved ivory, and snuffers of chiselled copper. Pictures stand on easels draped with velvet, the frames made conspicuous by some oddity, such as a spider in her web, a metal bunch of thistle-heads, and the like. In a corner a sort of temple is erected to a squatting or a standing Buddha. The boudoir of the mistress of the house partakes of the nature of a chapel and of a harem. The toilet-table is designed and decorated like an altar, a *prie-Dieu* is a pledge for the piety of the inmate, and a broad divan, with an orgiastic *abandon* about the cushions, gives reassurance that things are not so bad. In the dining-room the walls are hung with the whole stock-in-trade of a porcelain shop, costly silver is displayed in an old farmhouse dresser, and on the table bloom aristocratic orchids, and proud silver vessels shine between rustic stone-ware plates and ewers. In the evening, lamps of the stature of a man illumine these rooms with light both subdued and tinted by sprawling shades, red, yellow or green of hue, and even covered by black lace. Hence the inmates appear, now bathed in variegated diaphanous mist, now suffused with coloured radiance, while the corners and backgrounds are shrouded in depths of artfully-effected *clair-obscur*, and the furniture and *bric-à-brac* are dyed in unreal chords of colour. Unreal, too, are the studied postures, by assuming which the inmates are enabled to reproduce on their faces the light effects of Rembrandt or Schalcken. Everything in these houses aims at exciting the nerves and dazzling the senses. The disconnected and antithetical effects in all arrangements, the constant contradiction between form and purpose, the outlandishness of most objects, is intended to be bewildering. There must be no sentiment of repose, such as is felt at any composition, the plan of which is easily taken in, nor of the comfort attending a prompt comprehension of all the details of one's environment. He who enters here must not doze, but be thrilled. If the master of the house roams about these rooms clothed after the example of Balzac in a white monk's cowl, or after the model of Richepin in the red cloak of the robber-chieftain of an operetta, he only gives expression to the admission that in such a comedy theatre a clown is in place. All is discrepant, indiscriminate jumble. The unity of abiding by one definite historic style counts as old-fashioned, provincial, Philistine, and the time has not yet produced a style of its own. An approach is, perhaps, made to one in the furniture of Carabin, exhibited in the salon of the Champs de Mars. But these balusters, down which naked furies and possessed creatures are rolling in mad riot, these bookcases, where base and pilaster consist of a pile of guillotined heads, and even this table, representing a gigantic open book borne by gnomes, make up a style that is feverish and infernal. [...]

Appendix E: Literary Inter-Texts

[Perhaps the closest inter-text for *The Three Impostors* is Robert Louis Stevenson and Fanny Van der Grift Stevenson's *The Dynamiter*, an excerpt from which is reproduced below. Also notable, though, are the inter-textual elements across Machen's own texts. Dyson, for example, is a character that reoccurs in other works by Machen, extracts from two of which, "The Inmost Light" and "The Red Hand," are included below.]

1. From Robert Louis Stevenson and Fanny Van der Grift Stevenson, "Prologue of the Cigar Divan," *The Dynamiter*, in *New Arabian Nights: Second Series* (Longman's, Green and Co., 1885), pp. 1–12

In the city of encounters, the Bagdad of the West, and, to be more precise, on the broad northern pavement of Leicester Square, two young men of five- or six-and-twenty met after years of separation. The first, who was of a very smooth address and clothed in the best fashion, hesitated to recognise the pinched and shabby air of his companion.

"What!" he cried, "Paul Somerset!"

"I am indeed Paul Somerset," returned the other, "or what remains of him after a well-deserved experience of poverty and law. But in you, Challoner, I can perceive no change; and time may be said, without hyperbole, to write no wrinkle on your azure brow."[1]

"All," replied Challoner, "is not gold that glitters. But we are here in an ill posture for confidences, and interrupt the movement of these ladies. Let us, if you please, find a more private corner."

"If you will allow me to guide you," replied Somerset, "I will offer you the best cigar in London."

And taking the arm of his companion, he led him in silence and at a brisk pace to the door of a quiet establishment in Rupert Street, Soho. The entrance was adorned with one of those gigantic Highlanders of wood which have almost risen to the standing

---

1 Somerset's words echo a line from *Childe Harold's Pilgrimage: Canto the Fourth* (1818) by Lord Byron (1788–1824): "Time writes no wrinkle on thine azure brow."

of antiquities; and across the window-glass, which sheltered the usual display of pipes, tobacco, and cigars, there ran the gilded legend: "Bohemian Cigar Divan,[1] by T. Godall." The interior of the shop was small, but commodious and ornate; the salesman grave, smiling, and urbane; and the two young men, each puffing a select regalia, had soon taken their places on a sofa of mouse-coloured plush and proceeded to exchange their stories.

"I am now," said Somerset, "a barrister; but Providence and the attorneys have hitherto denied me the opportunity to shine. A select society at the Cheshire Cheese engaged my evenings; my afternoons, as Mr. Godall could testify, have been generally passed in this divan; and my mornings, I have taken the precaution to abbreviate by not rising before twelve. At this rate, my little patrimony was very rapidly, and I am proud to remember, most agreeably expended. Since then a gentleman, who has really nothing else to recommend him beyond the fact of being my maternal uncle, deals me the small sum of ten shillings a week; and if you behold me once more revisiting the glimpses of the street lamps in my favourite quarter, you will readily divine that I have come into a fortune."

"I should not have supposed so," replied Challoner. "But doubtless I met you on the way to your tailors."

"It is a visit that I purpose to delay," returned Somerset, with a smile. "My fortune has definite limits. It consists, or rather this morning it consisted, of one hundred pounds."

"That is certainly odd," said Challoner; "yes, certainly the coincidence is strange. I am myself reduced to the same margin."

"You!" cried Somerset. "And yet Solomon in all his glory—"[2]

"Such is the fact. I am, dear boy, on my last legs," said Challoner. "Besides the clothes in which you see me, I have scarcely a decent trouser in my wardrobe; and if I knew how, I would this instant set about some sort of work or commerce. With a hundred pounds for capital, a man should push his way."

"It may be," returned Somerset; "but what to do with mine is more than I can fancy. Mr. Godall," he added, addressing the salesman, "you are a man who knows the world: what

---

1 A smoking lounge and cigar shop (*OED*).

2 Biblical allusion to Matthew 6:29, part of the Sermon on the Mount, where Jesus tells his followers not to worry about food or clothing, as God provides for the needs of living things; using the example of lilies, he points out that while they do not work, they are better arrayed than Solomon in all his glory. (A similar passage occurs in Luke 12:27.)

can a young fellow of reasonable education do with a hundred pounds?"

"It depends," replied the salesman, withdrawing his cheroot.[1] "The power of money is an article of faith in which I profess myself a sceptic. A hundred pounds will with difficulty support you for a year; with somewhat more difficulty you may spend it in a night; and without any difficulty at all you may lose it in five minutes on the Stock Exchange. If you are of that stamp of man that rises, a penny would be as useful; if you belong to those that fall, a penny would be no more useless. When I was myself thrown unexpectedly upon the world, it was my fortune to possess an art: I knew a good cigar. Do you know nothing, Mr. Somerset?"

"Not even law," was the reply.

"The answer is worthy of a sage," returned Mr. Godall. "And you, sir," he continued, turning to Challoner, "as the friend of Mr. Somerset, may I be allowed to address you the same question?"

"Well," replied Challoner, "I play a fair hand at whist."[2]

"How many persons are there in London," returned the salesman, "who have two-and-thirty teeth? Believe me, young gentleman, there are more still who play a fair hand at whist. Whist, sir, is wide as the world; 'tis an accomplishment like breathing. I once knew a youth who announced that he was studying to be Chancellor of England; the design was certainly ambitious; but I find it less excessive than that of the man who aspires to make a livelihood by whist."

"Dear me," said Challoner, "I am afraid I shall have to fall to be a working man."

"Fall to be a working man?" echoed Mr. Godall. "Suppose a rural dean to be unfrocked, does he fall to be a major? suppose a captain were cashiered, would he fall to be a puisne judge?[3] The ignorance of your middle class surprises me. Outside itself, it thinks the world to lie quite ignorant and equal, sunk in a common degradation; but to the eye of the observer, all ranks are seen to stand in ordered hierarchies, and each adorned with its particular aptitudes and knowledge. By the defects of your education you are more disqualified to be a working man than to be the ruler of an empire. The gulf, sir, is below; and the true learned arts—those which alone are safe from the competition of insurgent laymen—are those which give his title to the artisan."

---

1 Cigar.

2 English card game.

3 Any judge or judgeship other than the most senior (*OED*).

"This is a very pompous fellow," said Challoner in the ear of his companion.

"He is immense," said Somerset.

Just then the door of the divan was opened, and a third young fellow made his appearance, and rather bashfully requested some tobacco. He was younger than the others; and, in a somewhat meaningless and altogether English way, he was a handsome lad. When he had been served, and had lighted his pipe and taken his place upon the sofa, he recalled himself to Challoner by the name of Desborough.

"Desborough, to be sure," cried Challoner. "Well, Desborough, and what do you do?"

"The fact is," said Desborough, "that I am doing nothing."

"A private fortune possibly?" inquired the other.

"Well, no," replied Desborough, rather sulkily. "The fact is that I am waiting for something to turn up."

"All in the same boat!" cried Somerset. "And have you, too, one hundred pounds?"

"Worse luck," said Mr. Desborough.

"This is a very pathetic sight, Mr. Godall," said Somerset: "Three futiles."

"A character of this crowded age," returned the salesman.

"Sir," said Somerset, "I deny that the age is crowded; I will admit one fact, and one fact only: that I am futile, that he is futile, and that we are all three as futile as the devil. What am I? I have smattered law, smattered letters, smattered geography, smattered mathematics; I have even a working knowledge of judicial astrology; and here I stand, all London roaring by at the street's end, as impotent as any baby. I have a prodigious contempt for my maternal uncle; but without him, it is idle to deny it, I should simply resolve into my elements like an unstable mixture. I begin to perceive that it is necessary to know some one thing to the bottom—were it only literature. And yet, sir, the man of the world is a great feature of this age; he is possessed of an extraordinary mass and variety of knowledge; he is everywhere at home; he has seen life in all its phases; and it is impossible but that this great habit of existence should bear fruit. I count myself a man of the world, accomplished, *cap-à-pie*.[1] So do you, Challoner. And you, Mr. Desborough?"

"Oh yes," returned the young man.

"Well then, Mr. Godall, here we stand, three men of the world,

1 From head to foot.

without a trade to cover us, but planted at the strategic centre of the universe (for so you will allow me to call Rupert Street), in the midst of the chief mass of people, and within ear-shot of the most continuous chink of money on the surface of the globe. Sir, as civilised men, what do we do? I will show you. You take in a paper?"

"I take," said Mr. Godall, solemnly, "the best paper in the world, the *Standard.*"

"Good," resumed Somerset. "I now hold it in my hand, the voice of the world, a telephone repeating all men's wants. I open it, and where my eye first falls—well, no, not Morrison's Pills[1]— but here, sure enough, and but a little above, I find the joint that I was seeking; here is the weak spot in the armour of society. Here is a want, a plaint, an offer of substantial gratitude: '*Two hundred Pounds Reward.*—The above reward will be paid to any person giving information as to the identity and whereabouts of a man observed yesterday in the neighbourhood of the Green Park. He was over six feet in height, with shoulders disproportionately broad, close shaved, with black moustaches, and wearing a seal-skin great-coat.' There, gentlemen, our fortune, if not made, is founded."

"Do you then propose, dear boy, that we should turn detectives?" inquired Challoner.

"Do I propose it? No, sir," cried Somerset. "It is reason, destiny, the plain face of the world, that commands and imposes it. Here all our merits tell; our manners, habit of the world, powers of conversation, vast stores of unconnected knowledge, all that we are and have builds up the character of the complete detective. It is, in short, the only profession for a gentleman."

"The proposition is perhaps excessive," replied Challoner; "for hitherto I own I have regarded it as of all dirty, sneaking, and ungentlemanly trades, the least and lowest."

"To defend society?" asked Somerset; "to stake one's life for others? to deracinate occult and powerful evil? I appeal to Mr. Godall. He, at least, as a philosophic looker on at life, will spit upon such philistine[2] opinions. He knows that the policeman, as he is called upon continually to face greater odds, and that both worse equipped and for a better cause, is in form and essence a

---

1 Somerset points to an advertisement for "Morrison Vegetable Pills," a remedy prescribed by "quack" doctor James Morison (1770–1840) for a wide range of ills.

2 One who is unenlightened, particularly in matters of art and culture.

more noble hero than the soldier. Do you, by any chance, deceive yourself into supposing that a general would either ask or expect, from the best army ever marshalled, and on the most momentous battle-field, the conduct of a common constable at Peckham Rye[1]?"[2]

"I did not understand we were to join the force," said Challoner.

"Nor shall we. These are the hands; but here—here, sir, is the head," cried Somerset. "Enough; it is decreed. We shall hunt down this miscreant in the sealskin coat."

"Suppose that we agreed," retorted Challoner, "you have no plan, no knowledge; you know not where to seek for a beginning."

"Challoner!" cried Somerset, "is it possible that you hold the doctrine of Free Will? And are you devoid of any tincture of philosophy, that you should harp on such exploded fallacies? Chance, the blind Madonna of the Pagan, rules this terrestrial bustle; and in Chance I place my sole reliance. Chance has brought us three together; when we next separate and go forth our several ways, Chance will continually drag before our careless eyes a thousand eloquent clues, not to this mystery only, but to the countless mysteries by which we live surrounded. Then comes the part of the man of the world, of the detective born and bred. This clue, which the whole town beholds without comprehension, swift as a cat, he leaps upon it, makes it his, follows it with craft and passion, and from one trifling circumstance divines a world."

"Just so," said Challoner; "and I am delighted that you should recognise these virtues in yourself. But in the meanwhile, dear boy, I own myself incapable of joining. I was neither born nor bred as a detective, but as a placable and very thirsty gentleman; and, for my part, I begin to weary for a drink. As for clues and adventures, the only adventure that is ever likely to occur to me will be an adventure with a bailiff."

"Now there is the fallacy," cried Somerset. "There I catch the

---

1 Open space in south London.
2 [Stevenson and Stevenson's note:] Hereupon the Arabian author enters on one of his digressions. Fearing, apparently, that the somewhat eccentric views of Mr. Somerset should throw discredit on a part of truth, he calls upon the English people to remember with more gratitude the services of the police; to what unobserved and solitary acts of heroism they are called; against what odds of numbers and of arms, and for how small a reward, either in fame or money: matter, it has appeared to the translators, too serious for this place.

secret of your futility in life. The world teems and bubbles with adventure; it besieges you along the street: hands waving out of windows, swindlers coming up and swearing they knew you when you were abroad, affable and doubtful people of all sorts and conditions begging and truckling for your notice. But not you: you turn away, you walk your seedy mill round, you must go the dullest way. Now here, I beg of you, the next adventure that offers itself, embrace it in with both your arms; whatever it looks, grimy or romantic, grasp it. I will do the like; the devil is in it, but at least we shall have fun; and each in turn we shall narrate the story of our fortunes to my philosophic friend of the divan, the great Godall, now hearing me with inward joy. Come, is it a bargain? Will you, indeed, both promise to welcome every chance that offers, to plunge boldly into every opening, and, keeping the eye wary and the head composed, to study and piece together all that happens? Come, promise: let me open to you the doors of the great profession of intrigue."

"It is not much in my way," said Challoner, "but, since you make a point of it, amen."

"I don't mind promising," said Desborough, "but nothing will happen to me."

"O faithless ones!" cried Somerset. "But at least I have your promises; and Godall, I perceive, is transported with delight."

"I promise myself at least much pleasure from your various narratives," said the salesman, with the customary calm polish of his manner.

"And now, gentlemen," concluded Somerset, "let us separate. I hasten to put myself in fortune's way. Hark how, in this quiet corner, London roars like the noise of battle; four million destinies are here concentred; and in the strong panoply of one hundred pounds, payable to the bearer, I am about to plunge into that web."

2. From Arthur Machen, "The Inmost Light" (John Lane, 1894)

[Published in the same volume as *The Great God Pan*.]

One evening in autumn, when the deformities of London were veiled in faint, blue mist and its vistas and far-reaching streets seemed splendid, Mr. Charles Salisbury was slowly pacing down Rupert Street, drawing nearer to his favourite restaurant by slow degrees. His eyes were downcast in study of the pavement, and thus it was that as he passed in at the narrow door a man who had come up from the lower end of the street jostled against him.

"I beg your pardon—wasn't looking where I was going. Why, it's Dyson!"

"Yes, quite so. How are you, Salisbury?"

"Quite well. But where have you been, Dyson? I don't think I can have seen you for the last five years."

"No; I daresay not. You remember I was getting rather hard up when you came to my place at Charlotte Street?"

"Perfectly. I think I remember your telling me that you owed five weeks' rent, and that you had parted with your watch for a comparatively small sum."

"My dear Salisbury, your memory is admirable. Yes, I was hard up. But the curious thing is that soon after you saw me I became harder up. My financial state was described by a friend as 'stone broke.' I don't approve of slang, mind you, but such was my condition. But suppose we go in; there might be other people who would like to dine—it's a human weakness, Salisbury."

"Certainly; come along. I was wondering as I walked down whether the corner table were taken. It has a velvet back, you know."

"I know the spot; it's vacant. Yes, as I was saying, I became even harder up."

"What did you do then?" asked Salisbury, disposing of his hat, and settling down in the corner of the seat, with a glance of fond anticipation at the *menu*.

"What did I do? Why, I sat down and reflected. I had a good classical education, and a positive distaste for business of any kind; that was the capital with which I faced the world. Do you know, I have heard people describe olives as nasty! What lamentable philistinism![1] I have often thought, Salisbury, that I could write genuine poetry under the influence of olives and red wine. Let us have Chianti; it may not be very good, but the flasks are simply charming."

"It is pretty good here. We may as well have a big flask."

"Very good. I reflected, then, on my want of prospects, and I determined to embark in literature."

"Really, that was strange. You seem in pretty comfortable circumstances, though."

"Though! What a satire upon a noble profession. I am afraid, Salisbury, you haven't a proper idea of the dignity of an artist. You

---

1 See p. 250, note 2, above.

see me sitting at my desk,—or at least you can see me if you care to call,—with pen and ink, and simple nothingness before me, and if you come again in a few hours you will (in all probability) find a creation!"

"Yes, quite so. I had an idea that literature was not remunerative."

"You are mistaken; its rewards are great. I may mention, by the way, that shortly after you saw me I succeeded to a small income. An uncle died, and proved unexpectedly generous."

"Ah, I see. That must have been convenient."

"It was pleasant,—undeniably pleasant. I have always considered it in the light of an endowment of my researches. I told you I was a man of letters; it would, perhaps, be more correct to describe myself as a man of science."

"Dear me, Dyson, you have really changed very much in the last few years. I had a notion, don't you know, that you were a sort of idler about town, the kind of man one might meet on the north side of Piccadilly every day from May to July."

"Exactly. I was even then forming myself, though all unconsciously. You know my poor father could not afford to send me to the university. I used to grumble in my ignorance at not having completed my education. That was the folly of youth, Salisbury; my university was Piccadilly.[1] There I began to study the great science which still occupies me."

"What science do you mean?"

"The science of the great city; the physiology of London; literally and metaphysically the greatest subject that the mind of man can conceive. What an admirable salmi[2] this is; undoubtedly the final end of the pheasant. Yes, I feel sometimes positively overwhelmed with the thought of the vastness and complexity of London. Paris a man may get to understand thoroughly with a reasonable amount of study; but London is always a mystery. In Paris you may say: 'Here live the actresses, here the Bohemians, and the Ratés;' but it is different in London. You may point out a street, correctly enough, as the abode of washerwomen; but, in that second floor, a man may be studying Chaldee[3] roots, and in the garret over the way a forgotten artist is dying by inches."

"I see you are Dyson, unchanged and unchangeable," said

---

1 One of the busiest roads in London. Dyson's education has been in the science or "physiology of London."

2 A ragout made with partly roasted game meat (OED).

3 Ancient language similar to Aramaic.

Salisbury, slowly sipping his Chianti. "I think you are misled by a too fervid imagination; the mystery of London exists only in your fancy. It seems to me a dull place enough. We seldom hear of a really artistic crime in London, whereas I believe Paris abounds in that sort of thing."

"Give me some more wine. Thanks. You are mistaken, my dear fellow, you are really mistaken. London has nothing to be ashamed of in the way of crime. Where we fail is for want of Homers, not Agamemnons."[1]

3. From Arthur Machen, "The Red Hand," *The House of Souls* (E. Grant Richards, 1906)

"There can be no doubt whatever," said Mr. Phillipps, "that my theory is the true one; these flints are prehistoric fish-hooks."

"I dare say; but you know that in all probability the things were forged the other day with a door-key."

"Stuff!" said Phillipps; "I have some respect, Dyson, for your literary abilities, but your knowledge of ethnology is insignificant, or rather non-existent. These fish-hooks satisfy every test; they are perfectly genuine."

"Possibly, but as I said just now, you go to work at the wrong end. You neglect the opportunities that confront you and await you, obvious, at every corner; you positively shrink from the chance of encountering primitive man in this whirling and mysterious city, and you pass the weary hours in your agreeable retirement of Red Lion Square fumbling with bits of flint, which are, as I said, in all probability, rank forgeries."

Phillipps took one of the little objects, and held it up in exasperation.

"Look at that ridge," he said. "Did you ever see such a ridge as that on a forgery?"

Dyson merely grunted and lit his pipe, and the two sat smoking in rich silence, watching through the open window the children in the square as they flitted to and fro in the twilight of the lamps, as elusive as bats flying on the verge of a dark wood.

"Well," said Phillipps at last, "it is really a long time since you have been round. I suppose you have been working at your old task."

"Yes," said Dyson, "always the chase of the phrase. I shall grow

---

1 Classical Greek epic poet Homer, author of the *Iliad* and the *Odyssey*. Agamemnon, leader of the Trojan army in Homer's *Iliad*.

old in the hunt. But it is a great consolation to meditate on the fact that there are not a dozen people in England who know what style means."

"I suppose not; for the matter of that, the study of ethnology is far from popular. And the difficulties! Primitive man stands dim and very far off across the great bridge of years."

"By the way," he went on after a pause, "what was that stuff you were talking just now about shrinking from the chance of encountering primitive man at the corner, or something of the kind? There are certainly people about here whose ideas are very primitive."

"I wish, Phillipps, you would not rationalize my remarks. If I recollect the phrase correctly, I hinted that you shrank from the chance of encountering primitive man in this whirling and mysterious city, and I meant exactly what I said. Who can limit the age of survival? The troglodyte and the lake-dweller, perhaps representatives of yet darker races, may very probably be lurking in our midst, rubbing shoulders with frock-coated and finely draped humanity, ravening like wolves at heart and boiling with the foul passions of the swamp and the black cave. Now and then as I walk in Holborn or Fleet Street I see a face which I pronounce abhorred, and yet I could not give a reason for the thrill of loathing that stirs within me."

"My dear Dyson, I refuse to enter myself in your literary 'trying-on' department. I know that survivals do exist, but all things have a limit, and your speculations are absurd. You must catch me your troglodyte before I will believe in him."

"I agree to that with all my heart," said Dyson, chuckling at the ease with which he had succeeded in "drawing" Phillipps. "Nothing could be better. It's a fine night for a walk," he added, taking up his hat.

"What nonsense you are talking, Dyson!" said Phillipps. "However, I have no objection to taking a walk with you: as you say, it is a pleasant night."

"Come along then," said Dyson, grinning, "but remember our bargain."

Works Cited and Recommended Reading

Ahmed, Sara. "The Orient and Other Others." *Queer Phenomenology*, Duke UP, 2006, pp. 109–56.

Altick, Richard D. *The English Common Reader: A Social History of the Mass Reading Public, 1800–1900.* Ohio State UP, 1957.

Anderson, Anne. "'Fearful Consequences ... of Living Up to One's Teapot': Men, Women, and 'Cultchah' in the English Aesthetic Movement c. 1870–1900." *Victorian Literature and Culture*, vol. 37, no. 1, 2009, pp. 219–54, https://doi.org/10.1017/S1060150309090147.

Aravamudan, Srinivas. "Fiction/Translation/Transnation: The Secret History of the Eighteenth Century Novel." *A Companion to the Eighteenth-Century English Novel and Culture*, edited by Paula R. Backscheider and Catherine Ingrassia, John Wiley & Sons, 2005, pp. 48–74.

Arnold, Matthew. "The Function of Criticism at the Present Time." *The Works of Matthew Arnold in Fifteen Volumes*, vol. III, Macmillan, 1903, pp. 1–44.

Ayto, John, et al. *Brewer's Britain and Ireland.* Weidenfeld and Nicholson, 2012.

Baldick, Chris. *The Oxford Dictionary of Literary Terms.* Oxford UP, 2015.

Bane, Theresa. *Encyclopedia of Mythological Objects.* McFarland, 2020.

Baudelaire, Charles. *The Painter of Modern Life and Other Essays.* Translated and edited by Jonathan Mayne, Phaidon Press, 1964.

Benjamin, Walter. *Charles Baudelaire: A Lyric Poet in the Era of High Capitalism.* Translated by Harry Zohn, Verso, 1983.

———. *Selected Writings, Volume 2: 1927–1934.* Edited by Michael W. Jennings, Belknap Press of Harvard, 1999.

———. "Theses on the Philosophy of History." *Illuminations: Essays and Reflections*, edited by Hannah Arendt, pp. 253–64.

Bernheimer, Charles. "Fetishism and Decadence: Salome's Severed Heads." *Fetishism as Cultural Discourse*, edited by Emily Apter and William Pietz, Cornell UP, 1993, pp. 62–83.

Black, Barbara J. *On Exhibit: Victorians and their Museums.* U of Virginia P, 2000.

Blackwell, Mark. "The It-Narrative in Eighteenth-Century England: Animals and Objects in Circulation." *Literature Compass*, vol. 1, 2004, pp. 1–5.

Cevasco, G.A. *The Breviary of the Decadence: J.-K. Huysmans's* A Rebours *and English Literature*. AMS Press, 2001.

Constable, Liz, et al., editors. *Perennial Decay: On the Aesthetics and Politics of Decadence*. U of Pennsylvania P, 1999.

Dawson, Gowan. "Intrinsic Earthliness: Science, Materialism, and the Fleshly School of Poetry." *Victorian Poetry*, vol. 41, no. 1, spring 2003, pp. 113–29.

Dellamora, Richard. "Productive Decadence: 'Of the Clear of Outlawed Thought': Vernon Lee, Max Nordau, and Oscar Wilde." *New Literary History*, vol. 35, no. 4, 2004, pp. 529–46.

Denisoff, Dennis. "The Dissipating Nature of Decadent Paganism from Pater to Yeats." *Modernism/modernity*, vol. 15, no. 3, September 2008, 431–46.

De Quincey, Thomas. *Confessions of an English Opium-Eater*. Edited by Joel Faflak, Broadview, 2009.

De Ridder-Vignone, António. "Incoherent Texts? Storytelling, Preaching, and the *Cent Nouvelles nouvelles* in Marguerite de Navarre's *Heptaméron* 21." *Renaissance Quarterly*, vol. 68, no. 2, summer 2015, pp. 465–95.

Dobson, Roger, et al. *Arthur Machen, Selected Letters*. Aquarian Press, 1988.

Donohue, Joseph. *Fantasies of Empire: The Empire Theatre of Varieties and the Licensing Controversy of 1894*. U of Iowa P, 2005.

Eckersley, Adrian. "A Theme in the Early Work of Arthur Machen: 'Degeneration.'" *English Literature in Transition, 1880–1920*, vol. 35, no. 3, Jun. 1992, pp. 276–87.

Ellmann, Richard. *Oscar Wilde*. Penguin, 1987.

Ferguson, Christine. "Decadence as Scientific Fulfillment." *PMLA*, vol. 117, no. 3, 2002, pp. 465–78.

Forlini, Stefania. "Modern Narratives and Decadent Things in Arthur Machen's *The Three Impostors* (1895)." *English Literature in Transition, 1880–1920*, vol. 55, no. 4, 2012, pp. 479–98.

Freedgood, Elaine. *The Ideas in Things: Fugitive Meaning in the Victorian Novel*. U of Chicago P, 2006.

———. "What Objects Know: Circulation, Omniscience and the Comedy of Dispossession in Victorian It-Narratives." *Journal of Victorian Culture*, vol. 15, no. 1, 2010, pp. 83–100.

Freedman, Jonathan. *Professions of Taste*. Stanford UP, 1990.

Freud, Sigmund. "Fetishism." *The Standard Edition of the Complete Psychological Works of Sigmund Freud*, edited and translated by James Strachey, vol. 21, W.W. Norton, 1989, pp. 152–57.

——. "The Uncanny." *The Standard Edition of the Complete Psychological Works of Sigmund Freud*, edited and translated by James Strachey, vol. 17, Hogarth, 1953, pp. 219–52.

Harman, Claire. *Robert Louis Stevenson: A Biography*. HarperCollins, 2005.

Hext, Kate, and Alex Murray, editors. *Decadence in the Age of Modernism*. Johns Hopkins UP, 2019.

Horne, H.P. "The Strand Improvements." *Fortnightly Review*, vol. 52, no. 309, Sept. 1892, p. 320.

Hurley, Kelly. *The Gothic Body: Sexuality, Materialism, and Degeneration at the Fin de Siècle*. Cambridge UP, 1996.

Huxley, T.H. "On the Physical Basis of Life." 1868. *Collected Essays*, vol. I, Greenwood Press, 1968, pp. 130–65.

Huysmans, J.-K. *Against Nature*. Translated by Robert Baldick, Penguin Books, 1959.

Im, Yeeyon. "Oscar Wilde's *Salomé*: Disorienting Orientalism." *Comparative Drama*, vol. 45, no. 4, winter 2011, pp. 361–80.

James, Henry. Preface. *The Spoils of Poynton*, 1897, edited by Bernard Richards, Oxford UP, 2008, pp. xxxix–l.

Johnson, Rebecca Carol, et al. "*The Arabian Nights*, Arab-European Literary Influence, and the Lineages of the Novel." *Modern Language Quarterly*, vol. 68, no. 2, 2007, pp. 243–79, https://doi.org/10.1215/00267929-2006-038.

Jones, Darryl. "Borderlands, Spiritualism and the Occult in *Fin de Siècle* and Edwardian Welsh and Irish Horror." *Irish Studies Review*, vol. 17, no. 1, Feb. 2009, pp. 31–44.

——. *Horror Tales: Classic Tales from Hoffmann to Hodgson*. Edited by Darryl Jones, Oxford UP, 2014.

Joshi, S.T. Introduction. *Arthur Machen: The White People and Other Weird Stories*, edited by S.T. Joshi, Penguin, 2011, pp. xi–xxviii.

Josiffe, Christopher. "Some Notes on Machen's 'Sixtystone.'" *Faunus: The Journal of the Friends of Arthur Machen*, vol. 18, 2008, pp. 32–37.

Kandola, Sondeep. "Celtic Occultism and the Symbolist Mode in the *Fin-de-Siècle* Writings of Arthur Machen and W.B. Yeats." *English Literature in Transition, 1880–1920*, vol. 56, no. 4, Oct. 2013, pp. 497–518.

Keene, Melanie. *Science in Wonderland: The Scientific Fairy Tales of Victorian Britain.* Oxford UP, 2015.

Keynotes Series of Novels and Short Stories / Twenty-One Designs by Aubrey Beardsley. John Lane, 1896.

Knowles, Elizabeth, editor. *The Oxford Dictionary of Phrase and Fable.* Oxford UP, 2005.

Kopytoff, Igor. "The Cultural Biography of Things: Commoditization as Process." *The Social Life of Things: Commodities in Cultural Perspective,* edited by Arjun Appadurai, Cambridge UP, 1986, pp. 64–91.

Leslie-McCarthy, Sage. "Chance Encounters: The Detective as 'Expert' in Arthur Machen's *The Great God Pan.*" *Australasian Journal of Victorian Studies,* vol. 13, no. 1, 2008, pp. 35–45.

Lodge, Oliver. "Experience of Unusual Physical Phenomena Occurring in the Presence of an Entranced Person." *Proceedings of the Society for Psychical Research,* vol. 6, 1894, pp. 300–60.

Lovecraft, H.P. "Supernatural Horror in Literature." *At the Mountains of Madness,* Modern Library, 2005, pp. 105–73.

Luckhurst, Roger. "Laboratories for Global Space-Time: Science-Fictionality and the World's Fairs, 1851–1939." *Science Fiction Studies,* vol. 39, no. 3, 2012, pp. 385–400.

Machen, Arthur. *Far Off Things.* Martin Secker, 1922.

———. *Hieroglyphics.* Grant Richards, 1902.

———. Introduction. *Notes and Queries,* Spurr and Swift, 1926, pp. ix–xx.

———. "The Little People." *Dreads and Drolls,* Martin Secker, 1926, pp. 42–48.

———. *The London Adventure, Or The Art of Wandering.* Martin Secker, 1924.

———. *Precious Balms.* Spurr & Swift, 1924.

———. *Things Near and Far.* Martin Secker, 1923.

———. *The Three Impostors.* John Lane, 1895.

McClintock, Anne. *Imperial Leather: Race, Gender and Sexuality in the Colonial Contest.* Routledge, 1995.

Miller, Carolyn R. "Genre as Social Action." *Quarterly Journal of Speech,* vol. 70, 1984, pp. 151–67.

Mitchell, Linda Elizabeth. *Voices of Medieval England, Scotland, Ireland, and Wales: Contemporary Accounts of Daily Life.* ABC-CLIO, 2016.

Mosse, George L. "Introduction: Max Nordau and his *Degeneration.*" Nordau, pp. xv–xxxiv.

Murray, Alex. *Decadence: A Literary History*. Edited by Alex Murray, Cambridge UP, 2020.

Nottage, Lynn. *Sweat*. Dramatists Play Service, 2018.

Nordau, Max. *Degeneration*. Translated by George L. Mosse, Howard Fertig, 1968.

"The Owl that Wrote a Book (A Fable)." *The Child's Friend*, vol. 2, no. 6, Jun. 1876, p. 90.

Oxford Dictionary of National Biography. British Academy and Oxford UP, 2004.

Pater, Walter. "The Bacchanals of Euripides." *Greek Studies: A Series of Essays*, Macmillan and Co., 1895, pp. 49–78.

Paxton, J., editor. *Penguin Encyclopedia of Places*. 3rd ed., Penguin, 1999.

Pfeifer, Michael J. *The Roots of Rough Justice: Origins of American Lynching*. U of Illinois P, 2011.

Pietz, William. "The Problem of the Fetish, I." *Res*, vol. 9, spring 1985, pp. 5–17.

———. "The Problem of the Fetish, II: The Origin of the Fetish." *Res*, vol. 13, spring 1987, pp. 23–45.

———. "The Problem of the Fetish, IIIa: Bosman's Guinea and the Enlightenment Theory of Fetishism." *Res*, vol. 16, autumn 1988, pp. 105–23.

Platizky, Roger. "Wilde's *The Picture of Dorian Gray*." *The Explicator*, vol. 60, no. 4, 2002, pp. 202–04, https://doi. org/10.1080/00144940209597714.

Potolsky, Matthew. "Introduction." *New Literary History*, vol. 35, no. 4, 2004, pp. v–xi.

Psomiades, Kathy Alexis. *Beauty's Body: Femininity and Representation in British Aestheticism*. Stanford UP, 1997.

Punter, David. "Gothic and Decadence: Robert Louis Stevenson, Oscar Wilde, H.G. Wells, Bram Stoker, Arthur Machen." *The Literature of Terror: A History of Gothic Fictions from 1765 to the Present Day*, Longman, 1980, pp. 239–67.

Quilter, Harry, "The Gospel of Intensity." *Contemporary Review*, vol. 67, Jan./Jun. 1895, pp. 761–82.

Raia, Courtenay Grean. "From Ether Theory to Ether Theology: Oliver Lodge and the Physics of Immortality." *Journal of the History of the Behavioral Sciences*, vol. 43, no. 1, 2007, pp. 18–43, https://doi.org/10.1002/jhbs.20207.

Rebry, Natasha. "'A Slight Lesion in the Grey Matter': The Gothic Brain in Arthur Machen's *The Great God Pan*." *Horror Studies*, vol. 7, no. 1, 2016, pp. 9–24. *EBSCOhost*, https://doi. org/10.1386/host.7.1.9_1.

Reynolds, Aidan, and William E. Charlton. *Arthur Machen: A Short Account of His Life and Work*. J. Baker for The Richards Press, 1963.

Royal Academy of the Arts. *Dante Gabriel Rossetti: Painter and Poet*. London, 1973.

Said, Edward. *Orientalism: Western Conceptions of the Orient*. Penguin, 1995.

Secord, James A. Introduction. *Vestiges of the Natural History of Creation and Other Evolutionary Writings by Robert Chambers*, edited by James Secord, U of Chicago P, 1994, pp. ix–xlviii.

Sharpe, Christina. *In the Wake: On Blackness and Being*. Duke UP, 2016.

Showalter, Elaine. *Sexual Anarchy: Gender and Culture at the Fin de Siècle*. Bloomsbury, 1990.

Silver, Carole G. *Strange and Secret Peoples: Fairies and Victorian Consciousness*. Oxford UP, 1999.

Stetz, Margaret, and Mark Samuel Lasner. *England in the 1890s: Literary Publishing at the Bodley Head*. Georgetown UP, 1990.

Stevenson, Robert Louis, and Fanny Van De Grift Stevenson. *The Dynamiter*. 1885. *The Novels and Tales of Robert Louis Stevenson: More New Arabian Nights*, Charles Scribner's Sons, 1909, 1–268.

Stocking, George W., Jr. *Victorian Anthropology*. The Free Press, 1987.

Sweetser, Wesley D. *Arthur Machen*. Twayne Publishers Inc., 1964.

Symons, Arthur. "An Apology for Puppets." *Plays, Acting and Music: A Book of Theory*, Constable & Company, 1909, pp. 3–8.

———. "The Decadent Movement in Literature." *Harper's Magazine*, Nov. 1893, pp. 858–67.

———. *The Symbolist Movement in Literature*. E.P. Dutton and Co., 1958.

Tales of Horror and the Supernatural by Arthur Machen. Edited and with an introduction by Philip Van Doren Stern, Knopf, 1948.

"The Three Impostors." *Saturday Review*, 11 Jan. 1896, pp. 48–49.

Tylor, Edward Burnett. "On the Tasmanians as Representatives of Paleolithic Man." *The Journal of the Anthropological Institute of Great Britain and Ireland*, vol. 23, 1894, pp. 141–52.

———. *Primitive Culture*. 1871. Harper and Row, 1958.

Valentine, Mark. *Arthur Machen*. Seren, 1995.

Vint, Sherryl, and Mark Bould. "There Is No Such Thing as Science Fiction." *Reading Science Fiction*, edited by James Gunn et al., Palgrave Macmillan, 2009, pp. 43–51.

Ward, John Powell. Series Afterword. Valentine, pp. 144–47.

Watson, Janell. *Literature and Material Culture from Balzac to Proust*. Cambridge UP, 1999.

Weir, David. *Decadence and the Making of Modernism*. U of Massachusetts P, 1995.

Wilde, Oscar. *The Picture of Dorian Gray*. Edited by Norman Page, Broadview Press, 2005.

Worth, Aaron. "Arthur Machen and the Horrors of Deep History." *Victorian Literature and Culture*, vol. 40, no. 1, 2012, pp. 215–27, https://doi.org/10.1017/S1060150311000325.

Yates, James. "Signa Militaria." *A Dictionary of Greek and Roman Antiquities*, edited by William Smith, Cambridge UP, 2013, pp. 883–84.

This book is made of paper from well-managed FSC® - certified
forests, recycled materials, and other controlled sources.